AN APOCALYPTIC NOVEL

DON ALEXANDER

OREN NATAS

Satan Incarnate As the Antichrist

A novel written depicting a colorful and witty cast of characters who live through *all the "end time" prophecies*

OREN NATAS

Satan Incarnate As the Antichrist

Don Alexander

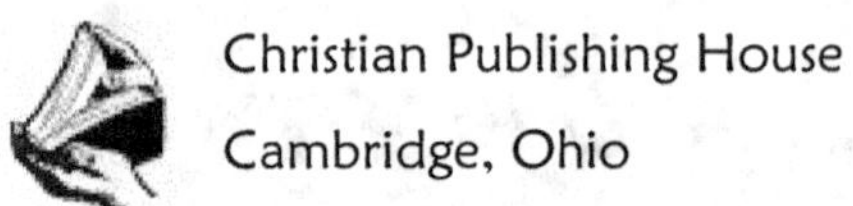
Christian Publishing House
Cambridge, Ohio

Unless otherwise indicated, Scripture quotations are from the Updated American Standard Version of the Holy Scriptures, 2018 edition (UASV).

OREN NATAS: Satan Incarnate As the Antichrist Authored by *Don Alexander*

This is a work of fiction. Names, locations, characters, and incidents are the product of the author's imagination.

ISBN-13: **978-1-949586-68-8**

ISBN-10: **1-949586-68-5**

Table of Contents

Introduction 1

CHAPTER 1 2

Through a Glass Darkly 2

CHAPTER 2 17

Wormwood and Nuclear War 17

CHAPTER 3 41

Anti-Christ by Global Acclamation 41

CHAPTER 4 69

Worship Anti-Christ or Lose Your Head 69

CHAPTER 5 75

Comes Now the False Prophet 75

CHAPTER 6 88

Death Squads Enforce the Mark 88

CHAPTER 7 95

Terminate the Seed of Abraham 95

CHAPTER 8 106

A Little Poison for Anti-Christ 106

CHAPTER 9 131

Global Reign of the False Prophet 131

CHAPTER 10 162

Back From the Dead 162

Chapter 11 183

Total Darkness and Blood to Drink 183

CHAPTER 12 205

Genocide by Divine Proclamation 205

CHAPTER 13 228

Torture and Decapitate All Christians 228

CHAPTER 14 253
Battle of Armageddon 253

Introduction

Today, there are more than *two billion individuals* around the globe who consider themselves to be *Christians.* More than *70%* of the people living in the United States poll as Christians. However, less than 18% of global Christianity *actually* read and understand "end time" Biblical prophecies. Consequently, when a novel is written depicting a colorful and witty cast of characters who live through *all the "end time" prophecies, such a novel can be very easy to read and understand.* Don Alexander wrote a single volume novel with the above storyline in 1992 and copyrighted the novel under the title "Oren Natas" [the *Anti-Christ character* in the novel]. Don Alexander did not have a literary agent and simply shelved the novel.

In 1995, two authors having some previous success with a major U.S. publisher teamed up and wrote a *serial novel* titled *"Left Behind"* based upon the *generic storyline* written into *Oren Natas* in 1992. Left Behind has now sold *over sixty million copies.*

Don Alexander has recently completed a major and final edit of his original and unpublished *Oren Natas* novel.

Dedicated to:

My wife, Elaine,

for her quiet patience and understanding

during the long and tedious hours

required to write this novel.

CHAPTER 1

Through a Glass Darkly

Thick fog shrouded the North Pacific 836 miles due west of North America while a mammoth nuclear carrier slipped quietly through the rolling water. The decks of the stealthy vessel were crammed with supersonic warplanes and guided missile launchers. Within the lower decks, anxious crew members manned a computer, radar, and sonar stations checking electronic signals, imagery, and coded transmissions.

Captain Josef Malinckoff continued his silent vigil atop the bridge as he sipped hot coffee laced with vodka. He shielded his eyes against the late afternoon sun and scanned the restless ocean. The overcast was breaking up earlier than predicted and the fading sunlight burned through the natural camouflage that had draped his carrier for more than thirteen hours. The enemy was down there somewhere watching his progress. Earth had become a dismal and dangerous planet. Disease and famine were now pushing the human race to illogical desperation bordering on the very brink of insanity. Social unrest among the masses had mushroomed out of control and threatened to further disrupt established governments and to rend the fragile fabric of ancient civilizations. Now that the nations within the eastern hemisphere had forged the Eastern Alliance and the wealthier nations in the west countered with the Western Alliance, he knew global war was imminent. Decades of wanton pollution had reduced agricultural output below the global survival level and depleted soils required an increase in manufactured fertilizers each planting season.

The Eastern Alliance cartels kept jacking up the price of raw materials needed by western industries. The west retaliated by sharply reducing agricultural exports and hoarding fertilizer. The resulting economic stagnation plunged both hemispheres into what was fast becoming a bottomless recession with both sides reluctant to make concessions for fear of perceived weakness which would undermine future bargaining positions. In the meanwhile, millions were facing starvation throughout Africa, Asia and Eastern Europe and western welfare resources were being drained by the flood of unemployed, hungry workers. The rich capitalists took long vacations while the working class massed in the streets demanding government handouts. The public mood grew darker with each passing day and the politicians, as usual, catered to the vested interest groups that could be depended upon to influence media coverage and to finance election campaigns.

Josef knew that his mission was a prelude to a first strike by the Eastern Alliance aimed primarily at the United States. If the American military could be caught by surprise and severely crippled, the remaining nations within the Western Alliance would certainly think twice before attempting to starve the east into economic surrender. Well, Josef thought to himself. A carrier skipper doesn't have to make war or peace decisions. Such matters would be decided by the heads of state who must cater to the will of the people. His job was simply to follow orders passed on by his superiors. He started to descend from the bridge and then stopped abruptly. He thought he heard something in the wind. Could it be his imagination.....or did he really hear the subtle sound of laughter?

The shadow of death spread over Joyce Roberts' drawn face. Her seven-year battle with breast cancer was nearly over, and for the first time in as many years, she appeared to feel no pain. Her minister sat next to the bed reading to her from the Psalms. He wasn't sure that she heard, but no other activity seemed appropriate. Her frail withered hands were folded over her flat breasts and her breathing was barely perceptible. He had been with her for hours and heard her final prayer along with instructions for the order of her funeral service. The squat, rotund preacher removed his wire-rimmed bifocals and wiped his forehead with a white handkerchief dampened with perspiration. His chubby buttocks ached from the long bedside vigil and his wrinkled pants clung to his clammy thighs. He stopped reading when he sensed a presence that he could not see, and he heard Joyce Roberts say: "Yes, I'm ready." The sound of her voice startled him because he could see that her lips were not moving and that her breathing had ceased. He leaned over, felt her pulse, and knew for certain she was dead.

Executive limos began arriving at the White House main entrance in rapid succession. High ranking politicians exited the limos and hurried into a prepared conference room. It was 5:40 pm, the sky was overcast, and a light rain fell upon Washington DC. The conference attendees seated themselves around a large, round, mahogany table. President James McCarron entered, strode briskly to his high-back, executive chair and sat down while mentally noting those present. Hanna Meecham, an elegant looking black woman in her mid-forties, entered and took the empty seat directly across from the President as everyone looked expectantly toward him. President McCarron was dignified, gray-headed, in his late fifties, and immaculately dressed.

"We're all pleased that you could join us, Dr. Meecham. Please update us concerning the present status of Wormwood." Hanna spoke quickly and with personal confidence: "The latest computer analysis indicates that Wormwood's solid core is approximately five and a half miles in diameter. The core composed of toxic, heavy metals and rock is surrounded by ice, dust particles and frozen gases. The comet's orbit is egg-shaped and crosses the orbits of Earth and the other known planets within our solar system. Wormwood was first detected by one of my students through the Hale Telescope during a routine field assignment. Its orbital period cannot be calculated since this is the first sighting, but the period is certainly longer than six thousand years." Hanna paused, took a deep breath and continued:

"As you know, all comets are invisible to us until they orbit close enough to our sun to reflect sunlight to Earth. At noon, Eastern Standard Time, today, Wormwood was roughly one hundred and thirty-four million miles from Earth. The comet is on a collision course with Earth and is closing the gap by four million, three hundred and twenty thousand miles each solar day. It will pass clear of Mars in approximately nineteen days, ten hours and thirty-four minutes; then collide with Earth eleven days, eight hours, and perhaps twelve minutes later. The precise moment of impact will depend upon the density of our atmosphere over the North Pacific at the time of Wormwood's penetration. In any event, at fifty miles per second, the comet will strike Earth between five and eight seconds following initial entry."

The prediction that Wormwood would smack into Earth was already known to everyone at the table, but Hanna paused to see if anyone doubted her statements. President McCarron stared blankly at the table top and, when no one voiced opposition, he looked up and nodded in Hanna's direction prompting her to continue. She radiated obvious concern: "Our atmospheric gases will slow the comet slightly, superheat its nucleus and melt away some of its outer mass. Taking into account the composition of the solid core, the computer calculates a sixteen percent loss in diameter; which means Wormwood will still be over four and a half miles wide upon impact with Earth."

President McCarron coughed and looked around but remained silent. Secretary of Defense, Harold Stevens, was seated next to Hanna. He sucked in his pot belly and sat up straight, tossing his pen onto his notepad. "My God!" he exclaimed.

McCarron ignored the outburst. His voice quivered in spite of his calm appearance as he asked for confirmation: "Dr. Meecham, what is the reliability factor concerning the software calculations?"

Hanna did not blink. "What I have stated is fact. There is absolutely no doubt about it." The President said nothing for a moment while he reflected upon the pending national disaster. Harold Stevens interrupted again: "Are you telling us that a chunk of rock and metal more than four miles wide will actually hit us traveling at fifty miles per second?

"Yes, Sir. That's precisely what I'm saying." Hanna sensed that Stevens could be a pompous adversary, but she maintained her professional demeanor. "The superheated core will plow into the North Pacific approximately eight hundred and ninety miles off the coast of northern California." Stevens yanked off his bifocals and pitched them onto the table. "Debris from such an explosion might block out sunlight! Life could become physically impossible!"

"Not necessarily," Hanna replied as she turned to face Stevens. "Earth is scarred with numerous craters from collisions with objects from space approaching the mass of Wormwood." President McCarron's eyes darted around the table, then focused on Hanna. "Give us your prediction of collision damage." His tone indicated no lingering doubt.

Hanna tried to swallow the lump in her throat, but her voice sounded strained: "Virtual destruction of our coastal cities bordering the North Pacific. But, we'll be spared the lethal dust clouds that would follow if Wormwood hit us anyplace but deep water. On the downside, tidal waves thousands of feet high will wash far inland polluting freshwater resources and drowning crops in addition to structural damage. The enormous shock from the impact will probably trigger earthquakes along major faults while vaporizing an enormous volume of salt water. Massive flooding will be followed by adverse weather patterns including tornadoes, hurricanes, and typhoons in unprecedented numbers. Large portions of our most fertile soil will be covered by salt deposits." McCarron squirmed in his executive chair and squinted at Hanna. Always the politician, he worried about public panic. "How long before the media will have similar information?" Hanna shrugged and replied. "My best guess is a day or so if we're lucky."

Andrew Mullen, Secretary of State, stopped scribbling notes and looked anxiously at Stevens while nervously rubbing his hawk-like nose that jutted above thin, drawn lips. He tried to scatter a few seeds of hope. "Is it possible, Harold, to intercept Wormwood with nuclear warheads and either break it up or divert it away from Earth?"

Stevens muffled a snort of amusement, then squinted back at Mullen. "Fifty miles per second is seventy times faster than a rifle bullet! Most comets orbit at less than half of Wormwood's velocity...but we all know Wormwood is a very unusual comet." Stevens glanced around the table to see if everyone made the connection. His tone turned slightly defensive. "To have even a remote shot at such an interception would require space stations already in orbit and equipped with scores of high megaton missiles.....which we have elected not to do because of budget restrictions and neither has any other government attempted such a project." He lowered his gaze to the table and picked up his glasses. He chewed at his lower lip and fixed his eyes on McCarron. "We're better off letting its entire mass smack into the ocean." Stevens clicked his pen shut and stuck it into his vest pocket as if to say that the topic was a dead end.

President McCarron ended the awkward silence. "That leaves evacuation as our only viable option and we'll be facing international upheaval as well as domestic panic. I expect a surprise attack from the Eastern Alliance."

The conference attendees exchanged quizzical looks. McCarron turned toward the man seated to his left. "The CIA warns me that sabers are already rattling. Let's fill everyone in, Walter." Walter Hickman, Director of the CIA, cleared his throat while shuffling through a folder of notes. He straightened his glasses, then smoothed back snowy patches of unruly hair with his stubby fingers. His barrel chest swelled with a deep breath that tightened his spare tire and his scowl of secrecy accentuated his flat nose, pudgy jaws, and pipe-stained dentures. The others looked at him with mixed expressions. His tone reflected self-importance and perceived superiority: "The Eastern dictators are definitely up to something nasty. Large-scale military mobilization is underway including heavy armor and transport aircraft. We have detected a high level of naval deployment and suspicious activity around missile sites. They are apparently getting ready for some major offensive, and we have enough intelligence feedback to point us to the Middle East.... and we know the target." Andrew Mullen leaned forward. "Oil or fertilizer?"

Hickman clenched his jaws. "They intend to confiscate the Dead Sea as well as the oil fields." "Surely, they know we'll intervene," Stevens said.

It was a statement, not a question. Hickman scratched his thick lips with his left fingertips. "They're acting out of desperation. They need massive quantities of fertilizer for minimal agricultural output, and they want the oil fields for bartering with us; oil in exchange for food."

McCarron raised his eyebrows and shifted his attention from Hickman to Stevens. "Are we fully prepared for a surprise attack?" "Yes," Stevens answered without reserve. "We're on full alert without tipping our hand." He smiled wanly at McCarron. "Your command plane can be airborne within thirteen minutes with all key personnel. We can stay aloft as long as we have service tankers for in-flight refueling." McCarron looked toward the ceiling while squinting thoughtfully. "Have every available tanker filled and standing by. Transfer all military equipment and personnel along the west coast to non-threatened sites. Leave sufficient troops and transport vehicles to conduct an orderly evacuation of the impact area."

The President now seemed to be measuring his words carefully as he eyed Hickman, Mullen, and Stevens. "Let's show them we know their intentions. Order strategic and tactical naval vessels out to sea along with supply ships. Keep the maximum level of offensive and defensive aircraft aloft and position the remainder to present difficult targets. Avoid any mass concentration of troops and tighten up security around our military assets.... especially nuclear weapons. Button up Unified Air Command including food, water, and medical inventories. Put munitions and other supply plants on a twenty-four-hour schedule and prepare for immediate activation of all reserve and guard units."

The President paused while notes were furiously compiled around the table. Hanna Meecham took the opportunity to speak out. "Won't this action by us just trigger a larger response? What happened to the premise that serious negotiation is better than escalating tension between opposing forces?"

The urgency of his own orders wrenched McCarron's bowels. "The world is being pushed to the brink of nuclear war by a few madmen who believe they have nothing to lose, and they have control of enough nuclear firepower to decimate the human race. The Eastern Alliance dictators rate human life below achievement of strategic goals, regardless of the body count. Of course, we'll negotiate as long as they're listening. But, we can't simply cave into their demands. There would be no end to such bullying until they rape our entire hemisphere."

The President pushed back from the table, stood up and leaned forward, supporting his weight with his palms against the tabletop. "We appear rather short on time. Our most immediate problem is panic control. You know what needs to be done. We'll meet here again at eight this evening."

General Oren Natas sat at a plain metal desk inside a small rectangular office with a single door that opened into a spacious working area furnished with the latest electronic gadgets. His white military uniform was decorated with emblems and medals befitting his rank. Black, curly hair and Roman features blended well with his six-foot, three-inch frame, muscular physique, and olive complexion. His light gray eyes reflected sensitivity and intelligence as he studied military maps of the world fastened to the wall opposite the desk. There was his kingdom -- the planet, Earth. Soon, he would again rule supreme. A military aide appeared in the open doorway. "Oh, there you are, General. I've been looking everywhere for you. The Prime Minister is waiting in your private office."

Natas' unblemished teeth were perfectly framed by his sinister smile. "I'm never late.... for anything." Natas' smile seemed to reassure the aide. "Yes, Sir. I put the current agenda on your desk along with the latest information on the big comet." Natas folded his arms over his large, firm chest. "I knew about Wormwood six thousand years ago. Tell the Prime Minister that I'll join him shortly." The aide blinked in puzzlement. "Yes, Sir. Your limo is waiting."

Wormwood's orbit decayed slightly as the mighty comet pierced deeper into the solar wind. The hot gases expanding outward from the sun continued melting the outer layers of Wormwood's coma, adding to the tail behind the comet. The thin molecular structure of the tail streamed through space as the frozen gases trapped within the coma absorbed the tremendous heat carried by the solar wind. The gravitational force exerted by the inner planets further decayed Wormwood's orbit steering the monster toward the planet, Earth.

Marge Rosen sat quietly watching the evening news. Mary had been taking care of personal business since shortly after eight o'clock. The telephone rang. Marge got up to answer, thinking it would be Mary. "Roberts' residence..." Silence. Then, a male voice asked softly: "Who's this?" "I'm Marge Rosen, Mary's friend. Neither Paul nor Mary is home right now. May I take a message?" The soothing, masculine voice continued: "This is Jack Roberts, Paul's brother. Do you expect either, Paul or Mary, back soon?" Wow! He's nice, Marge decided. "Paul flew to Colorado Springs this morning, but Mary should be back around ten-thirty." "Tell Mary to call me as soon as she comes in. Do you have a number where I can reach Paul?" "No, but I'll make sure Mary calls right away. Does she have your number?" "Yes. It's very important that I get in touch with Paul. Our mother died this afternoon." Marge was caught off guard and didn't respond immediately. "Don't tell Mary.....just have her call me. This is something she should hear from a family member." Marge found her voice. "Yes ... I understand. I'm terribly sorry. Is there anything else I can do?" "Thank you. No, there isn't. Just tell Mary I'll be waiting for her call." The gentleness in his tone soothed her. "Yes, I'll be sure to tell her."

All the television networks broadcast the President's special address. The Speaker of the House announced his arrival. "Ladies and Gentlemen....the President of the United States." McCarron stepped quickly to the podium and adjusted the main microphone. "Thank you.....and good evening my fellow Americans. I have a few brief statements and then I'll answer a limited number of questions from the press. Events are somewhat hectic at the moment and my schedule is extremely heavy." He paused for effect, then continued:

"First, let me bring all of you up to date on Wormwood. For those of you who haven't yet heard the full story, Wormwood is the name given to a large comet by the folks at the Palomar Observatory. One of Dr. Meecham's graduate students first spotted the comet several days ago. Some of our astronomers predict that Wormwood will collide with Earth if its present course remains unchanged. As of this moment, there has been no deviation from Wormwood's projected orbit, but that could easily occur since the comet is still over ninety-eight million miles from Earth. We are assuming the computerized predictions to be accurate. Plans are being finalized for evacuation of our west coast because predictions are that Wormwood will hit us in the North Pacific roughly eight hundred and ninety miles offshore."

McCarron carefully avoided any awkward pause that might signal indecisiveness. "The Secretary of Defense has been charged with the responsibility for providing sufficient military personnel and support equipment to assist civilian authorities with an orderly evacuation in the event that evacuation becomes desirable. Second, I believe that some comments on the reported Eastern Alliance military deployments are timely and appropriate. Our satellite cameras indicate that Russia and China are massing troops, heavy armor, and transport aircraft. We have further detected a consolidation of strategic and tactical naval vessels and suspicious activity around nuclear weapons facilities."

McCarron paused for fifteen seconds to indicate his next statements had been carefully considered. "It is quite possible that this threatening deployment represents no more than a new war game since no borders have been violated. The present maneuvering is entirely within their own backyard. On the other hand, the CIA tells me that the military posturing is in preparation for an offensive in the Middle East to grab fertilizer deposits and perhaps the oil fields. We have not yet discovered a reliable method for reading the minds of the Eastern dictators, so we shall simply have to wait and see what actually develops. And, as you would expect, we are pursuing all the appropriate diplomatic channels to avert any unwarranted international tension concerning the matter." The President paused and looked at his watch to emphasize his limited time.

"Just in case the CIA might be right this time, I have initiated sufficient defensive precautions including a full military alert, maximum production scheduling at all munitions and supply plants, and active duty status for reserve and guard units. This response by the United States to the threatening military maneuvering within Russia and China should not be interpreted to be anything more than it actually is -- routine defensive preparation while assuming, until proven wrong, that the Eastern Alliance has nothing devious in mind."

McCarron modified his tone slightly to indicate a change in subject matter. "We will also be transferring military personnel and equipment from the west coast to locations not threatened by predictions concerning Wormwood. This transfer is only a public safety concern and has nothing to do with our defensive deployments."

His tone shifted from informative to dogmatic. "We are acting in the interest of peace, not war. Let me reassure the American people and all the world that the United States has no aggressive intentions. We desire nothing more than world peace. We will do everything within our power to achieve that goal, and we join hands with every nation striving toward peaceful coexistence. However, we will never be impotent in the face of naked aggression. We are fully committed to the defense of our allies in the Middle East. Let no one doubt the resolve of the United States to protect our national interests regardless of how small or how great the powers that threaten us. Thank you all for your continuing support."

The President smiled passively during a standing ovation. When the clapping and cheering began to subside, he looked at his watch once more, then held up his hands indicating he wished to continue. "Thank you! Thank you all! I have just a few minutes to take some short-answer questions." He flashed his best presidential smile hoping the media would give him a break.

"Mr. President! Mr. President!" Every correspondent tried to get his attention. He spotted an elegant lady who appeared on the surface to have at least a trace of civility. He pointed to her. "Mr. President, can you tell us something about the size of Wormwood? Just how big is this runaway comet?" McCarron tried to sound nonchalant. "I can only give you the rough computer analysis which is being constantly updated as the sun melts away the coma around the comet's core. The icy coma is two thousand times larger than the solid nucleus, but the coma will melt away entirely, adding to the comet's tail."

The newswoman insisted on her right to a follow-up question: "How large is the coma?" McCarron coughed out his reply: "About 11,000 miles in diameter." The elegant lady uttered an audible gasp. "Are you saying that the nucleus is over five miles in diameter?" She scribbled furiously on her notepad. The room echoed with exclamations, shuffling of chairs and muted exchanges of amazement between correspondents.

"Mr. President! Mr. President!" The correspondents wildly waved pens and notepads hoping to attract the President's eyes. He pointed to a familiar face in the front row.

"Mr. President, can you tell us something about the composition of the nucleus?" McCarron swallowed to relieve inner tension. "Computer analysis indicates a rocky type core mingled with heavy metals that are yet to be identified." The follow-up question was very direct. "How much of the nucleus will melt away assuming that Wormwood maintains its present course and does, in fact, collide with Earth in the North Pacific?"

President McCarron knew that the word game was over. The media would never forgive him if he withheld the truth in responding to this pointed question. After all, the public did have the right to know; and they would find out anyway regardless of how much panic followed.

He tried to maintain an optimistic outlook. "Wormwood would enter our atmosphere with a nucleus roughly five and a half miles in diameter, and the comet will be traveling at fifty miles per second. For comparison, Earth orbits the sun at slightly under nineteen miles per second. Wormwood is an extremely high-velocity comet requiring only a few seconds to pass through our atmosphere. It will be traveling seventy times faster than a rifle bullet....too fast to intercept it with nuclear warheads or any other method currently available to us. The only practical protective measure is a complete evacuation of the impact area."

Mr. President! Mr. President!" The media wanted more. McCarron pointed to another familiar face in the third row. "Mr. President, might a collision with such a large comet cause major earthquakes, tidal waves, and other types of disturbances?"

McCarron answered in an upbeat tone. "That is certainly a possibility, but the evacuation of the impact area will minimize the potential damage. I have time for one more question." He pointed to an ABC anchorwoman. "Mr. President, could Wormwood be something other than a comet? We have never seen a comet with such a large nucleus. Where did Wormwood come from?"

McCarron had been prepped for this very question by Dr. Meecham. He gave her the credit: "Dr. Meecham tells me that some comets have orbital periods that exceed a million years, and our recorded history covers less than six thousand years. Some comets are never visible because their orbits never bring them close enough to our sun to reflect sunlight on Earth. Therefore, we have seen only a tiny fraction of the comets that actually travel through space. Wormwood's orbital period cannot be calculated until it passes our sun during a subsequent orbit. Since we are seeing Wormwood for the first time, its orbital period could well exceed hundreds of thousands of years.....and if Wormwood collides with Earth, its orbital period will forever remain a secret."

"Mr. President! Mr. President!" McCarron held up his hands and apologized: "I'm terribly sorry, that's all the time I can give you for now. I must attend a very important meeting with the Joint Chiefs and my cabinet. Again, thank you all, and I promise to keep you informed." The President smiled, waved, and hurried out of the room.

A light breeze blew from the south across Jerusalem, stirring the olive branches and rustling through patios where elderly Jews took refuge during the heat of the day. At first, few seemed to notice the two strange appearing men walking near the ancient site of Solomon's Temple. Both were dressed in flowing sackcloth and open sandals. Their bearded faces appeared old, but their movements were as sure and supple as young warriors. The two odd characters were engaged in casual conversation. They abruptly walked away from each other, one facing south and the other facing north. The one facing south lifted his hands skyward and began to speak in a loud, clear voice:

"Hear the words of him who sits upon the circle of the earth, who gave energy to the atom, who fashioned all orbits, and formed man from the dust. Hearken unto him for he knows your every thought and the rebellion in your heart. The politicians speak of peace, but war will decimate mankind. Those who remain will cry for bread and languish for water. The bear has risen up against the eagle, but the jackal shall feed upon their flesh."

A few spectators gawked out of curiosity, but no one laughed. The seed of Abraham had seen many strange and wonderful things. No, the words of this witness apparently claiming to be sent by the God of Abraham did not provoke laughter. A growing crowd quickly gathered around the temple site and listened passively. The focus of attention shifted when the stranger facing north began to bellow out in a ringing voice:

"Now, in the mouth of two witnesses, shall each judgment be established. Think not that the tares shall always choke the wheat, for the reaper is upon you and all his garments are red with blood. Listen to laughter from heaven as the scavengers gather in the valley of decision. Assemble all nations and let all the men of war draw near. God shall give them to the ravenous birds and to the scavengers to be devoured. He has seen you give a boy for a harlot and sell a girl for wine. Because of the hardness of your hearts and your bloody ways, he will visit you in the Valley of Jehoshaphat.....at Armageddon." A sudden gust of wind caused the onlookers to shield their eyes from blowing dust. The wind died away and those gathered at the temple site again looked for the two witnesses. The areas where the two had stood were empty.

The sleek 727 passenger jetliner descended to the lighted runway and taxied to the arrival gate. Captain Raymond Marcus shut down all engines as the jet-way operator guided the covered walkway over the front cabin door. Mary Roberts stood on her tiptoes inside the passenger lounge trying to see over the heads of people crowded into the space ahead of her. She saw Colonel Paul Roberts step into the lounge in full dress uniform. Paul carried a briefcase in his left hand. His right arm reached out for her. She pressed her body against him, kissed him lightly on his lips, then stepped back holding onto his right arm. "I 'm so sorry, there was nothing anyone could do. Jack and Ruth are handling all the arrangements in Boise." Paul nodded his approval. "How's Jack taking it?"

Mary's voice suggested she was close to tears. "Pretty hard at first. He was upset because no one in the family knew she was so close to death.

He lightened up a little when her minister explained she wanted it that way." Paul smiled. "That's just like her. No sympathy, no tears." He blinked repeatedly, and Mary noticed a wetness in his eyes. His right arm squeezed her against his side. "Can you bring the minivan around in front while I get my luggage?" "Okay, Honey. I'll take your briefcase, so you don't have to fool with it at the carousel." Paul kissed her forehead and handed her his briefcase. "We'll stop on the way home and get some dinner. I don't want you cooking tonight. I've got other plans." "Sounds good to me." She kissed his right cheek, turned and headed for the terminal entrance.

Paul snatched his luggage from the carousel and made it to the pickup area just as Mary arrived with the minivan. He chucked his bags into the rear and took over behind the wheel. Mary snuggled close to Paul making it difficult for him to concentrate on traffic along the expressway. Paul switched to the right-hand lane. "There's a truck stop at the next exit. Let's eat there and not order anything that has to be cooked."

Inside, they found an empty booth next to the buffet. Paul scanned the hot offerings. "We stopped at the right place.....smells delicious."

Paul selected fried chicken, mashed potatoes with gravy, corn, green peas, salad, and hot dinner rolls. Mary opted for roast beef, carrots, green peas, and a small salad. They settled back into their booth and spread their napkins. Mary sliced her meat and looked at Paul with apparent concern. "What's going on, Honey? Are we facing some sort of military threat?" Paul munched on a drumstick, wiped his mouth and sipped some hot coffee. "McCarron and the CIA seem to think so. They believe Russia and China are preparing to invade the Middle East." A slight frown wrinkled Mary's pretty nose. "What do you think? Is there a real possibility of nuclear war?" Paul's mouth was full, giving him time to decide how much to tell her. He chewed slowly and studied her pensively. He knew she'd not be satisfied with an evasive answer. This wasn't going the way he'd planned. Her timing was rotten. "It's beginning to look that way. Russia and China are massing millions of troops backed up by carrier groups and heavy armor. The CIA and Israeli intelligence believe the Middle East will be invaded. There's little doubt that Israel will defend its borders with nuclear weapons, and McCarron has already committed us to repel any Middle East invasion."

"I think McCarron will back down at the last minute," Mary said wistfully. "Neither side can survive a nuclear attack. Let the Jews and Arabs defend themselves. We've got our own problems. Like Wormwood. Why commit suicide?"

"It's like bluffing in a poker game," Paul explained. Mary loved to play poker and would easily follow his logic. "If the bluff works, you win the pot while holding a losing hand. But, if the bluff is called, you lose everything you gambled on the hand. Russia and China are gambling that we'll fold our cards. On the other hand, we can't afford not to call their bluff unless we're willing to let the Eastern Alliance rule the entire world. They won't stop in the Middle East once we back down because we're the only nation with enough firepower to really threaten them with total destruction. It's our nuclear subs that provide the main deterrence."

Mary was beginning to feel sick to her stomach. "Other nations in the Western Alliance have nuclear subs..... like France and Great Britain. Don't they count for something?" Paul sipped coffee and considered her question. "Other than Israel, I doubt that any nation would attempt to take on Russia and China once the United States gives in. The war would simply be too one-sided. The Israelis are stubborn enough to protect their own borders regardless of the odds against them." Mary marveled at Paul's calm demeanor. "What are we going to do? Shouldn't we get out of San Francisco?"

"I was going to bring that up later tonight," Paul admitted. "I can see that you're upset, so we'd better talk about it now." "I'm sorry I asked, but I'm really getting scared." She pulled a handkerchief from her purse and blew her nose. Paul reached across the table and caressed her right hand. "When we leave for the funeral in the morning, I think we should secure the house and rent an apartment in Boise. We'll load our small stuff worth stealing into the minivan and I'll arrange for a moving company to haul everything else within a week. If Wormwood does hit Earth in the North Pacific, San Francisco will be demolished by tidal waves. Besides, if nuclear war breaks out, you'll be a lot safer in Idaho. The house will be a total loss unless the insurance company pays off.....which I seriously doubt. War damage isn't covered, and if tidal waves wash over San Francisco, a lot of insurance carriers will go belly-up."

Tears welled up in Mary's eyes. "What about you? I don't care about anything else. We can always replace the house." Paul took both her hands into his and squeezed gently. "I'll have to go wherever they send me, but I'll be back. You can count on that. Jack will look after you for me until things work themselves out. Jack' s a good man, and smart. He'll know how to survive if anyone can. If war breaks out, you stick with Jack and Ruth until I come for you." Mary dried her eyes and picked at her food. "What if you don't come back?" Paul knew that question was coming, and he didn't have a good answer. "I'll be a lot safer in the air than most civilians on the ground. I won't do anything too daring because I'll be thinking about you. I'm well trained and know how to stay out of trouble. I promise you.....I'll be back."

The American submarine slithered quietly through the blue water 650 feet below the surface of the North Pacific. Admiral John Wallace sat in the control center enjoying a glass of orange juice while monitoring incoming signals and imagery. He pondered the latest information concerning the big Russian carrier. What was Malinckoff up to? What was he doing in the North Pacific so close to the area where Wormwood was going to smack into the ocean at fifty miles per second? A chilling thought suddenly occurred to him. What if Malinckoff was gathering data for attacking our subs in connection with a first strike against our mainland during the confusion created by Wormwood? Was the current military maneuvering inside Russia and China just a ploy to sidetrack us? The far-reaching destruction and public panic caused by the comet presented a golden opportunity for such deception.

The evacuation would tie up a lot of our military assets and the rest would be concentrated in the wrong place. Malinckoff would have time to complete his mission and retreat from the North Pacific before Wormwood's arrival. Then, he could move in behind the tidal waves and launch his heavy load of nuclear missiles and bombers against American cities. Yes! That makes a lot of sense. If our subs could be taken out by a carefully coordinated surprise attack, it would break the back of our retaliatory strike.

"I'm going to kill him! Wallace promised himself. I'm going to follow that weasel wherever he goes and keep him in my sights, and I don't care if he knows it. Maybe, if I push him hard enough, he'll fire on me on his way to hell!"

CHAPTER 2

Wormwood and Nuclear War

Colonel David Solomon was recognized as a top-drawer intelligence officer. He knew what the General wanted to know and felt sure that he had the correct information. The cool air felt good after the hot Sabbath. The skies were clear over Jerusalem and the forecast called for more of the same. Maybe tomorrow, he would take a badly needed day off and go to the beach.

He passed the first security checkpoint and walked through the garden toward the rear entrance. The guard recognized him and waved. "Good afternoon, Colonel. The General's expecting you." "Thank you, Thomas. Nice to see you again."

General Aaron Hartstein, himself, greeted him at the rear door. "Shalom, David. We'll talk in the library." "Shalom, General. I hope I'm not intruding upon your rest." "Not at all. I've been anxious to hear from you." Hartstein led the way to his favorite room containing wrap around bookshelves and antique reading table. The oval walnut table was ringed with reading lamps and well worn, comfortable looking leather chairs. A fully stocked liquor cabinet adorned the east corner of the room.

David eased himself into one of the luxurious old chairs while the General fetched two crystal wine glasses and a bottle of fine sherry from his private stock. "What do you think, David? Where will the Russians and Chinese concentrate their forces?" Hartstein poured the wine, pushed a glass toward David and sat down across from him. David raised his glass toward Hartstein and they touched the rims together. "To your health, General." "May Jehovah grant us wisdom and courage," Hartstein added. They drank the toast together. The General wore a short-sleeved military blouse and the familiar concentration camp tattoo was plainly visible on his forearm. He had watched his parents starve to death and had seen their corpses pitched onto a disposal wagon like garbage. He had survived only because a Nazi officer found him sexually desirable and preferred him over the other child prisoners he regularly sodomized. Now, at seventy-five, his health was failing. Bald and overweight with splotched skin and slightly stooped, he appeared shorter than six feet. Trifocal lenses distorted his watery, blue eyes.

Colonel Solomon just turned thirty-nine, a Sabra with eighteen years in the Israeli armed services. A fierce warrior at five feet, eleven inches, he had suffered numerous combat wounds during hand to hand fighting and had been decorated seven times. His brown hair, blue eyes, slightly hooked nose, and thin lips were typical of many native-born Israelis. He was in excellent health, trim and unusually strong. He lowered his glass to the table following the toast and addressed Hartstein's question: "The Plain of Esdraelon near the hill of Megiddo where the British defeated the Turks in 1918......the battlefield of Armageddon." Hartstein grunted. That is what he anticipated. "What's the source of your information?" David grinned. "My contact in the CIA."

General Hartstein rubbed the tattoo on his arm and squinted at David through half-mast trifocals. "Where did the CIA get the information?" "From a high-ranking Russian officer who's been a CIA mole for the past seventeen years." "Are you convinced this information is reliable?" David sipped some sherry and thought about how much hinged upon the reliability issue. "Yes, General. I am. The Americans are also positive that the information is accurate." Hartstein was pleased. A secret agent nurtured on the inside for seventeen years should be reasonably trustworthy. "How large a force are we talking about, David. ... approximately?

David frowned at him. "Roughly twenty million ground troops, mostly Chinese, supported by six Russian carrier groups and most of the Russian air force."

"A tidy little force!" Hartstein mused. "They mean to overwhelm us. Maybe we should be flattered," David quipped. "The ground troops will include waves of paratroopers and twelve armored divisions. The Chinese forces will cross the border into southeastern Russia. The paratroopers will be dropped into the Plain of Esdraelon. The rest of the combined ground forces will form an offensive line from the Russian border on across the northwestern tip of Iran, and through central Iraq and Jordan. The general invasion will be carefully coordinated with a nuclear first strike against the United State and other nuclear powers within the Western Alliance following the arrival of Wormwood."

Hartstein whistled softly. "Do you know what the Americans are planning since they obviously know all this and more?" David gave an affirmative nod. "President McCarron has been completely briefed. He has ordered preparation for a massive retaliatory strike and the American military is on full alert around the clock. It is certain that the Americans will hit the invading forces with nuclear weapons. It's unclear whether McCarron will consider a first strike by the United States without more hard evidence from the CIA and other U.S. intelligence agencies."

"Too bad..." Hartstein murmured. "Do you have any suggestions regarding an appropriate Israeli strategy?" David toyed with his wine glass as if pondering the question. He didn't want to appear to answer flippantly. Sure, he had a suggestion......nuke the invaders! "I appreciate your compliment, General, but I'm not qualified to formulate such strategy," Hartstein grunted affectionately. "You're as qualified as anyone I know. You've been formulating a response since you first collected the information." "Sometimes, you scare me, General." David grinned. "You gonna tell me or evade the question?" Hartstein kidded.

David drank his glass empty. "I think we should surprise the paratroopers as they're landing with everything, we've got short of nuclear weapons. No need to make our own backyard radioactive. We can ambush them with planes, tanks and ground troops. Once they have committed their paratroopers, their planes can't do much more than dogfight with our planes without killing their own troops. The key to a high kill rate is a total surprise. We should wait and move into position at the latest practical moment. The Americans may shoot a lot of them down before they penetrate our airspace, but there is apparently enough of them to go around. In any event, we can decimate their paratroopers before they can land and reorganize. The Americans will take care of the other ground forces before they reach our borders. For insurance, in case the Americans botch the job, we should hold enough of our planes in reserve to hit their carrier groups with nuclear weapons while simultaneously attacking the balance of their ground forces in Iran, Iraq, and Jordan. We'll no doubt suffer some heavy losses, but nothing like we'd lose if we fail to strike the first blow."

The General listened attentively, nodding his approval along the way. He had complete confidence in David Solomon. "We can beat them, General. Even if McCarron is foolish enough not to strike first, the American submarines will rain long-range missiles over Russia and China. In addition, the Americans will launch many of their large land-based missiles before the incoming missiles actually arrive on target. Moreover, the bulk of American aircraft equipped with nuclear weapons is now airborne and being refueled by air tankers. Russia and China will be annihilated by the United States and we should be able to eliminate the invaders isolated in the Middle East. It is quite possible that we can emerge from this conflict with our military capability reasonably intact."

Hartstein liked what he heard. "I'm truly glad you're on our side, David. The Prime Minister will be impressed." He reached for the bottle of sherry. "Have another glass with me and tell me how Martha and the boys are doing."

Vatican City covered forty-four hectares in northwestern Rome just west of the Tiber River. The Pope ruled Vatican City and it was foreign soil to Italian citizens. The tiny independent state was enclosed by high stone walls partially obscuring an irregularly shaped one-sixth square mile containing St. Peter's Church, stately and picturesque buildings, several courtyards, landscaped gardens and quiet, manicured streets. On the same ground, Nero had walked among his public gardens and the Emperor's Circus where Christians were butchered by gladiators and wild beasts.

A thunderstorm had drenched Vatican City chasing tourists and residents indoors. A cold wind whipped across The Square of St. Peter's Church as people emerged from the various buildings into the open areas. Some of them paused to gape at two men dressed in sackcloth and sandals. They stood about ten yards apart, one facing east and the other looking west. The chilly gusts of wind stirred up their sackcloth, hair, and beards giving them a wild appearance. They seemed to radiate power and virility.

Several of the spectators laughed at them and shouted insults but got no response. A brilliant bolt of lightning crackled above the square and the witness facing east proclaimed: "Hear the words of him who sent us for we are his witnesses. What is man that he should defile all creation? You have made a covenant with death and hell has enlarged itself. The treasures of hail and fire have been opened to mingle with blood. A third of trees and grass shall perish. The waters shall become bitter and a third of all creatures therein shall die. One-third of all ships shall be destroyed. A third of the day shall be darkened and a third of the night shall be bright."

Many of those who stood by booed and jeered. Others listened in wonderment and tried to get a closer look at the two witnesses. One tourist was busily capturing the event on videotape. The heckling became louder as media crews arrived. The cameras began whirring while the witness looking west spoke. His message was clearly heard above the noisy distractions:

"Let the bowels of the earth be opened and let the great smoke arise to darken the sun. Let the locusts go forth to work their torment one hundred and fifty days. Beware of the mark of Oren Natas for he is not as he appears. Be not deceived. The mark is the number of his name.....six hundred and sixty-six. Receive it not; neither in the right hand nor in the forehead. His mark is everlasting, and the blasphemy endures forever." Hoots and laughter filled the air and the media crews moved in to question the witnesses. The heckling ceased, and a hush fell over the square. The two witnesses had simply vanished.

The Roberts' minivan hummed along the interstate twenty miles west of Boise. Mary worked at a crossword puzzle while Paul drove at a leisurely speed to avoid spending much time in the church before the service began. He glanced at his watch. Yes.....he had it figured about right. They should arrive at the church just in time to be seated without feeling rushed. He dreaded the thought of viewing his mother's corpse. Paul remembered her comment when he questioned her faith in God. "It is appointed unto us once to die," she said. "Then, we shall inherit our immortal bodies, without spot or blemish and indestructible." He wasn't sure he understood what she said, but that thought gave her an inner peace which reinforced her faith and carried her through life's tragedies.

The minister, family members, and close relatives stood under the pavilion next to the fresh grave. The other mourners gathered on the grassy perimeter to listen to the graveside service. The minister read the familiar passage from the King James Version of the Gospel of John. Paul tried to think of his mother as she was the last time, he saw her. His mind wandered, and he couldn't concentrate. The final portion of the graveside scripture caught his attention: "I am the resurrection and the life: he that believes in me, though he were dead, yet shall he live. And whosoever lives and believes in me shall never die." The minister closed his Bible and stepped back from the grave. Paul, Jack and other relatives stepped forward and, in turn, dropped a handful of fresh dirt onto the casket.

The funeral procession wound its way around the cemetery circular drive and headed back toward Boise. Paul and Mary joined Jack and his wife, Ruth, inside the courtesy limo for the ride back to the church. They rode in silence for a few minutes, and then Jack laid his left hand on Paul's right shoulder. "Why don't you and Mary visit us a couple of days before you head back? It may be a while before we get another chance to spend some time together. How about it? Ruth and I would really appreciate it." Paul smiled his relief. "Matter of fact, Jack, we were going to invite ourselves if you didn't offer. I've got some pressing matters to discuss with you and Ruth." "Great!" Jack exclaimed. "Then, it's settled. We'll pick up your van and head over to our place."

The American submarine surfaced within twelve hundred yards of the Russian carrier. It was an unusual and daring confrontation. The cat and mouse game had ended. Malinckoff now knew the identity of his enemy and that Wallace intended to shadow his every maneuver and would fire on him at the least provocation. And yes, Wallace wanted to make sure that he knew it. He shivered in the damp air and thought about the warning. This is a dangerous game we're playing, Admiral. Neither of us can win but we play on. Well, I'm finished here for now. Get your finger off the trigger and follow me to safety. We shall have our little shoot-out soon enough.

His unmistakable message delivered, Admiral Wallace leveled out the sub seven hundred and fifty feet below the surface and called a closed-door meeting with his subordinate officers. After coffee and sandwiches were sent in, the room was secured, and guards were posted. Wallace got straight to the point: "Naval intelligence confirms that Russia and China are preparing to invade the Middle East. President McCarron has committed us to repel any such invasion attempt."

The officers had already concluded as much and their faces revealed neither surprise nor reluctance to carry out their predictable assignments. Wallace reviewed with them all the intelligence reports spanning the previous seventy-two hours. Then, he laid out his future strategy and supporting logic.

"Millions are starving within the Eastern Alliance due to the global food shortage. The populations in those regions are willing to follow Russia and China to war with the hope of gaining access to the food supplies of other nations. A Middle East invasion will, if successful, provide both short and long-term resources if the United States can be neutralized by a first strike while we're preoccupied with the multiple threats posed by Wormwood. It is common knowledge that our nuclear subs represent our major retaliatory capability. Neither does it require any particular military genius to predict that those same subs will cluster to protect our exposed west coast after Wormwood smashes into the ocean off the California mainland. The enemy air force and navy will try to take out our subs in the North Pacific. Their basic strategy assumes the benefits of predictable reactions, close coordination, and precise timing. They must also preposition their invasion forces to seize and hold Middle East assets. The Chinese are contributing over eighteen million troops, and Russia roughly two million. Those conventional forces are now being deployed. While we're crippled by Wormwood, the Russians will launch a sweeping attack upon our subs just prior to a general attack upon our major cities and military installations. They're gambling that our subs will wait for confirmation of a nuclear first strike which will not be forthcoming until they actually launch the attack against our mainland. It is during this time lag that they hope to surprise us with a first strike. Well....we're going to arrange a little surprise party of our own. We're going to continue to shadow Malinckoff's carrier and eavesdrop on his incoming and outgoing communications. We'll keep him in our sights at all times, day and night. When they make the first move against our subs, we'll hit his carrier with a spray of torpedoes and then immediately launch our full complement of missiles against our designated targets. It is unlikely that we'll survive, but there will be nothing to return to anyway. Our biggest contribution will probably be posthumous. No one in the future will ever doubt the suicidal nature of a nuclear first strike."

Admiral Wallace picked up his coffee mug while scanning the faces of his officers. He drank a mouthful while peering over the rim of his mug. A young officer asked meekly: "What if you're wrong, and the pressure we exert on Malinckoff causes him to fire on us?"

Wallace set his mug down and gazed at the officer. "I pray to God that he does fire on me and gives me the opportunity to screw up their surprise strategy. Even the most fainthearted politician in Washington knows that an attack upon a nuclear submarine is an act of war." He settled back into his chair and looked directly into each officer's eyes, from left to right. "I expect each of you to keep his men under control regardless of what transpires. Anyone who disobeys an order is to be shot to death on the spot.....and that goes for officers as well as enlisted personnel. Do I make myself clear?"

Again, Wallace eyed each man. There was silence indicating submission to proper authority. "All right," Wallace said flatly. "When the time comes, we shall all do our duty. Under the circumstances, we simply have no other choice. That will be all for now."

General Robert Norris scanned the checklist of emergency supplies and the stores of food and water. President McCarron's orders had been explicit. This was no drill. It was really happening. The President of the United States was actually preparing for nuclear war. Tough way for an old general to go out. His retirement was scheduled for the 30th of next month. Now, it looked like he might die with his boots on, along with lots of other folks. He had controlled Unified Air Command operations for four uneventful years.

Every week, he had checked and rechecked the sufficiency of security measures, often halfheartedly. This time, it was no mere routine. He had better be absolutely sure everything was accounted for that would allow him to operate underground for at least ninety days. The Joint Chiefs assumed that the mountain covered stronghold could withstand the pinpoint attack that was sure to come with the first wave of hostile missiles. He wasn't so sure. The UAC fortress was supported by giant steel coils deep within the mountain sanctuary. The ceilings, walls, and doors were heavily reinforced with thick, tempered steel that could absorb the energy released by a nuclear explosion. Whether several high megaton warheads could gut the mountain and destroy UAC headquarters was certainly open to question. Satisfied that nothing had been overlooked, Norris returned to his office. He inspected his image in the wall mirror, fastened the top button of his dress blouse, adjusted his tie, and picked up his briefing notes. It was time to address the troops.

The war room was buzzing with activity. High-speed military computers sorted out an endless stream of incoming information in the form of radar blips, satellite imagery, coded messages, intelligence photos, and transmissions from electronic detection devices around the world. The condensed information was projected onto huge video screens encircling the walls around the spacious working area. The video display was continuously updated as the Russians, the Chinese and the Americans maneuvered their most secret military assets in frenzied preparation for a fight to the death.

From the elevated control platform in the center of the working area, it was possible to identify the military assets deployed by both sides anywhere on Earth. Aircraft, ships, missile silos, mobile missile launchers, heavy artillery, armored divisions, and ground troop concentrations were tracked and geographically pinpointed around the clock.

General Norris entered the war room through the south door and walked briskly to the control platform. All military personnel snapped to attention and the room became quiet. Norris mounted the platform and stood with feet spread and hands clenched behind his back. He looked somewhat comical. At five feet, ten inches; two hundred and sixty pounds; sixty-five; bald; puffy cheeks; red nose and trifocals; he resembled Santa Claus without a white beard. His military posture and tone belied the Santa image. His voice was clear and steady.

"At ease, Ladies and Gentlemen." An aide stepped forward and adjusted the microphone suspended from the ceiling. "It is now certain that Wormwood will hit us in the North Pacific approximately nine hundred miles off the California coastline. The President has ordered full and immediate evacuation of our entire west coast. The media has already told you what will happen when Wormwood collides with Earth. I'm sorry to say that the tidal waves and probable earthquakes will be the minor problems facing our nation. The dictators who have grabbed power in Russia and China believe we will be more vulnerable in the wake of this comet than at any time in the past or the foreseeable future. They will attempt to neutralize us and seize the Middle East. High-level negotiations are ongoing at this time, but the Eastern Alliance keeps denying anything but war games. The President does not expect negotiation to be productive. We now anticipate a nuclear first strike by the Eastern Alliance and believe it will coincide with the earthquakes and tidal waves. However, considering the remote possibility that we may be wrong, we will not launch any of our nuclear arsenals prior to the actual attack. When we detect the launching of enemy missiles, we will commence a retaliatory strike by land, sea, and air. There is a slight chance that the dictators may decide to hold off when they discover that our nuclear submarines are not going to cluster in the North Pacific. Instead, the fleet is maneuvering into position to fire on all designated targets inside Russia and China."

The General's aide stepped forward and whispered a message in Norris' left ear. Norris nodded, and the aide retreated. "Before coming to brief you, I ordered UAC operations buttoned up and secured for the duration. We shall live and work together here until our duties have been accomplished. We have an adequate store of food, water, and medical supplies and our regular medical personnel will be here with us. We have a dreadful job to do, and it is always possible that some individuals may refuse to obey orders. I regret to inform you that such persons will be summarily executed. I sincerely hope that discipline of this magnitude does not become necessary. Thank you, and God bless each and every one of you.....in this life and the life hereafter."

General Norris stepped back from the microphone and all military personnel again snapped to attention. He descended the control platform and headed toward his office.

Paul and Mary cruised along the highway toward the cemetery. Paul drove, and Mary looked through the morning paper. Fresh flowers for Joyce Roberts' grave lined the back seat. "That was a fabulous breakfast," Paul remarked. "I wonder if Ruth really cooks like that all the time?" "I'm sure she does." Mary folded up the paper, laid it on the dash and slid over next to Paul. "It's my rotten cooking that keeps you so sexy."

Paul checked the rearview mirror and passed an old farmer in a pickup. "We'll stop by and look at the apartment Jack recommended on the way back. The price sounds right." "I really like Jack and Ruth," Mary ventured. "They're very nice. Jack's my kinda guy.....intelligent but modest." "Ruth's a real charmer and one fine lady," Paul added. "They assured me they'll look out for you.....no matter what." Paul pulled out and passed a truck, then wheeled back into the right-hand lane behind a late model, red Chevy sedan. The car was rounding a curve well under the speed limit causing Paul to slow down. Both Paul and Mary could clearly see the elderly couple in the front seat. The man was driving, and the woman appeared to be napping. Beyond the curve was a passing zone. Paul checked his rearview mirror and pulled out to pass. Mary screamed at him: "Watch out!!" The red Chevy was weaving back and forth. It swerved off the pavement, careened across the shoulder into the woods, sideswiped a large tree near the gas tank, bounced off another tree and erupted into flames.

Paul jammed on his brakes, pulled off onto the shoulder, jumped out of the minivan and sprinted back to the burning car. He threw up his left arm to protect his eyes and tried to open the door on the driver's side. The door was locked, and the window was closed. Paul beat on the window, then backed away from the flames with an expression of astonishment. He raced around to the other side and tried to open the passenger door. It was locked, and the window was up. He stared into the flames in amazement and horror.

Mary ran toward Paul along the shoulder of the road. She stopped directly above the flaming vehicle and called out. "Paul! Paul!! Get away..... before it blows up!!"

Paul began running and stumbling toward her. There was very light traffic along the roadway. Two cars and a truck came upon the scene, slowed down and drove onto the shoulder beyond Mary. When Paul reached Mary, his face was still frozen in shock and disbelief. "It's empty!!" he croaked hoarsely. "I saw inside! It's empty!! There are no bodies.....doors all locked and windows closed!!" He clasped Mary in his arms. She sputtered in trembling bewilderment while pushing against his chest. "But.....we....we saw them!! Both of them!!" More traffic pulled onto the shoulder. A group of onlookers gathered around Paul and Mary. They gawked at the flaming car and a passing motorist used a cell phone to call the state police.

Paul slumped in the back seat of the State Patrol cruiser. Down below, firemen were inspecting the interior of the burned-out sedan. The patrolman turned sideways and looked at Paul. "Are you sure you saw two occupants?" Paul spoke slowly and calmly. "Yes, I'm sure. We got a good look at both of them. A man and a woman.... appeared to be in their sixties. The man was driving. We saw them go out of control and hit the trees. When I got down there, the car was in flames, but I could see inside. I tried every door and window. The doors were all locked and the windows were up." His voice faltered slightly. "There was no one inside. It was empty." He leaned back in the seat and shut his eyes.

The patrolman took notes with a blank expression. "Okay. We'll take it from here." He looked again at Paul's driver's license. "Is this your current address in San Francisco, Colonel?" Paul opened his eyes. "Yes, but we're in the process of moving to Boise. If you'll give me your card, I'll forward our new address and phone number soon as we get settled." "That'll work out fine. I'll be on the lookout for it." He opened his glove box, selected a business card and handed it to Paul. "You and Mrs. Roberts can be on your way, Colonel. No need to detain you any longer." He smiled politely. "I'll be in touch if we need anything further."

Paul drove along the traffic lane inside the cemetery. Neither he nor Mary had come up with a rational explanation for what they had just witnessed. Tears had smeared Mary's eye makeup and she was trying to repair the damage with the aid of the visor mirror. Paul stopped the minivan alongside the private road a short distance from Joyce Roberts' grave. His eyes widened in stark amazement. He bolted from the minivan and dashed to the grave. There was fresh dirt scattered over the plot as if an internal force had flung the dirt aside. At the bottom of the hole, the lid was open on an empty casket. Stunned, he fell to his knees and stared into the hole. There was no trace of a body.

Mary was startled and frightened. She scrambled from the passenger side and ran across the grass toward him. Upon reaching his side, she leaned over and peered into the grave. She gasped, fell to her knees, grabbed his arm to keep from collapsing and buried her face in his shoulder. "My God!!" Paul's voice was barely audible. "Look over there!" Mary raised her head and followed his eyes. The sight made her shiver and she breathed hard to keep from fainting. Nearby, contrasted against the well-manicured grounds, were several other burial plots littered with fresh grave dirt. Paul squeezed her gently. "Wait here. I'll be right back." He trotted around the cemetery grounds and looked into more than a dozen open graves.....all without corpses.

Mary had followed behind but couldn't keep up. Her eyes were filled with tears and confusion, her heart pounding in her throat. Paul stopped to catch his breath, noticed her trailing behind and walked back to meet her. She stumbled into his arms and he supported her while she steadied herself. "Wh... what's happening?" she gasped. "Wh... where're the bodies?" Paul hugged her tightly. "There's nothing we can do here. Let's go to the police."

They hurried back to the minivan and Paul took the driver's seat. Mary got in and Paul headed for the cemetery exit. "How would the cops know anything?" Mary asked in an uncertain voice. "What else can we do?" "I don't know," Paul murmured. "I'm so shaken up I can't think clearly." He reached over and switched on the radio. "Let's see if there's anything being reported by other people." He dialed the indicator across AM frequencies trying to find a local station.

He paused at a clear station broadcasting a special announcement that quickened his pulse: "... to report immediately to their assigned units. All leaves have been canceled without exception. We repeat: The President of the United States has declared a national emergency and has ordered all military personnel to report immediately to their assigned units. All leaves have been canceled without exception. Also, at this hour, local authorities are being flooded with reports of missing persons, grave robbing, and accidents involving unmanned motor vehicles, boats, and aircraft. We will update you on these unusual stories as more information becomes available. We repeat The President of the United St..." Paul switched off the radio and checked his wristwatch. "We've got to head for the airport right now," he said curtly. "Most of my luggage is in the back except for some personal items that I can replace at the base." He slipped a flight schedule from his hip pocket and glanced at the card. "The next flight to Colorado Springs leaves in thirty-two minutes. There should be seats available this time of day." He encircled Mary with his right arm, drew her close to him and kissed her cheek. "Don't worry.....there's got to be a logical explanation for all this craziness. I'll call you the first chance I get after reporting in." Mary dug a handkerchief out of her purse and wiped her eyes, then blew her nose softly. "I'm sorry to be so scared," she said, snuggling up close to Paul. "I just can't help it."

Captain Marcus was completing his departure checklist as Mary and Paul entered the passenger lounge. The gate agent picked up the intercom. "Don't close the door yet, I think we may fill another seat or two." He smiled at them. "One passenger or two?"

Paul carried luggage in both hands and Mary carried his briefcase. "Just me." Paul set his luggage down and fished out a credit card. "She's just seeing me off. I didn't have time to go to the ticket counter and still make the flight." He handed the credit card to the agent and watched him fill in a ticket. "Please go aboard right away, Colonel Roberts. We're ready to depart." The agent picked up Paul's luggage and headed for the service door. Paul took his briefcase from Mary, hugged her once more and kissed her good-bye. "Don't forget to give my note to Jack and Ruth. I'll call as soon as possible."

Through the window in the passenger lounge, Mary watched the jet-way retract. The ground crew moved in and backed the Boeing 727 away from the gate. Tears had smeared her mascara leaving dark blotches under her eyes. She felt a strange chill and a troubling thought lingered. Her husband wasn't coming back. The 727 reappeared on the active runway. She watched as it gathered speed, lifted off and quickly faded into the southeastern horizon.

Jack Roberts opened the door and Mary entered. Jack glanced around. "Where's Paul?" Mary dropped her purse onto a black marble coffee table and flopped on the soft leather couch. "Haven't you heard the news?" "We've been reading in the garden," Ruth replied. "What news?"

"McCarron declared a national emergency and canceled all military leaves." The strain was apparent in Mary's voice. "I dropped Paul off at the airport." Jack and Ruth exchanged a look of concern and waited to hear more. Mary's composure crumbled. She began sobbing and collapsed on her side. Jack knelt down by the couch and gathered Mary into his arms. He comforted her until her hysterical weeping subsided. Ruth looked on with moist eyes. Mary regained some semblance of self-control. Jack gently maneuvered her into a sitting position and sat down beside her. He slid a handkerchief from his shirt pocket and placed it in her left hand. She dabbed at her eyes and nose. Her voice was unsteady and still ragged. "Your mother's grave is empty."

Jack's mouth fell agape, and his heart fluttered. "Her body's gone?" He felt sudden panic but didn't show it. Mary looked from Jack to Ruth with blurred eyes. "Yes. When we got there, her grave was open and fresh dirt was scattered over the top. The lid on her casket was open...and it was empty." Jack got up from the couch with an awed expression. "Did you see any other graves with fresh dirt around them?" Mary wiped fresh tears away and looked up at Jack. "Yes, several. We looked inside them too. They were empty."

Jack blinked at Ruth. She stifled a sobbing noise and clasped her right hand over her mouth. Jack sat down by Mary again. "Did you see or hear anything else that seemed strange?" Mary sniffled and blew her nose. "On the way to the cemetery, a car ran off the road in front of us. It hit some trees and started burning. We saw an elderly couple inside before they lost control. Paul stopped and tried to help, but he couldn't get a door open. They were all locked.....windows too. Paul was able to see inside. He said the car was empty. The firemen and state police couldn't find any bodies either. Then, we heard on the radio that the cops are being flooded with reports of missing persons, grave robbing, and accidents involving empty vehicles, boats, and planes. None of it makes any sense."

Ruth had been intently listening to every word. She stared wide-eyed at Jack. "No......no! It can't be! Oh, My God!"

President McCarron stood on the White House lawn peering into the night sky. The comet, Wormwood, was now plainly visible and people were beginning to believe it would collide with Earth. Civilian authorities no longer doubted the prediction and the west coast evacuation was underway. Canadian, Central and South American governments had initiated similar evacuations. McCarron had watched the mad scramble on the evening news. The widespread panic had overshadowed public concern over strange accidents involving unmanned vehicles, grave robbing, and the sudden disappearance of nearly ten percent of the population. Well... first things first. Those mysteries would have to be addressed after the evacuation.

All roadways, waterways, and airports along the west coast were jammed with people fleeing with whatever valuables they could carry. Police, firemen, federal troops, National Guard units from every state and the Coast Guard worked frantically to keep the human tide flowing into ships, planes, railroad cars, buses, trucks, and automobiles. All commercial transportation equipment had been pressed into service by presidential order along with all inventories of unsold new or used vehicles capable of transporting people.

The army, navy and air force contributed all available aircraft, ships, trucks, buses, and miscellaneous motor vehicles. Hundreds of thousands fled on foot toward the mountains and other high elevations. Those with sufficient money, power or influence took off in private boats, airplanes, and helicopters. Individuals who couldn't take refuge with family or friends away from the impact area were routed to government land and national parks throughout the west and southwest. Federal troops set up temporary shelters and trucked in food and water supplies. It was the greatest evacuation effort in modern history and it was proceeding as smoothly as could be expected under the circumstances. The troops-maintained order and provided security within the temporary shelter areas.

The American nuclear submarine had shadowed the Russian carrier over fifty-seven hours since the initial encounter. Admiral Wallace sat in the control center monitoring coded messages being transmitted to and from the carrier. The frequency and length of the transmissions led him to believe that Captain Malinckoff was relaying to his superior's information gathered during the intelligence portion of the carrier's mission.

Wallace removed the electronic headset, leaned back and closed his eyes. He let his mind drift to relieve the tension headache that had been building for the last hour. The big, rawboned Texan from Dallas was well respected by both superiors and subordinates. His overall image was magnetic. The ladies were attracted by his brown eyes; bushy, brown hair; broad forehead; high cheekbones and square chin. He was powerfully built, standing six feet, two inches; thick chested; two hundred and twenty pounds and no extra fat.

"Admiral Wallace. . ." The sound of his name jarred him back to reality. It was Lieutenant Walker, his intelligence officer. "Admiral, we've broken their code. You are right, Sir. They're going to attack our subs just prior to a strike against our mainland. It sounds like they may hit us before Wormwood does. They're afraid that we might launch a first strike and consider it a trade-off to attack before the comet arrives while a lot of our conventional assets are tied up with the evacuation."

"Are they still transmitting, Lieutenant?" "No, Sir. All communications to and from the carrier have ceased." "Very well, Lieutenant. Do you have anything further?" "No, Sir. I'll inform you immediately if we pick up another transmission, but I think there won't be anymore." "Thank you, Lieutenant ... good work!" Wallace leaned back and closed his eyes again. What should he do? If the Eastern Alliance moved up the timetable, the attack could commence at any time. They are going to launch a sneak attack. The only question is when. Should he contact Admiral Meeker and run the risk of transmitting? We decoded their communications. Have they broken our new codes? Is that how they discovered we know their initial plan? If he took the risk, what would Washington do? How fast could the politicians react? Fewer Americans would die if we strike first and knock out some of their nuclear capability. Did he have the raw nerve to steal the initiative? He wrestled with himself and tried to think of another way.

Admiral Wallace ordered all personnel to battle stations, and ordered torpedoes and missiles readied for launching. USS Liberty turned about into launch position while final preparations for firing were completed. Firing keys were inserted and the countdown began. Eight seconds before he gave the command to fire, Admiral Wallace transmitted a coded emergency message to Admiral Meeker, companion nuclear subs and Unified Air Command: "UNDER FIRE BY RUSSIAN CARRIER. RESPONDING.....ALL WEAPONS.....WALLACE."

When Captain Malinckoff discovered that the American submarine had locked in on his carrier from a launch position only fifteen hundred yards away, he did not get overly concerned. Wallace had bird-dogged him for days and sighted in on him several times. No. He would not allow Wallace to goad him into action prematurely. The planned attack upon the American submarines would commence in less than two hours; and four minutes later, the strike against the mainland would be launched. Timing was extremely important. No.....Wallace would not fire on him without provocation. The shoot-out must be delayed a little longer.

Assuming that the American officer would not actually fire on his carrier was the last mistake Captain Malinckoff would ever make. It took a few seconds for him to realize that Wallace had fired four torpedoes and all four were going to hit his carrier broadside. He immediately initiated defensive tactics, but it was too late to return fire or escape from the swift torpedoes. The carrier sent out its last transmission: "ATTACK BY AMERICAN SUBMARINE. NUCLEAR STRIKE...... The exploding warheads ripped the carrier apart within a few heartbeats. Amidst the blinding fireballs and thick smoke, the charred remains of the great vessel slipped beneath the North Pacific.

After firing the torpedoes, USS Liberty had dived as a tactical maneuver and to avoid the heat and shock waves on the surface. It now ascended back toward the surface to launch its long-range missiles. Wallace leveled out the sub well below the radioactive surface and commenced the firing sequence. The water above the sub churned as the first missile emerged. It rose vertically above its billowing fireball before tilting eastward. Sleek and awesome in the afternoon sun, the cargo of death accelerated to attack speed and streaked into the eastern horizon. Within a matter of minutes, USS Liberty's total complement of long-range missiles was flaming eastward carrying a total of ninety-six high megaton warheads.

The unthinkable had now been triggered and "mutual assured destruction" was transformed from military theory to shattering reality. The nuclear war commenced by air, land, and sea. Around the globe, the Western Alliance unleashed its powerful arsenal upon the Eastern Alliance. Theoretically, the west enjoyed the first strike advantage; but again, theory proved unreliable. The ferocity of the first strike was matched by the fury of the retaliatory strike. The population of the world was about to shrink by several billion.

Captain Marcus leveled out the Boeing 727 at twenty-nine thousand feet. Colonel Paul Roberts sat near the middle of the plane in an aisle seat. He appeared to be in another world, oblivious to his surroundings. Flight attendants moved throughout the cabin serving soft drinks and cocktails. Some passengers dozed while others read or engaged in casual conversation. An attractive female attendant paused at Paul's seat and leaned toward him. "Something to drink, Sir?" Paul looked at her with an empty expression, gave her a negative nod, and turned his eyes back to the cabin window.

A hollow sadness had settled over him and his eyes felt watery. He slumped back into his seat and tried to doze, but he felt the heat from the burning car and recalled the horror that gripped him when he realized the car was unoccupied. He saw himself kneeling in the fresh dirt staring into his mother's empty grave, trembling in amazement. The cabin speakers emitted an electronic beep that caught his attention. The flight attendants paused, and the passengers stopped talking. The static click of the flight deck microphone was followed by the calm voice of Captain Marcus:

"Ladies and Gentlemen, may I please have your attention......this is Captain Raymond Marcus. I regret to inform you that the Eastern Alliance has just launched a surprise attack upon the United States and our allies. Our flight control center reports that numerous missiles have crossed over Alaska and are expected to reach our mainland within a few minutes. Missiles apparently launched by their carriers and submarines are also headed toward the United States. For your protection, I have altered our flight plan to head for the interior of Canada. Counting our reserves, we should have enough fuel to land at the Calgary airport in Alberta Province. We will make every effort to ensure your safety. Please help us by remaining calm and by following every instruction from the flight deck and your flight attendants."

The passenger cabin buzzed with startled exclamations, praying, weeping and cursing. Paul stared at the front wall of the cabin, thinking of Mary and mouthing a silent prayer. "Please, God. Don't let her die.....not like this." Behind him, an elderly woman mumbled the Lord's Prayer.

Gradually, the mixed outcries died away, and the cabin became quiet except for muffled praying and the shuffling of passengers trying to see out the windows. Captain Marcus had taken the 727 to forty thousand feet as a safety measure and to conserve fuel by avoiding lower altitude turbulence. Far below the jetliner, two missiles were visible in the western horizon.

Civil defense systems broadcast their ominous message and warning sirens blared as the plummeting warheads approached their targets. The streets teemed with people.....young, old, male and female running in all directions seeking shelter.....any kind of shield. Inside industrial, commercial and residential buildings, people rushed to the ground floors and huddled in corners or under any protective shield. By and large, their efforts were both pitiful and futile.

Each exploding warhead produced a brilliant flash of light, gigantic fireball and a thick column of smoke topped by a huge mushroomed cloud. The monstrous heat and shock waves radiated out from the center of each explosion, leveling and charring everything in their wake. Each fireball burned at the core temperature of the sun and was visible over a two-hundred-mile radius. Thousands of warheads rained down upon military, industrial and other strategic targets within the eastern and western hemispheres.

Supersonic bombers ran the gauntlet of fighter planes and surface-to-air missiles in order to drop high megaton bombs upon seats of government, naval ports, missile fields, air force bases, and military-industrial complexes. Many got through and released their payloads before being shot down. Among the scores of governmental centers that perished were London, Paris, Berlin, Peking, Washington, DC, and Moscow. Hundreds of other heavily populated cities were reduced to ash and radioactive rubble.

Earth wobbled in its orbit from the nuclear explosions jarring its surface. Secondary explosions at military warehouses, air bases, oil and gas storage yards, military-industrial sites, and naval facilities sent up enormous clouds of heavy, black smoke that mingled with gray, mushroom-shaped clouds dotting Earth's atmosphere. The thick smoke clouds and fine particles of airborne debris ascended into the troposphere blotting out the light and heat from the sun. The super-heating of the troposphere allowed massive precipitation to escape into the stratosphere making possible the formation of huge hailstones when the vapors condensed back into the top of the troposphere.

The planet became cold and dark, and an eerie glow from burning structures flickered about the corpses strewn in every direction. People caught near the epicenters of the heat and shock waves were totally consumed. Miles away from the epicenters, the eyes, tongues and outer flesh of the dead were burned away by high-level radiation. Beyond the killing radius, victims staggered about with sightless eye sockets, blistered faces, and disfigured mouths void of soft membranes. Over three billion persons were either dead or dying and hundreds of millions suffered lethal exposure to radiation that would kill them within a matter of days.

The Eastern Alliance had not directly targeted the Middle East during the nuclear attack. The invasion armada was pressing into the area, and it would have been foolish to jeopardize the oil fields and mineral deposits. Israel held back its weapons and waited in ambush for the invaders.

The Russian, Chinese and American governments disintegrated during the Holocaust along with closely allied military powers. Israel escaped due to its strategic location within the Middle East. UAC headquarters had been penetrated by two hydrogen bombs and President McCarron's plane landed in neutral Sweden seeking sanctuary.

After exhausting their firepower, the surviving nuclear submarines cowered in the oceans' depths, and surface vessels sought to conserve fuel while hiding under cover of thick cloud banks. Weaponless and cut off from command centers, naval vessels were sitting duck targets. Military aircraft not capable of vertical landing that escaped the murderous air-to-air and surface-to-air fire ran out of fuel. With no place to land, the lethal weapons crashed into the oceans or wherever the engines failed for lack of fuel.

The Chinese and Russian ground forces concentrated in Iran, Iraq, and Jordan was methodically slaughtered by nuclear bombs dropped from American aircraft which had been circling in friendly airspace. The carrier groups were destroyed by long-range American missiles, and American pilots shot down nearly half of the transport planes in spite of their fighter escorts.

Only one-sixth of the invasion force survived. The Israeli ambush was enhanced by the dark, debris-filled clouds circling Earth. Israeli warplanes equipped with infrared targeting devices attacked the surviving invaders scattered throughout Iran, Iraq, and Jordan. Israeli pilots shot down scores of transport planes and escorting fighters. Nevertheless, over a half million armed paratroopers dropped into the Plain of Esdraelon. The darkness saved many of them from Israeli ground fire. The situation was further complicated by a deadly storm moving into the area. The atmosphere quickly took on a greenish hue pierced by continuous thunder and streaks of lightning while monstrous hailstones hammered the invaders. The icy bombardment plucked aircraft out of the sky, sending the fiery fragments into the terrain below. The paratroopers were caught in the open plain and squashed by the huge stones. The astonished Israelis withdrew and regrouped their forces.

The moon tugged at Wormwood's mass as the big comet flashed by the lunar orb toward the dark clouds circling Earth. Stretched between the gravitational forces of Earth and its moon, the outer clusters of rocks and metals separated from the inner core of Wormwood's nucleus. The trajectory of each cluster widened, forming an irregular umbrella pattern around the inner core. The monolithic fragments blazed through Earth's atmosphere appearing as seven mountainous balls of fire. The solid core buried itself in the North Pacific eight hundred and twelve miles west of northern California sending up vast clouds of steam and concentric walls of water more than one thousand feet high. Tidal waves flowed outward from the point of the impact rising over sixteen hundred feet in height. The molten mass blasted a crater in the ocean floor more than twelve miles wide and two thousand feet deep. The awesome impact rocked Earth on its axis a full sixty degrees causing the planet to wobble along its orbit.

The six clusters plowed into the Pacific a fraction of a second later with an explosive force exceeding sixty hydrogen bombs, creating craters in the ocean floor several miles wide and twenty-two hundred feet deep. The clusters vaporized additional billions of gallons of salt water and triggered towering tidal waves that roared across the ocean's surface like erupting volcanoes as the destructive walls of water raced toward the coastlines. The raw power of the killer waves inundated and smashed every surface vessel between the crater sites and the surrounding land mass. The relentless waves washed across coastal cities uprooting everything in their paths, drowning air-breathing creatures caught in their wakes, and polluting rivers, streams, and lakes. Radioactive rubble and debris, along with millions of charred human and animal corpses, were scattered upon the face of the waves and mingled with dead and dying marine life.

The odor of decaying flesh putrefied the air as the great walls of water were gradually leveled out by gravity, flooding the lowlands. The extensive clouds of vaporized ocean water mixed with the debris-laden clouds circling Earth producing tornadoes, hurricanes, and typhoons which hammered the continents.

The raging flood waters drove survivors to higher elevations, inundated more agricultural lands, and spread additional pollution upon freshwater supplies. The lowlands became covered with a layer of salt. Another billion or so humans died from exposure to lethal radiation, hunger, and thirst. Millions more suffering from blindness, nausea and internal hemorrhage were swept away by the flood waters. Much of the livestock and wildlife that escaped the killing radiation drowned. Uncontaminated food and water became more precious than pure gold.

Gradually, over ninety-seven days, the dark clouds scattered, letting more sunlight through to Earth's surface. The lighter gases filtered into the stratosphere and the moisture-laden debris settled out of the atmosphere. Rain, sleet, and snow precipitated out the finer particles causing the darkness to further dissipate. The prevailing winds scattered the remaining clouds, letting normal sunlight warm the earth.

Earth continued to rock on its axis in the vacuum of space like a spinning top poked by a child's finger. The rocking initiated by colliding with Wormwood introduced four hours of sunlight during night hours and four hours of darkness during each day. Radiation levels diminished, and human scavengers openly foraged for food and water. The strong preyed upon the weak and unarmed by robbing, raping and killing.

The flood waters finally abated and drained back into rivers, lakes, and oceans. The natural cycle of evaporation and precipitation slowly redistributed Earth's waters. The lowlands dried up revealing the unprecedented carnage wrought by Wormwood and the nuclear war. The natural environment was littered with bloated human and animal corpses as far as the eye could see in every direction. Millions of dead fish and other marine life remains were strewn among the litter, sending forth a suffocating stench in addition to the noxious odor of rotting human flesh and the repulsive aroma of decomposing animals. Earthquakes had opened up yawning chasms filled with putrid water, corpses and miscellaneous debris. Man-made structures had been flattened, toppled or gutted. Utility networks and communications systems were virtually wiped out.

Geographical areas that escaped direct nuclear attack had been contaminated to varying levels with radioactive fallout. Millions of humans and animals exposed to lethal radiation died slowly, their remains dotting the landscape. Most of the survivors suffered radiation burns, hair loss, and radiation-related illness. Earth's carrion scavengers swarmed around the unattended dead, feasting upon the flesh and blood of the fresher, less contaminated corpses.

The monumental pollution and radioactive contamination inflicted upon the planet reduced Earth's habitable regions by two thirds. Naturally shielded mountainous terrain, remote wilderness areas, third world countries without military significance, and isolated, non-militarized islands contained the largest supplies of uncontaminated food and water as well as the natural environment capable of sustaining the normal population of living creatures. In North America, human scavengers migrated into Canada, Alaska, Oregon, Idaho, Utah, Montana, Wyoming, and New Mexico.

Local civilian authorities struggled to maintain control of limited food and water supplies. Armed guards protected seasonal inventories and mobile patrols roamed about watching over crops, livestock, wildlife, and freshwater resources. Individual consumption was carefully rationed at the survival level and prices were frozen. Slowly, the wheels of ordered society began tuning again and idle manpower was organized into work crews engaged in mass burials and general cleanup of the environment.

Social institutions were overburdened caring for the sick and dying, monitoring radiation levels and inspecting food and water supplies for signs of contamination. In geographical regions where civilian governments had crumbled, social institutions had collapsed, and law enforcement had vanished, the law of the jungle prevailed. The dead were left to carrion scavengers and the elements. Humans hid out wherever they could and fought like wild animals over meager sustenance.

Inside the Calgary airport, officials had set up an information booth for the Americans who landed there with Captain Marcus. For one hundred and sixty-four days, the passengers had slept in the Boeing 727, ate and drank in the airport and used airport restrooms. The airport manager arranged for laundry service and for showers in six designated restrooms.

Paul Roberts sat in his seat inside the 727 thinking about Mary. He felt sure she was still alive. Boise had never been a prime military target in spite of its nuclear power plant and highly specialized research facilities. He closed his eyes and tried to visualize Mary and what she might be doing at the moment.

Jackie Mason interrupted his train of thought. "Hi, Paul. May I join you?" Paul pushed the button to lower his seat back, settled into a semi-reclining position and closed his eyes hoping to relieve the pounding in his forehead. "By all means, ... you're always welcome. Matter of fact.... I'd like you to stay with me. We should be able to leave the airport anytime now, but it'll be a while before they let us leave the country." He opened his eyes and grinned at her. "I don't have much cash, but I've got some credit cards.....if they're still good. I haven't tried to use them here." "Why won't they let us leave the country? All airborne radiation should have settled out by now. What are they waiting for now?"

Paul gazed out the window at the far horizon. "The Canadians feel responsible for our general safety. They're afraid conditions inside the United States are too unstable to risk re-entry." "You think it's dangerous?" She sounded more relaxed and was picking at her nails. "It's hard to say for sure," Paul answered with a look of uncertainty. "Safe food and water will be very hard to come by, and so will any type of transportation. They don't want us trying to hoof it back from here." "Won't this plane fly back?" Jackie asked hopefully. "Not for some time.... maybe months."

Paul's headache had faded allowing him to feel comfortable again. He rotated in his seat slightly to face Jackie. "The war, tidal waves, and earthquakes have severed international communications. Rebuilding won't begin until law and order have been restored. Since the United States was directly targeted during the war, the condition of any airport remains suspect until visually inspected. The only social order, for the time being, will probably be in primitive areas remote from military or industrial targets. The civilian death toll won't be known yet, but it'll be in the billions. Lawless scavengers will be a major problem until local and national governments have been reorganized."

"When do you think that'll be likely? Will the military regroup and impose martial law?" Jackie crossed her legs and smoothed out her skirt. An air force Colonel would probably know the answer. "That possibility is pretty remote," Paul answered quietly. "Washington, DC probably caught some high megaton bombs and any surviving military personnel will be widely scattered and completely disorganized. Military operations are ineffective without a rigid chain of command. Surviving civilians will eventually band together for protection from scavengers. Only then will it become possible to impose law and order throughout the country."

Jackie's yen to return to the United States faded somewhat as she considered his logical explanation. She respected his opinion and considered him highly intelligent and exceptionally handsome. She remembered noticing him when he boarded the plane in Boise, attracted by his tall, muscular frame, virile aura, and UAC emblems. Her admiration grew upon discovering he also flew jet fighters. She wasn't sure what the future held, but she was very sure about Colonel Paul Roberts. Now might be the right time to open the door a little wider. "The Alberta and Calgary governments appear to be in control. Why not just settle down here and begin a new life?"

"I'd never be content without knowing what happened to Mary. I promised her that no matter what I'd be back. I left her at the Boise airport when the emergency alert voided my funeral leave. My brother, Jack, who lives in Boise promised me he'd look after her until I return.....and Jack has never let me down on a promise." Jackie swallowed hard but managed a smile. "Is Jack anything like you? Maybe I should be introduced." Paul chuckled softly. "He's more talented, couple years older, and has the natural instinct to survive most anything. He's an orthopedic surgeon and his wife, Ruth, is a shrewd lawyer. They're both sensitive, brilliant, witty and care about people. Jack's an outdoorsman, loves to hunt and fish....which will probably come in handy about now. He's very gentle and considerate but, when cornered, he's a wild man. That's why I made him promise to look after Mary. If anyone can bring her through this mess, Jack can."

Mother Roberts raised a couple of real gentlemen, Jackie concluded. Being around the Roberts brothers would suit her just fine. "Where do you think Jack is now? In Boise?" "I think he's probably in that general area." Paul wished he had stayed behind with Mary. "Jack seldom gets caught unprepared. Before the missiles landed, he probably hid out in the mountains with Ruth and Mary. We often discussed practical ways to survive a nuclear war. Jack always favored heading for the mountains. Of course, there's no assurance he made it to the wilderness or survived after he got there. But, there's a good chance he did ... I've got to know one way or another." "Any other relatives around Boise?" "None that I'm close to. I was in Boise attending my mother's funeral. The only relatives I keep up with are Jack, Ruth, and Mom. Dad died before my fifth birthday....an accident."

"I'm sorry," Jackie mumbled. "I didn't mean to bring up something unpleasant.... just being nosy." "No need for an apology." Paul reached out and folded his hands over hers. "Life is here and now. The dead are beyond our reach and know nothing of our tears. Sorrow and grief can't help them." A tear glistened on Jackie's right cheek. "I know that's true but it hurts just the same."

Paul decided to change the subject. "Guess it's too much to hope that such a beautiful woman likes to hunt and fish?" The inflection in his voice indicated a question rather than a statement. She hoped she didn't sound too anxious. "I'd enjoy doing anything with you ......including your hobbies."

CHAPTER 3

Anti-Christ by Global Acclamation

General Oren Natas relaxed within the splendor of his private office in southern Sicily, looking over the list of statesmen scheduled to attend the emergency conference in Geneva. He reclined in a soft, red leather, chaise lounge sipping 75-year old brandy from a huge crystal snifter. The white carpet was thick and luxurious and rare paintings adorned the spacious walls. The wallpaper was white velvet above darkly grained, mahogany paneling. The massive mahogany desk was equipped with silver hardware, and the red leather, executive chair was mounted on solid silver castings. The large, exquisitely grained, solid mahogany conference table and matching red leather chairs along with the white leather sofa, matching chair and heavy, mahogany end tables gave the room a balanced look of pure luxury. The elegant lamps, solid silver coffee urn, and delicate china service indicated that Natas had a taste for opulent decor.

Natas smiled to himself as he mused over the list of names. There would be no one at the conference who would detract from his ingenious plans to restore world order and to provide sufficient food and water for everyone. His army had been held in reserve, was well equipped, well-disciplined and quite capable of eliminating the lawless scavengers that plagued local authorities, plus rounding up and inducting the remnants of the armed forces that had plunged the earth into nuclear war. Yes, he would display his understanding of difficult problems, offer plausible solutions, and overcome all doubts concerning his ability to function as the benevolent dictator of the world. Even the worthiest opponents would succumb in the face of his power to give life and to vanquish dissenters with whirlwinds of fire.

Yes, he alone would determine the destiny of mankind and he would humble the seed of Abraham. They would worship at his feet and Jerusalem would cease to be a thorn in his side. First, he must rise to power, establish one secular ruler, one spiritual leader, and a mark to distinguish loyal subjects from dissenters. Then, he would track down the two witnesses who opposed him and celebrate their demise by proclaiming a memorial holiday. He chuckled to himself at the thought of their dead bodies being desecrated in the streets while his followers watched on television. After his victory over Enoch and Elijah, no one would dare speak out against him.

Jack Roberts carefully removed a portion of the brush and rocks that concealed the small entrance to the cave and peered through the hole looking for any sign that other humans might be nearby. He watched for several minutes, then removed four large rocks and a tangle of brush. He looked and listened for another five minutes, then quietly crawled through the remaining debris into the damp woods outside the cave. The mid-August air was cool and refreshing. The late evening sun filtered through the lodgepole pines casting soft shadows about the tree trunks. Jack laid aside his bow and quiver of arrows while quickly replacing the cover over the cave entrance.

He stood motionless looking and listening, then slipped stealthily into the woods above the cave. His camouflaged jumpsuit, cap, gun belt, and knife scabbard blended into the trees making him virtually invisible until he moved forward. He carried a .45 caliber pistol in his gun belt and a large hunting knife in the scabbard on his left hip. He hunted with the bow to avoid the scavengers a gunshot might attract. He walked slowly and silently, scanning the soft ground for tracks or droppings. The morning rain had drenched the woods and the ground was still damp enough to deaden his footsteps. He stopped a half mile north of the cave and inspected some fresh tracks. Two does and a fawn had passed by after the rain stopped. The tracks led northeast and then circled south toward a small lake east of the cave. Jack circled wide to keep the wind in his face as he approached the water from the northeast. He paused beneath a drooping red cedar and watched the open spaces between the water and the surrounding pines.

A slight rustle to his left turned out to be a squirrel chewing on a pine cone. He sat down beneath the cedar and leaned against its trunk. He enjoyed the woods and loved to hunt. Under other circumstances, the hunt would have been a relaxing outing even if he came up empty. But, this was no pleasure hunt. If he returned to the cave empty-handed, he and the women would go to sleep hungry again. The supplies they had backpacked in had been consumed except for coffee, tea, and spices. For the past six weeks, they ate fish and wild game. All those years he and Ruth spent studying, scheming and sacrificing now profited them nothing.

Everything had been left behind, they used pocket money and credit cards to buy what they could carry into the cave before pushing the Jeep over a cliff two miles from the entrance. Their hasty departure from civilization proceeded the incoming missiles by less than ninety minutes.

He wondered what would become of his property and other assets. What did it matter? They weren't going back. He knew they must hide out for seven years when Mary returned from the cemetery and reported the empty graves. He was no longer Dr. Roberts, but rather a vagabond, a hunter and gatherer. They would have to live off the land like the early Indians. The cave provided adequate shelter and was well hidden. He and Paul had discovered it by sheer accident three years earlier while bear hunting in the Sawtooth range. The underground spring flowing through the cave provided all the fresh water they needed to hide out indefinitely as long as they were careful about leaving no trails or other signs of human presence pointing to the entrance.

A flash of brown in the pines directly across the lake interrupted his thoughts. He froze and squinted at the shadow like figure moving toward the water in the dusky twilight. It appeared to be a young four-point buck. The deer stopped at the edge of the water and sniffed the air, prancing nervously. Jack was downwind from the animal and it could neither see nor smell him. When the buck lowered its head to drink, Jack raised up on one knee and took careful aim through the crossbow sights. He knew he would only get one shot, and in the fading light, he aimed for the lungs.

The twang of the bowstring startled the buck. It jerked its head upward as the arrow pierced its left flank. The shock knocked the animal to its knees, but it regained its balance, wheeled and bolted into the woods. Jack moved slowly and quietly toward the spot where the deer entered the woods, giving it enough time to weaken from internal bleeding and instinctively lie down. Trailing by moonlight, Jack had difficulty spotting the blood spatters. He nearly missed the buck lying in a pool of blood about three hundred yards inside the pine thicket. He dragged his prize out of the brush, slit its throat to bleed it, removed his arrow and quickly field dressed the carcass. In the darkness, he dragged the buck to the lake, washed it and stuffed the body cavity full of grass to soak up any remaining blood. He hung the bow and quiver on his gun belt and began dragging his prize toward the cave.

He stopped every thirty yards, released the deer and backtracked, using pine branches to smooth out his tracks and the trail made by the carcass sliding along the ground. It was tedious work but absolutely necessary to avoid leaving a visible trail to the cave entrance.

The quarter moon hung high in the night sky as Jack approached the cave. He stopped in the trees and listened intently, then left the buck behind, walked to the entrance and uncovered a crawl space. He placed the bow and quiver inside, returned to the carcass, dragged it to the opening, pulled it inside, then swept the ground with a branch all the way from the trees to the entrance. He crawled inside and closed the opening again with rocks and brush. Jack dragged the deer through the dark, narrow tunnel toward the inner room. When he could see the glow from the campfire, he left the deer, went back for the bow and quiver, then continued on, dragging the animal with his right hand and carrying the hunting gear in his left hand. By the time he reached the opening to the inner room, he was totally exhausted.

Up ahead, he heard giggling and splashing. Ruth and Mary were apparently bathing in the spring. He laid his load aside and sat down in the dark tunnel to wait until they finished. His thoughts turned to Paul. Was he really dead? If not, where was he? Had he returned to Boise in search of Mary? That didn't seem very likely. After he discovered the deserted house, he would have looked for them here. That was the main reason for selecting this particular cave. Paul knew its location and would definitely check it out. He surely hadn't returned to Boise. If he did survive the war, he wouldn't bother trying to report to military authorities. For all practical purposes, the United States military no longer existed. Could he be wounded and laid up somewhere unable to travel? Had his plane crashed for lack of fuel or serviceable runway? There was just no way to answer such nagging questions.

Billions of persons had perished and would eventually be buried in mass graves. He would never know for sure what happened to Paul. Something had kept him from returning and the only thing that could stop him was death or serious injury. The lump in his throat passed into his stomach as he faced up to reality. Paul wasn't coming back, or he would have shown up by now. It was time to end the wishful thinking and make decisions based on logic, not false hope.

Ruth and Mary waded out of the spring, dried off and put on their bathrobes. As they walked toward the campfire, Jack picked up his gear and began dragging the fresh meat into the inner room. The room temperature always seemed warm compared to the cold spring water. Somewhere in the small, rocky tunnels off the inner room, tiny openings to the outside world vented the cave. Jack had ringed the fire with large, flat rocks and it burned continuously for lighting, cooking and physical comfort.

Jack removed the ashes daily, dropping them into the toilet area where the spring flowed underneath the north wall. The swift water was waist deep and the fast current cleansed the area they used for personal hygiene. The floor of the inner room was dry, hard and cluttered with several natural rock formations which came in handy for storing various supplies. Jack had dragged in dozens of heavy, flat rocks for makeshift furniture. They slept in sleeping bags spread on the floor and washed the bags and their clothing in the spring. The ceiling was about seven feet high and covered with colorful stalactites that hung as much as two feet below the ceiling. Between the icicle-shaped calcite formations, Ruth had strung wire for drying laundry and strips of meat.

Ruth and Mary spotted Jack and met him between the fire and the tunnel. "Thank goodness! You really got something!" Ruth gushed. "We were beginning to worry about you when it got so late." "We were coming to get you," Mary teased. "Thought maybe you ran into something interesting." She kissed his right cheek while taking the crossbow and quiver. "I got lucky," Jack explained. "I found fresh tracks and followed them to the lake. This beauty showed up just before dark. Took a while to track it down and bring it back without leaving a trail to our front door." "We'll make ourselves pretty while you slice up some steaks," Ruth suggested while helping Jack hang the carcass. "We're ready for a little nourishment."

Jack skinned and quartered the deer while the women dried and combed out their hair. He carved out three thick steaks and washed them in the spring. Ruth placed a metal grill on the rocks above the campfire while Mary set out plates, knives, and forks. Ruth turned the meat and made a pot of fresh coffee while Jack washed down the remaining venison. He spread the skin in the south corner of the room and salted the underside. Mary carried three cups over to Ruth, then sat down, savoring the aroma coming from the grill.

“Meat's ready,” Ruth announced. Mary and Jack walked their plates over to Ruth. She forked a portion onto each plate, filled the cups with hot coffee and took the third steak. They ate in silence, too hungry for casual conversation. There wasn't anything pressing to talk about anyway. They had exhausted the usual topics of conversation during the long days and nights underground and now struggled to come up with something new to relieve the boredom.

Ruth and Mary washed the plates, cups and flatware in the spring, then helped Jack slice up the rest of the meat, salt it down and hang the cuts over a wire suspended between stalactites. "We're getting low on firewood again," Ruth reminded Jack. He nodded. "I'll take care of that tomorrow. I've picked up all the loose wood within a mile radius, so I'll have to use the ax and saw again." "Won't that be a lot more dangerous?" Ruth worried. "Yes," Jack admitted. "I better not cut anything close to here. It's much too risky. By scattering the cutting over a wide area, it'll look like scavengers did it. I'll take the shotgun along in case someone hears the ax and saw noise." They finished with the meat and the women got out the toothbrushes. Jack sat on a flat rock, puffed at his pipe and thought about his mother and Paul.

Switzerland's long-standing policy of steadfast neutrality concerning political or military turmoil among other nations had saved the Swiss from direct attack during the nuclear war. Nevertheless, the Swiss people, like all other neutral population centers, were war victims. Generations of dependence on international markets, global banking services and other aspects of modern commerce left Switzerland in economic chaos. Moreover, the Swiss countryside had been exposed to radioactive fallout. Food supplies were running dangerously low and drinkable water was in short supply. The Swiss were in deep trouble and they knew it. They were not alone in their dilemma. Every nation that survived the nuclear holocaust faced similar problems. The ability to remain a self-sufficient island within the global sea of commerce had long since vanished. The future of all surviving population centers was inexorably linked to international trade, and such trade perished along with most governments.

Responding to the recognized crisis, surviving nations sent their civilian leaders to Geneva to address seemingly unsolvable problems. The global summit had entered its third week. Common problems had been clearly identified: contaminated food and water; radioactive farmlands; unburied corpses; rubble and debris; lawless human scavengers; structural damage; inoperable transportation and communications systems; overburdened social institutions; civil unrest; economic disorder; inequality of natural resources; breakdown of essential commerce between geographical regions; mass starvation; mass dehydration; and the possibility of additional wars unless solutions were formulated.

President McCarron had escaped to Switzerland and he spoke for survivors within the United States. Israel chose not to participate in the summit. The other attendees came mostly from non-nuclear, neutral and third world countries not targeted during the nuclear war. General Oren Natas was the single exception. He commanded the largest remaining force in existence outside Israel. His army possessed no nuclear firepower but was otherwise heavily armed and completely loyal to Natas. By the time Natas spoke, no plausible solutions had been forthcoming. The summit appeared to be ending in confused bickering, each attendee mentally, physically and emotionally exhausted.

Natas stepped briskly to the podium. His white military uniform was unwrinkled and spotless. He radiated an image of determination and enthusiasm. He stood tall and straight before the bank of microphones. His voice was clear and authoritative:

"Thank you, Ladies and Gentlemen, for this opportunity to share with you a survival plan for the human race. I need not add to what has already been said concerning the importance of this summit. It is clear that civilized members of the human race cannot survive unless we come up with answers to the problems the prior speakers have so precisely described. In order to conceive solutions, we must first look behind each problem to determine the cause. When we do that, we shall discover that the single cause of all the problems before us is inequality. We are here today because a human being is not a wild animal driven by instinct and fixed behavior patterns. Rather, mankind is capable of intelligent thought, logical reasoning, and a deep sense of what is fair and reasonable when interacting with other humans. We have witnessed the most destructive war in human history because we have failed to recognize that we all belong to a common family wherein every individual has the right to have access to an equal share of those things absolutely necessary to sustain life. It is neither fair nor logical that one should be gluttonous while another starves. Such inequality among individuals leads to similar inequality among nations and a disproportionate consumption of natural resources based on claims of ownership backed up by military might. The concept that might make right has caused members of the human family to war upon each other since the beginning of recorded history. From the same history, we also know that war never brings about a permanent peace. War results in one side being defeated and humiliated thereby planting the seeds of future wars. We have plundered each other, polluted our environment and nearly destroyed our planet. There must now be an end to war and a new beginning for the human family......a peaceful reordering of society within environmental limitations." Natas was interrupted by applause that escalated into a standing ovation. He looked on, fresh and unruffled, waiting for complete silence.

When the applause ended, and the attendees sat down again, he continued without the use of notes or props:

"If within the brotherhood of humanity, we forge one social order, one government, one law, one faith and equality of opportunity, there will be no reason to war upon each other. It is within the logic of this postulate that I present a plan for restoring world order and perpetual peace." Again, Natas was interrupted by a standing ovation. He beamed with appreciation and waited patiently for the noise to abate. This is going to be easier than I thought, he mused. He decided to ask for a grant of power by acclamation. The wild cheering and clapping subsided, allowing him to continue without distraction:

"Our new beginning must offer every individual clean air, clean water, healthy diet, adequate housing, education, medical care, choice of employment and retirement security within a system of free enterprise. We have learned the hard way that neither socialism nor communism provides equality of opportunity. However, before we can guarantee equality, we must survive the aftermath of the nuclear madness. We are well aware of our dependence on the natural environment for the necessities of life..... air, food, water and shelter from the elements. Yet, in the attempt to impose inequality, we have severely damaged a large portion of our planet. Only a third of Earth's land surface remains habitable and over sixty percent of the planet's waters is totally polluted. For the purpose of establishing environmental limitations, we can define Earth's land surface in terms of four zones. A zone does not have a geographical boundary but rather represents only a description of the natural environment within each hemisphere. Zone one areas are presently habitable, meaning that pollution and nuclear contamination levels are low enough to allow normal plant, animal and human life. Zone two is in the hazardous category, meaning that pollution and radiation levels are high enough to cause health problems, but not so severe as to preclude controlled use of the land, taking into account sufficient protective measures. Zone three is not presently habitable but will become partially habitable following extensive cleanup and is therefore reclaimable. Zone four regions are completely uninhabitable, now and in the future. Zone four land is forever lost and can be used only for dumping and burial of contaminated matter. Consequently, we must relocate Earth's surviving populations in zone one regions while planning to expand into zones two and three as quickly as the environment can be cleaned up."

Natas paused for a drink of water and to let everyone catch up with his logic. When the attendees began looking up from their notepads, he continued:

"In order for such relocation to become possible, there must be one government, one law, and one police force. All weapons must be banned other than normal police equipment needed to protect society from the criminal element which surfaces within any human culture. My troops can form the core of the global police and they can be supplemented with other surviving military personnel since they are already disciplined, trained and committed to a definite period of service. This will allow time to recruit and train replacements. All scavengers and military personnel in hiding must be given the opportunity to surrender to the police and join our new world order. We cannot tolerate criminals or individuals who refuse to conform to our law. In order to ensure peace and safety, the penalty for breaking our law is death. We must not burden ourselves with the cost of attempting to rehabilitate criminals. We need to conserve our resources in order to provide every world citizen with those things which ensure equality of opportunity. All political waste must be eliminated. We will have no need for bureaucracies because all necessary government functions can be planned and scheduled by completely computerized control centers. The global police will maintain order and enforce our law. We have no need for a costly and corrupt legal system. The choice is simple and easy to comprehend ..... obey the law or die. The police will track, apprehend and execute criminals. The tremendous portion of our total resources that have previously been squandered on military budgets and government bureaucracies can be allocated to fund free education and medical care. There will be zero unemployment. Workers not employed in the private sector will provide government and community services. The minimum pay level will be calculated to allow for a comfortable standard of living. All citizens of retirement age and those who are disabled will receive a government subsidy to ensure the same minimum income level as workers. All able-bodied citizens above college age and below age seventy will be employed forty hours each week. There will be no welfare programs other than the subsidy for retired or disabled citizens. There will be no taxes except an income tax. The minimum income will be tax-exempt and there will be an eighty percent tax on all personal income above the minimum level. Private business income will be taxed at sixty-five percent of gross profit. The income tax plus fees for goods and services provided by government workers will be sufficient in the absence of bureaucratic waste to sustain the public treasury. Individual productivity will be monitored by computers. Those performing above the public standard will receive an incentive payment, and those performing below the standard will receive a cut in wages. There must be only one currency and all diverse currencies will be converted at a fixed exchange rate. Income tax will be collected during the exchange. The assets of all former governments will be transferred to the public treasury to cover the expense of initial government services. Thereafter, the income tax and fee structure will provide adequate funding. To ensure equality of opportunity and to conserve our natural resources, the public will own all agricultural lands and government workers will perform all agricultural activities including the breeding and slaughtering of animals suitable for human consumption. The public will also own, and government workers will operate and manage sewage and water treatment facilities, educational and medical facilities, and public transportation systems. Government workers will also provide mail service, fire and police protection. All other public services can be provided by free enterprise. All public works and private business must rely on solar, thermal and electrical energy. There must be zero air or water pollution. All new industrial, residential and commercial facilities will conform immediately. All existing facilities must conform within three years. Self-propelled transportation vehicles will be powered by nonpolluting energy sources and nonconforming vehicles must be junked within three years. Due to pollution and nuclear contamination of zones three and four severely restricting Earth's capacity to sustain life, the human population of the planet must be fixed at a level not to exceed the carrying capacity of our natural environment. This means the birth rate must be controlled relative to the death rate. This ratio will be continuously monitored by computers. Females of childbearing age must have an equal opportunity to have children. Computerized figures will be published monthly detailing the number of new births allowed per thousand eligible women. Violators will be sterilized, and the children placed for adoption. Women wishing to bear children must register at their assigned birth control center. When the number of new births desired exceeds the allowable birth rate, new births will be scheduled by lottery over successive nine-month periods. Fully computerized, government operated control centers will replace bureaucracies. Existing hardware and software is sufficient for control center needs and can be set up immediately. There will be one control center for each hundred thousand citizens and every individual must register within thirty days from today. Each citizen will be assigned a personal identification number and the number will be imprinted on the right hand or forehead. The number will be invisible to the eye but easily read by electronic scanners. The first nine numbers will identify the specific individual and the last three numbers will indicate compliance with control center regulations. The compliance number is six hundred and sixty-six. The assigned number entitles the individual to receive his or her personal share of food and water rations and the right to engage in commercial transactions. Thereby food and water rationing are accomplished and personal income is monitored for income tax collection. The control centers will assign and pay government workers and track address, employment status, income, commercial transactions and income tax for all citizens regardless of age, disability or employer. Because millions are presently dying for lack of food, water, and medical attention, it is imperative that we act at once in an orderly and prioritized manner. The control centers must be set up while our police locate mobile food and water supplies for routing through government-operated distribution points. Armed guards will protect non-mobile supplies. Every citizen must set up containers to collect rainwater until public water supplies are adequate. Water suitable for drinking must not be used for any other purpose. After food and water supplies are secured and emergency medical attention is provided, our police will hunt down and execute anyone who does not surrender all weapons and report to a control center for registration. Surviving military personnel must also surrender military weapons and register at a control center. Government workers assisted by all citizens will initially concentrate upon the production, distribution, and protection of food and water supplies including the purification of all water which can be treated to make it potable. All land capable of food production must be fully utilized and privately-owned land suitable for agricultural use must be sold to the government at fair market value. Our next priority is the mass burial in zone four of all human and animal corpses. Rubble, debris, and junk will be collected and deposited in zone four. All military weapons will be dismantled, rendered inoperative and buried in zone four pits. Private, nonmilitary weapons will be collected and also buried in zone four. All military equipment, vehicles, aircraft, and naval vessels not easily converted to nonmilitary use will be rendered inoperative and buried at sea in zone four waters. Then, we can concentrate on the repair or replacement of public sewage systems, public transportation, medical and educational facilities, and public works. Low cost, government-underwritten loans will be available for residential, commercial and industrial construction so that war damage does not create long-term economic depression."

Natas paused for effect before concluding his speech. The attendees were captivated and there was no indication of opposition throughout the entire assembly. Natas knew it was time to take control. His tone became more adamant:

"There are, of course, many mechanical details to work out and time is extremely precious. I ask for your immediate approval to take control and carry out the peace plan with each of you serving as a permanent adviser for your geographical population. There can be only one head of state in our new world order. I ask you to give me that authority now."

Natas stepped back from the bank of microphones and waited to become world dictator by acclamation. The attendees began rising to their feet cheering, applauding and chanting: "Natas! Natas! Natas!

"Let's go home," Paul suggested to Jackie. "I'm tired of waiting for the Canadians to give their blessing." Jackie sat up in surprise. "You mean leave on foot?" "No. Let's use bicycles. It'll be slow, but we won't have to worry about scavenging fuel below the border.

"Hey, all right! Let's go!" Jackie sat up and smoothed out her long, black hair. Paul stood up and scratched the stubble under his chin. "We'd better eat here. It'll take all day to round up supplies. We'll use backpacks and fender bags. We'll also need a pistol and shotgun with lots of ammunition." Jackie wondered if the guns were really necessary. She hated both guns and violence. "Do I need to carry one?" "Not unless you want to. I need the pistol in case we run into scavengers and the shotgun for hunting. We also need some fishing line and hooks. I can make poles out of tree limbs. Our ration coupons won't get us very far. We'll have to depend on nature for most of our food and water."

Reasonable doubt crept into Jackie's eyes. "What if Mother Nature doesn't cooperate?" "Don't worry," Paul assured her. "There's lots of wildlife in these parts and plenty of springs along the way. We'll buy the guns from native sportsmen who need cash more than extra firearms. I've got three credit cards that should be good in Canada for cash advances."

Bishop Julius Romas was somewhat apprehensive as two of Natas' armed bodyguards led the way to the top floor of a luxurious office building overlooking the western shore of Lake Geneva. Why had Natas summoned him? Why should a busy dictator give him a special audience? He had neither spoken for nor against the new world order. It seemed to be working out okay. It surprised him that Natas knew he existed.

Although the top floor was cool, his armpits were damp beneath his dark gray suit and his palms were moist with perspiration. He had dressed carefully for his meeting with the most powerful man in human history. His custom-tailored suit fit nicely and was perfectly matched by his white, silk shirt, medium red tie, gray knee-length socks and freshly polished black leather shoes.

He wore no religious ornaments. He wasn't sure how Natas felt about organized religion. It would be unwise to provoke him with a pompous costume. The guards stopped in front of Natas' temporary office. Two more bodyguards-controlled access to the door. "Bishop Romas," said one of his escorts to the men at the door. The man on the left opened the door and then stepped aside. "Come in, Julius," Natas said without looking up. "Make yourself comfortable. I'll join you in a moment." The door closed behind Romas. He walked over and sat down on the plush blue velvet couch to the left of Natas' large glass covered executive desk.

"May I offer you a brandy, Julius?" Natas scribbled his signature on several documents, looked up and smiled broadly. He wore his white uniform and gold-braided general's cap. He must know more about me than I imagined, Romas concluded as his comfort level increased. "Thank you, Your Majesty. I would be honored. Brandy is my favorite crutch."

Natas swiveled in his executive chair, opened the sliding doors on his desk credenza, pulled out a bottle of fine brandy, took two large crystal snifters from the top shelf, and poured two drinks. He replaced the bottle, selected two silver casters and linen napkins, then got up and joined Romas. He set Romas' drink on the ornate convenience table and settled into the opposite end of the couch. Romas picked up his snifter and extended it toward Natas. "To your great victory, Your Majesty." Natas lifted his snifter and clinked the rim against Romas' drink. "To a new beginning and peace on Earth," Natas added. They sampled the brandy and set the snifters on the casters.

"I suppose you're wondering why I sent for you?" Romas nodded. "I'm completely puzzled, Your Majesty. I watched your speech on TV. You were truly magnificent. But I fail to see what that has to do with me."

Natas was pleased with Romas' demeanor and image. He fit the part well and could be easily manipulated. The Bishop was middle-aged, white-headed, non-offensive features, a visage of benevolence and anxious to please him. Yes, Bishop Romas could be very useful, but he needed the proper orientation. He gazed thoughtfully at Romas for a moment. "Our new beginning can be retarded by religious dissension. That must not happen. I'm counting on you to see that it doesn't."

Romas was not prepared for such a direct proposition but managed to conceal his surprise. "That would take a greater miracle than the crossing of the Red Sea, Your Majesty. I'm afraid you overestimate my meager ministry." Natas chuckled softly. "The people await a new spiritual leader. The Pope and his Cardinals were cremated in the war. Other religions are too splintered to rally around a single spiritual figure. They all quarrel among themselves like the Protestants. Thus, I agree with you. It will take a miracle or two to encourage diverse fanatics to accept you as my prophet and their leader."

Romas was getting somewhat nervous. "Miracles are wrought by faith ... and I'm sorry to admit that mine is less than the proverbial mustard seed." Natas' gray eyes twinkled as he controlled the urge to laugh. "What sort of miracle would you like? Call fire down upon dissenters? Raise the dead?" Romas' nervousness escalated into chilling fear. "I'm more than willing to serve you, Your Majesty. I've already seen you in action."

Natas' visage changed from humor to impatience. "Do you recognize the statuette on the left corner of the credenza?" Romas looked carefully at the image. "No, Your Majesty." "It is Epiphanes, the Syrian king who wanted to stamp out Judaism one hundred and sixty-seven years before Christ was born." Natas beckoned to the image. "Epiphanes, come forth!" he commanded.

"Here am I, Master." The hollow voice behind him startled Romas. He turned and saw the brutish Syrian holding a sword dripping with fresh blood. Romas mustered all his strength to remain calm. He was, in fact, terrified. Natas barked a command. "Prepare for the final extermination." "Yes, Master," Epiphanes replied. "The time has come." Cold sweat beaded Romas' brow. Epiphanes vanished and Romas stared in horror at the blood seeping into the thick, white carpet.

Natas stood up and looked down at Romas. "Go now and purge yourself of all fear. Soon, you will stand by my side and call all families of the earth unto me."

The Israelis refused to recognize Natas as anything more than an opportunist, a usurper of power during chaos. Natas fumed at the very thought of the Jews as he monitored dozens of TV screens mounted in the wall opposite his desk. Everyone had complied with his proclamations except Israel. His peace plan was being broadcast every four hours on all TV and radio stations that remained operable outside Israel. Government engineers and work crews were quickly rebuilding TV and radio facilities in zones one, two and three, in that order.

Mass media was the best way to reach his subjects around the world and to announce his proclamations. The Jews hid behind their nuclear weapons and openly defied him. The arsenals of all other nuclear powers had been depleted during the war. Israel had sandbagged and let the United States carry most of the burden in the Middle East, leaving the tiny Jewish state the world's greatest military power. Even he dared not attack them. He gritted his teeth and cursed the Children of Abraham. He would have to negotiate with them and convince them to trade their weapons for something more precious to Jews ... security and prosperity.

He must be unopposed in order to remain global dictator. If he allowed the Jews to defy him, others were sure to follow after he filled their bellies and slacked their thirst. He pushed the buzzer under the corner of his desk. The office door opened, and the two guards snapped to attention. "Bring me, Bishop Romas," Natas ordered. "Yes, Your Majesty," one of them responded. They wheeled, and the door closed behind them.

Natas' eyes narrowed and a frown creased his brow. He would send Romas to negotiate with the stiff-necked Israelis. Romas would promise them that they could maintain their religious independence as long as they outwardly recognized Romas and voiced no objection to his status as global spiritual leader. The Jews were accustomed to compromise when it suited their most basic principles. He, Natas, would guarantee their borders and peaceful coexistence. With their homeland and their religious integrity thus secured, they would have no need for military weapons. They must give them up to ensure their future protection. If they refused, he would cut them off from the world market and confiscate all their assets outside Israel. And, they had to report to control centers set up inside Israel and submit to the mark of acceptance. Natas felt refreshed. Yes, he would promise that......for now.

Paul and Jackie stood in line inside the restaurant waiting for a table. Canadian television was back in operation and the TV set mounted on the north wall of the dining room was tuned in to a local news broadcast. Paul glanced at his watch. It was 9:55 am, September 12th. The newscast was just ending and a special broadcast was announced .....the videotape of the emergency summit in Geneva between world leaders two weeks earlier. The hostess guided Paul and Jackie to a table being vacated by another couple. Paul smiled at the hostess as she handed them menus. "Your waitress will be right with you," she promised.

"Ham, eggs over easy, hash browns, toast and coffee will be just fine," Paul urged. "We're in a bit of a hurry. She wants the same. Will you relay that to our waitress?" The hostess flashed them an accommodating smile. "Yes, I'll give her your order right now. It'll be ready in about seven minutes." She now looked apologetic. "You do realize we'll have to translate your order into the allowed rations, don't you?"

Paul handed her ration coupons for both orders. "Yes, we know. It's kinda hard to adjust to eating half a meal." "Helps my waistline." She patted her stomach, smiled, took the coupons and headed back toward the front. Paul and Jackie could now see the TV off to the left of their table. Natas was just beginning his speech before the world assembly. The conversations around the dining room stopped abruptly and everyone listened to the video playback. Paul was impressed by Natas' oration and sweeping proposal. When Natas outlined the control centers and the identifying mark, Paul's mouth fell open and his blood ran cold. Had he heard correctly? A mark required to buy and sell? A mark ending in the numbers 666? He looked quickly around the room at the other guests. No one else seemed to understand the significance of an identifying mark in the right hand or forehead. A mark ending in 666! He broke out into a cold sweat. Jackie noticed his discomfort. "What's the matter, Honey? Are you okay?" "It's nothing," he said quietly. "Just a sour stomach."

Their waitress set their breakfast on the table and poured the coffee. My God! Paul thought. Jackie's never heard it before! She has no idea who Natas really is. If I try to explain it, she'll think I'm nuts! They ate while listening to the rest of Natas' speech. Paul's senses were numb, and he felt sick to his stomach. He couldn't taste the food, but he forced it down anyway. He would need all his strength for the dangerous journey ahead. He must find Jack as quickly as possible. Soon, there would be more than scavengers to worry about......the execution squads hunting down anyone without the mark. He tried to concentrate on a list of essential supplies, but his thoughts kept returning to Mary. Natas finished his speech and stepped back from the podium. When the videotape showed the world leaders rising and cheering, the people in the restaurant, including Jackie, stood up and joined in the chanting: "Natas! Natas! Natas!"

Paul got up and grabbed Jackie's arm. "Let's get out of here! Right now!" Jackie looked puzzled but followed him back to their room. Paul unlocked the door and Jackie entered behind him. "Let's get ready and hit the road," Paul advised. "We'll get organized and while you pack I'll go get the guns and ammo."

From his change in pace, Jackie sensed he was worried about something Natas said on TV. She dug a pen and paper out of her purse. Paul sat down and thought about essential supplies. "The weather is unpredictable in the high elevations this time of year. Let's think about clothing first." Jackie nodded and began to organize the list. Paul quickly rattled off items. "We'll need thermal underwear and socks; insulated jumpsuits; waterproof, insulated hiking boots; thermal gloves; tennis shoes; sunglasses, snow goggles; and ski caps."

"How many of each?" Jackie asked. "Three sets of underwear and socks, two jumpsuits, one of everything else. We'll wash our socks, underwear and jumpsuits every other day. If we run into really cold spells, we'll wear two sets of underwear and socks." "Sounds like fun," Jackie commented. "What's next?" "That should cover inner and outer clothing. Let's think about sleeping and bathing. Let's see. . . arctic sleeping bags; two bath towels and hand towels; month's supply of shampoo, soap, toothpaste, mouthwash and deodorant; shaving kit; toothbrushes, hairbrush, and comb."

"That should do it," Jackie agreed. "I'll just add some liquid laundry soap. How about cooking and cleanup?" "The heavy stuff." Paul frowned. "Besides guns, ammo, short ax and hatchet, hunting, skinning and fillet knives; we'll need a can opener, plastic spoons, forks, cups, and plates; fishing lines, hooks and sinkers; quarter-inch steel rod two feet long; plenty of matches; salt and pepper; aluminum coffee pot and skillet; aluminum foil; month's supply of coffee; two canteens; two flashlights with supply of bulbs and batteries; and all the canned goods we can buy with our supply of ration coupons. And, if we can find some. ... crackers, cookies and candy bars. There may still be some in Canada."

"Sounds like we need a pickup," Jackie quipped. Looking at Jackie reminded Paul of another item. "Better include a hand mirror with your cosmetics. Also, jot down rope, hunting belt, toilet paper, and handkerchiefs." "How should we pack it?" Jackie queried. "Sounds like a load." "Packing is the trick for making it lighter," Paul replied. "It's all in the balancing... and it'll get lighter as we go."

"Tell me how and I'll do it." "We'll buy two off-the-road bicycles with tire repair kits, front and rear baskets, and plastic fender slings," Paul explained. "We'll tie the sleeping bags on the left side of the rear fender slings. We'll wrap our tennis shoes inside our extra clothes and tie the bundles on the right side of the rear slings. We can plastic-bag light items like toilet paper and towels and tie the bags on the right front slings. On the left front slings, we'll strap on the short ax, hatchet, steel rod, coffeepot, and skillet. One bike can handle the ax, hatchet, and rod. The other can carry the skillet and coffeepot. We'll strap the tire repair kits and air pump to the frames under the seats. Things like gloves, goggles, and sunglasses can be carried in our jumpsuit pockets. The front and rear baskets will carry the canned goods and other packaged food. I'll strap the pistol and knives to my hunting belt, and you can hang the canteens on yours. The shotgun can be strapped behind my backpack. Everything else will easily fit inside our backpacks. . . the heavier items in mine."

"Sounds like you've roughed it on a bicycle before," Jackie noted. "It's really simple once you know how. Jack and I used bikes on hunting trips.

Off-the-road bikes are solidly built and will balance a lot of weight if it's not one-sided. The load will get lighter along the way as we eat the canned food."

"You think it'll take a month to get to Boise? How many miles is it?" Jackie liked the idea of spending a month on the road with Paul. It sounded like a long picnic. "It's not around the corner," Paul replied. "I memorized the route last week. By highway, it's roughly eight hundred miles from Calgary to Boise. We can shave off some miles by cutting across country part of the way, but we'll have to stay close to the road over rough terrain." "Are the roads all paved?" "Pretty much. We'll follow local highways south and west through Crow's Nest Pass just east of Sparwood, then south across the border near Roosville into northwestern Montana. We follow U.S. 93 through western Montana, cross the Bitterroot Mountains over Chief Joseph Pass into east-central Idaho. Then, south on U.S. 93 to Idaho 75; head west on 75 to the Sawtooth Wilderness Area northeast of Boise. Where 75 turns south and heads toward Galena Summit, we should find Jack, Ruth, and Mary in a small one-room cave with an underground spring. It's actually located six and a quarter mile northwest of Galena Summit."

"Sounds like an easy route to follow," Jackie commented. "How many miles can we average per hour?" "Probably three," Paul answered. "We'll have to walk the bikes up steep grades, coast downhill and pedal on fairly level ground. We should average thirty miles a day traveling between 9:00 pm and 7:00 am. That'll allow six hours each day to hunt, fish, cook, eat, bathe and wash our clothes plus eight hours for rest and sleep. If we stick to that schedule, we should reach the cave in just under twenty-seven days, around October 10th. By traveling at night, we can use the paved roads more than we would want to during daylight. In any event, we must get there before the heavy snows begin at the lower elevations."

"How come?" Jackie asked. "Does the cave get snowed in?" "That's not the major problem. Deep snow makes the trails impassable. We couldn't get up to the cave." Paul got up from the bed. "I'd better go after the guns now. Then, we'll buy the bikes and use them to gather up the rest of our supplies. We'll hit the trail soon as it gets dark." Jackie nodded agreement. "I'll start gathering up everything we have here that's on the list." "I won't be long," Paul promised. He opened the door. "See you soon. Lock the door behind me."

Admiral Wallace sat in his cabin looking over the remaining inventory of USS Liberty. The ultimate weapon was now just a defenseless underwater hideout. Since April 10th, its torpedoes and missiles all launched, USS Liberty had slunk through the ocean depths maintaining radio silence to minimize the danger of detection by enemy vessels. Wallace was sure that all surviving naval units stopped transmitting when cut off from command centers. There were no winners among the superpowers. An attack now upon an enemy vessel would be an act of vengeance without military significance.

The real danger was the tendency in such situations to fire before being fired upon. He had been rationing food and water for five months leaving his crew weak and demoralized. He would have to surface soon. Fuel was no problem, but he had barely enough food and water for three more days. He had to head for a port.....but where? He needed information concerning environmental contamination, port damage, location of hostile forces, available supplies, and a few other important details......such as whether the port selected even exists anymore. If he guessed wrong, there would be no reprieve. His current position was five hundred and sixty miles off the Florida coast. He pushed the button on his cabin intercom. "Yes, Admiral?" "Send Lieutenant Walker to my cabin." "Yes, Sir. Right away, Sir."

Wallace opened the last can of orange juice while he waited for the officer he trusted without reservation. He thought once more about Janet, Billy, and the grandchildren. Did any of them survive? If so, were they maimed? blind or disfigured? A gentle knock on his door indicated Lieutenant Walker was waiting. "Come in, Lieutenant." Walker stuck his head inside the cabin. "You sent for me, Sir?" "Yes. Come in and pull up a chair. There's fresh coffee in the pot. Help yourself."

Walker entered, poured a cup of coffee, moved a chair from along the wall to the cabin table and sat down opposite Wallace. "Yes, Sir?" Wallace rubbed his cheek and downed the last drops of juice. "How do you read the crew morale?" "They're hungry, thirsty and scared, Sir." "Scared of what?" Walker sipped some coffee and arched his eyebrows. "Of the unknown. We've been down a long time. They know we'll have to surface soon and they're afraid of what we'll find. We all know billions have died. Every man is convinced his family and friends are among the dead."

Wallace rubbed his fists together and gazed blankly at Walker. "How about you, Lieutenant? What do you believe?" Walker couldn't miss the sadness in his commander's eyes. He cradled his cup with both hands and thought about his own family. He had no doubt that New York had been wiped out. "I gave up all hope when we fired on the carrier." "Do you think now that we should have waited?" "No, Sir. We had no choice.

There was nothing we could do but try to kill them first. No one blames you, Sir. We're alive because you made the right decision. They held a gun to our head and were squeezing the trigger when we finally acted. It makes no difference to the dead which side struck the first blow. We didn't sacrifice anything but some of the enemy in order to save ourselves. That's the way we all feel, Sir."

Wallace wanted to believe he had no other choice. "Maybe fewer on our side died because we fired first." "Certainly, you saved us. The civilians were beyond our help anyway but knocking out some of their weapons had to make a difference. We'll never know how big a difference, but we did our very best."

Wallace found some comfort in Walker's words, but his heart had turned to stone. "I understand how the crew feels. There's not enough of Dallas left to shelter a stray dog." Walker knew that Wallace did not want a reply. He looked at his watch. "I'd better run a security check," he mumbled. "Some of the men are near the breaking point." He got up and opened the cabin door. "Will that be all, Sir?" "Tell the other officers we're going to surface in ten minutes. We have to choose a port. We're breaking radio silence. We'll ride the surface for a few hours and try to pick up land-based transmissions before making our final decision." "Very well, Sir." Walker went out and shut the cabin door.

Wallace leaned back and stared at the cabin wall. Suppose he lucked out and chose a safe port. Where would he get a supply of food and water? It would be like prospecting for gold. Any uncontaminated military stores would have been raided by this time. He couldn't hold the crew on board without supplies, and he couldn't just turn them loose to become wandering scavengers. They were still his responsibility. What if he made it into port and found the surrounding area uninhabitable? Then, what? He didn't have enough water to search for an alternate haven. They could go a few more days without food ... but not without drinking. He decided to take things one step at a time as he reached for the cabin intercom. "This is Admiral Wallace. Prepare to surface."

USS Liberty ascended toward the surface like a huge gray ghost. It was shortly after 10:00 pm and it was pitch dark. The heavy overcast and gently rolling waves added to the sense of total isolation. The sub's electronic ears scanned every frequency but heard only faint background static. "There's nothing on the screens, Sir.....except static." Wallace doubted that commercial radio stations were operational in the area or they would have heard more than normal background static. He didn't really expect any military transmissions, and communications between commercial vessels were infrequent during calm seas. He had hoped to at least pick up some chatter between ham radio operators. The unbroken static within five hundred miles of the Florida coast also indicated the absence of commercial air traffic. Maybe Florida was no longer there. . . just radioactive rubble.

"It's time to start transmitting," Wallace instructed his communications officer. "Rotate frequencies every three minutes and send an SOS under the name Southern Prince. Let's see if anyone's listening." "Yes, Sir. I'll pass the word."

The firm tug at his shoulder ended Wallace's dozing. "We've got something, Sir." "Anything on the screens?" Wallace sat up and rubbed the sleep from his eyes. "There appears to be a recorded message on the UAC frequency." "Any indication where it's coming from?" "No, Sir. It's not coming from UAC. There was no protocol, just a recorded announcement that an emergency broadcast would follow in three minutes." "Very well, Lieutenant. Put it on the speakers so the crew can hear. There are no more military secrets."

The speakers throughout the sub emitted an electronic buzz catching the attention of every crew member. "This is Colonel Carl Wirtman, Security Center Fourteen, speaking for our new world government. Many are hearing this broadcast for the first time, so I will begin by repeating the most current estimate of the death toll in connection with the nuclear suicide. Five billion, one hundred and thirty-seven million, six hundred and thirteen thousand have been murdered by the warmongers. Approximately thirty-nine percent died from exposure to lethal radiation. Twenty-one percent died from starvation, dehydration, or consumption of contaminated food and water. The remaining forty percent were killed outright during the nuclear folly. Sixty-seven percent of Earth's land is uninhabitable, and sixty-four percent of the world's oceans, rivers and lakes is totally polluted. With respect to the planet's surviving population, approximately one billion, three hundred and ninety-nine million, nine hundred and eighty-seven thousand are believed to have survived the mass murder."

Every individual aboard USS Liberty listened in stony silence. They knew the death toll would be enormous and the damage to the environment cataclysmic. Many heads were bowed, cheeks streaked with tears. The recorded voice continued: "Earth's survivors are committed to a new beginning wherein peace shall be perpetual and every person's security guaranteed. There shall be one law, one government, one head of government and one police force. The new world order was established by representatives of surviving populations meeting in Geneva, Switzerland. During this global summit, General Oren Natas' peace plan was adopted by acclamation and General Natas was elected to preside over our new beginning. Following is a rebroadcast of the peace plan which has now become law on this planet."

Heads raised throughout USS Liberty and every person listened carefully to Natas' speech delivered at the global summit. At the segment of the recording where the world leaders began chanting "Natas! Natas! Natas!," the sub's crew caught the fever and joined the acclamation. Wallace and Walker exchanged looks of suspicion and wonderment. The crew quieted down when Colonel Wirtman continued:

"There are still lawless scavengers and surviving military personnel that have not surrendered to our police force so that they can be granted amnesty, be registered at the appropriate control center, and be freely admitted to our new society. The amnesty offer expires at midnight on September 29th. After that date and time, all individuals that have not been officially registered at one of our control centers will be hunted down by our global police and executed on the spot. This is one of several former military frequencies that may be utilized for contacting our security forces. We invite all to take advantage of our amnesty offer. The designated frequencies are available around the clock. For those wishing to surrender, please identify yourselves, give your exact location and state that you are accepting our amnesty offer." The recording abruptly ended and only static emitted from the speakers. Wallace looked curiously at Walker. "What do you think, Lieutenant?" Walker looked dismayed. "A world dictator? Isn't that what we've been fighting to avoid? Over five billion dead for nothing!"

Wallace stared down at his feet. "We either accept the amnesty or die inside this sub. As long as we're alive, there's still a chance to fight again. We'll have to play Natas' game for the time being." He flicked a switch on the communications control panel. "This is Admiral John Wallace, USS Liberty nuclear submarine, United States Navy, nineteen degrees North Latitude, eighty-nine degrees West Longitude, accepting amnesty offer."

A now familiar voice responded over the frequency. "This is Colonel Wirtman, Security Center Fourteen. How much food and water do you have, Admiral?"

"Less than three days at quarter rations." "Is your vessel intact?" "Yes. Our only emergency is food and water." "Okay, Admiral. We'll get you in right away. Head directly for the port at New Orleans at full speed.

We'll receive you there and you'll be given further instructions." "I understand, Colonel. Is the port free of wreckage?" "No . . . the area is uninhabitable. Do not try to enter the port. A supply vessel will meet you outside the port and then move on to your final destination." "Very well, Colonel. We're proceeding full speed ahead."

A disquieting fear gnawed at the pit of his stomach as Admiral Wallace followed armed guards to Natas' headquarters. "Wait here," the lead guard commanded. He left the escort standing in the main entrance to the Palace of Nations while he checked with the four lobby guards. Watching passively, Wallace pondered the possible motive for this private meeting with Natas. They had never met and knew nothing about each other except the general biography compiled by intelligence agencies. Natas was generally believed to be an intelligent and capable military officer but Wallace had never heard of any exceptional military operations commanded by him. His only remarkable achievement was the powerful speech before the world body that vaunted him to power. It was a carefully planned and executed maneuver. A man that clever worried Wallace. What did Natas have in mind for the commanding officer of the USS Liberty? To punish him? To pick his brains? Some special assignment? The thought of catering to a witty dictator turned his stomach.

The lead guard returned. "His Majesty will see you now." His Majesty? Wallace mused to himself. Nothing modest about Natas' assumed title. The escort proceeded through the elegant lobby, up an ornate elevator and handed Wallace off to the two guards in front of Natas' working office. One of the armed men quickly frisked him and the other opened the office door. "Admiral John Wallace, Your Majesty." "Send him in," a mellow but authoritative voice replied. "You may enter," the guard conceded.

Wallace glanced around the spacious office and opulent decor. An armed guard stood in each corner of the room. Natas rose from behind his pompous desk and strode toward Wallace, his eyes beaming and his hand extended. "Just in time for lunch, John. Will you join me?" He gazed casually at Wallace's naval uniform seeming to take particular note of the medals and emblems. "I'd be honored," Wallace replied while firmly shaking Natas' hand. "I'm sure my stomach won't object. It's a bit empty at the moment." "Not for long," Natas promised.

He led the way to a large mahogany conference table furnished with soft, red leather chairs. The table had been previously draped with an elegant covering and set with fragile china and solid silver service. A corner guard stepped forward and pulled out the chair at the left center of the large, round table. "Enjoy your meal, Admiral," he said softly, then walked to the right center and pulled out a chair for Natas.

His Majesty smiled warmly. "May I order you a drink, John? Perhaps some potent brandy?" "At this point, I'd gladly drink wood alcohol," Wallace admitted. "Not much booze where I've been." "We can do much better than that," Natas chirped. He motioned to the guard who had positioned himself directly behind Wallace's chair. The guard walked to the office door, opened it a few inches and passed a silent signal to the outside sentries, then returned to his vigil. Natas relaxed in his seat across from Wallace. The egomaniac does have a touch of class, Wallace thought. Moreover, he timed this meeting perfectly. He knew I'd be famished. What does he want from me?

Natas looked studiously at Wallace, sensing his uneasiness. "What would you have done, John, if USS Liberty had not been depleted of food and water?"

This opening question irritated Wallace but he remained cautious. "What would you have done if the world body had rejected your proposal to restore law and order?" "The outcome was never in doubt," Natas replied with a sly smile. "Neither was the outcome of a nuclear war," Wallace countered. "But you pushed the first button, John. Why?"

The door opened, and a maid entered carrying a large silver tray bearing two linen napkins, two silver casters, two crystal snifters and a fifth of very old brandy. She arranged the napkins, casters and snifters on the table, poured the first round of brandy and set the bottle in the center of the table. She paused and looked attentively at Natas. "Anything else, Your Majesty?" Natas smiled politely. "You may serve lunch whenever it's ready. Our guest has a hearty appetite." "Yes, Your Majesty. It's on the way." She bowed and headed for the door.

Natas lifted his snifter and extended it toward Wallace. "To a new beginning." Wallace returned the gesture. "To all those who died without knowing why." They swallowed the toast, then Natas asked again, "Why, John?" "So, you could rise to power." Wallace looked directly into Natas' cold gray eyes. Natas roared with laughter. It wasn't the answer he anticipated, and it was very clever.

"You're a fearless but prudent man, John. That's why I sent for you. I need your help." "For what?" Wallace warmed the hollow in his stomach with another sip of brandy. Natas looked blankly at him. "I notice that you avoid using my royal title. Does it offend you?" "I'm just not accustomed to dining with dictators," Wallace replied. "Give me a little time. . . I'll adjust." Natas feigned a smile. "No harm. You may call me Oren if that's more comfortable." "What do you want from me, Oren?"

Natas was impressed with Wallace's candor and apparent lack of humility. "I want you to command our new global police force. I have good regional commanders, but I need a top gun to pull everything together. I need a tough, independent decision-maker who doesn't need wet nursing. You're capable of understanding our overall mission, assessing foreseeable risks, outguessing the enemy, and taking decisive action. . . like spoiling the first strike strategy of the former Eastern Alliance."

Wallace still felt uneasy. "Who is the enemy?" "Anyone who breaks our law?" "Who makes our law?" Natas concealed his irritation. Wallace was the right man. He just needed a little more convincing. "The main points of the law were set down before the world body in Geneva and accepted by acclamation. I'm willing to leave the mechanics to your judgment along with the responsibility for hunting down and executing all lawbreakers." "Without a trial?" Wallace asked blandly.

"One breaks the law by choice knowing that the penalty is certain death. Rarely will guilt or innocence truly be in doubt." Natas spoke slowly to emphasize his logic. "But anyone not caught in the act will be presumed innocent until sufficient evidence is compiled to convince you that there is no question of innocence. You must rely on the wisdom of Solomon to decide truly difficult cases, but there won't be many that require such effort. Few persons will risk certain execution for the sake of temporary gain. Our concept of equality among all eliminates the poor and underprivileged which formerly constituted the vast majority of lawbreakers. There will be few executions after lawless scavengers and those who refuse to join our global society are hunted down and eliminated."

The maid returned with a serving cart laden with broiled lobster tails, golden fried shrimp, fresh salads, assorted side dishes, hot rolls, butter, and desserts. The sight and odor of the banquet made it difficult for Wallace to concentrate on the harshness of Natas' legal policy. He sipped his brandy and gazed at Natas. "What about civil disputes? Do you have a policy to avoid civil litigation?"

Natas spread his napkin on his lap as the maid served the meal. "Civil matters will be heard and decided by the regional commander assigned to the control center where the dispute arises. There are 14,000 control centers and 100,000 persons to be registered at each center.

Approximately 47,700 will be disabled, retired or minors. Roughly 52,300 will be employed. Of those employed at each center, on the average, 33,985 will be employed by private enterprise; 14,393 will be providing government services, and 3,922 will provide police protection."

Wallace dipped a fork loaded with lobster meat into a dish of hot butter. "That figures out to be roughly one police officer per twenty-six persons registered at the center." Natas washed down some shrimp with hot coffee. He knew that Wallace already saw the whole picture. "It will be most difficult for criminal acts to escape police scrutiny. The cost of such heavy police coverage is a mere fraction of the funding for layers of bureaucratic incompetents, corrupt lawyers, judges, and overflowing penal institutions. We don't want political scalawags meting out justice driven by campaign contributions or appointment payback. In our new world order, the scales of blind justice must never be tipped by grubby politicians hidden beneath judicial robes. Our objective is equality under the law and death to every lawbreaker. There is no moral justification for rationing food to law-abiding citizens while feeding criminals."

Wallace savored the lobster and considered legal policy. Natas' planning was more detailed than he had anticipated. "Handling all the civil disputes for 100,000 persons might be a heavy load for one individual." Natas had considered this concern. "Under the previous, corrupt social order, it would be much too heavy. But most civil liability also involves some criminal behavior. The blanket of police coverage combined with the death penalty for any infraction of our law will minimize civil complaints. Negligence, property and contract disputes will generally be settled between the parties without an official hearing. The knowledge that a regional commander rather than a corruptible judge conducts hearing will tend to promote early settlement. Adoption of no-fault divorce and community property rights allows divorce to be handled by computer at each center. Both parents will have the continuing responsibility for supporting minor children. Marriage is irrelevant to the issue of child support. The computers will calculate child support as a fixed percentage of each parent's income and each parent will have equal custody rights. Paternity questions will be rare because perjury is a criminal act as well as nonsupport. I don't really expect civil disputes to become a burden upon our regional commanders."

"What about juvenile crime?" Wallace asked, knowing that Natas had a ready solution. "Those old enough to commit a crime are old enough to pay the penalty." Wallace was beginning to appreciate Natas' concept of law and order. "How about disputes where the parties are registered in different control centers and cannot agree as to where the dispute is centered?" Natas was pleased with Wallace's concern for sticky details. "The hearing, when one is necessary, will be conducted in the control center where the original complaining party is registered."

Wallace helped himself to dessert and a fresh cup of coffee. Natas finished off his lobster and shrimp. Wallace remained silent until Natas selected dessert. "I'm very interested, Oren. What are your priorities?" Natas topped his strawberry pie with whipped cream. "Pretty much as I laid out before the civilian leaders on August 29th. Your military background and intimate knowledge of nuclear weapons will be most helpful in rounding up the remnants of military forces that survived the war but haven't yet accepted our amnesty offer. The mass destruction of military weapons also requires a man with your training and special skills. I want you to concentrate on those tasks first. You may hand-pick all the personnel you need, and you will report directly to me. You will also be personally responsible for my security at all times."

Wallace leaned back in his chair and wiped his mouth with his napkin. "How do you know you can trust me with that much power and unquestioned authority?" Natas' gray eyes took on the texture of granite. "It's a risk I'm willing to take. I have to trust someone, and I believe you're the right man."

Wallace made up his mind. "I'll have to move quickly before dispersed military units can regroup and pose a threat to our security." Natas beamed with satisfaction. "Your working office is next to mine. I think you'll find it well suited to your needs. If you need anything at any time, it will be provided immediately without question." "I'd like my crew from USS Liberty to work closely with me. They're well trained and very capable."

Natas stood up and extended his right hand. "I've already made arrangements for them to join you here. After you get settled in, come back and we'll discuss the Israeli problem." Wallace rose from his chair and shook Natas' hand like an old friend. "The lunch was excellent, Your Majesty. I'd best get to work." Natas walked him to the door, immensely pleased to hear his royal title from Wallace's mouth. "Why don't we chat again over dinner?" "Thank you, Your Majesty. I look forward to it." He followed the guard to his new office.

Bishop Romas stared out the port window of the Boeing 747. It was going to be a long flight from Geneva to Tel Aviv. His thoughts were scrambled, and he couldn't shake the image of the strange figure that Natas had conjured up. How did he do that? It had seemed so real. Where did the blood on the carpet come from? Had he been hallucinating? Natas scared him! That much he was sure of. He stared at the white clouds streaming past the window and tried to collect his wits. What if the Jews refused to negotiate? What then?

He began rehearsing his proposal and supporting logic. History indicated that Israeli negotiators could be quite stubborn. He must convince them that their national interests are linked to the new world order and not retention of their nuclear arsenal. They must understand that Natas is bending over backward to accommodate their special interests. Humanity would no longer tolerate war regardless of the political justification. Any type of violence is criminal and punishable by immediate execution. If Israel insisted on keeping military weapons, it could only mean that Israelis contemplated war.

The rest of the world would rise up and destroy Israel. Nuclear weapons would not save them. Consider the superpowers that perished while relying upon nuclear firepower. No lawbreakers would ever again be allowed to disrupt global security. Wallace would not dismantle salvaged nuclear weapons while Israel hid their rebellion behind unlawful arms. The nuclear madness would have to be prolonged until Israel was properly punished. Jews would be branded as outlaws and completely exterminated. The world would understand and support Natas should such drastic action become necessary to stamp out a rogue nationality threatening the new beginning. Cut off from the world market and with all assets outside their borders confiscated, Israel could not possibly compete with Natas, a reasonable man totally dedicated to world peace. Why commit suicide? Accept his offered compromise or perish. Do not count on future negotiations. There won't be any. Natas would make no further concessions. What more could he concede and still comply with the world mandate? He could not allow rebellion at the very moment the new world order is being implemented.

He is offering what Jews always prayed for ... peace, security and prosperity. They could maintain their religious beliefs and rituals. They could even control their own affairs inside Israel as long as they didn't openly violate global law. They had everything to gain and nothing to lose by accepting Natas' compromise. He would guarantee their safety, but crime would not be tolerated. Obey the law or die. That was Natas' final word.

CHAPTER 4

Worship Anti-Christ or Lose Your Head

The grizzled Israeli Prime Minister listened politely to Bishop Romas' presentation. They met in private in the executive conference room at the Knesset Building in Jerusalem. No one inside Israel had yet been exposed to the proposed compromise. Romas knew that the Prime Minister must be sold, or the question would be stonewalled during lengthy debates in the Knesset. The elder statesmen in Israel were more concerned with religious tradition than with stark reality.

Romas' oration alternated between logical reasoning, supplication, and cold threats. When he felt that Natas' position had been made quite clear, he posed a question, hoping to channel the Prime Minister's thoughts. "Isn't peace, security and prosperity more important to the people than the questionable value of your military weapons?"

The old man looked back with unblinking eyes. "An Egyptian Pharaoh promised us peace, security and prosperity, and the Egyptians enslaved us for four hundred years. The Romans were going to protect us, but they destroyed our homes, plundered our temple and drove us into exile among hostile nations. The Germans protected us for a time before they burned us in their ovens. The United Nations guaranteed the return of a portion of our homeland but stood by while we were attacked by armies that outnumbered us more than twenty to one. By the grace of God, we have survived all the plots to exterminate us. There has been no end to the sacrifices exacted of us under the promise of peace and prosperity. We exist today only because we have learned to defend ourselves rather than rely on empty promises. Now, Natas wants us to make ourselves defenseless again in exchange for another promise of protection. Out of one side of his mouth comes a promise to defend us. Out of the other side comes a threat of extermination. Which side of his mouth should we listen to? Which side is the real Natas? We're a tiny nation that has fashioned a big stick to beat back those who say we have no right to exist. Now you ask us to lay down that stick because a single man says we can be secure on his bare promise. We no longer need anyone's protection. We are quite capable of protecting ourselves. You say our weapons threaten world peace. We say those weapons are the only guarantee of our own peace. Wars have been fought with sticks and stones, then with swords and spears, followed by guns and bombs, and finally nuclear weapons. It is not the existence of weapons that triggers war, but rather the desire to rule one's neighbor. Natas wants to rule the world and demands that we give up our weapons so that he may proclaim himself to be our king. If we wish to have a king reign over us, we will anoint one of our own to sit upon the throne. Our law is handed down in Jerusalem, not in Geneva. You say Natas can build nuclear weapons to destroy us if we do not accept his demands. We have survived among nuclear powers that could and did murder over five billion people simply because a few men wanted to rule over their neighbors. Now, Natas says he won't murder us if we let him rule over us, but if we don't, he will kill us all. It might be somewhat dangerous to rely upon his promises. We do not fear Natas, but we do fear what he represents."

Romas was stunned by the harshness of the response. He stood up and extended his hand. "I will carry your message back to Natas." The Prime Minister rose slowly and shook Romas' hand. "I do not speak for the Knesset. The Knesset does not speak for the people. We are a democracy. The people speak for the people. I will ask the people to decide by popular vote. Then Natas shall have his answer. That is the message I ask you to take back to your master."

Romas fought back the urge to curse. What should he tell Natas? That the mission was a success? That would be stretching the truth more than he dared. How many Israelis would share the Prime Minister's opinion of the proposed compromise? A simple majority was usually sufficient on issues decided by popular vote. A lot of people wanted peace at any price. . . even in Israel. The nuclear war had made doves out of a lot of hawks. Surely the Jewish people would be violently opposed to another nuclear battle where Israel would be the primary target. If superpowers such as the United States and Russia perished when directly targeted, how could Israel expect to survive? Jews might be stiff-necked, but they were not generally suicidal.

He caught the driver's eyes in the rear-view mirror. "Open the window, please." The electric motor hummed as the glass panel receded into the door cavity. A breath of fresh air filtered through the limo. Romas took a deep breath and settled back into the soft leather. He would tell

Natas that the Jewish people would accept the offer. A formal vote would be the method of acceptance.

"Lieutenant Walker is here, Chief." The door sentry stepped back, and Walker appeared in the doorway. Wallace smiled broadly, got up from his desk, and greeted Walker with an affectionate handshake. "Welcome to my new quarters, Jim." He turned to the guard. "Thank you. That will be all." The man nodded and closed the door. Wallace motioned toward two spacious guest chairs upholstered with thick, white velvet. The chairs faced each other, separated by a knee-high convenience table constructed of heavy, polished glass supported by hand-carved walnut legs. Atop the table were piles of computer printouts.

"Have you had dinner, Jim?" Wallace inquired while settling into the cushioned luxury opposite Walker. "Yes, Sir. But, I wouldn't turn down a glass of your scotch." "I'll join you." Wallace got up, walked over to his desk credenza, took out a fifth of whiskey and two six-ounce glasses. "Are all the men okay?" He poured the scotch while looking back at Walker. “Yes, Sir. The men are fine. They're well fed and enjoying first-class accommodations, but anxious to know what's going on. They know that you sent for me."

Wallace handed a glass of straight whiskey to Walker, then sat down again. He leaned over and tapped his glass against Walker's. "To our new careers, Commander." "To my good friend... and father image," Walker replied. "I assume you took note of your new title." Wallace grinned. "I have a big job for you if you're interested."

Walker set down his glass and chuckled. "You know I'm always interested in a promotion.....assuming that Commander outranks Lieutenant within your police force."

Wallace's expression became ambiguous. "There's no parallel between military rank and titles within our police force. Your authority will be whatever I say it is. The issue is whether you are willing to take on a very difficult and distasteful responsibility."

Walker bought a few seconds to think by downing more scotch. "That sounds pretty ominous. What do you want me to do?" Wallace was pleased with Walker's cautiousness. Ambition was not objectionable as long as it was subservient to prudence. "Natas is a powerful and extremely dangerous man. However, his peace plan makes a lot of sense. His intelligence is frightening. He knows precisely what you're going to do before you make a conscious decision. He understands the nature of the human spirit and he uses that knowledge to manipulate and control the masses. What's left of the human race has unconditionally accepted him as a benevolent dictator."

Wallace gestured toward the stacks of computer printouts. "Over eighty percent of the surviving population around the world has already registered at the control centers and accepted his proclamations. His word is undisputed law, and the penalty for noncompliance is summary execution. We are more than a police force. We're judge, jury, and executioner. We enforce the law, execute criminals and provide continuous security for Natas. He has entrusted me with his very life. I need a loyal and trusted assistant who can follow my orders without question. Someone who can wield my authority in my absence without aborting basic objectives......enforce the law and keep Natas alive."

Walker was overwhelmed by Wallace's frankness. He masked his surprise by asking the anticipated question. "Doesn't the summary execution of lawbreakers without a trial trouble you a bit?" Wallace's face turned to stone. "No. It's a simple matter of priorities. In order to provide adequate food, water and suitable shelter for everyone, all bureaucratic waste must be eliminated. One breaks the law by choice knowing that the penalty is execution. The severe environmental limitations within our new society prohibit the tolerance of criminal behavior and the expense of attempted rehabilitation. In order for everyone to be equal before the law, everyone must obey the law."

"How about the accused where there is a question of guilt?" Walker interrupted. Wallace was not concerned. "False criminal charges, in themselves, are a crime punishable by death. In those rare cases where guilt is truly in doubt, we will provide the accused with a fair and impartial hearing before a police tribunal. Failure to provide a fair and impartial hearing is also a capital offense. I will never tolerate corruption within those we entrust with the duty to judge impartially." "Who decides if the hearing was unjust?" "I will. . . and in my absence, you will." "A one-man supreme court?" "Yes. There will be no dissension as to what the law is or what constitutes a fair and impartial hearing. There will be no appeal unless there is some evidence to support the charge of malfeasance. Where corruption exists, execution will follow."

Walker was chilled by the coldness in Wallace's eyes. "That's quite a departure from our constitutional values." Wallace continued: "Democracy has its faults. When the deviants, the morally bankrupt, the welfare sponges, the politically inept, and the judicial incompetents outnumber the productive, law-abiding population, democratic principles and constitutional guarantees become empty illusions. Throughout history, democracy has preceded anarchy and anarchy is usually ended by a dictator. The political incompetents within the United States led us into a nuclear war that produced global anarchy which can only be ended by a global dictator. The most morally corrupt within the United States gravitated to the positions of lawyers, judges, and politicians. Their single motivation became personal enrichment while clothed with the public trust. They catered to the politically powerful and groveled very low before the rich and famous. Judgeships were handed out as political favors and the price of justice barred the courthouse door to the poor and underprivileged. One of my continuing priorities will be the meting out of impartial justice to former lawyers, judges, and politicians. It is my fervent hope that such societal parasites attempt to circumvent our law. I will personally handle those executions."

Walker had heard enough. He knew Wallace was more to be feared than Natas. Perhaps Natas had reached the same conclusion. He hoped Wallace never became his enemy.

Wallace leaned forward, and his visage changed from flint to thoughtfulness. "We have fifty-four million, nine hundred and eight thousand policemen at our disposal. They're located at fourteen thousand separate control centers throughout zone one. The average police strength at each control center is three thousand, nine hundred and twenty-two. I want you to take half of them and hunt down every person who has not registered as the law requires. They're all criminals and are to be executed wherever they're found.

Concentrate on the nomadic scavengers first. You may structure your own chain of command and work out your own strategy. Just get the job done as quickly and efficiently as possible. Anyone who has registered at a control center will have an identifying mark in the right hand or forehead. The mark is invisible to the naked eye but is highly visible to an electronic scanner. The amnesty period for registration ends at midnight on September 29th. You need to have your organizational structure and general strategy mapped out by then.

We'll leave a thousand men at each center to provide routine police protection while we round up those who refuse our amnesty terms. Colonel Wirtman and I will use the remaining thirteen million, four hundred and fifty-four thousand policemen to flush out all surviving military personnel who haven't yet surrendered, and to transport, dismantle and bury all military weapons and equipment that cannot be easily converted to industrial use or properly utilized by our police force. We will destroy all nuclear weapons and bury the remains in zone four areas. The only weapons suitable for our men will be those formerly utilized by conventional police personnel. Weapons of war are totally banned from our new world order. There will be no exceptions."

Walker nodded his approval. "I understand, Sir." Wallace smiled warmly. "You may call me John. You and I and Colonel Wirtman will provide the brains behind law enforcement. Our orders will be transmitted by computer to each control center. Supervisory personnel at each geographical location will see that the orders are immediately communicated to local field personnel. There will be a clear division of responsibility along with complete authority. You will manage routine law enforcement. Wirtman will handle all recruiting and training. I will coordinate with Natas, manage internal security matters as well as global security; monitor civil and criminal hearings; and preside twice each week at skull sessions between the three of us. The meeting times will vary each week so that we do not become predictable."

Wallace rose to his feet indicating that the conference was over. "I have a meeting with Natas in five minutes. Get some rest and we'll have breakfast together."

“Thank you, John. I will not disappoint you.”

CHAPTER 5

Comes Now the False Prophet

The bar was lively but peaceful when Marge entered. It was amazing how docile drunks had become once they learned that the penalty for assault was immediate execution. Oren Natas certainly knew how to keep the peace. The policeman in the corner kept a watchful eye on the patrons. She unzipped her jacket and hung it on the coat rack. There was an empty seat at the center of the bar. She made her way to the spot, sat down and placed her purse on the bar.

The bartender, Jeff Arnold, spotted her and moved down to her stool. He was a young, handsome guy with brown hair, brown eyes and tall, muscular build. Jeff winked at her and then smiled. "Hi, Marge. You look fantastic. . . as usual. Whiskey sour?" "Every time, Jeff," Marge answered. "And keep 'em coming." "You got it, Pretty Lady. Any news about Mary?" "Nothing yet, but I still have hope." He poured her drink and set it on a napkin. "The first one's on me. It's worth it just to see you at my bar." "Why don't I fix you a special drink at my place later?" Marge suggested.

"I'd like that very much. I'm off at ten. Why don't you write down your address while I wait on that guy waving his glass at me?" He moved away while she searched her purse for a pen and some paper. She scribbled her address on an old business card and laid it on the bar next to her napkin, then sipped her drink and waited.

He returned and poured her another whiskey sour. Marge gave him her teasing look. "Now that you've hooked me, what are you doing on Saturday?" He picked up the card and stuck it into his shirt pocket. " Whatever you're doing.... I hope." "How about taking me up in the mountains to look for Mary?" "Is she anything like you?" "Younger and more beautiful." Marge pretended to pout. "We're headed for the mountains," he chuckled. "What makes you think she's up there?" "Just a special feeling that came over me. I think she's been playing Daniel Boone since the missiles crossed the Pacific."

Bishop Romas was both relieved and pleased that the Israeli people had voted to accept Natas' proposed compromise. He knew that Natas was aware of the acceptance although no comment had been forthcoming. Why? Did Natas secretly hope the Jews would defy the law and provide the excuse to attack them? The memory of the bloody sword still made him queasy. He hoped the feeling didn't linger too long. Natas liked to hold conferences over lavish meals served in his private office where security was well established.

Romas checked his watch. The conference was still eight minutes away. He looked over his notes and tested his memory. Natas didn't like a briefing from notes. He expected his subjects to know the answers to questions without relying on props. Anyone could recite from notes. Natas showed respect for intelligence, not the ability to read. He had no patience with anyone who couldn't engage in an anticipated conference without cluttering up the table with written memory joggers.

They could review the Israeli situation over the brandy appetizer. Then what? Did Natas have something else to review with him? If not, why a dinner meeting? Natas never wasted time and seemed to be perpetually preoccupied with his own schemes. He never spent time with women or attended social activities that did not require his personal appearance. Maybe Natas was too taken with himself to feel desire for anyone else. He always felt inferior in Natas' presence, and the man frightened him. He seemed to read a person's secret thoughts as easily as reading a newspaper. That thought revived his nausea. He looked at his notes again.

The rapping of the guard's knuckles on the thick door of the executive lounge ended his short wait. The guard opened the door and looked inside. "He's waiting for you, Bishop." "Thank you, Hanzel. Lead the way." Romas got up and followed the guard. "Sure wish I could join you," Hanzel said. "Tonight's menu includes flame-broiled sirloin with all the trimmings. It's nice to dine with royalty. If the cook's too generous, save me a morsel," Hanzel said, trying to look agreeable. "I'll see to it," Romas promised.

Hanzel knocked on Natas' private door, paused and then opened the door. "Bishop Romas is here, Your Majesty." "Come in, Julius," Natas invited. "I'm sorry for the delay." Hanzel retreated and closed the door behind him. Natas rolled his chair back from his desk, stood up and greeted Romas with a firm handshake. "It's been a busy time. Sit down and join me in a little relaxation." Romas sat down in the guest chair to the left of the desk. "These are exciting times. The world owes you a lot. You have achieved the impossible."

Natas smiled as he reached inside his credenza for the brandy and snifters. "There is nothing that is truly impossible once fear and ignorance have been properly channeled. He poured the brandy and raised his snifter. "To my loyal subjects." Romas joined the toast. "To one law, one faith, and one ruler." He drank heartily, hoping the brandy would increase his confidence level. His armpits were damp again. Natas raised his snifter again. "And to the Children of Abraham. May they rest in peace." "Forever," Romas added. He drank the second toast with Natas. The remark did not really surprise him. He no longer had any doubt where the Jews stood with Natas. They were marked for extermination. Why? They were no longer a threat to world peace. What was Natas' true motive? Whatever the reason, Romas had made a conscious choice. He would be an accomplice in the murder of an entire nationality. A modest price to pay for Natas' trust and favor.

Natas poured more brandy. "Tell me, Julius. What did you think of the Israeli Prime Minister?" Romas arched his eyebrows and stroked his chin. "A tough negotiator with a hide like a rhino and stubborn as a mule." "Did he give you a history lesson?"

The question startled Romas. How did Natas know that! The Prime Minister had never met Natas and he, himself, had never told anyone about the negotiation dialogue. "Yes. As a matter of fact, he did ramble through a bit of ancient history. He thinks you're just another pharaoh who can't be persuaded to let the Hebrews prosper."

"Raamses only killed the newborn males." Natas chuckled. "A halfway measure that led to his ultimate demise. We shall be more thorough." The brandy gave Romas a false bravery. "Why is extermination the only solution?" "A legend does not die easily. Like a precious gem, it is handed down from generation to generation. To kill a legend, one must kill those who are succored by it. When Abraham's seed is extinct, the promises to his children are also extinguished."

Hanzel knocked on the door and opened it for the servants. "Dinner is ready, Your Majesty." Natas nodded and smiled at Romas. "We can continue our more serious business over dinner." He rose and led the way to the table which had been prepared before Romas' arrival. They seated themselves across from each other at the center of the table and spread their napkins. "I hope the brandy sparked your appetite," Natas remarked. "I ordered the sirloin thick, juicy and man-sized." "Hanzel offered to eat my leftovers," Romas replied. "I noticed that the corner guards are absent.....a change in security?" "More a question of privacy. The corner guards have been made unnecessary by beefed up security outside my office. A suggestion by Chief Wallace."

Their waitress arranged the fresh garden salads, spices, selection of dressings, baked potatoes, sour cream, butter, and hot rolls. Another attendant brought in a red dinner wine for Natas to inspect and taste. Natas' eyes scanned the label and checked the integrity of the seal. "1967. . . was that a good year, Julius?" "I was a young altar boy in 1967. Yes. As I recall, that was an excellent year."

The attendant broke the seal and poured a sample into Natas' glass. He swirled it, sniffed it, and swished it over his taste buds. "That will do just fine," he said. He looked back at Romas while the attendant filled their glasses. "What kind of reception are you getting around the kingdom, Julius?" "More or less indifferent at this point, but the concept of one faith is more difficult to impose than one law and one ruler." "Have you seen any evidence of significant resistance?" Romas tasted his wine. It was very smooth and delightful. "What I see is blind adherence to tradition. Very few people can explain precisely what they believe or why they believe it. However, tradition is like a bad habit. People won't turn loose even though they know that death may result."

Natas spread chunky blue cheese dressing on his salad and buttered his potato, then smothered the potato with sour cream and chives while appearing to ponder Romas' statement. Romas now knew that Natas didn't need to ponder anything. He knew exactly what he was going to do regardless of what anyone said or did. He understood the human spirit and wanted his subjects to follow willingly. Romas sprinkled his salad with Italian dressing and garlic salt, then garnished his potato with heaping portions of butter and sour cream. He added salt and pepper and buttered a hot roll.

Natas tasted his salad and potato. "We need to strip the tradition away one layer at a time. It's much easier to skin a carcass from the outside than from the inside. First, we get rid of all religious books, writings, symbols, and ornaments. Then, we destroy all religious shrines and convert places of worship into government property for rehabilitation. Next, we provide the public with an exhibition of your power to raise the dead. Finally, we seal the coffin by making it a crime to speak or write anything contrary to your spiritual guidance."

Romas forked his mouth full of salad to give himself time to think. Raise the dead? Is he serious? "I might fall a little short on my end. Raising the dead is a pretty tall order ......not something I do on a routine basis." "Do you believe in life after death, Julius? Do you believe that humans have an immortal soul?" Romas dabbed at his lips with his napkin. "I used to think so. That's why I became a priest. Now, I worry more about staying alive and enjoying the life that I have now."

Natas studied him pensively. "What disillusioned you?" "I suppose the lust of the flesh overcame my longing for immortality. I have never seen any evidence of life after death or witnessed any miracles outside of Hollywood productions." "Suppose you had witnessed someone raise the dead. Would that have duly impressed you?" Natas refilled their wine glasses. Romas became more and more uncomfortable. Natas was testing his fickleness. "It would have certainly captured my attention." "Do you believe that Jesus raised Lazarus from the dead after Lazarus had lain in his tomb for four days?" Romas' armpits were wet again. "Isn't that the same as asking whether I believe in life after death?" Natas*' eyes* became more intense and more piercing. "That's not exactly what I had in mind. I'm more interested in whether you believe that it is possible to restore life to a dead body."

The waitress brought the steaks and gave Romas a breather. His palms were now damp with nervousness. What was Natas driving at? He knew he was beginning to appear inept and hypocritical. Natas had earlier referred to a public display of his power. What power? If this line of questioning continued, he would need assistance to get up from the table. Did Natas really expect him to perform some sort of miracle as evidence of his competence to function in his assigned role? His appetite was fading fast.

The steaks were broiled to perfection and garnished with steamed mushrooms. Natas applied a liberal layer of steak sauce and sliced into his sirloin. The outside was slightly charred, and the center was pink and moist. He tasted the meaty flavor and grunted with approval. Romas dug into his steak and tried to come up with an intelligent response to Natas' last question. Did he believe that it is possible to restore life to a dead body? Did he? No. He did not. He sliced off another bite of meat and answered. "Death is the absence of life. Whatever spiritual awareness follows physical life cannot be of the same quality. Physical life involves nurturing of the flesh, bones, organs and blood chemistry. In the absence of life, such nurturing ceases and the body undergoes irreversible corruption. No. I do not believe that a dead body can be restored to physical life after the brain and organs die for lack of oxygen."

Natas chewed his meat and gazed at Romas. "Where does that leave morality?" Romas locked eyes with Natas. "Morals are the product of environment and culture. Culture is the mixture of religious fables, man-made law, physical needs, and social structuring while environment is the geographical boundaries separating mature cultures. In one society, it is moral to kill and eat other humans. In another social order, it is immoral to eat the flesh of hogs. Morality is whatever the majority of people within established social boundaries proclaim it to be. The norms become confused when diverse cultures are fused into a global society."

Natas was not impressed with Romas' attempt to evade the question. "What is morality for Julius Romas?" Romas reached for his wine glass. "To be cool in summer, warm in winter, work very little, eat and drink what pleases me, and to die at a ripe old age." "Then, what?" "Then, I am dead. Julius Romas no longer exists. I mix forever with the elements. My lovers and closest friends will soon forget that I ever lived and move on to new relationships."

Their waitress brought in an assortment of desserts and hot coffee. She poured the coffee into fragile china cups and removed the abandoned plates, side dishes, and condiments. Natas helped himself to apple cobbler and vanilla ice cream. "You have just described the life of a sheltered stud. Does it really matter whether such an animal lives long enough to die of old age? How often must a living creature experience the same pleasures before life becomes meaningless and monotonous? If continuous enjoyment of carnal lusts is the essence of life, then wouldn't old age be a curse rather than a fervent hope?"

Romas had chosen strawberry pie and whipped cream. He savored the richness and sipped hot coffee. "Old men have the erotic desires of young stallions. Fantasies of eternal youth distort the true image in the mirror. Old men do not really see the wrinkled skin, the sagging flesh, and withered muscles. They see themselves being pursued by young virgins as they snort, paw the earth and display their masculine virility. Unlike the lower animals, humans have the capacity to believe themselves to be something that they are not. It is the pride of life that warms the breasts of old men."

Natas was tiring of Romas' human vanity. It was time to move on to thoughts more relevant to his purpose for entertaining Romas. "For the purpose of deeper meanings, let's assume that humans do have a spiritual existence that survives the physical body. In such an eternal state, would you prefer to serve in heaven or reign in hell?"

Romas' heart skipped and his hand trembled slightly. He set his cup down and lowered his hands below the table. "I have no firm concept of either habitation. I cannot choose between status levels of which I am ignorant." "Well said, Julius," Natas replied. "Where you profess your ignorance, I declare my specific knowledge. I have both served in heaven and reigned in hell. You need only to read my name backward to see that I speak with authority and experience. I have come from my everlasting habitation to save willing souls from the bondage of heaven. To that end, I shall bestow upon you the power to destroy your enemies with the flames of hell and to raise me from the dead."

Natas' declaration shook Romas to the very core of his being. He was beginning to understand the significance of the sudden appearance of Antiochus Epiphanes at the command of Natas. That display of power was a prelude to this revelation. A subtle sense of strength and calmness swept over him and he was no longer afraid of Natas. He resisted the urge to flatter him with praise. Natas perceived his change in comfort level. He watched as Romas moved his hands back into view and continued consuming his coffee and dessert.

"Do you wonder why your dread of me has vanished, Julius? A man always dreads what he doesn't understand. There is no dread when the inevitable is accepted. Your soul belongs to me. My mark is forever in your forehead. Heaven is eternally barred to you and hell awaits your coming. In the meanwhile, there is much to be accomplished. It is time to elevate your status in the eyes of all mankind."

"Is hell truly a reality?" Romas inquired. Natas flashed a devilish grin. "Hell was created as a temporary prison for those who rebel against heaven. The immortality of fallen humans is confined there until the great battle for human souls is ended. The full measure of Lucifer's struggle will be decided less than seven years from now. A great lake of fire has been created to swallow up hell and to imprison Lucifer and the fallen angels. Our task is to help Lucifer conquer human immortality."

Romas began to see the total picture. "We will share Lucifer's earthly kingdom and then join him in the lake of fire?" "Yes. And so, will all humans who side with him. Thus, you can see why I must leave to prepare for the quantitative victory. Lucifer will succor you as he has been with me in the earth. He is in me and he shall be in you."

The late evening sun over northern Idaho painted the sky crimson red. The snow-covered mountain peaks glistened in the scarlet horizon. The soft breeze was unusually warm for early October. A bull elk trumpeted his rutting call across the expanse of wilderness. The forlorn plea echoed through the thick woodland sheltering a swift mountain-fed stream where Paul Roberts fished for trout. The sound gradually died away and Paul glanced toward Jackie. She had been sleeping nearby since noon. She stirred in her sleeping bag but did not awaken. She had begun sleeping more soundly since they decided to take turns resting and keeping watch. Elk steaks would be a welcome change in their diet of fish and roots, but he dared not leave her unprotected to look for the bull.

The hunt would take hours and would sap his energy. The odds were small that he would find the animal anyway, and it would be a shame to butcher such a magnificent creature for the small amount of meat they could consume in a day. It would be too dangerous to try and dry strips of the carcass out in the open; and without being processed, the meat would spoil quickly in the warm air. His mouth watered at the thought of charred elk steaks. It had been twenty-two days since they left Calgary and their supplies were dangerously low. The canned foods had been consumed during the first eleven days along with the cheeses and dried fruit. Only seasoning and a few sticks of beef jerky remained in the backpacks.

They made better time with the lighter load, but it was still five hard days to Galena Summit. Ten hours of travel, five hours sleeping, five hours standing watch, and a total of four hours for meals, bathing and conversation didn't leave much time for hunting game. Anyway, they had made out fine fishing and digging up edible roots. It was just getting awfully monotonous.

He raised the fishing pole fashioned from a birch limb and checked his bait. The worm he had dug up was still wriggling on the hook. He lowered the line again and scanned the surrounding trees. A flash of golden brown in the pines beyond the stream drew his eyes. The young cougar looked back at him and then moved on. Paul watched the cat disappear into the trees. His left arm jerked upward instinctively at the gentle tug on the line. The hook was solidly set and the limb bowed downward. Paul began slowly walking backward while keeping the line tight. He knew from the amount of resistance and the deep bow in the limb that he had hooked a fairly large fish. A three-pound rainbow trout broke the surface of the stream and splashed helplessly in the clear, cold water.

The sun faded from the horizon as they sat on Jackie's sleeping bag and ate the fish. Paul passed a canteen of water to Jackie and then looked around the campsite. It was too dark to see anything moving in the trees and the red glow of the fire made the twilight period appear shorter in duration. Jackie moved closer to him and laid her head on his left shoulder. "It won't be long now. . . just a few more days. What if Mary's at the cave, Paul? What will we do?"

He stroked Jackie's hair with his right hand. "I don't know at this point," he answered truthfully. In the darkness far beyond the stream, the report of a large caliber rifle shattered the stillness. Five seconds passed, and a second shot rang out. "What's that?" Jackie asked. "Sounds like gunshots!" "Can't tell," Paul answered. "It's about a mile away. Could be scavengers, or maybe police chasing scavengers. Whatever it is, we don't want to run into them. Let's move on.

It was almost noon when Jack spotted fresh moose tracks. It was a lone bull with a crippled leg. The bull only set the left rear hoof down every twenty yards or so. Probably got gored in the left hip by another bull, Jack surmised. He picked up the pace and tracked the wounded animal with confidence. It wouldn't roam over a very large area and would not try to run unless spooked.

As he gained ground on the moose, Jack saw something that troubled him and made him extremely cautious. A big male grizzly was also trailing the crippled bull. Jack swore softly to himself. He'll spook the bull for sure. Jack began trotting along the trail, hoping to spot the bear before the bull did. Luck was with him. Less than four hundred yards ahead, he saw the grizzly moving through the trees. He ran faster, knowing that the big bruin would either flee the vicinity or attack him. If the bear charged, he would climb a tree and then try to shoot it at close range when it stopped beneath the tree. Otherwise, he would aim for the heart when it reared up to challenge him. He hoped the bear would just take flight.

He slowed down a little to catch his breath. The grizzly caught his scent, spun around, rose on its hind legs and sniffed the air. The brute was still more than a hundred yards away.... too far for an accurate shot using a crossbow. Jack waved his arms and ran directly toward the grizzly. To his amazement, the bear dropped on all fours and continued along the trail, seemingly unconcerned with anything but the moose scent. What an idiot! Jack chuckled to himself. Guess I'll have to shoot him in the rump.

He ran faster while fitting a hunting arrow into the crossbow. When he closed the gap to within forty yards, he stopped and took aim. The grizzly stopped suddenly and wheeled around just as Jack squeezed the trigger. The arrow lodged in its right shoulder without inflicting a serious injury. It reared up and swatted at the nuisance with its huge left paw.

Jack knew he didn't have time to restring the crossbow before the bear attacked. He spotted a large white pine with thick branches within a few feet of the ground. He slung the crossbow around his neck and scampered up the tree as the grizzly charged. Jack wrapped his legs around the trunk about twenty feet up and held onto the branches until he could wedge his boots between some limbs and the trunk. The grizzly reared up, growled at him and began trying to shake him loose from the tree by shoving mightily against the trunk. The tree swayed back and forth slightly, but its thick trunk absorbed the furious assault. The angry grizzly backed off and sat down.

Jack managed to restring the crossbow and load another arrow. He was anxious to get back to his moose hunt and the situation was beginning to irritate him considerably. The grizzly eyed him with disdain and the thick branches made it difficult to position and aim the weapon. Jack finally got a clear shot at the grizzly when it rose on its hind legs again. The arrow pierced the animal's massive chest just about dead center. The grizzly dropped on all four paws again, growled savagely at Jack, and lumbered off into the woods to lick its wounds. Jack watched the bear until it was totally out of sight. Well, at least I got him off the bull's trail, Jack thought with relief. He waited a few minutes before climbing down to see if the grizzly might double back. He lowered himself to the ground, circled around, found the moose tracks again and continued after the bull.

Jeff Arnold shifted the GMC pickup into 4-wheel drive as he veered off the mountain road and headed northeast toward a small lake he had spotted last fall while trailing a wounded buck. The secluded spot would be a romantic place to rest and eat lunch. He and Marge had left Galena Summit at dawn and had searched for a hidden cave in every likely spot he could remember on both sides of the road.

Marge had packed a picnic basket that included three bottles of fruity wine, which indicated to him that she expected lunch to be long and delightful. "Where to now?" Marge asked as the pickup bounced over a fallen spruce. "I know a perfect place to stop for lunch. A little spring-fed lake surrounded by pines and cedars. We can get within a quarter mile in the truck, then backpack in from there. After lunch, we'll check out some rough terrain that might conceal a cave. The spot I'm thinking of lies about half a mile northwest of the lake."

The wounded grizzly waddled through the thick timber, stumbling against tree trunks and crashing through the underbrush. Suddenly, it stopped, reared up and turned a full circle on its hind paws. Bloody foam oozed from its muzzle and its eyes were wild with bestial rage. The bear snarled and exposed its teeth as the odor of humans filled its nostrils. It dropped back on all four paws and continued on toward the southwest, the direction it sensed the hated scent was coming from. The animal's natural fear of humans was overcome by blind fury.

Jack stayed well behind the injured moose hoping for a change in direction or a shift in the wind. The gentle breeze out of the southwest would carry his scent to the bull if he closed the distance too quickly. He walked slowly and scanned the woods in all directions to make sure no one else was around. The mature bull would yield nearly a thousand pounds of meat, but it wasn't worth being spotted by anyone who might follow him back to the cave. His camouflaged outerwear made him invisible except when he was in motion. He had blackened his face, hands, and crossbow with ashes from the cave, and wouldn't be spotted unless he got careless. He continued on and found a spot where the moose had laid down. There was a smear of blood on the pine needles. So, the wound is fresh, Jack concluded. That means the left hip should still be edible.

Just ahead, the bull had turned south. Now, he would be downwind of the wary animal and could move in for a shot at close range. Jack picked up the pace and became more cautious. He knew this would be his best chance to bag the bull, and he had to get within killing range before the moose changed directions again. He pressed on with a keen sense of urgency.

Sixty yards or so ahead, Jack stopped and frowned with disgust. Familiar bear tracks cut across the trail. He muttered to himself. "That grizzly's still around and heading straight for the lake." Jack began trotting faster and with apprehension along the game trail knowing that bear and moose would wallow in water to soothe and cleanse a fresh wound. He had to catch up to the bull before it circled east toward the lake.

Jack slowed to a walk to rest for a moment. He heard a throaty bellow and saw the bull struggle to its feet from beneath the drooping branches of a red cedar. He quickly raised the crossbow and stood motionless. The bull hobbled out from under the cedar and looked back in Jack's direction giving him a clear view of its left shoulder and flank. Jack took careful aim at the lung area and fired. The twang of the bow was followed by a solid thud as the arrow sank deep into the animal's ribs behind the left foreleg. The bull bellowed loudly and lurched out of sight among the evergreens. Jack restrung the bow and inserted another arrow. The first shot had been right on target. The bull would drown in its own blood within a half hour.

The stricken moose left great splotches of blood along the trail as it headed for the small lake less than three hundred yards away. Jack was certain the grizzly was still close by, but the nature of his concern had changed. The bull would not get away, and he would have no difficulty following the bloody trail.

The bear would also eventually die. The second arrow that embedded in the brute's chest would cause fatal internal hemorrhage. In the meantime, it would be very prudent to avoid the grizzly and stay within sprinting distance of a climbable tree.

A rumbling growl caused Jack to halt in his tracks. Off to his right, he saw the great bear stumbling through the trees near the north side of the lake. The arrow had done its job and the beast would soon die. He decided it would be safer to keep the bear in sight until it finally collapsed. The grizzly stopped, rose on its hind legs and sniffed the breeze. Jack began looking for a suitable tree.

Then he saw what caught the bear's attention. . . a couple sleeping on towels beside the water. The wobbly grizzly let out a threatening growl, dropped on all four feet and charged. Jack shouted and waved his arms, but the grizzly had zeroed in on the couple.

Jack's shouting awakened Jeff and Marge, and they sprang up just in time to face the grizzly's fury. "Run, Marge!" Jeff yelled as he frantically looked for something to swing at the charging bear. The closest thing was his backpack. He snatched it up and hurled it at the grizzly's massive head. Marge was petrified with terror and cowered beneath a bushy cedar. Jack ran toward them with his crossbow raised and ready to fire. The backpack bounced off the side of the bear's head as it bore down on Jeff. At the last terrifying second, Jeff tried to sidestep the lumbering grizzly. It reared up and clubbed him on the right side of his head with a powerful swipe of its left forepaw. The force of the blow lifted Jeff off his feet and hurled him into the shallow water. The grizzly immediately pounced on him, sinking its razor-sharp teeth into the back of his neck while ripping at his back and shoulders with its huge claws.

Jeff's neck bones snapped with a sickening sound as the enraged bear flung its head from side to side while crunching Jeff's neck between its teeth. Jack stopped less than forty feet from the water, aimed, and sent an arrow whizzing into the grizzly's thick neck. The bear released Jeff and reared up, snarling at Jack. He quickly restrung the bow and shot another arrow into the front of the grizzly's neck halfway between its head and shoulders. The dying bear lowered itself into the water and thrashed violently for a few seconds, then got back onto its feet, galloped out of the lake and into the woods on the south side of the water. Jack had only one arrow left as he watched the bear disappear into the trees.

He knew the grizzly would bleed to death before long, and if it circled back, he would be forced to use his pistol. Seven .45 caliber slugs would surely be enough to finish off an enraged beast that was already dead on its feet.

Jack waded into the water and dragged Jeff's dead body out of the lake. Jeff's neck was totally crushed, and his body was badly mangled. Jack lowered the limp corpse to the ground and looked toward Marge. She was still huddled under the cedar, weeping hysterically with her hands over her face. Jack walked over and lifted her to her feet. She clung to him and sobbed into his chest. "It's over," Jack reassured her in a gentle voice. "The bear is gone." Marge gradually regained some self-control and her sobbing subsided. She wiped her eyes with the back of her hands and looked toward Jeff's body. "Is he dead?" "Yes," Jack said, "He's dead. There's nothing we can do for him." He took Marge by her shoulders and looked her over. "Who was he. . . and who are you?"

For the first time, Marge looked straight into the face of the man who had been comforting her. My God! she thought. It's Dr. Roberts! She blinked back more tears and looked away. "His name is Jeff Arnold, and I'm Marge Rosen . . . from Boise. We were just on a picnic." Jack released her shoulders and looked toward the spot in the trees where he had last seen the grizzly. "Get your clothes on," he said with a note of urgency in his voice. "We're in great danger here."

CHAPTER 6

Death Squads Enforce the Mark

Jack stopped the pickup in the trees below the cave entrance. He got out, opened the rear, bundled up two chunks of moose meat inside the beach towel, slung the load over his right shoulder and closed the back end again. The night air had turned cold and damp and heavy storm clouds blotted out the moon and stars.

Marge stayed close to Jack in the thick darkness to avoid stumbling as they approached the cave. Jack lowered his bundle to the ground and uncovered a passageway through the entrance, then shouldered the meat again and turned to Marge. "Keep your head down and stay close. We have to go through a long, narrow tunnel and you won't be able to see a thing. The ceilings about five feet high, so stoop over a little and hold onto my gun belt."

"No problem," Marge responded. "I'm right behind you all the way." No wonder they chose this place to hide, Marge thought. We never would have found it. She quietly followed Jack through the darkness toward the inner room. After several turns, she saw a faint glow up ahead and her heart began to pound with excitement. Her search was over!

Mary and Ruth were napping when Jack sang out: "It's Jack! With dinner!" Both women jumped up from the sleeping bags and ran to meet him, then stopped short when they saw someone behind him. "Marge! It's Marge!" Mary cried with delight. She ran up and threw her arms around Marge. Jack grinned at Ruth. "I found her hiding from a grizzly, and she followed me home. . . didn't know what else to do with her."

He walked over to the fire, set the bundle of meat down and opened it up. Ruth followed him and gawked at the huge pieces. "Oh, Jack! It's beautiful! What is it?" "Moose," Jack replied. "I've got over a thousand pounds of moose and bear meat outside in a pickup that Marge and I borrowed. The owner doesn't need it anymore." Ruth's eyes teared as she threw herself into Jack's arms and bubbled with joy. "Oh, Baby! I knew you could do it! That's more than enough for the whole winter."

Mary and Marge were still standing by the tunnel, chattering with exhilaration. Jack went to the spring to wash the dried blood from his hands, and Ruth walked back to Mary and Marge. She extended her hand to Marge. "I'm Ruth Roberts, Jack's wife." Marge shook her hand warmly. "I'm Marge Rosen, Mary's best friend. "We don't have much to offer you," Ruth said. "We've been here for some time and our supplies are exhausted."

Jack came back and interrupted. "I need help carrying in meat and wood. There's a storm coming that should cover our tracks, and we need several truckloads of wood. I won't have to cut any. We'll just drive around and pick it up. With all of us working together, we can get it all in before daylight. It's a good night for gathering. There won't be many people wandering around in the wilderness tonight."

Jack and the three women toiled throughout the night. The rain began falling shortly after 4:00 am. The bountiful supply of meat was stacked along the west wall, and six truckloads of wood had been piled against the east wall. They gathered two more truckloads of wood in the rain before Jack parked the pickup under a rock ledge obscured by a heavy stand of cedars about a mile northwest of the cave. He locked the truck, removed the distributor wire, stuck it into his pocket, and walked back to the cave.

The cold rain was falling faster as Jack recovered the cave entrance and headed for the inner room. He removed his wet clothes and warmed himself by the fire. The women were busily washing the meat in the spring and arranging it on fresh pine branches. Ruth walked back to Jack carrying a choice chunk of meat. "How about slicing up some moose steaks, Honey? We'll keep on washing meat if you'll handle the grill." "That suits me." Jack agreed. Ruth handed Jack the meat and positioned the grill over the fire, then went back to the spring.

During the activity around the fire, two rain-drenched figures appeared in the opening between the tunnel and the inner room. "What the dickens is this? A hotel or a cave?" Ruth and Jack stared at the two people in astonishment and Marge's mouth fell open. Mary's face turned white as she jumped to her feet. "Oh, my God!" she screamed. "Paul! Paul! It's Paul!" She ran with exuberance, leaped into his arms, buried her face between his chin and neck and wept with pure joy. The rain battered woman looked on with tears of happiness streaming down her cheeks. Jack, Ruth and Marge gathered around them.

When Paul finally set Mary back on her feet, Ruth moved up and hugged him with her head pressed sideways against his chest and her arms wrapped around him. "Oh, Paul!" she cried. "We thought you were dead!" Paul squeezed her in his arms and kissed her forehead. "Not yet," he chuckled. "Just a little tired and hungry. Do I smell broiled steak?"

Ruth released Paul and Jack grabbed him in a masculine embrace as tears watered his eyes. "Welcome home, Paul. Furnishings are a little shabby, but the company's great. Come over to the fire and dry out."

Paul drew Jackie to him with his right arm and held her close to his side. "This is Jackie Mason. She's been my friend and constant companion for the last six months." Jack smiled at her. "Hello, Jackie. . . this is Mary Roberts, Paul's wife," he said, putting his arm around Mary. He placed his other arm around Ruth. "I'm Jack Roberts, Paul's brother, and this is my wife, Ruth." He turned to Marge and motioned for her to step forward. "And. ... this is Marge Rosen, our friend."

Marge moved up and kissed Paul lightly on the cheek, then turned and hugged Jackie. Ruth and Mary also embraced Jackie to make her feel welcome. "Come over to the fire, Jackie," Mary urged. "Let us dry you out before you catch pneumonia."

Jack and Paul could easily pass for each other. Each of the four women was striking in appearance......all medium height, shapely figures, flawless skin, sparkling white teeth, and finely chiseled features. Mary's natural blond hair tumbled around her shoulders in complete harmony with her creamy skin and sky-blue eyes. Jackie's silky black hair cascaded down her back to her waist, and her lightly tanned skin blended perfectly with her pale green eyes. Marge and Ruth wore their brunette hair shoulder length with a petite flip. Both women exhibited pampered skin, gorgeous figures, and hazel eyes.

Jackie followed the women toward the fire and Jack accompanied Paul. "I'll broil you and Jackie some steaks while you dry out," Jack said. "We were about ready to eat breakfast when you surprised us." "We're famished," Paul admitted. "We ran out of supplies, and the fishing's been lousy." He sucked in his breath and whistled with awe when he spied the pile of fresh meat. "Looks like the hunting has been better than fishing." "Actually, it's been rotten for several weeks. I got lucky last evening and found a grizzly tracking a crippled bull moose. I killed the moose for food and the bear in self-defense."

Paul removed his backpack and set it aside, then sat down on a rock and began shucking his boots and socks. He looked over at Jackie and saw that the other women had removed her backpack and were helping her out of her wet clothes. Marge set Jackie's wet boots by the fire and spread the socks out to dry. Ruth and Mary hung up her wet garments and Jackie stepped up to the fire, shivering slightly.

"I love Mary very much, Paul. But I certainly haven't taken your place. . . . nobody can. Mary had just given up all hope, and so had Ruth and I. Here, let me hang those up to dry." He took the soggy clothes and hung them over the wire next to the woodpile. Paul set his boots out to dry and warmed himself across the fire from Jackie. Mary spread a towel for Paul and then handed him her plate. "Go ahead and finish my steak, Sugar. We'll broil some more." Ruth fixed a place for Jackie to sit and gave her plate to Jackie. "Eat this, Sweetie, while I help Mary."

Jack ate with Paul, Marge, and Jackie while Ruth sliced six more steaks and Mary placed them on the grill. Paul looked at the stack of meat again and turned to Jack. "Have you got enough supplies to preserve that much meat?" "Not at the moment," Jack answered. "But I've got an idea about how to get some now that you're here to help me." Paul glanced at Mary and looked at Jack out of the corners of his eyes. "Do I wanna hear this?" Jack laughed softly and gestured toward the stack of meat. "Sure, would be a shame to let that spoil and it's gonna be mighty tough finding game this winter." "You planning to hole up here indefinitely?" "You got a better idea?"

Paul chewed his steak and looked around the cave. "It is kinda homey, isn't it?" He looked at the four women and then back at Jack. "It appears that we won't be lonesome."

Mary came over and reached for Paul's plate. "Ready for another, Sweetheart?" "You bet," Paul answered with a big grin. He reached out and caressed her left arm. "Then, I'll be ready for you." "Looks like you've been well taken care of." She stuck out her tongue at him and went back to the grill to refill his plate.

Paul looked over at Jackie and saw that she and Marge were chattering like magpies. Mary and Ruth served the second batch of steaks, then sat down with Marge and Jackie. Paul and Jack gazed at the women and continued eating. "Looks like a hen party," Paul remarked. "I hope they continue to get along that well."

Jack nodded and changed the subject. "Have you heard any news as to what's going on?" "Not much. We've been on the road from Alberta for nearly a month. My flight from Boise to Colorado Springs was diverted there when the war broke out. That's where I met Jackie. She was on my flight and we were cooped up at the airport most of the time. The Canadians refused to give us permission to leave Alberta. We finally rounded up a couple of bicycles and left anyway. It's taken us twenty-seven days to get here. I figured I'd find you here if you survived the missiles, the death squads, and the scavengers."

"Where're the bikes?" "Just inside the entrance with our sleeping bags and extra clothes. I had to take the fender slings off to get the bikes inside. I guess I'd better bring them on in and dry out our bags and clothes." "I'll help you soon as we finish eating," Jack offered. "Were you able to get any news in Canada?" "A little . . . enough to know that I won't take the mark that's required to buy, sell, and receive food rations."

"You mean the mark's already been announced?" Jack queried with a startled expression. "In the right hand or forehead?" "How long have you been here, Jack?" "Since the bombs started falling." "Then you haven't heard about Oren Natas?" "No. Who's Oren Natas?"

"He's one bad dude, Jack . . . and the undisputed ruler of the planet, Earth. Roughly five billion people died in the war, and all the nuclear powers except Israel were annihilated. Two-thirds of the earth's surface and over sixty percent of the water on the planet are uninhabitable. World governments were in shambles and people who survived the bombs and radiation were fighting over the limited food and water. Law and order broke down and lawless scavengers were everywhere......robbing, raping and killing. Natas came up with a peace plan to cope with most of the problems, and the world accepted his plan along with a total dictatorship. All military forces are being disbanded and the law of Natas is being enforced by a worldwide police force. The penalty for any infraction of Natas' law is immediate execution. Natas' primary information network and his rationing system are handled by fully computerized control centers with a hundred thousand people being tracked by each center. The law requires every person to be registered at a control center and receive an invisible mark in the right hand or forehead that is read by electronic scanners. The first nine numbers are personal identification and the final three numbers indicate compliance with registration requirements. Those three numbers are six hundred and sixty-six."

"The mark of the beast," Jack said, shaking his head with disgust. "Sure, looks that way, Jack and the deadline for registration expired on September 29th. Now, death squads composed of police from each control center are hunting down anyone without the mark and conducting field executions. . . after a little torture to get information on the whereabouts of others in hiding."

Jack was silent for a moment then looked at Jackie. "Did Jackie take the mark?" "No, but she doesn't know why?" "You didn't tell her?" "No. She'd think I'd lost my mind. How about Marge?" Jack looked over at Marge and shook his head. "I don't know for sure, but I would assume that she has it . . . and has no idea what that means. She's only been here since last night, and I haven't discussed it with her. She was picnicking with some guy by the lake and got in the way of the grizzly I had to kill. The bear got her friend and I brought her here since I couldn't let her go blabbing around Boise about some hunter saving her from a bear. She claims she was hunting for Mary and had thrown in a picnic for good measure."

"That's probably true. Marge is Mary's best friend. But, how did she know Mary was hiding out?" "Beats the dickens outta me, Paul......but she was pretty sure about it, and the guy with her was rigged for a long search. I've got his propane-powered four-wheeler stashed about a mile from here."

The women had finished eating and were still chattering and giggling. Jack got up and put more wood on the fire, then turned back to Paul. "Let's get your stuff in by the fire."

When Paul and Jack returned with the bicycles, the women had washed up the plates and were busy washing more meat in the spring. Paul and Jack watched them for a minute and then spread out the wet sleeping bags and clothes by the fire. "Ready to get some supplies?" Jack asked. "Like robbing a warehouse or hijacking a grocery truck?" "Sounds like fun, Jack. But, isn't that a little risky?" "Everything is risky these days. We gotta have some supplies." "I'm game," Paul committed. "Let's get it done so we can process the meat. Got some dry clothes I can borrow?"

Jack gave Paul his extra jumpsuit, boots and socks and they began dressing. The women saw them and walked back to the fire. "You guys sneaking out on us?" Ruth teased. "You won't find any better action than you've got right here." "We're going after supplies to cure the meat," Jack informed her as he and Paul strapped on their gun belts. "And maybe some coffee and other things we're out of." "Gonna rob a grocery store?" Mary kidded. Jackie and Marge listened with apprehension. "We considered that," Paul answered with an expression that told the women they were not joking. "But, since we can't wait for darkness, we're gonna hijack a grocery truck. We can't leave that meat unprocessed much longer."

"How will you know if you're getting a straight or mixed load?" Marge asked with a worried look. "We'll have to find a truck loaded for a store delivery rather than one headed for a warehouse," Jack replied. "And that's going to require a little detective work." "Maybe I can help," Marge offered. "I was working in a supermarket in Boise. A mixed load came in every day about one o'clock. I checked it in occasionally and remember the driver talking about stopping for a coffee break at the restaurant in Ketchum on Highway 75. The tractor is solid red, and the trailer is green with red trim."

"Any guards on the truck?" Paul inquired. "One usually. . . and fully armed. Paul hugged Marge with appreciation. "That takes care of the detective work. The rest we can handle." "Better keep washing down the meat," Jack said. "We'll be back as soon as possible." He turned to Paul. "We'll need my binoculars and six pieces of wire about four feet long for tying up the driver and guard." Ruth got the binoculars for Jack while Mary cut some wire from the supply spool. "Be careful," Marge pleaded. "The police are everywhere."

CHAPTER 7

Terminate the Seed of Abraham

David and Martha Solomon watched the evening news while Reuben and Benjamin studied their synagogue lessons. David had found it difficult to adjust to his new status as an unemployed civilian and spent most of his time pouring over old intelligence reports trying to solve the riddle of recent events. He and Martha were still undecided about registering at the control center and accepting the mark required to work and receive food rations. For the first time since boyhood, he was truly afraid.

Their savings were meager, and he couldn't even apply for employment without the mark. The deadline for Israeli registration would expire next week then, he wouldn't be able to buy food rations anyway. They had decided to stretch their food supply by eating just once each day. For days, he had been physically sick with anger and frustration. Now he was just plain scared as his ordered world unraveled. The Jewish people had bet their very lives on the compromise with Natas. The votes had been cast and the issue was officially decided. He and Hartstein had led the opposition against the disarming of Israel, but the people were terrified at the prospect of facing the wrath of the entire world. He felt a sudden urge to run somewhere fast! Natas was going to murder the Jews and he was now isolated, unarmed and helpless. Registration warnings were flashed on the TV screen every fifteen minutes.

He tried to clear his head and absorb the latest news concerning implementation of the compromise. The existing population would be allocated among forty control centers and the Israeli borders were closed to new immigrants since all Jews outside Israel were already assigned to other control centers. Natas had signed formal documents guaranteeing their borders and continuation of religious rituals as long as lip service was paid to Natas and Bishop Romas and there was no open defiance of official proclamations. On all other points of global law, the Jews inside Israel were to fully comply, and summary execution would be meted out to lawbreakers.

More than fifty thousand Israeli had been continuously employed in connection with mass burial activity in Israel, Iran, Iraq, and Jordan. The onerous task had been ongoing for a hundred and eighty days. Another thirty days would be required to search out and safely bury the radioactive skeletons of the Sino-Russian forces that died from radiation exposure while fleeing through the mountain and desert terrain seeking refuge from the American and Israeli warplanes. Five-sixths of the Sino-Russian troops were killed outright by the murderous nuclear bombardment and the giant hailstones. The majority of the sixth part that fled were cut down by killing radiation.

The Plain of Esdraelon had now been cleared of the skeletons of the half million paratroopers whose flesh and blood had been consumed by great clouds of ravenous birds that moved in behind the hailstorm. By the time the ice melted, the birds had descended upon the corpses strewn throughout Iran, Iraq, and Jordan. The scavenger feast went on for weeks and scientists had no explanation as to why the birds were seemingly unaffected by the radiation contamination. The horrible stench of rotting human flesh still permeated the Middle East war zones.

Burial crews dressed in protective suits gathered up the radioactive remains and transported the skeletons to zone four burial pits. The work was slow and tedious, and workers frequently vomited inside their helmets. The work crews inside Israel were primarily Jewish, and Jews constituted a large percentage of the work crews inside Iran, Iraq, and Jordan. The civilian death toll was enormous in the Middle East nations hosting the invading ground forces.

Jewish industrialists contracted to recycle war debris that was convertible to energy, and private enterprise work crews supplemented the government workers and police personnel assigned to environmental cleanup in the Middle East. The remains of the carrier groups destroyed by American warplanes were dismantled with underwater torches and recovered by heavy cables hooked onto the wreckage by divers.

The skeletal remains of ship crews were hoisted from the waters and transported to zone four burial grounds. The war debris left by the twenty million ground troops which moved into the Middle East now choked Israeli warehouses and salvage yards. All weapons and equipment not suitable for use by the global police force were dismantled and rendered inoperative by police personnel and nuclear technicians before being buried or released as salvageable raw materials. In addition, Israeli industrialists began dismantling Israel's war machine worth billions of dollars in salvageable materials......under the watchful eyes of police supervisors and salvage experts.

The night air in Jerusalem was warm and still under a full moon and starry sky. Aaron Hartstein shuffled past the Knesset building and remembered how proudly he used to visit with the Prime Minister. Now, the building stood dark and empty like a dead body without a soul. Parliament had handed down its last decision when it approved the Natas compromise as mandated by popular vote. He was no longer General Hartstein, the most respected voice in the Israeli military. . . just a broken-down old man with nothing to do. The good people of Israel deemed it safer to rely on Natas' goodwill than his military strategy, and they had no further need for old generals.

The nation of Israel had ceased to exist at the very zenith of its military might. The Jews were once more outcasts without a country.....just numbers in a computer to be manipulated at the whim of a ruthless gentile dictator. He wondered if David Solomon might be right. David believed Natas to be the last gentile ruler foreseen by the prophet, Daniel, and that Natas would establish a false peace to disarm the Jews before launching a genocide campaign.

He had great respect for David's understanding of Hebrew prophecy and his detailed knowledge of Old Testament history. Daniel had written that the last gentile kingdom would be a mixture of strength and weakness, like trying to mix iron with miry clay. It would only endure for a short period, about forty-two months, and it would be divided into ten political units which would tear the kingdom apart. The dictator would proclaim himself to be God and would desecrate the holy places while seeking to destroy every Jew. He would be more brutal than Hitler and possess great intelligence which would be focused on total extermination efforts. Hartstein sighed, turned the corner and walked south toward his home. There was nothing he could do about it now. He felt as helpless as he did in the concentration camp as he watched the wanton murder of more than half a million of his people......men, women and children.

There were no longer any paid servants or security personnel at the Hartstein residence. Aaron walked through the moonlit garden, entered through the unlocked rear entrance and headed for the library. He wanted to read the prophecy of Daniel very carefully before deciding whether to register at the control center and accept the mark of Natas. The thought of having his body marked made him very uneasy, and it was a humiliating experience which he wasn't anxious to repeat. Life for him was about over anyway and he wanted to face death with some self-respect and dignity. He poured himself a glass of sherry, found the prophecy of Daniel in the Old Testament, relaxed in his favorite chair and adjusted his reading light.

Bishop Romas was adorned in a plain, black robe without ornaments, emblems or headdress as he smiled into the TV cameras and greeted his worldwide congregation:

"Peace to all citizens everywhere. May tolerance and wisdom fill our hearts as we strive together against ignorance and bigotry, and against misguided violence. Let us knit our hearts and minds together to forge a lasting brotherhood among all families of the earth. Where there has been hate, let there be an abiding love. Where there has been greed, let there be abundant charity and unselfish sacrifice. Where there has been envy and malice, let there be togetherness with humility and patience. Let us cast out from among us all things contrary to this unity of faith and singleness of purpose. We must not allow contentious writings and religious fables to corrupt the minds of our youth and breed mistrust between neighbors. Our law should be our book of faith in order to ensure spiritual unity and peace on earth. Let us purge our society of all religious books, writings, symbols, ornaments, and shrines as the first step toward one faith under one law. Let us deliver up these items of bigotry and cast them into a great fire kindled within each control center to consume such trash."

David Solomon could hardly believe his ears as Bishop Romas' voice droned on with more platitudes in connection with the wholesale destruction of religious artifacts. The deadline for Israeli registration had not expired yet, and already the compromise provisions were being disregarded by Romas. It didn't make any political sense! More than a million Orthodox Jews within Israel hadn't registered yet.....and would never register now! Surely both Natas and Romas had anticipated as much. Why make such an announcement now? Was Natas seeking an excuse to attack Israel so soon after disarmament? Nothing else seemed logical. David was elated at the thought of more than a million Jews standing together to defend themselves. The rush of excitement quickly faded into frustration. Weapons! They needed something to fight with! Where would they get guns and ammunition?

Martha entered the living room followed closely by Reuben and Benjamin. Martha got out her sewing and the boys sat down quietly on the couch. The special broadcast had lasted less than fifteen minutes, and regular programming had resumed. Martha relaxed in her easy chair, spread her sewing on her lap and looked over at David expectantly. "What did His Majesty have to say?"

David picked up the remote control and clicked off the TV. "He announced the ten divisions of his kingdom that John foresaw on the Isle of Patmos in 96 A.D. along with his false prophet, Bishop Romas. The good Bishop called for the burning of all religious books, writings, ornaments, emblems, and shrines."

Martha blinked with astonishment. "So soon?" "That was my reaction," David replied. "Nata reeled off the latest registration figures. He knows full well that only 2.1 million Jews in Israel have registered so far. My guess is that he's looking for a reason to attack Israel, and figures that over a million unregistered Jews is a politically safe excuse."

"Do you think the orthodox Jews will band together and fight?" Martha asked with a hopeful expression. "With what? We gave up our weapons." "Can't we make some more?" "Not fast enough to arm a million men before Natas attacks."

Reuben and Benjamin listened intently but didn't interrupt their parents. Martha glanced at her sons' faces and then looked back at David. "We've got kitchen knives, and so do the other families. Why don't we use the knives to get some guns from the police? Then, use those guns to get more?" "We need a battle plan," David answered. "I'm going to visit Aaron Hartstein."

Two adjoining luxury hotel suites had been reserved for Romas' private party. The menu included Peking duck, exotic dressing, gourmet side dishes and discriminating desserts plus a wet bar with brandy, scotch and sparkling wines. The attendants were all young, attractive women who looked more like fashion models than servants.

Bishop Romas drained his brandy snifter, motioned to the barmaid and glanced at his watch. His guest was already a half hour late and he was becoming slightly irritated. Dinner was ready to be served in the north suite and would be less than elegant if not consumed on schedule. The carefully selected entourage had been well paid to function both as attendants and entertainers.

The twin set of sliding doors between the suites had been locked into the open position to ensure a full view of the south suite from the dining table. Romas had planned the entertainment to be as delightful and satisfying as the succulent meal.

"Don't worry," the redheaded barmaid consoled him. "Very important people are always late. It's like a status symbol." She winked at Romas and refilled his snifter. Romas squirmed in his overstuffed, white velvet chair and sipped some brandy. He wore white leather shoes, blue socks, gray slacks, white turtleneck sweater, and powder blue sports jacket.

"Getting a head start on me, Julius?" Wallace kidded as he entered through the north suite. "Looks like I'm in the nick of time.....since I'm partial to redheads." "I was just telling her your preferences," Romas explained. "She's Vivian Riley, our liquor hostess, and head attendant. We'd just about given up on you." "Dinner is ready," she said sweetly. "Let me seat you and then I'll bring your scotch." "Make it a double," Wallace instructed as he and Romas followed her to the table adorned with lace, flowers and lighted candles.

The two chairs were adjacent to each other on the north side of the table to give both men a comfortable view of the south suite. Wallace looked very casual in his suede shoes, brown socks, beige slacks, light brown silk shirt, and tweed jacket. He smiled apologetically at Romas and unfolded his white satin napkin. "Sorry about the time, Julius. I had an unexpected call from Natas on my way out. He's concerned about the halt in Israeli registration following your telecast. Looks like the registration deadline will expire with only two-thirds compliance."

"What did he expect?" Romas responded with disgust in his voice. "It was less than cunning to make such an announcement prior to the deadline. A novice politician could have anticipated the Israeli reaction." Vivian returned with Wallace's scotch and a fresh snifter of brandy for Romas. Wallace tasted his scotch and looked at Romas. "Perhaps His Majesty is feigning his disappointment. Maybe he wanted a goodly number of Jews to defy him in order to achieve some hidden objective."

Romas gulped some brandy to steady his voice. He knows! Romas surmised. He's testing me to see if I'm honest with him. If he mistrusts me, I'll get nothing from him. He lowered his snifter and gazed intently at Wallace. "Is it acceptable for His Majesty to break his own laws?"

"It is never acceptable for a lawgiver to function as a lawbreaker because the public rightly loses all respect for law and order. Those who would bind others must also bind themselves." Wallace drank more scotch without looking away from Romas' eyes. "What do you know about it, Julius? What are Natas' plans for the Jews? Can they trust him?"

Romas both feared and respected Wallace. He totally controlled all security forces and could easily usurp Natas' power. If he lied to Wallace now, what would become of him when Natas moved against the Jews and Wallace reflected on the obvious lie. He had heard that Wallace personally executed corrupt officials. He sipped more brandy and considered a second possibility. Natas might be using Wallace to test his loyalty when it came to a choice between Natas and Wallace. He decided to buy more time to think by responding to a question with another question. "Do you think Natas really wants to exterminate the Jews?" The tone of Wallace's voice became deadly. "Is that what you and he are planning, Julius?"

The look in Wallace's eyes helped Romas make up his mind. Wallace was going to find out shortly anyway, so he might as well confide in him rather than risk his wrath. "Natas believes that total extermination of the Jews is the only way to kill the Hebrew legends and make sure that the divine promises to the Children of Abraham can never be fulfilled. For some reason, Natas fears those promises and is convinced that spiritual unity is impossible as long as the Jewish seed can be propagated."

"Other than leading them to the slaughter, Julius, what other role are you playing in this mass murder?" A sudden fear engulfed Romas as he struggled to appear poised. Wallace would be Natas' executioner. . . and his too if he admitted any part in the genocide. He sighed to relieve some tension and drank his snifter empty. Vivian brought them fresh drinks. She smiled at them modestly. "Shall we begin serving and commence the entertainment?

"Serve the food but hold the dancers for a few minutes," Romas answered. "We're in the middle of something rather important." Vivian nodded agreement and retreated. Romas turned back to Wallace and continued in a confidential tone: "I was unaware of Natas' underlying motive when I negotiated with the Israeli. It was after I returned that he declared to me that he is Lucifer, the fallen angel and that he intends to kill all Jews."

Wallace's eyes softened somewhat, and his tone became ambiguous. "How do you feel about that, Julius? Do you believe that Natas is immortal.....or just a man drunk with power?" Again, Romas weighed the balance of power between Wallace and Natas. What if Natas was simply a fake and used magician's tricks to create a supernatural aura about himself. What if there really was nothing beyond the grave? No heaven, no hell, just an eternity of nothingness? He was in no hurry to fill his grave. "I think Natas has become a very dangerous man and is no longer predictable, but he's a mortal human like the rest of us." "You're a careful and prudent priest,

Julius. This is a party, not a funeral. Let's enjoy the food. . . and the women."

Romas caught Vivian's eyes, lifted his right hand and rotated his index finger in the air to signal that the dancing could begin. She nodded, smiled back at them, and turned on the tape player with its auxiliary speakers. The music was soft and relaxing with a smooth beat conducive to slow, graceful dancing. The table attendants served the duck, dressing and side dishes while Vivian poured the sparkling wine.

Concern over Oren Natas' integrity kept Wallace from enjoying the meal. Was the man losing his grip on reality? Why would he risk his kingdom in order to persecute the Jews? Unmasked genocide would divide rather than unite his subjects. The only way Natas could murder the Jews was by using him and his troops. He no longer thought of his men as police. They were security forces dedicated to maintaining law and order and preservation of the human race. Natas had now become a threat to global security and his hatred for Jews had warped his political competence and common sense.

Who would be next? Suppose Natas decided that he disliked Africans or Orientals......or perhaps all humans except those of Italian descent? Where would the genocide stop? Six million Jews only whetted Hitler's appetite for murder. The populations of Poland, Hungary, Russia, Czechoslovakia, and other nations could not be allowed to copulate with his carefully bred master race.

Natas had to be stopped, and he was the only man on earth in a position to prevent Natas from killing law abiding citizens. Over two million Jews had totally complied with global law and depended upon him for security in reliance upon Natas' written guarantees. He and his men represented law and order. Natas would comply with the law or be removed from power. If necessary, he would personally kill him. He believed Romas had spoken the truth out of fear for his own life, but such testimony was not sufficient to convict Natas of breaking the law. He would have to hear such statements out of Natas' own mouth.

It was shortly after seven in the morning when Wallace arrived at his office. He checked the latest computer reports while Hanzel made a fresh pot of coffee. During the past twenty-four hours, Walker's roving search squads had apprehended and executed twenty-eight thousand, nine hundred and seventeen lawbreakers. The situation in Israel had not changed. Only sixty-six Jews had registered since Romas' telecast calling for the burning of historical artifacts connected with religious doctrines.

Hanzel brought the coffee pot over and filled his cup. "Would you like breakfast now, Chief?" Wallace glanced up and smiled in appreciation. "No, thanks. I have a breakfast conference with Natas this morning. Has he arrived yet?" "Not yet. He must be running late. I'll let you know when he shows up and I'll tell the servants about your breakfast meeting." Hanzel placed the pot back on the burner and laid the morning paper on Wallace's desk. "Will that be all, Chief?" "Until after breakfast," Wallace replied. "If Walker calls in while I'm with Natas, tell him to hightail it back here." "I'll take care of it," Hanzel promised as he waved, went out and shut the door.

Over ham, eggs, gravy, and biscuits, Wallace updated Natas on the status of all security matters. Natas nodded his approval and transferred a trace of gravy from his chin to his napkin. The waitress cleared the table, poured more coffee and left the office with her load of dishes. Natas watched her depart and turned back to Wallace. "How long is it going to take to eliminate the rest of the scavengers and religious fanatics still hiding out? We've got half our manpower tied up on that task."

Wallace sipped his coffee and gazed directly into Natas' eyes for a moment, then lowered his cup. "We're facing the first winter since the nuclear war, which means that snow and ice will become our greatest ally. Those hiding out will have to forage over a larger area and we'll be able to track them much easier. We'll have the cold climate areas cleaned out by spring, then we'll concentrate on those areas that never freeze. The job should be finished within six to nine months." "Isn't there any way to root them out faster?" "Not without doing irreparable damage to the environment and getting a lot of good men killed by sniper fire."

"I'll leave the strategy up to you," Natas replied. "You've done a magnificent job thus far.....as I knew you would." He smiled at Wallace, got up and began pacing the floor with his arms folded over his chest. Okay, Wallace mused to himself. Let's get down to the more serious business of murdering law-abiding citizens. Natas stopped pacing, turned and looked at Wallace with a poker face. "What strategy would you recommend for dealing with the Jews, John?"

Wallace returned the deadpan look without blinking. "Leave them alone and let them handle their internal problems using our security forces stationed inside Israel." "But the police assigned to the forty control centers are mostly Jews. Shouldn't we send in reinforcements?" "You've already violated the compromise provisions and your personal guarantees. Sending additional troops into Israel is the best possible way to start a war."

Natas unfolded his arms and spread his hands in a questioning gesture. "They have no weapons to wage war against us!" Wallace's respect for Natas' military genius was rapidly disappearing. "There are over a million unregistered Jews over the age of eighteen. Israeli women fight alongside their men. The only prerequisite for fighting an enemy recognized in Israel is to be alive and breathing. How long do you think it would take them to kill every member of our police force inside their borders?"

Natas returned to his chair, sat down and stared at Wallace with a puzzled expression. "How can a million unarmed civilians overpower four hundred thousand men armed with machine guns?" Wallace bit his tongue to keep from laughing in Natas' face. "It would not be a battle between opposing armies across a defined battlefield. The Israeli underground will get a printout of our personnel listing inside Israel......where they live, where they work and their work schedule. Two Israeli will be assigned to each of our men. At a predetermined signal, each of our men will be ambushed by two assassins using butcher knives, clubs, garrote wires, or anything else suitable for killing. Then, the underground will have four hundred thousand machine guns plus all our extra stores and munitions. Then, our reinforcements would be facing a well-armed guerrilla organization fighting on their home turf. It would be a long and bloody war."

"Do you really believe their resistance leaders are capable of conceiving and executing such a maneuver?" Wallace thought he caught a trace of fear in Natas' eyes. "Their military leaders studied the same guerrilla tactics that I did. . . and that's exactly what I would do in their shoes. I noted with great interest that nearly all of the unregistered population is composed of orthodox Jews and former military personnel. That's the same mix of dedication that carved out the nation of Israel in 1948 when the Arabs outnumbered them twenty to one. The Jews were essentially unarmed in 1948 while the Arabs were armed to the teeth." Wallace paused and sipped his drink.

"The situation is not so one-sided today. While the guerillas hold down the fort, Israeli factories will operate around the clock pumping out modern arms including nuclear weapons. . . don't forget, it was Jews who conceived and designed the first nuclear bombs. Moreover, Aaron Hartstein and the former Prime Minister are among the unregistered Israelis. There is a high probability that they did not surrender all of their weapons. They were the only ones who knew the complete inventory. In anticipation that you would breach the compromise, they could easily have hidden a large store of arms including nuclear weapons while the negotiations and voting were underway. Just like the Arabs in 1948, our troops greatly outnumber unregistered Israelis, but our manpower is scattered across several continents and not massed along Israel's borders. What reason have we to believe that we would be more successful than the Arabs who geographically surrounded Israel?"

Natas' eyes narrowed and his tone revealed a growing rage. "You speak as if these lawbreakers are invincible!" Now, we're getting somewhere, Wallace reasoned. His composure is slipping. He would have his answer shortly. "I'm simply pointing out that the cost to invade Israel would be very high and the outcome uncertain. If we simply wait, the underground will crumble under the will of the majority who have accepted your mark and your proclamations."

"Would the will of the majority keep the Israeli factories from producing weapons in violation of the law which they have adopted?" Wallace chuckled softly to further irritate Natas. "Not after the underground kills off our men inside Israel and gets control of their firepower. The power of persuasion will pass to the resistance movement, and the registered Jews will do whatever they are told as long as they remain unprotected inside Israel."

Natas got up and began pacing the floor again. He watched Wallace out of the corners of his eyes. "Do you know the substance of the Hebrew writings, John? The foundation of Orthodox Judaism as well as Christianity?" "Yes. I have read the Old and New Testaments in various translations of the Bible." "Then, you must appreciate the fact that there can never be spiritual unity on Earth until the Jewish seed is totally exterminated. Where there is no unity of spirit, there is no lasting peace. Religious friction has spawned more wars than all other causes combined. That is why all Jews must be eliminated. Their religion is more important to them than world peace."

Natas' statement was sufficient for Wallace, and he no longer doubted his intentions. The man stood convicted out of his own mouth. The lawgiver had reduced himself to a common criminal. The two-faced dictator was planning to murder millions of innocent, law-abiding citizens.....not only in Israel but throughout the world. He would humor Natas while he planned his execution. "I understand your intentions, Your Majesty. I will develop a definitive plan to address the problem." "Excellent!" Natas exclaimed. "Let's review strategy again in a couple of weeks."

CHAPTER 8

A Little Poison for Anti-Christ

Jack and Paul Roberts headed back toward the cave with a heavy load of firewood on their backs. The wood was carefully stacked inside a carrying frame constructed from thick limbs laced together with strips of deer hide. The front center of the rigid frame was fitted with shoulder straps to make balancing and carrying easier while leaving the hands free. Both men carried a shotgun in one hand and wore a gun belt equipped with handgun and knives. They had gathered wood throughout the night and had made three round-trips between the cave and the area they searched a mile and a quarter to the northwest. They were stockpiling firewood in anticipation of the winter snows. They managed to gather several truckloads before the pickup ran low on fuel and had to be abandoned in the hollow southwest of the lake. After giving up the truck, they resorted to the carrying frames.

They stopped to rest twenty minutes before dawn under a grand fir about a half mile from the cave entrance. A hot, blustering wind whistled through the evergreens and the sky looked dark and ominous. Paul wiped the sweat from his brow and studied the threatening sky. "Looks like a real humdinger's coming, Jack. We'd best keep humping if we wanna stay dry."

Jack adjusted his shoulder straps and shifted his shotgun to the opposite hand. "Sure, is a strange wind for this time of year. I'll bet it's close to eighty degrees." They began walking briskly toward the entrance as a series of lightning bolts streaked the sky followed by deafening thunder. The wind increased in intensity and the lightning became incessant amid continuous claps of ear-shattering thunder.

By the time Paul and Jack reached the entrance, the endless flashes of lightning brightened the morning twilight and illuminated everything as far as the eye could see as if a myriad of gigantic strobe lights were focused on the earth. Countless trees were set ablaze and lightning ran along the ground in all directions creating whirlwinds of fire driven by the relentless wind. Paul and Jack hurriedly shed their frames, uncovered the entrance, shoved the frames into the tunnel, scurried inside and looked back with awe. The outside world had become an inferno of wind and fire.

"Look at the sky!" Jack shouted. "Did you ever see anything like that?" They gaped at the eerie green overcast made plainly visible by the constant lightning as the hot air seared their faces. "There's nothing we can do but wait it out," Jack advised. "Let's get the wood on in and check on the women." They strapped the frames on again and trudged to the inner room.

The women were busy around the campfire making coffee, grilling meat and heating canned vegetables. The living space inside the cave had become extremely cramped due to the large store of winter firewood and the space occupied by meat storage and processing. The large smoke-blind which Jack and Paul had rigged up in the northwest corner made the room look much smaller than its actual dimensions. The blind was constructed from blankets sewn together and suspended from the ceiling with wire strung between stalactites.

The edges of the blankets were taped snugly against the ceiling and the floor to hold the smoke inside where the cuts of meat were hung from the ceiling by various lengths of wire. The bottom four feet on the southeast corner of the blind was pinned rather than sewn to permit ease of entry and exit. The smoke that escaped from the blankets drifted into the natural vents within the small tunnels branching out from the northwest corner of the cave. The setup was crude, but it got the job done without smoking up the living space.

Paul and Jack unloaded the wood, leaned the frames against the woodpile, and walked over to the women. Mary handed Jack and Paul a cup of coffee while Jackie and Ruth loaded their plates. "From all the thunder we've been hearing, we thought you'd come in dripping wet," Mary commented. "What's it doing outside?" "We're lucky we didn't get scorched," Paul replied. "There's a phenomenal lightning storm going on, and the woods are on fire. I've never seen such a storm and the sky is green like it's gonna hail any minute."

"Lightning fires are common in the wilderness," Jack explained. "But, this one's pretty widespread. Everything around us is on fire. We're fortunate to have a supply of meat and wood because both are gonna get a lot harder to find." "It's really strange," Paul added. "A hot, gusty wind came up just before the lightning started. It felt like the middle of July. There's generally heavy snow in these mountains by the middle of October." "Maybe Wormwood and the nuclear explosions altered Earth's orbit enough to affect normal weather cycles," Marge offered. "Isn't that a possibility?"

Jack swallowed a juicy bite of bear meat and looked thoughtfully at Marge. "You could be right about that because it wouldn't take much of an orbital deviation to alter seasonal temperatures. Whatever the cause, it's a lucky break for us..... gives us more time to replenish our supplies."

"The constant temperature in this cave sure gets monotonous," Marge complained. "Good thing the company is so stimulating." She walked to the grill to refill her cup and Jack's thoughts returned to the fire outside and the resulting damage. He sipped his coffee and looked over at Paul. "Maybe we ought to go out when the fire dies down and look for game that we can salvage. . . especially anything that dies from smoke inhalation and isn't too badly burned. We've got plenty of salt to work with and could possibly double our meat supply."

"That's a good idea," Paul answered. "If we work fast, we can even save some choice cuts on large game that's charred on the exterior. We need to get out there as soon as possible. Too bad we don't have a vehicle."

"Let's grab a couple hours sleep and get at it," Jack said. "The fire won't be out, but maybe we can work around it if the smoke isn't too heavy." Suddenly, Jack stiffened and looked toward the tunnel. He thought he heard a thumping sound. The others noticed his concern, stopped talking, and listened carefully. They all heard a noise coming from the tunnel that sounded like continuous blows against a solid surface. Jack and Paul sprinted back to the rocks, grabbed their shotguns, and ran into the tunnel. When they rounded the first bend, they knew the noise was outside the entrance. They cautiously approached the entrance and peered outside. Their mouths fell open with wonderment and they couldn't believe their eyes. The entire surface of the ground was littered with huge chunks of ice.

"Hail!" Jack said with amazement. "It's hailstones!" He looked up at the sky and saw that the greenish hue was beginning to dissipate. The air was calm, and the hailstorm appeared to be over. "All this ice will come in handy," Paul said cheerfully. "We can use it to keep the meat good and cold while we're doing all the cutting and hauling." "Let's carry one of these stones back to show the women," Jack suggested. "They'll never believe us otherwise."

Oren Natas peered through the gaping holes in the north wall of his office and scanned the streets below. Work crews were attempting to clear the streets to allow ambulances and other emergency vehicles to get through. The hail damage was astronomical and there was no practical way to remove the hailstones except to physically carry them from the streets and pile them up for transport after main arteries had been cleared for traffic. Workers were severely hampered by sections of roofs and walls that had collapsed when pelted by the heavy chunks of ice.

Broken glass from shattered windows mingled with crushed motor vehicles and the bloody remains of motorists and pedestrians who had been moving along the streets when the hail began falling. Stretcher bearers were frantically trying to remove the dead and injured from inside heavily damaged buildings before the unstable structures toppled. The outer layers of the hailstones had begun melting away and the water that flowed into the sewers was red with the blood of the dead and dying.

Hanzel appeared in the open door with a handful of computer printouts. "Preliminary reports are coming in from the control centers, Your Majesty. . . and it doesn't look good." Natas brushed off his executive chair, sat down and glared at Hanzel. "Spare me the details," he said sharply. "What's the damage?"

“It appears that both the lightning and hail were widespread. Nearly half of all manmade structures in zone one has been destroyed or heavily damaged. At least one-third of all trees have burned and ground vegetation has been destroyed. The death toll is estimated at over six million with another twelve million badly injured." "Any looting taking place?" "None reported at this time."

Natas reflected on the information and slapped his right palm against his left fist. "Oxygen depletion is going to be a major problem. Prepare a transmittal under my authorization code and send it to all control centers. I want all commercial and industrial consumption of oxygen to cease immediately. All inventories of oxygen are to be released into the atmosphere. Every plant that is capable of oxygen production is to be operated around the clock until further notice and the output released to supplement the oxygen produced by our surviving trees. All low priority government workers are to be assigned to replanting forests and ground vegetation.”

Natas scribbled some instructions for Hanzel. “Find Wallace and tell him that I want half of his police personnel assigned to the replanting project and general cleanup of the storm debris. After the dead are identified, they are to be buried in mass graves in zones three and four. We can't afford to tie up precious land in zones one or two with millions of graves. All solid hailstones are to be dumped into our fresh water supply systems."

"Yes, Your Majesty. I will transmit the message immediately." As Hanzel turned to leave, the building began to shake and sway. "Earthquake!" Hanzel shouted. "Follow me!" He ran down the hallway to the stairwell, descended two flights of stairs, and huddled down under a large steel beam. Natas crowded in beside him while the building shook violently for one and a half minutes.

When the quake ended, Hanzel got up and looked around. "Looks like the building's okay. Let's check the computer to find the quake focus." Natas followed him to the computer center and stood by while incoming messages were printed out. Hanzel quickly scanned the printout. "Here it is! Avezzano, Italy along the Alpide belt; major quake.....heavy damage." "That's all the information we'll get for a while," Natas said. "Go ahead and send my message and get me set up in another office until the north wall is repaired. I'll be in Wallace's office for now."

Natas relaxed in Wallace's office, sipping brandy and thinking over the day's events. Hanzel knocked on the door and stuck his head in. "There's more information coming from Avezzano, Your Majesty. I thought you'd want to know." "What have you got?" Natas rocked forward in Wallace's desk chair and set his snifter on the desktop.

Hanzel stepped inside the office and sat down in a guest chair across from Natas. "The quake was over nine on the Richter scale and opened up a chasm in the earth nearly a mile wide extending from Avezzano to Melfi. Dense black smoke is pouring out making it difficult to measure the depth, but scientists believe the chasm is several miles deep. Everyone is fleeing the location because the smoke is filled with some kind of armor-clad mutants that resemble locusts. They are about six times larger than seven-year locusts and are equipped with a large stinger in their scorpion-shaped tails. They appear to number into the millions and are spreading out in all directions from the chasm site." Perspiration beaded Hanzel's forehead indicating that the big, blond Swede was less calm on the inside than he outwardly appeared.

Natas sipped more brandy and studied Hanzel. "No need to be frightened yet, Hanzel. The locusts can't get here today. They'll only be around for about five months and won't kill anyone. . . just torment us a bit. Tomorrow, you can worry. Right now, we need to disseminate the information to all control centers, so people can anticipate the problem and avoid unnecessary exposure."

Natas' statement puzzled Hanzel. How did Natas know about the strange monstrosities and their limited threat to humans? He looked with awe at Natas. "You already knew, Your Majesty?" "Yes, Hanzel. The little monsters are the work of the two troublemakers that the media refers to as witnesses. We shall soon end their reign of terror. Send the message and bring me another bottle of brandy."

The thick smoke that continued to billow from the chasm ascended over Italy and began spreading over the continents, blotting out the sun and lowering the surface temperature of the earth. Enormous swarms of mutants emerged from the black clouds and scattered to the north, south, east and west. The sound of their wings was like the noise of horse-drawn chariots thundering across a battlefield.

The chilly darkness echoed with human screams as those bearing Natas' mark were sought out and stung by the mutants while they dispersed over zones one and two. The pain resulting from the sting was similar to that produced by a poisonous scorpion. Hospitals were inundated with stricken individuals seeking pain medication and began turning away the growing tide when drug supplies were depleted. People sought shelter inside residential, commercial and industrial structures, but the hail damaged buildings were easily entered by the mutants. Even undamaged property was invaded through chimneys and air vents. The thick smoke continued to rise from the chasm until the entire earth was dark and cold. . . and with the smoke came the mutants.

Jack Roberts stirred in his sleep and turned over on his back. He blinked and opened his eyes as he felt a weight on his chest and sensed that something was watching him. In the shadowy light from the campfire, he saw something sitting on the cover in the middle of his chest staring at him. He held his breath and became motionless as his eyes focused on the hideous creature. It was about four inches long and its body was armor plated except for its wings and tail. The top of its head was dome-shaped and covered by yellowish armor with hair growing from beneath the armor. Its profile resembled a large locust, but it had fangs like a serpent. A scorpion-type tail with a visible stinger curled over its back.

Jack was transfixed by the creature's eyes as it stared back at him. Suddenly, its wings began whirring as it rose vertically, moved over Marge's head, dropped down near her face, uncurled its tail and stung her squarely in the forehead. Jack instinctively reached out to swat it away, but it darted upward, hovered out of reach, looked back at him, and then flew into the rocks beyond the spring.

Marge seemed initially paralyzed by the sting, but as Jack started to reach for her, she sprang forward into a sitting position. Her eyes bugged out and her tongue protruded out of her mouth as she shook with an uncontrollable spasm. Jack picked her up, cradled her against his chest and stomach, rushed to the spring and splashed cold water over her face and forehead. Her arms and legs flailed wildly while she screamed in fear and agony. Jack tried to quiet and comfort her, but she was oblivious to his presence. Her screaming woke up Ruth, Jackie, Mary, and Paul. They all ran to the spring to see what had happened. Jack kept bathing Marge's face and forehead with spring water. "Help me get her back to the covers," Jack said, looking at Paul. "We need to keep her warm and cool her forehead with a wet towel."

Jack and Paul lifted Marge's thrashing body between them and headed back toward the sleeping bags while she screamed and convulsed with irregular spasms. Ruth ran ahead, got a towel, ran back to the spring and wet down the towel. Mary and Jackie followed alongside Jack and Paul. "What happened?" Mary inquired in a loud voice in order to be heard above Marge's screams. "What's wrong with her?"

"She's been stung by something I've never seen before," Jack shouted. "Maybe I can quiet her down with some morphine. Bring me my medical bag." Jack and Paul lowered Marge onto the sleeping bags, held her down and covered her up while Ruth bathed her forehead with the wet towel.

Mary brought the doctor's bag over to Jack and then helped hold Marge while Jack injected the morphine. They continued to hold Marge's arms and legs and comfort her until the large dose of sedative began to take effect. When she finally stopped screaming and thrashing about, they released her and sat down on the sleeping bags. "Is she going to be all right?" Paul asked, looking over at Jack.

"I think so." Jack answered. "I'll keep giving her morphine, so she can sleep for a while. The sting of the creature that attacked her doesn't kill. It only torments." "How do you know that?" Mary asked. "You said you'd never seen one before." "I haven't. No one has until now. I'm sure the thing I saw is one of the hellish locusts described in the Bible. . . in the book of Revelation. John prophesied that such mutants would arise out of the bowels of the earth to torment all those who worship Satan during the great tribulation period."

Mary's face was ashen, and she humped forward to keep from shaking. "Where did it go? Is it still around?" "Probably not," Jack reassured her. "I last saw it flying into the rocks near the air vents beyond the spring, so it must have exited there." "Do you think it'll come back?" Mary asked in a trembling voice. Ruth remained calm, but Jackie's facial expression revealed she had no conception of what Jack was talking about. Jack rubbed his hands together and massaged his fingers while glancing over at Ruth and Paul. "It might return repeatedly to sting Marge because she has accepted Natas' mark. The rest of us have nothing to fear from such locusts since we have neither worshiped Natas nor his image, nor accepted his mark."

Jackie could contain her puzzlement no longer. She looked quizzically at the others, covered her face with her hands and shrilled at them: "What on earth are you talking about?" She doubled over and began sobbing incoherently. Paul moved around to her, slipped his right arm around her shoulders and cradled her head against his chest with his left hand, then looked back at Jack. "Now might be the best time to explain exactly what's happening, Jack. Why don't you lay it out? You're the one here who knows it best."

Jack got up, put more wood on the fire, sat down again, pursed his lips and tapped his fingertips together. "There is much about life, death and eternity that I simply don't understand. The Bible has always fascinated me because it does give an explanation of great mysteries that are otherwise unfathomable." Jack paused, looked around and saw that everyone except Marge was listening with rapt attention. He leaned over Marge, felt her pulse, then continued:

"I have read the Bible all my adult life, but never really convinced myself that I sincerely believed the scriptures. Consequently, when those who had accepted Christ were raptured from the earth, I was left behind because I was more concerned with my physical life than spiritual truths. Then, when mom's body disappeared from her grave and I heard the other things that Paul and Mary witnessed, I knew without any remaining doubt that the prophesied period of great tribulation was unfolding. We are not hiding out to escape the aftermath of the nuclear war, but rather to hide from Natas who I fully believe is the Anti-Christ described in the book of Revelation. Otherwise, I would have remained in Boise to defend my home and possessions. Natas has required humanity to accept his mark. . . six hundred and sixty-six. . . in the right hand or forehead. Once the mark is accepted, the gift of redemption through Christ is no longer available. Anti-Christ has a companion false prophet who encourages the world to worship an image of Anti-Christ, and the false prophet has the power of death over all who refuse to do so." Anti-Christ promises peace but will actually plunge the world into a global war."

Jack checked Marge's temperature, then continued his explanation: “Anti-Christ will make peace with the Jews and then violate their temple while demanding that they worship him. Many of the Jews will refuse and try to flee, but he will kill roughly two-thirds of all Jews. During the seven-year reign of Anti-Christ, two witnesses sent by God appear repeatedly and call down a series of devastating, supernatural plagues upon the earth. Anti-Christ will overcome and kill these witnesses, but they will be revived after three and a half days before the eyes of the world. There are ten divisions of Anti-Christ's kingdom which will become splintered and war upon each other. The opposing armies will meet in the Middle East and encompass Jerusalem where Anti-Christ will be sitting in the temple proclaiming himself to be God. Jesus will appear the second time, overthrow Anti-Christ and his false prophet, cast them into the lake of fire prepared for Satan's final habitation; and then reign over the earth for one thousand years. During this millennium reign of Jesus, Satan will be powerless. God will fulfill all the prophecies remaining unfulfilled prior to the second coming of Christ due to human rebellion and the rejection of Jesus by the Jews. . . the very people who were chosen to proclaim him to the world as being the sacrificial lamb of God."

Ruth, knowing what Jack was going to say, had gotten up to prepare fresh coffee. Marge was still sleeping under morphine sedation. Mary was anxious to hear more and started to say something when Jackie blurted out a question. "Who will participate in the thousand-year reign?" Jack swallowed some coffee, set his cup down and answered:

“The Jewish remnant protected from Anti-Christ; those who died after accepting Christ and were raised up during the rapture; those who were translated during the rapture; those who are martyred by Anti-Christ. . . .and people like us who refused Satan's mark and survived. Satan will gather all who will follow him into a great army and again encompass Jerusalem to fight against Christ. This will be the final battle between God and Satan wherein Satan will be forever defeated. Satan and his followers are then cast into the lake of fire where Anti-Christ and his false prophet spend the millennium, and the second general resurrection of humans then occurs. All those participating in the second resurrection will be judged according to their works in the flesh and then cast into the lake of fire to spend eternity in torment and separation from God. All those redeemed through the body and blood of Christ spend eternity with God and Christ in the unending kingdom of heaven."

"I'm not sure I understand the second resurrection," Jackie said with a frown. "Are you saying that every single individual who takes part in the second resurrection will be cast into the lake of fire with Satan?" "Yes," Jack replied. "The only individuals who appear at the second resurrection are those who physically died after rejecting Christ and those who will be killed during the final battle between God and Satan. They will be brought before the throne of God and formally judged in order to show that their eternal punishment is just. Since they have rejected the body and blood of Christ as an atonement for their sins, they are without a savior and therefore will spend eternity with Satan in the lake of fire."

Jackie still looked puzzled. "What is the difference between hell and the lake of fire?" Jack sipped more coffee and considered her question. "Hell is a place of temporary confinement for lost human souls who must later appear at the final judgment before being formally condemned and sentenced to the lake of fire. . . like being held without bond prior to trial. Since the human soul is immortal, it must be confined somewhere awaiting judgment. Paradise was the waiting place for those souls separated from their physical bodies after accepting the sacrificial atonement provided by God before Jesus actually appeared on earth and sacrificed himself. After Jesus offered himself up before God, the souls in Paradise were allowed to enter the kingdom of God. At the time of the rapture, these souls, along with the souls of those who later died believing in Christ or were translated during the rapture, were given new bodies which are not subject to death."

"You speak as if the rapture has already occurred!" Jackie responded with a startled expression. "That's true," Jack replied. "It has. We are now into the reign of Anti-Christ. . . into the seventh month; and Anti-Christ is Natas. That's why we're here together in this cave. All of us except Marge have not taken his mark and the penalty is death. Natas has death squads searching everywhere for those who haven't registered and received his mark." Mary looked down at Marge with sadness. "Marge now belongs to Satan and we can't do anything about it. She probably had no idea what she was doing when she accepted the mark. I feel so sorry for her. I hope the locust that stung her doesn't come back."

Two men dressed in flowing sackcloth and sandals walked along the harbor in Kowloon, Hong Kong seemingly unconcerned with the mutant locusts that buzzed through the city. Nearby, a media crew wearing protective suits was filming workers engaged in cleanup activities. The media crew recognized the two witnesses and followed along after them hoping to film something newsworthy.

The two witnesses ignored the camera crew and ambled along the walkway quietly conversing with each other. Their beards rippled in the crisp breeze that blew across the harbor and the sackcloth curled around their muscular legs. They stopped near the center of the harbor, faced toward downtown Kowloon and lifted their hands skyward in an act of supplication. The camera crew crept forward and began filming the witnesses as the one closest to the camera called to the heavens:

"We give you thanks, Lord God Almighty because you are and were and shall be; and because you have exercised your great power in this final time of tribulation; and because you have reigned over the heavens and the works of your hands. And the nations are angry that your wrath is upon them, and that the time of the dead is come that they should be judged, and that you should give rewards unto your servants, the prophets, and to the redeemed in Christ, and to them that fear your name, small and great. . . and that you destroy them which destroy the earth. Who shall not fear God and give glory to him? For the day of his judgment is upon the proud and the arrogant, and upon the faces of the blasphemers; upon those who worship the beast and his image. For they shall drink of the wine of the wrath of God, which is poured out without mixture into the cup of his indignation; and they shall be tormented in the presence of the holy angels, and in the presence of Jesus. The smoke of their torment ascends up forever, and they have no rest day nor night. Now, Lord God, let there be a noisome and grievous sore upon those with the mark of the beast, and upon those who worship his image. Let the proud be abased by the odor of his own body and the arrogant be humbled likewise. Let the blasphemers lift up their voices in pain and sorrow at the sight of their bodies and the smell in their nostrils."

Thunder rumbled across the heavens and lightning streaked the cloudless sky for several minutes. When the ominous noise faded away, the other witness delivered his message:

"Blessed are the dead which die in Christ from henceforth; that they may rest from their labors; and their works do follow them. But, upon the beast and those with his mark, let there be thirst and famine. Let them wail for bread and cry for water with parched lips and swollen tongues. Let the heavens be brass above and the waters putrid beneath, that they evaporate not, neither condense upon the earth. Let the waters in the seas become as the blood of the dead and let the poison waves cast forth every living thing as vomit; lest blasphemers feed upon the innocent, and stuff their bellies at the table of the Lord of Hosts. For they have disdained his grace and mercy and his outstretched hand and profaned his holy sacrifice. Let them, therefore, eat of the fruit of their own way and be filled with their own devices. But, unto them who flee from Natas, and from his mark, let there be found a refuge in the wilderness, that the earth may bear them up and succor their flesh until the time of their testimony, and the shedding of blood; that their sins may be blotted out and their transgressions forgotten. Fear God and give glory to him; for the hour of his judgment is come; and worship him that made heaven, and earth, and the sea, and the fountains of waters."

The camera crew tried to move closer, but the two witnesses turned, continued along the walkway a short distance and then vanished.

Natas and Romas had been groomed and made up for a prime-time broadcast that would be carried live around the world via satellite distribution. Natas looked like a political candidate fresh from a landslide victory over a worthy opponent. He stood poised and confident before a podium with rows of microphones set up in the impressive lobby of the Palace of Nations. A network celebrity introduced the broadcast, praising Natas for his wise leadership and compassionate understanding of the recent misfortunes endured by global society. Natas beamed into the cameras and flashed his most charismatic smile while the cameras zoomed in for a close-up, then he began his appeal for patience and understanding:

"Good evening to all our citizens around the world, and my special thanks for allowing me to intrude upon your evening. I know that many of you would like to know what's being done to cope with the series of natural disasters that we have recently endured and that you are grieving over the loss of loved ones who perished in the storms and great earthquake. My heart goes out to those who have suffered a personal loss during these freak occurrences, and I know that all of you will face the future with the same strength and courage with which you have overcome previous difficulties. There have been diverse explanations offered by our scientific community as to what caused the rare phenomena which we have witnessed. We all know that the four hours of darkness during daylight hours and matching light during normal night hours were caused by the impact of Wormwood which rocked Earth on its axis and slightly modified its orbit around the sun. You can easily see how Earth was caused to rock back and forth by shoving a spinning top with your finger. The top continues to spin but rocks back and forth in proportion to the amount of force exerted by your finger. The top eventually stops spinning and falls over due to friction, but Earth orbits in the vacuum of space and does not stop spinning although the centrifugal force of the planet's spinning does gradually dissipate the abnormal rocking motion. The small deviation in orbit about the sun has caused some variations in seasonal temperature; and we will not know the maximum variation until Earth completes a full orbit around the sun."

Natas paused for a sip of water while checking the expressions of his media attendants. He noted their awed state and continued with his monologue:

"With respect to the global lightning and hail storms, the cause and effect relationship is a little more complex. Normal weather patterns occur in the lower atmosphere where the gases making up our air are more condensed causing molecules of water vapor to precipitate out before they ascend more than a few miles above the earth's surface. Because water from our oceans, rivers, and lakes evaporates at different rates depending upon climate and surface water temperature, specific weather varies widely between geographical locations. The normal circulation of air within the troposphere, the ten-mile thick layer of air closest to the earth's surface, causes collisions between masses of hot and cold air. The electrical current produced by these collisions is seen as lightning, and we all know that lightning is capable of starting fires. Hail is formed when precipitated water vapor is prevented from falling as rain because strong air currents carry the drops of water back to higher altitudes where they cluster together, freeze, and then fall as hail."

Natas paused again for effect to let what he had said thus far sink in, then continued: "The air in the stratosphere, which extends upward from the troposphere twenty miles, is much thinner and warmer, and thus is capable of holding more water vapor than the same volume of air in the troposphere. However, the stratosphere is normally not laden with water vapor because of precipitation within the troposphere. Recently, the nuclear war caused an unusual warming of the troposphere which allowed water vapor to pass into the stratosphere where the humidity was too low to precipitate it out into the troposphere. The massive evaporation of our surface waters in the form of steam caused by Wormwood's molten masses plowing into the North Pacific allowed more water vapors to reach the stratosphere. Like the end of a drought, the humidity in the stratosphere finally became high enough to precipitate the moisture back into the troposphere where the denser air caused a clustering of the condensation. The frozen clusters grew in size as they descended through the troposphere picking up additional moisture while falling through the ten miles of humid air. The precipitation of the stratosphere resulted in the phenomenon we experienced as a hailstorm of gigantic proportion. The accompanying lightning storm was produced by the sudden temperature changes within opposing air masses. The prolonged intensity of the lightning storm started numerous lightning fires which further impacted on air temperatures as a third of our forests burned, and lightning running along the surface of the earth burned away the grass and surface vegetation."

Natas adopted a “thoughtful professor” expression and pivoted toward the main camera. “With respect to the earthquake with its focus in Avezzano, Italy, it is important to remember that one of the hot spots in the Alpide belt runs through Avezzano. Disturbances within the earth's crust have previously been recorded as deep as twenty miles. The nuclear war and Wormwood caused unprecedented shifts along both the Circum-Pacific belt and the Alpide belt; so we should not be terribly surprised at a chasm a mile wide and six miles deep running from Avezzano to Melfi. Finally, we all know that there are seven-year locusts and fourteen-year locusts which come out of the ground in great numbers at those intervals of time. The mutant locusts which now plague us no doubt resulted from radiation within the earth's crust and the emergence of the mutants happened to coincide with the opening of the chasm by the earthquake. Volcanoes are also produced by disturbances within the earth's crust, and black smoke pouring out of a volcano for days or weeks is a familiar sight. We should expect to see smoke pouring from a great chasm caused by a massive disturbance deep within the earth."

The media crew seemed duly impressed, shaking their heads up and down with expressions of appreciation as Natas concluded his speech:

"As we have frequently seen in the past, there are always those who seek to derive personal gain from natural disasters. It does appear that one of these charlatans has some ESP capability and senses some phenomena before the events actually occur. The so-called witnesses thereby try to take credit for the events by claiming they are prophets sent by God. They appeared in Hong Kong today predicting that the seas will become putrid and all marine life will die; and that our citizens will develop sores on their bodies that will be noisome and grievous. No doubt they are aware that our scientists are very concerned about the existing levels of pollution and radioactive contamination of the seas. They also employ some sort of magician's trick and appear to vanish after proclaiming their self-serving predictions. I promise you that when our police catch up with them, they will disappear forever. I should also mention that a new virus has been discovered that causes the type of flesh sores which these two fakers have learned about, and they seek to use that knowledge to vindicate themselves as prophets."

Natas paused again while the media personnel applauded his comments concerning the two witnesses. When the hand clapping ended, he again smiled into the cameras and ended his speech like a master politician:

"Your government is doing everything possible to lighten the burden imposed upon you by the natural disasters I have just spoken about. I have ordered all industrial and commercial use of oxygen halted, and all inventories released into the air to offset the oxygen depletion due to the loss of trees, grass and ground vegetation. In addition, all factories capable of oxygen production will operate around the clock while government workers replant forests and ground vegetation. The grass will grow back on its own. We are making excellent progress in cleaning up the storm damage and providing emergency care for the injured. The large number of people killed during the rampage of nature have been respectfully removed and properly buried. Sufficient government-insured loans have been authorized to fund the rebuilding of homes, factories and commercial buildings by private enterprise. Our scientific research into the mutant locusts shows that they have a lifespan of only five months, and their sting is never fatal. Every factory which produces drugs used in treating sting victims will operate around the clock until the mutants are gone, and the production of protective clothing will also be scheduled around the clock. In the meanwhile, residential, industrial and commercial buildings are being sealed up tight, and anyone moving around in the open air should take care to wear protective clothing. Thus far, none of our insecticides has proven effective against the mutants, and it is highly unlikely that a killing spray can be developed from scratch within five months. The great chasm is no longer billowing smoke into the air, and our atmosphere is rapidly clearing up while we are building a protective fence around the chasm. In closing, let me implore you to ignore gloom and doom rumors and self-serving predictions spouted by those who wish to disrupt our global society. Please return to your places of employment as quickly as possible so that we can maintain an adequate supply of essential food, water and consumer goods. Good evening to all of you and thank you for giving me this opportunity to update everyone on our efforts to make your life more peaceful, prosperous and pleasant."

The media personnel clapped and cheered as Natas smiled, waved, and left the lobby surrounded by several security guards. The cameras followed Natas until he moved out of sight, then returned to the network spokesman, who lavishly praised Natas and prepared viewers for a brief address by Bishop Romas.

Romas spoke for roughly five minutes, making an impassioned plea to all world citizens to unite behind Natas thereby ensuring world peace, law and order, and equal rights for all. He ended his brief address by calling for spiritual unity and the total destruction of all religious artifacts contrary to that unity.

Aaron Hartstein peered through the glass in the rear door of his residence looking for David Solomon who was already fifteen minutes late. Hartstein was becoming more and more uncomfortable with each passing minute. He had never known David to be late for a scheduled conference with him. Maybe he had been picked up by the police. . . or worse. But that didn't make much sense. Chief Wallace had extended the deadline for Israeli registration for another thirty days while he personally reviewed Israeli complaints that Natas was violating the principal provisions of the peace agreement.

It was obvious that Wallace didn't want to rush into a death struggle with a million Israeli on their home soil. He was a hard and decisive man, but also prudent and cautious. David had compiled a complete file on Wallace since he had become Natas' right-hand man. He sighed with relief as he spotted David walking briskly through the garden.

"Shalom, David. You were beginning to worry me some." He held the door open as David entered, shook hands, and then looked back into the garden. "I'm sorry, General. The police have a tail on me, and It took a while to shake loose before heading your way."

"They're watching me too, David." He patted his shoulder affectionately and guided him toward the library. "Probably think we're the most likely ones to lead a resistance movement and form a guerrilla army." "Well, we were a little vocal about disarmament," David admitted. "Too bad we couldn't get more doves to listen."

Hartstein fetched the sherry and two glasses. "How's Martha and the boys?" he inquired while pouring the wine. "We're all still eating since the deadline extension, but our finances are a little skimpy." He raised his glass toward Hartstein and smiled wanly. "To Jehovah. . . and all those who haven't forgotten him." "And to all who will die in his name," Hartstein added. They drank the toast and sat down across from each other at the reading table. "How's the statistical project coming along?" "No luck so far in breaking into the software security codes, but I did manage to spend your bribe money and set up an inside contact. It took several days just to piecemeal the printouts together. I have summary statistics on the general population and complete details on security forces."

"On all forty control centers?" Hartstein asked hopefully. "Yes. There are three hundred and ninety-nine thousand, eight hundred and seventeen security troops inside our borders of which two hundred and seventy-eight thousand, seven hundred and thirty-three are Israelis. The rest are mostly Arabs who were born in Israel, with some minor exceptions. The summary data shows two million, two hundred and sixteen thousand, four hundred and fifteen registered Israelis, and one million, one hundred and twenty-three thousand, six hundred and ninety-two unregistered as of last Wednesday. The records are merged every twelve hours."

"How many of the unregistered are children under twelve?" "I was just coming to that," David answered. "There's no way to get that information from just the summary sheets, but I think that the number is less than a hundred thousand. . . which means we should be able to put together a substantial fighting force to tackle the security troops."

Hartstein was encouraged by the statistics and David's enthusiasm. "Do you have some method in mind for making contact with our potential guerillas?" David leaned back, tapped his fingertips together and frowned. "Whatever method we use will be dangerous, but I think we can minimize the risk by using personal contact to spread the word." "Won't that take too long?" "If set up properly, it is really one of the quickest ways to contact a large number of people who are widely dispersed."

"Explain," Hartstein said with a doubtful expression. David pulled a pen and pad out of his shirt pocket and smiled politely. "Who are the individuals most likely to know that you aren't registered?" "My family members and the friends that I trust with my life." "And approximately how many would that be?" "My three daughters and half a dozen very close friends . . . also unregistered. Less than a dozen for sure."

"Fine," David responded with a positive nod. "How long would it take you to get an emergency message to at least six of them?" "Thirty minutes, *perhaps.* I might have to call around to locate some of them." "That's about what I figure it'd take me to do the same thing. That means that once we're organized, we can get word to over a million individuals in approximately four hours."

"I don't follow you, David." "Six to the eighth power is one million, six hundred and seventy-nine thousand, six hundred and sixteen." Hartstein nodded his sudden grasp of David's line of thought. "Exponential progression from the top of a pyramid! Sure! That'll work and limit our risk as long as everyone keeps their six contacts strictly confidential." "We should allow ourselves a week to get the initial word out because of duplication of contact until everyone has locked in six individuals for whom they will have the sole responsibility for down-line communications like a platoon leader with six personal recruits, where each recruit then fills two roles; recruit to his platoon leader, and platoon leader to his recruits."

"That's a fantastic concept!" Hartstein praised David. David nodded agreement while marking out eight descending parallel lines on his pad. "Line one represents six individuals who are the brains behind the guerrilla army, and function as six generals with an equal vote. Where there is a disagreement in strategy, the majority rules. If the votes are tied, then one man's vote is voided by drawing lots. On line two are the six platoon leaders that each individual on line one recruits, for a total of thirty-six. Each individual on line two then finds six recruits that show up on line three as two hundred and sixteen individuals that are recruits to line two and platoon leaders to line four. Thus, on line four we wind up with one thousand, two hundred and ninety-six individuals that are recruits to line three and platoon leaders to line five. Then, on line five are seven thousand, seven hundred and seventy-six individuals that are recruits to line four and platoon leaders to line six. Line six contains forty-six thousand, six hundred and fifty-six individuals that are recruits to line five and platoon leaders to line seven. Line seven then has two hundred and seventy-nine thousand, nine hundred and thirty-six individuals that are recruits to line six and platoon leaders to line eight. Line eight contains the recruits produced by line seven, and there will be less than six recruits per individual on line seven because every potential guerrilla will have been accounted for somewhere between six to the seventh power and six to the eighth power. Since every single platoon leader on each line will be communicating to his or her recruits simultaneously, communications can easily pass downward from one line to the next line in the time it takes one platoon leader to contact his or her six recruits . . . about a half hour per line, and roughly four hours total elapsed time between line one and line eight." David paused, looked at Hartstein and waited for him to respond.

"That's remarkable," David. "It's simple, and it's effective, and the risk is controlled because each platoon leader recruits only six people that he or she knows well and trusts completely." David handed his pad to Hartstein. "We need to get started immediately so we're organized and functional at least five days before the deadline extension expires."

Hartstein was thrilled with David's plan and anxious to hear more. "Have you worked out a strategy for eliminating the security forces inside Israel?"

"The sheer numbers make anything other than a general communication down the lines too risky," David answered thoughtfully. "Secrecy and determination will be essential. In round numbers, there are four thousand armed security troops and twenty-five thousand unarmed, unregistered Israelis in each of the forty control centers. We must surprise the armed troops, kill them, and take their weapons. We can accomplish this difficult feat by setting a specific time, down to the second, for a general attack throughout Israel. We pass the word that every recruit is to target one security person and be aware that the same individual may also be targeted by other Israelis. The targeted individual should be the one with whom the recruit is the most familiar in terms of location, habits, and work schedule. Each recruit should be armed with some sort of concealed item that can be used as a weapon. . . butcher knife, ice pick, screwdriver, letter opener, hammer, or whatever else is both lethal and easily concealed. At the appointed time, each recruit makes an innocent approach to his or her target, suddenly attacks using the concealed item, dispatches the target, and picks up the target's weapon. Once the security forces inside Israel are eliminated, we can publicly communicate with our guerillas, take over all weapons and munitions stored inside Israel by the security forces, organize our people, and seal our borders. While security forces outside Israel are being organized to move against us, we can begin producing more weapons, including nuclear devices. Our factories can easily be converted over for production of weapons since we still possess the necessary raw materials, technology, skills, and manpower. Because of logistical problems, wide dispersion of forces, sheer distance, and scale of operations, Wallace will need weeks, or perhaps months, to prepare to attack us. Even when he does attack, we can hold him at bay by using guerrilla tactics while we continue producing weapons. Trying to subdue a million armed Israelis inside our own borders will prove to be quite a challenge. . . even for Wallace."

Hartstein beamed with satisfaction, grinned amicably at David, and poured more wine. "We'll have something else to hold him off for a while. Wallace had no way of knowing exactly what we used up out of our military arsenal during the nuclear war. Amid the confusion immediately following the last nuclear explosion, my hand-picked officers crated up complete components for four hydrogen bombs, marked the crates as nuclear waste and buried them. The men who actually did the work thought they were crating up and burying junked parts containing radioactive materials. We can modify commercial jetliners for delivery capability until we produce appropriate aircraft, and we can use the bombs against any army advancing toward Israel. In the meanwhile, we'll run our factories at maximum capacity."

David poured their glasses full again and proposed another toast. "To Israeli independence and the future of our children." "And to those who will prepare the way," Hartstein added.

John Wallace was bone tired when he returned to his office and removed his protective clothing. It was after eight in the evening and he hadn't eaten all day, but a stiff drink was what he wanted at the moment. He took a bottle and glass from his credenza and slouched in his executive chair with his feet propped on top of his desk. He poured the glass half full, slugged it down, then massaged his neck with both hands while the whiskey relaxed him. I've got to act pretty soon, he convinced himself. If I don't attack the Jews at this point, Natas will replace me with someone who will......maybe murder me also. He swigged more scotch and made up his mind to kill Natas and take his place. He leaned back, closed his eyes and began thinking about various ways to achieve the objective.

He must make it appear that Natas died of natural causes and not by his hand. Otherwise, it would be much more difficult to take control without using force. If he was even suspected of killing Natas, there would be a public clamor for his head, and his own subordinates might try to arrest him.

It wouldn't be easy to pull it off without casting suspicion upon himself unless he could secretly poison Natas without using an accomplice. No one must know. He began thinking about various poisons that might be appropriate. . . something that he already had access to so that no procurement trail was created. Something that could be used to spike a bottle of expensive brandy.

Coniine! That would work! He had seen a three-foot poison hemlock among the plants in the lobby. He could prune away a few leaves and extract the poisonous alkaloid. With a little liquid sugar added, the alkaloid bitterness would be masked when mixed with a potent brandy.

Natas would suspect nothing if he drank with him from the same bottle. He could protect himself by coating his stomach with an antidote, then vomiting right after Natas' fatal heart seizure. Then, he could empty the bottle into Natas' executive toilet, thoroughly rinse the bottle and snifters at the sink, pour some brandy from Natas' private stock into the bottle and snifters, push the button for the guards and begin giving Natas futile mouth-to-mouth resuscitation. He'd have everything in Natas' office seized to be analyzed for foul play. The rinsed out sink and well flushed toilet would leave no evidence behind. When no suspicious evidence turned up, he would order Natas' corpse spared the autopsy mutilation and let him lie in state while he assumed control.

Wallace went over and over the details in his mind looking for possible flaws. He saw two critical points where he was vulnerable . . . when he picked the leaves, and when he cleaned up the evidence.

If someone intruded during those activities, his plan would unravel. He'd make sure he wasn't disturbed. A phony bomb threat could be used to temporarily clear the lobby, and he'd arrange for Hanzel to guard the office while he met with Natas. Hanzel would never intrude on such a meeting unless he was directly summoned. He capped the bottle of scotch and reached for the telephone.

"Yes Chief?" Hanzel bit his lip to keep from yawning into the telephone. "Get over here and check out the building. We've just received an anonymous bomb threat over the lobby telephone. I was on my way out to dinner when I heard the phone ringing, and the guard was busy elsewhere. I'll get the search started and stay until you get here." "Yes, Sir. I'm on my way."

Wallace hung up the lobby phone, then dialed line two from line one. The center lobby guard was right on schedule at the security checkpoint located between the elevator banks. He heard the phone ringing and was hurrying to pick it up when he saw Wallace lift the receiver. "Who is this?" Wallace inquired in a curt tone, then listened a few seconds before slamming the receiver back into place.

"Trouble, Chief?" The guard called to him as he hustled toward the security desk. "Just another nuisance bomb threat . . . but we'd better check it out. I'll call Hanzel and start searching the lobby areas until he arrives. Get the guards started on the top floor and begin working downward." "Okay, Chief. We're on it."

Wallace began systematically searching the lobby until all the guards were on the elevators and headed up. Then, he picked a dozen leaves from the poison hemlock plant and stuck them into his inside coat pockets. He continued going through the search routine until he saw Hanzel enter the lobby. "Anything so far?" Hanzel asked as he approached.

"Nothing yet. The guards are working downward from the top floor. There's no one inside but security and housekeeping personnel. I'll see you in the morning." "Okay, Chief. We'll make sure it's clean. Have a nice dinner." "Sorry to bother you at home," Wallace apologized. "But I haven't eaten all day and I need to be fresh for an important meeting with Natas tomorrow." He started to depart, then turned back to Hanzel. "By the way, I'd like a little gift to soften him a bit. On your way home, pick up the most expensive brandy you can find, charge it to my account and leave it on my desk." Hanzel grinned and then winked at Wallace. "No problem, Chief. He'll love it."

"Chief Wallace is here, Your Majesty." "Come in, John," Natas invited as Wallace entered and Hanzel withdrew. He glanced at the bottle in Wallace's hand and smiled broadly. "I hope the news isn't so bad that it needs to be chased with such expensive brandy." Wallace sat down across from Natas and set the brandy on the corner of the desk. "I think the problem's solved, Your Majesty. So, the news is all good. I'm always sucking up your private stock, so for this occasion, I had Hanzel pick up a bottle of the best . . . on me. I sampled it this morning, and it's the pick of a man who knows fine brandy."

Natas swiveled around in his executive chair, extracted two snifters, coasters and napkins from his credenza, placed them on his desktop and looked over at Wallace. "Tell me more about your trip. . . and your solution."

Wallace uncapped the brandy and poured the snifters half full. "I listened to civilian spokesmen complain about violations of the compromise provisions while I studied internal security and the possible defensive positions available. We're not ready to attack yet, so I extended the registration deadline to avoid a premature clash between our forces and potential Israeli guerillas. I believe it is prudent to concede the fact that Hartstein has hidden some nuclear weapons. If we try to land our forces from ships in the Mediterranean, we would be sitting ducks for such weapons launched from modified commercial jets. On the other hand, if we attempt to march troops through Egypt, Jordan, Lebanon or Syria, we would be badly mauled by guerillas dug into the rugged, mountainous terrain."

"But you have devised an attack plan?" Natas queried with hopeful visage. "Yes. We'll use the short-range missiles that Wirtman and I saved for such an occasion. We'll transport them to Egypt and launch from less than sixty miles outside Israeli borders. Then, we'll move ground troops in from Jordan and mop up behind the missiles." Natas was ecstatic with the thought of such a slaughter. He picked up his snifter and extended it toward Wallace. "To the demise of a troublesome people."

Wallace lifted his snifter and touched rims with Natas. "To law and order and the death of all criminals." They drank heartily and lowered their snifters. Wallace smiled and proposed a second toast. "To Your Majesty's health and the future of mankind."

"And to my loyal subjects," Natas boasted. They drank the second toast with the same gusto. Natas lowered his snifter and smiled pleasantly. "How soon will you make your move?" Wallace was beginning to feel nauseated from the heavy ingestion of antidote and his palms became moist. He grinned at Natas and lowered his snifter. "I have already cast the die."

Natas raised his right hand to his brow as his body quaked with intense muscular spasms. Wallace jumped up, ran around to Natas and lowered his jerking body onto the carpet. Spittle drooled from the corners of Natas' mouth and his eyes rolled upward in their sockets.

Wallace snatched up the brandy bottle along with the two snifters and dashed into Natas' private toilet. He set the bottle and snifters on the sink, then stuck his finger down his throat and gagged himself to induce vomiting. He retched repeatedly and continued gagging himself until his stomach was completely empty. He then poured the brandy from the bottle and snifters into the toilet and flushed it several times.

He carefully rinsed the bottle and snifters with hot water and then with cold water, rinsed out his mouth and drank a snifter full of cold water. He used a fresh washcloth to wipe the bottle and dry the snifters. He took a small paper funnel from his inside coat pocket, placed it in the neck of the brandy bottle and carried the snifters and bottle back to Natas' desk.

He hurriedly opened a bottle of brandy from Natas' private stock and refilled the rinsed bottle half full, removed the funnel, wrapped it inside his handkerchief, returned it to the same pocket, poured a small amount of brandy into each snifter, capped the substitute bottle and returned it to the credenza shelf. He quickly picked up the cap from the original bottle, returned to the toilet, rinsed the cap out, flushed the toilet again, rinsed out the sink, wiped off the basin and toilet bowl, wrapped the washcloth around his right calf and pulled his sock over it. He returned to the desk, recapped the original bottle, rearranged the bottle, snifters, coasters, and napkins, closed Natas' credenza and checked to make sure he hadn't forgotten any telltale clues. He checked Natas' pulse to make sure he was dead, then pushed the button for Hanzel and began giving Natas mouth-to-mouth resuscitation.

Moments later, Hanzel knocked on Natas' office door. "Quick, Hanzel! Give me a hand!" Wallace yelled out. Hanzel burst inside took one look and reached for the telephone. "It's his heart!" Wallace shouted. "Call an ambulance and help me with him! And call the other guards!" Hanzel made the calls, then helped Wallace apply the CPR routine while they waited for the ambulance.

Six other guards appeared and secured the office area. Wallace and Hanzel continued the CPR until the ambulance crew arrived on the scene, then moved aside while the paramedics took over. Two of them maintained the CPR rhythm while the other two hooked up a resuscitator and portable monitors. The four of them then loaded Natas onto the stretcher and headed for the elevator. Wallace turned to Hanzel and the other guards. "I want four men to seal this office and make sure no one goes in or out until we've had a chance to check it out. Hanzel and two men will go with me to the hospital and watch over Natas. Let's go!"

Wallace, Hanzel, and the two other guards stood by in the emergency room while the medical team examined Natas. The lead doctor removed his mask and looked toward Wallace. "There's nothing anyone can do. He's been dead for at least fifteen minutes and exhibits all the symptoms of a massive heart attack that apparently killed him instantly."

Wallace stared at Hanzel with a feigned expression of grief and then walked over to the table where Natas was lying. "I want him placed in a private room and guarded closely while we conduct an investigation to determine if an autopsy is necessary. I see no need to desecrate his body unless there's some evidence to suggest foul play."

He turned to the guards and eyed them sternly. "Hanzel and I will commence the investigation. You two stay with the body and protect it until you're relieved. See that it's covered with a drape, taken immediately to a secure room and watched constantly unless you receive personal instructions from me otherwise."

While Hanzel called the guards back at Natas' office, Wallace stepped into the men's room in the hospital lobby, removed the handkerchief, paper funnel and washcloth, and dropped them into a covered trash container, then rejoined Hanzel in the lobby. "The media is swarming all over the place," Hanzel warned. "Our men are fending them off outside the building, and we may run into some reporters outside the entrance here." "We won't give them anything but a brief statement," Wallace replied. "Nothing more until we're sure of our facts."

Media crews began arriving at the hospital and encircled Wallace and Hanzel just outside the main lobby doors. A large band of security troops appeared along with reporters and secured the perimeter. Wallace held up his hand requesting silence, then spoke into the cluster of microphones extended toward his mouth by network celebrities: "His Majesty, Oren Natas, approximately thirty minutes ago, died following a major heart attack. He collapsed in his private office, was given emergency CPR, was transported here by ambulance attended by four paramedics and pronounced dead upon arrival by attending physicians. His body is presently under guard pending the outcome of a complete investigation which is now underway. There is nothing to indicate that His Majesty died from other than natural causes. He will lie in state in the lobby of the Palace of Nations and then be enshrined in a memorial tomb to be erected on the Palace grounds. We have suffered a great loss, but there is no need for panic. The law and order established by His Majesty will be perpetually maintained by our global police and the ten regional administrators will report to me until further notice. That's all we can give you at the moment."

Wallace and Hanzel ignored the barrage of media questions, made their way through the reporters, entered a security van under heavy guard and headed toward the Palace of Nations.

CHAPTER 9

Global Reign of the False Prophet

Bishop Romas had been in seclusion within his private residence for three days following the announcement of Natas' untimely death. He tossed down a glass of Irish whiskey, sat down on the end cushion of the couch, and poured himself another drink. The sweet taste freshened his mouth as he yawned widely, settled back, propped his feet on the plush ottoman and thought about the death of Oren Natas. The whiskey he'd already consumed made him feel relaxed and sleepy.

He remembered his meeting with Natas when Natas predicted his own death and subsequent resurrection. He shivered slightly at the vivid memory of Natas' eyes when he made the predictions. No doubt about it, he concluded. Natas was murdered. But who? How? The doctors said he died from a heart attack, and the elaborate investigation spearheaded by Wallace, himself, had turned up nothing suspicious.

But, why no autopsy? he asked himself. Wallace claimed there was no need to desecrate the body. Was he trying to hide something? No, that didn't seem logical. Wallace was too honest. . . all law and order. He already had a free hand to enforce his vision of public morality, and he never exhibited any inclination to enlarge his role as Natas' head of security.

Who else might think of benefiting from Natas' departure? A spiritual leader desiring to become a secular dictator? That thought made him so cold that he gulped down a half glass of whiskey. No worldly stature was worth being pursued by Chief John Wallace. No, he was quite content to stay a mere bishop and do his small part in the larger order of things.

He poured another drink and grunted contentedly. Let someone else solve the riddle and struggle for recognition. It was police business anyway, not a spiritual issue. He finished his drink, positioned a couch pillow, swung his legs from the ottoman onto the cushions, laid back and closed his eyes.

The whiskey worked its magic and he drifted off to sleep while thinking sluggishly about the upcoming funeral for Natas.

Strange images formed in Romas' mind as he slept. Seemingly unconnected objects took shape, disappeared and then reappeared: parsley shaped leaves, a paper funnel, brandy bottles, and a washcloth. The objects merged into each other and became a dark mass that reformed itself into the likeness of John Wallace's face. A curtain of flames descended over the likeness and consumed it, leaving only smoking vapor which slowly condensed into an ebony statue of Natas, except for the eyes which appeared as coals of fire. The image spoke to Romas in a hollow voice that seemed to originate inside an endless tunnel:

"He that poisoned me with coniine prepared his stomach and vomited up his portion. My stock replaced the gift of death. You must proclaim his guilt and call down fire upon him before the eyes of my subjects lest he usurps my power and cast you down. Go to Rome and reign there until I join you. Give my image to the people that they may worship me in preparation for my coming. Rebuild the city and raise my temple, for it is in Rome that all shall see me. Encourage the people and let the ten divisions stand until my return. Despair not, for Lucifer shall sustain you and make you great in the earth. None shall prevail against you."

Romas awoke and sat upright, trembling with fear. His robe was damp with perspiration and his flesh felt clammy as he poured himself a drink. He gulped the whiskey to calm his nerves, then went into his bathroom, stripped off his robe and stepped into the shower. The spray of hot water warmed his skin and helped clear his head as he tried to sort out his thoughts. The death of Natas was no longer a mystery as he fit the objects into the message. Wallace had extracted coniine from poison hemlock leaves and spiked a bottle of brandy which he gave to Natas.

He drank an antidote just before drinking with Natas from the bottle, vomited up the alkaloid, dumped the tainted brandy, washed out the bottle and glasses, and refilled the clean containers with some brandy from Natas' credenza using a paper funnel. He must have used the washcloth to clean up Natas' private bathroom to eliminate any traces of coniine.

Pretty slick, Romas admitted to himself. The leaves probably came from the hemlock growing in the downstairs lobby, and the absence of autopsy would allow the secret plot to be buried with Natas. Wallace had been with Natas and vouched for his heart attack in addition to ordering the follow-up investigation.

No one had any reason to suspect that Wallace would poison Natas, which made the no autopsy order seem innocent under the circumstances of his death. Romas turned off the shower, stepped from the stall and reached for a towel. He was still puzzled concerning Wallace's motive. Why kill Natas when he already had all the power and status that he desired? Then, he remembered his conversation with Wallace at their private party. Genocide!

Natas' intent to slaughter the Jews had make him a criminal in Wallace's eyes. . .. and he had accepted the responsibility for executing all criminals. Yes! That would be consistent with Wallace's nature. He could rationalize a plan to make the death appear accidental in order to avoid a public outcry. Caught between the choices of murdering law-abiding citizens or eliminating Natas, Wallace would deem it morally justified to kill Natas. By usurping Natas' power, he could ensure the administration of justice throughout every level of society. . . the end would certainly justify the means since Natas was already guilty of a capital crime. . . conspiracy to commit murder. He was simply carrying out the sentence in such a manner as to avoid more violence and subsequent executions.

Romas felt refreshed and admired his image in the full-length mirror as the cloudy water vapor faded from the glass. Chief Wallace was a brilliant and dangerous enemy, but Lucifer's bishop was no slouch either. The vision of calling Satanic fire down upon Wallace made him feel invincible. Go to Rome and reign there, Natas had said. That order he was both willing and anxious to obey. He hung up the towel, walked to his dressing room and laid out his bishop's apparel. The spiritual leader of humanity was about to unmask a murderous traitor.

He picked out a fresh robe to lounge away the early morning hours. The cook wouldn't be in until six, but she had set up the coffee service so that it only needed to be plugged in. He walked into the kitchen, stuck the plug into the socket, then returned to the living room, picked up a magazine and sat down on the couch.

A noxious odor wafted into his nostrils, causing him to instinctively sniff for the source of the obnoxious stench. His body suddenly felt on fire with sharp pain and he had an uncontrollable urge to scratch himself all over. The offensive smell was coming from his own body!

He sprang from the cushion, peeled off his robe, and stared at the open sores that were popping up on his chest, stomach, arms, thighs and legs. He dashed to the bathroom, looked into the mirrors and saw that his face, neck and backside were covered with the noisome sores. He gritted his teeth to resist the desire to scratch himself as the pain seared every fiber of his being. He made his way to the telephone to call an ambulance but got no answer. He groaned in agony as he hung up, went back to his closet and began gingerly putting on some clothes. He'd have to walk the five blocks to the neighborhood hospital.

The emergency room was already teeming with people seeking salves and pain medication. Everyone, including the handful of doctors and nurses on duty, exhibited the same affliction. . . . open, stinking sores covering their entire bodies. The medical staff had treated their own sores with soothing medication and deadened their pain with drug injections. The anguished cries, moans, and groans of those seeking treatment made the hospital sound like a huge torture chamber. One of the nurses recognized Romas and immediately led him to an examining booth. "I'm sorry, Bishop, I have to leave you here and get back to the other patients. The doctor will be in as soon as possible." Romas grimaced with pain and nodded as she went out and closed the curtain.

Eleven minutes later, a young doctor pulled the curtain aside and entered, carrying a tray containing a jar of salve, swabs and a filled syringe. He managed a half smile though his facial sores set the tray down on the examining table, and helped Romas out of his clothes.

"I know it probably hurts to talk, so I'll just tell you what I can," he said as he uncapped the jar of salve and began swabbing Romas' sores. "The salve contains a pain medication that will give you some temporary relief. I'll give you a prescription which I suggest you get filled immediately before supplies are depleted. I'll also give you a prescription for syringes and morphine which will also be in short supply. Make the salve and morphine last as long as possible because we have no idea how long it will take for the sores to heal. Neither do we know what is causing them, so we can't do anything except try to ease the pain and discomfort. Stay off your feet as much as possible to allow healing time. Don't take a tub bath or shower because that will wash away the salve and deplete your supply much quicker. Use a clean washcloth and warm water to wash between the sores. We can't do anything about the odor, but it will not really offend others because they have the same odor on their bodies. The entire population appears to be afflicted, so there is nothing peculiar about you that caused the sores to appear. It may be some type of new virus that we simply have to endure until it has run its course. It's a bit early to promise anything, but the condition appears to be of a temporary nature and not fatal."

He injected the dose of morphine and checked to make sure that each individual sore had been thoroughly swabbed. "Okay, Bishop. You can get dressed and pick up your prescriptions at the front desk. The pain killers will begin to take effect within a few minutes. Sorry to be so abrupt, but I'm a little swamped and shorthanded at the moment." He picked up the tray and disappeared through the curtain.

Romas clenched his jaws against the pain and began easing his clothes on again. The confrontation with Wallace would have to be delayed for a while. The wheels of society were going to grind to a halt until the plague ended. No one would be able to perform manual labor. . . just drink enough water to stay alive and wait it out.

Romas awoke on the morning of the seventh day following his trip to the hospital. His skin felt tight and crusty and his pain had diminished. He sat up in his bed and looked over his body with growing elation. The sores had scabbed over and appeared to be healing. He got up and examined his face and neck in the mirror. The ugly scabs made his face look hideous, but that would be temporary also. . . perhaps a week or two.

He put on a fresh robe, went into the kitchen and began preparing himself coffee, toast, and jelly. He switched on the kitchen radio to catch the eight o'clock news while the coffee finished brewing and was startled by the lead story. The unregistered Jews in Israel had taken over the government following a surprise attack by more than eight hundred thousand Israeli guerillas against the police inside Israeli borders.

The guerillas were somehow immune to the disabling sores that afflicted the rest of the population, including the police. They killed every single member of the police force inside Israel using butcher knives, ice picks, screwdrivers, hammers, choke devices and other lethal objects. Each victim was caught off guard by one to three guerillas during the widespread attack which was apparently triggered by some predetermined signal.

The rebels then armed themselves with automatic weapons taken from the bodies of their victims and from police armories located inside Israel. Guerrilla forces had now sealed off Israeli territory, taken over all manufacturing inside Israel and were producing more weapons.

While Romas' head was still spinning from that tidbit of news, the next report stunned him even more. All of the world's oceans and seas had become totally polluted from some catastrophe of undetermined origin. The waters had become thick, sluggish and poison causing the death of all saltwater marine life, which now floated on the surface adding to the pollution and malodorous air. The unexplained sores, poison waters, and death of Natas had resulted in public panic over adequate food and water inventories. The combination of natural disasters and large number of people unable to work had greatly reduced those supplies.

Moreover, scientists were predicting a prolonged drought due to the retardation effect the thick, putrid waters would have on the natural evaporation of ocean and sea water which falls back to earth in the form of rain, snow, sleet, and hail. The police had not reported any rioting, but the public mood was becoming darker and more unstable.

Romas sat down at the breakfast bar to ponder his strategy. The most important thing was to reassure the people that things were under control, and rhetoric would not accomplish that. The public needed to see a raw display of power and authority to convince them to follow after him, and the event must receive worldwide television coverage. The upcoming confrontation with Wallace would certainly be newsworthy if he staged it properly.

He could leak enough information to the press to obtain international coverage when he accused Wallace on television. Then, the actual destruction of Wallace and his power base could be similarly staged. He got up, applied butter and jelly to his toast, and poured himself a hot cup of coffee. There was no longer any reason to fear Wallace now that he had the upper hand.

Bishop Romas mustered up his most benevolent visage. He faced the TV cameras from behind the modest desk in the working studio adjacent to the living room inside his private residence. He sat with his hands folded and positioned on top of the desk in front of the row of microphones. The makeup seemed to highlight rather than obscure the scabs visible on his face, neck, and hands. Nonetheless, he looked worthy of reverence in his bishop's attire as he maintained his pious expression and waited for his cue from the media crew. He breathed deeply and exhaled slowly until the cue was flashed, then began his live address on worldwide television:

"Good evening, fellow citizens throughout the world. I address you tonight with a heavy heart and sadness of spirit. It is my most unpleasant duty to lay before you the insidious and traitorous plot which resulted in the murder of our beloved and inspired leader, His Majesty, Oren Natas. It was not a dreaded enemy that robbed us of his wisdom and farsightedness which he so unselfishly lavished upon us; neither did he succumb to sudden heart failure as we have been led to believe. Rather, a public official of high standing in whom His Majesty placed complete trust murdered our benevolent king by tricking him into drinking a deadly poison which induces heart failure and virtually instant death. That poison was coniine, a highly toxic alkaloid extracted from the leaves of the poison hemlock plant growing in the lobby of the Palace of Nations. In an attempt to usurp His Majesty's leadership role, our Chief of Police, John Wallace, used the coniine to poison a bottle of brandy which he then gave to his trusting superior as a personal gift. He knew that His Majesty would suspect nothing if he drank with him, so he first coated his stomach by drinking a powerful antidote, then vomited up the poison brandy as soon as His Majesty was fatally stricken. He then flushed the poison drinks and residue in the bottle down the toilet in His Majesty's private office, rinsed out the bottle and glasses and refilled them with untainted brandy from His Majesty's desk credenza. Chief Wallace used a paper funnel which he had concealed in his pocket to transfer the liquid, and then wiped away all clues with a washcloth from the bathroom. He hid the cloth on his body under his clothes until he could safely dispose of the evidence. He then sounded an alarm and pretended an attempt to revive our beloved king when he knew in fact that His Majesty was already dead. To further conceal his guilt, Chief Wallace accompanied the lifeless body to the hospital, proclaimed that His Majesty had suffered a heart attack in his presence, then ordered that the corpse not be desecrated by autopsy."

Romas fumbled for a handkerchief, wiped feigned tears from his eyes and blinked into the cameras. "The truth of what I now share with you can easily be established by exhuming His Majesty's body and checking it for traces of coniine. I know that what I speak is the truth because His Majesty appeared to me in a vision, unmasked his murderer, and further revealed to me that he is, in fact, god; and that he will return to us at such time that we show ourselves to be worthy of his presence. He commanded me to fashion his likeness and distribute the images to the control centers so that all may pray in his name for continued peace, prosperity, and unity of spirit. He further made it known to me that the natural disasters which are befalling us are due to the forces of evil which seek to discredit his name, and that the spokesmen for these evil forces are the two sorcerers who call themselves witnesses. They possess no power within themselves but simply proclaim plagues on behalf of the evil powers that fight against us. Geneva is no longer worthy to be the seat of our government, and our divine king has instructed me to build his temple in Rome and minister unto you from there until his return. He desires that his chosen administrators enforce our laws and his divine proclamations throughout the ten divisions of his kingdom here on earth. They shall rule on his behalf as he reveals his divine will to me until we show ourselves worthy to receive him again. He has appointed Boris Malinsky as the new Chief of Police to replace John Wallace who must be executed for his treachery among us. I call upon all citizens to rise up and make sure that this seditious crime does not go unpunished. We have endured the plagues with which we have wrongfully been afflicted, and we must continue to face these phenomena with stout hearts and unyielding courage. The poisoning of our oceans and seas has exterminated our marine life in those waters and will reduce our rainfall. We must endure further sacrifice and conserve our inventories by a thirty percent reduction in our daily food and water rations. This necessary measure will not affect public health and will ensure that all of us have access to adequate food and water. Our scientists are working diligently to speed up the reclamation of zone three land, so we can expand our agricultural production. In addition, we are now producing synthetic foods in large quantities that contain all the necessary vitamins and minerals for healthy bodies. These synthetic foods will be available for purchase with your ration coupons. We must all pray to His Majesty for strength and guidance during these troubled times. The images of our god will be delivered to the control centers shortly. I implore each of you to worship before his image daily and pray for our divine king to return and minister unto us on earth. It is His Majesty's will that I be joined in Rome by four hundred and seventy-six workers drawn by lot from each of the fourteen thousand control centers plus two thousand additional police officers selected in lots of two hundred from the ten control centers that have suffered the largest population loss due to natural disasters. Six million of these workers will rebuild Rome and erect a temple to our god, His Majesty, Oren Natas. The remaining six hundred and sixty-six thousand individuals drawn from the control centers will provide extra security until the project is completed. I do expect that the criminal, John Wallace, will rally some loyal supporters around himself and move against me in an effort to retain control of our police force. Our god has instructed me to call down fire from heaven to destroy Wallace and his supporters. When you see this actually come to pass, you will know in your hearts that I speak the truth and that I do indeed reveal to you the will of our god. Before him only you must worship and pray for deliverance from the evil forces that now plague us. In closing, let me remind everyone to wear your protective clothing whenever exposed to the mutant locusts still among us. Stay away from the poison waters and do your part to conserve our food and water supplies. I bid you goodnight in the name of our king and our god."

John Wallace rocked back in his executive chair, dumbfounded and speechless. He had been glued to the television set in his private office ever since Hanzel warned him that Romas was going to accuse him on television of murdering Natas. Wallace dug out his scotch, poured himself a stiff drink, tossed it down, and tried to calm himself. How did that blathering hypocrite figure out how he executed Natas? It didn't seem possible.

The plan was flawless and perfectly executed. He alone knew the details. Romas' babbling about a vision was preposterous. If Natas knew or even suspected anything, he would not have drunk the spiked brandy. Besides, he died just like any other mortal man, so the nonsense about him being divine defied logical reasoning.

Would the unwashed public actually be swayed by Romas? Jesus died like any other mortal man, yet countless millions believed him to be divine. Yes. . . the general population was gullible enough to believe Romas. But, how did Romas find out?

Wallace poured more scotch and sipped it slowly, trying to envision the impossible. It was no wild guess. Romas knew the precise details. How? Damn him! How? Suddenly, a rational explanation occurred to Wallace. What if Romas had his own plan to kill Natas and take over his kingdom? And, suppose that plan involved the use of poison. Romas frequently ate and drank with Natas, so he would naturally consider poison as an option.

The poison hemlock was there in the lobby for all to see. . . and Romas was well educated. He would know that the leaves contained deadly coniine, and it was, therefore, conceivable that he might have devised the precise plan which he, himself, had put together. Once Romas decided to poison Natas with coniine, spiking some brandy would no doubt enter his mind as the best way to get Natas to drink the poison. Naturally, he would have to drink the same brandy with Natas to avoid suspicion. The rest of the details would occur to Romas just like it had popped into his own mind.

"The rotten hypocrite!" Wallace muttered to himself. "I simply beat him to the punch." All the pieces fit, he thought. What a lousy break! He must have begun to suspect me when the autopsy question arose because he would have the same concern about an autopsy showing up the coniine. Then, when I assumed control, he knew he'd have to make his move to keep me from taking over. Even if I was totally innocent, by accusing me of killing Natas, he could rally the people behind him anyway.

Then, if Natas' body was actually exhumed and autopsied, and coniine was present, my fate would be sealed and his claim to a divine revelation from Natas would certainly be vindicated. On the other hand, if no coniine was found, the pathologist could be bribed to report some anyway. Every person could be bribed if the price was right, and Romas would definitely be in the position to pay a handsome bribe.

Wallace felt somewhat relieved as the scotch mellowed him out. One sticky detail remained as he rehashed the scenario. Why would Romas put himself into the trick bag by telling the public on television that he would destroy me by calling down fire from heaven? Then, shove himself farther into the hole by saying that people could judge the truth of his statements by whether the fire fell upon his command. Why make such an asinine statement?

Was it a bluff? ... a high stakes gamble that no one would support me and he therefore never has to make good his claim? The very fact that he dared make such a statement would lend credibility to everything else he said as long as he wasn't put to the test. The people could easily believe that the threat of divine wrath was enough to keep me from confronting him. Thus, if my subordinates deserted me, he would win, hands down. The crafty snake! He's counting on the public outcry to keep me from getting any significant support. . . in which case I could easily be arrested and quickly executed as Natas' murderer.

"Wow! I'd better come up with a solid counter strategy," Wallace concluded, talking to himself. He began searching his mind for a logical plan of attack. What if Natas' body vanished? That would create some possibilities, he mused. No body. . . no coniine!

Then, he could proclaim to the world that Romas fabricated the charges against him in order to seize Natas' power. Romas and his accomplices had done away with Natas' body because an autopsy would prove him innocent. Enough of his men would believe that feasible defense and join in a full-scale attack against Romas and anyone who dared side with him. Then, when that windbag couldn't deliver the heavenly fire, his goose would be cooked for sure. Good fortune! Walker and Wirtman were in town for tomorrow's scheduled meeting with him. He'd fill them in on everything except the fact that he did kill Natas.

It was important that Walker and Wirtman believed him to be innocent and yet fully understood his dilemma. They would select a group of trusted subordinates and make Natas' body disappear forever. . . and do it tonight! Wallace pushed the button for Hanzel, then leaned back in his chair with a contented grin.

"Yes, Chief?" Hanzel responded over the intercom. "Would you step into my office? I need your help." "Yes, Sir. I'm on my way."

Less than a minute later, Hanzel knocked and stuck his head inside the door. "Yes, Chief?" "Come on in and have a seat. I need your advice." Hanzel entered, shut the door, and sat down in a guest chair with an expectant look. Wallace got another glass from his credenza, poured Hanzel a drink, refreshed his own, then looked Hanzel squarely in the eyes. "What did you think of Romas' statements on television?"

"He's plain nuts!" Hanzel answered, sipping some scotch. I was with you that day, so I know what happened, and I know you're innocent of everything except trying to save Natas' life."

"For the purpose of understanding Romas' motive, let's assume that Natas' body is exhumed, autopsied and coniine is found. What would you say to that?" "I'd say someone had to plant it, but you'd certainly be in big trouble. It would be tough to explain under the circumstances. Practically everyone would believe Romas."

Wallace stared at the ceiling and laced his fingers behind his head. "How hard do you think it would be to plant some coniine in the corpse since it is practically fresh as a daisy?" "No problem at all," Hanzel admitted. "Matter of fact, Romas could have done it himself. He spent some time alone with the body before it was interred. . . .at least a half hour." "You see my problem? We can't take the chance that coniine might show up during an autopsy. Romas has come up with a very clever plan to discredit me so he can take over."

Hanzel pursed his lips and thought about the situation for a moment. "Why don't we get rid of the body? We can always claim that Romas somehow disposed of it to keep an autopsy from proving you innocent. No one could ever prove otherwise."

"That's an outstanding idea!" Wallace praised him. "Get in touch with Walker and Wirtman, explain the situation to them just as you've explained it to me. Suggest to them that they gather up some men that they trust completely, relieve the guard detail around Natas tomb and then make sure that Natas' corpse is never seen again after tonight."

Hanzel gulped down the remainder of his scotch. "Consider it done, Chief. No one will even know the body is gone unless there's an exhumation order. . . in which case the guard detail will have been changed numerous times before such an order could be carried out."

Wallace smiled gratefully. "Thank you Hanzel. I really appreciate your help in bailing me out." Hanzel got up, opened the door and looked back at Wallace before leaving. "Glad to help out anyway I can, Chief. Don't worry about a thing. We'll take care of the problem."

Wallace napped on and off at his desk between reading the latest computer summaries and thinking about the situation in Israel. He admired the guerrilla leaders for their courage and brilliant tactics. Too bad they weren't on his side. It was going to be a bloody and costly war, but he had no choice. No outlaws were going to slaughter that many of his men and not pay the price. He had hoped for more time to renegotiate the compromise provisions that Natas had violated, and to reassure the Israelis that the peace agreement would not be breached in the future.

His phone rang. It was Commander Walker. "Evening, Chief. The object of your concern is in a van headed for zone four where it will be permanently disposed of. Wirtman sends his regards. We'll see you at the scheduled time tomorrow."

Wallace was elated. "Thank you, Commander. I appreciate your loyalty and understanding. Please pass along my thanks to Colonel Wirtman."

Bishop Romas arose at six in the morning and enjoyed a warm shower. He lathered his body gently to avoid loosening the scabs over his sores which were not yet completely healed. The cook had returned to work and was busily preparing breakfast for two. Boris Malinsky would be arriving shortly for a strategy conference in connection with the inevitable confrontation with Wallace.

He adjusted the shower head to rinse away the soap, then turned off the water and reached for a soft towel. He examined his body in the mirror as he gingerly dried himself. The dark scabs scattered over his body made him look like a refugee from a war zone where napalm was the weapon of choice. He frowned at his grotesque image, slipped on his robe and checked with the cook.

Breakfast would be ready by the time he got dressed. He donned his bishop's attire and returned to the dining room just as the cook was opening the front door for Malinsky. Romas met him in the vestibule and greeted him warmly: "Good morning, Boris, and welcome to my home. Breakfast is just about ready," Romas said, shaking his hand like an old friend. "Let me take your coat while Rosie shows you to the dining room."

The cook seated Malinsky at the dining room table and poured him a cup of fresh coffee, then poured a cup for Romas. Malinsky was born in Poland and had served as a general in the Russian army before becoming a secret agent. He was fifty-four, tall, thin and swarthy with a hooked nose, crooked teeth, and thin, gray hair. His high forehead, irregular jaw line and thin lips made him rather unattractive. He positioned his napkin as Romas settled into the opposite chair at the elegant table.

"I hope you like scrambled eggs," Romas ventured. "If not, Rosie can whip up whatever you prefer." "Scrambled will be fine," Malinsky replied with a friendly smile. "I seldom eat breakfast, so my stomach will appreciate the treat."

The cook brought in platters full of scrambled eggs, bacon, sausage, biscuits and gravy followed by salt, pepper, honey, and jellies. "May I get anything else for you?" she asked, looking first at Malinsky, then at Romas.

"That's more than enough. You'll spoil me rotten," Malinsky said, helping himself to the scrambled eggs. "Looks just fine to me, Rosie," Romas complimented her. He looked across at the sores on Malinsky's face as she withdrew. "How are your sores healing up?" Romas asked with a sympathetic grin. "Mine have been kinda hard on my social life."

"Social events have been the least of my discomfort," Malinsky responded while placing biscuits around his eggs and spooning gravy over them. "I'm just glad to be able to sit down again. Does anybody know what caused them?" "Not to my knowledge," Romas admitted while buttering two biscuits. "My doctor passed them off as connected with some type of new virus. But I don't think anyone really knows the cause. Sure, hope they're like the measles so we only suffer through them once. I'm not sure I could handle a second batch."

Malinsky wiped a dribble of gravy from his pointed chin with the corner of his napkin. "I watched your speech on TV yesterday. You were magnificent. . . almost had me believing Natas spoke to you in a vision." "That's precisely what happened," Romas assured him. "Natas told me exactly how Wallace murdered him. He appeared to me again in the same manner and told me that you were to replace Wallace. He also gave me other instructions along with political advice. I never even suspected Wallace, much less all the intricate details. It was quite an ingenious scheme."

Malinsky swallowed some eggs and sausage, sipped some coffee, and gazed inquisitively at Romas. "If Natas knew all the details of Wallace's scheme, why did he go ahead and drink the coniine?"

Romas smiled serenely over the rim of his cup. "So, I can raise him from the dead and convince everyone that he is divine." Malinsky nearly choked on his bite of biscuit and gravy. This charlatan has got more than just one loose screw, he thought to himself. Next, he'll be telling me that he really can call fire down upon Wallace. Maybe he should take a hike. Still, it wasn't every day that one gets a chance to command a worldwide security force. . .power beyond his wildest imagination. He decided to humor Romas. "When does this modest display of your capabilities take place?" Romas buttered a third biscuit while masticating some bacon and eggs. He chased the morsels with a swallow of coffee. "Whenever Natas tells me that he's ready to return."

This guy's too much, Malinsky mused as he finished off his biscuits and gravy. Wonder why he doesn't just flap his wings right up to heaven and haul the fire back in person? He really should have a guardian. "You actually going to scorch Wallace's traitorous hide with fire?"

Romas' visage indicated that he was quite serious. "More than simply scorch him. I'm going to give him a preview of hell. However, the action must be properly staged so that people around the world can watch the entire sequence of events on television."

"That'll require mighty close coordination with the media. Do you have something specific in mind?" Romas topped off his breakfast with a biscuit stuffed full of bacon and honey. "Yes. We need to provoke him into trying to arrest us out in the open. . . like in front of Natas' tomb. That particular location would have a favorable psychological effect upon our audience as well as allow excellent media coverage."

Malinsky thought over the possibilities while finishing his coffee. He really thinks he can pull it off. There's one sure way to find out while forcing the showdown with Wallace at the same time. "Walker and Wirtman are very close to Wallace and will also have to be replaced. Why don't we schedule some sort of ceremony in front of the tomb where you formally announce to the world that I am taking over command of all security forces and that I will be appointing immediate replacements for Commander Walker and Colonel Wirtman? In Wallace's mind, we won't have committed any crime worthy of arrest until we actually make the announcement and call upon all security personnel to support us. That's when he'll move in to make the arrest. The networks will have crews spotted to cover the ceremony as well as speculate concerning Wallace's reaction to the announcement. Such speculation on international TV will surely force his hand if nothing else does."

"That's very clever . . . I like it," Romas agreed. "We need to move quickly while the controversy is still fresh in the public mind. Let's set it up for tomorrow afternoon."

Anchorpersons on the television networks analyzed the contest between Romas and Wallace with commentaries that exacerbated the conflict. Speculation as to whether Natas' body would or would not be exhumed and autopsied was bantered back and forth with the fervor of bookies placing bets on their favorite horses. The big question centered around the issue of authority. The world community had no political process for replacing a total dictator. Both Romas and Wallace were Natas appointees and neither had been given a public mandate to succeed Natas. Had Romas come up with the charges against Wallace purely for a political advantage? As yet, there was no solid evidence to substantiate Romas' personal accusation.

Who had the proper authority to issue an exhumation order? Coroner offices had been eliminated along with county and state governments. In any event, what would an autopsy really prove. If coniine was indeed found in Natas' body, that did not prove Wallace guilty. Romas could have poisoned Natas as easily as Wallace, and then accused Wallace of his own crime in order to achieve two major objectives. Namely, to eliminate a powerful competitor and, at the same time, produce a scapegoat for the public to pounce upon thereby masking his own guilt.

Romas was asking the world to convict Wallace on the basis of his self-proclaimed vision wherein a man who was known to be dead appeared and accused his murderer. If Romas was being truthful, when did Natas identify Wallace as the culprit? After his death? If so, by what process or means? If Natas knew before his death, why did he drink the poison?

Romas was asking world citizens to swallow a big pill with some pretty sharp edges. Wallace was the most logical person to issue an exhumation order. After all, he was in charge of global law and order. Wallace was not naive and would consider the possibility that Romas could have poisoned Natas. If he let Romas goad him into exhuming the corpse, and poison was found, public opinion would favor Romas. On the other hand, if Wallace resisted the exhumation, he would only cast more suspicion upon himself.

Moreover, if Wallace was indeed guilty as Romas claimed, how could Romas wrest the power away from Wallace? Wallace had the power, the position, and the guns; and he was charged with the responsibility for law enforcement. Romas must prove his charges against Wallace, and simply finding poison in Natas' corpse would not be sufficient without additional evidence. If Romas continued to encourage the people to rise up against established officials charged with maintaining the public peace, he would be guilty of a capital crime sufficient to warrant his own execution. . . unless he could back up his personal accusation with adequate evidence.

The struggle between Romas and Wallace was shaping up to be the biggest public controversy since law and order had been established by Natas. The showdown would occur in less than twenty-four hours. Romas had announced a formal ceremony in front of Natas' tomb on the grounds outside the Palace of Nations.

He had stated his intention to proclaim Boris Malinsky as the new Chief of Police, and it was further rumored that Malinsky would name replacements for Commander Walker and Colonel Wirtman. Romas was claiming authority for the ceremony on the basis of his self-proclaimed vision wherein Natas revealed his divine nature and claim to immortality as god of the planet. Did Romas have more surprises in store for Wallace? If so, what? Whatever transpired, the networks would be there to cover the story.

John Wallace's respect for network anchorpersons grew as he watched the evening news. They were making all his arguments for him and preparing the public mind to accept the execution of Romas. He felt like the ax buried between his shoulder blades had just been extracted without any loss of blood. The autopsy issue was now overshadowed by Romas' announcement of a public ceremony which plainly constituted sedition.

All he needed to do now was to carry out the public execution. Romas had bet his life and lost. Now that the network celebrities had properly analyzed the legal nature of the power struggle, no one would dare side with Romas unless he could produce more evidence.

The media had destroyed the credibility of potential autopsy findings. Romas was trapped. There was no other evidence except his claim to a divine revelation, and that wouldn't count for much after his head was severed. He, Walker, Wirtman, a hooded executioner and a hundred armed subordinates would apprehend Romas and anyone crazy enough to stand with him at the scheduled ceremony. Natas' tomb should stand for law and order, not sedition. It was quite appropriate that the demise of Romas occur before the tomb of Natas. He had counted on a dead man's claim to immortality to justify his insurrection against lawful authority. If the public missed that psychological link, the media would surely point it out. He wondered if Walker and Wirtman had been watching the media commentaries. He buzzed for Hanzel. It was time to start organizing for tomorrow's showdown.

Throughout the long morning hours, the spectators gathered in a crowded circle, jockeying for standing room to watch the clash between Wallace and Romas. They looked like aliens from another planet in their heavy, protective clothing, helmets and face shields. The cool November air was insufficient to keep them from sweltering inside their well-padded garments, gloves, and footwear. The media crews arrived early and vied for the choice camera positions. Live network coverage commenced at noon although the ceremony was scheduled for two o'clock. A local production studio hired by Romas set up a platform for the ceremony along with microphones, speakers and amplifiers. A twenty-foot square was roped off around the platform to hold back the crowd.

At 1:58 pm, the studio crew commenced playing an audio tape of Romas' TV address containing his accusations against Wallace and his testimony to the divine status of Natas. At 2:05 pm, Romas and Malinsky arrived by limo and made their way to the platform. Neither Romas nor Malinsky was wearing protective clothing. Romas was decked out in his ceremonial bishop's robes with full headdress, and Malinsky was wearing a modest business suit. They stood tall and straight on the platform while the audio tape concluded.

Romas began his address with a loud, impassioned prayer to Oren Natas, god of the planet. Then, he touted Malinsky's good character, accomplishments, and his deep devotion to law and order. Next, he referred to Wallace's treachery and the need for his immediate replacement by Malinsky in accordance with the divine will of Oren Natas.

The threatening sound of tramping boots turned the heads of the spectators. Wallace, Walker, and Wirtman were moving up the street toward the Palace of Nations. Behind them marched a rectangle of police officers, twenty men across and five men deep. Bringing up the rear were two burly executioners wielding long-handled, heavy bladed axes. Their black hoods were clearly visible underneath their plastic face shields. The protective outer gear worn by the entire assembly did not detract from their menacing appearance. Each man, except the executioners, was armed with an automatic rifle in addition to a heavy caliber service revolver. The crowd shrank back before the advancing force.

Bishop Romas raised his hands skyward in supplication and bellowed out a prayer to Natas: "Lord Natas, our divine king, and god of Earth, behold your betrayer who now seeks to silence your faithful servant. His heart is filled with deceit and his hands are full of innocent blood. Rise up from your eternal throne beyond the stars and grant my supplication. Send down a whirlwind of consuming fire upon those who seek to defy your divine will and cast down your loyal bishop. Let the people witness your mighty power so that they may know you are their god and that you have appointed me to minister unto them in your name."

The crowd looked on with utter astonishment as a churning cloud of crackling flames appeared in the sky and descended upon Wallace and his men, completely engulfing the entire force within a whirling inferno of white-hot fire. A cocoon of flames enveloped each man; and every individual that had appeared with Wallace was totally consumed as the spectators watched in shocked horror.

The TV cameras followed the entire episode, preserving every detail for the eyes of the entire world. The spectators fell upon their knees and began chanting praises and prayers to Lord Natas, king of humanity and god of Earth.

Malinsky was petrified with stark amazement and disabling fear. Romas surveyed the scene before him with both pleasure and satisfaction. He had just become the recognized spiritual leader of the human race.

Throughout zones one and two, the people built great bonfires in sacrifice to Natas, casting into the flames all religious artifacts in their possession. They burned all religious shrines except those dedicated to Natas, and the security forces converted all buildings formerly dedicated to religious purposes into government warehouses. Romas proclaimed it to be a capital crime to worship any deity other than Natas and Malinsky enforced the proclamation with vigor. At least one factory in each control center was dedicated to the production of images of Natas fabricated from heavy metals and painted with a glossy black enamel. The statues varied in size with none smaller than six inches.

Romas gave Malinsky and the ten regional administrators a free hand while he concentrated on the spiritual leadership of humanity. Whatever proclamations Romas issued as being the will of Natas became law, and each new proclamation was relentlessly enforced by Malinsky.

Israel became the only exception. Romas and Malinsky negotiated a new peace agreement with the Israelis. They were allowed to manage their own affairs inside their borders, but any Israeli traveling outside Israel would not be covered by the provisions of the agreement and would have to comply with world law. They were also permitted to worship as they saw fit inside Israel as long as they didn't speak out against world law or openly defy Romas or Malinsky. In return, the Israelis gave up their weapons, pledged to abstain from any production of war materials and to abide by world law pertaining to food and water rationing.

Hartstein and Solomon surrendered the four hydrogen bombs and all the remaining nuclear weapons on earth were dismantled, rendered inoperative and then safely buried in zone four pits. The peace agreement contained provisions for random visits by inspection teams to ensure that Israel neither concealed nor manufactured any weapons. Outside Israel, Malinsky's security forces enforced the ban on all military weapons.

The seat of world government was moved to Rome, Italy and the fourteen thousand control centers contributed a total of six million, six hundred and sixty-six thousand workers to rebuild Rome and to construct Natas' temple. Global society settled down into a period of relative stability wherein the top government priorities became the production of synthetic foods to supplement agricultural output and the conservation of potable water.

Bishop Romas, surrounded by a guard escort, toured the newly constructed temple erected to Natas. No expense had been spared in order to produce a temple of breathtaking wonder and beauty. It was designed to be occupied only by Natas and those making supplication to him. The exterior was constructed with white marble, and white onyx steps led to the entrance arch which was overlaid with solid silver and trimmed with gold. The exit arch was an exact duplicate of the entrance arch, and a life-sized image of Natas stood between the two arches. The statue was sculptured from exquisite black onyx, and the physical features depicted were chiseled with astounding detail.

The temple interior was spacious and circular with a domed ceiling lined with pure gold. Stained glass skylights framed with polished silver circled the interior of the dome at its midpoint and the walls were polished white marble garnished with precious stones embedded in carved images. The floor was made of black marble inlaid with seams of gold. In the center of the interior, circular steps ascended to Natas' throne which was fashioned from solid silver and overlaid with pure gold. The perimeter of the throne was studded with precious stones and the footstool was solid gold ringed with flawless diamonds. Behind the throne were two graven images of archangels with uplifted wings that joined at the wing tips. The images were solid silver draped with chains of gold.

On the right side of the throne platform was a graven image of Lucifer carved from white onyx and on the left side was a matching image of Natas. There were six ascending steps to the throne. The first three were fashioned from silver and the top three were gold, encrusted with rubies, emeralds and diamonds. Engraved upon a golden scroll suspended between the archangels above the throne was an inscription: "You are the anointed cherub that went forth upon the holy mountain and walked up and down in the midst of the stones of fire."

Rising from the floor in front of the throne were twelve supplication pedestals consisting of black marble blocks one foot high and three feet across arranged in semicircles, four across and three deep. One hundred and forty-four witness seats made of polished brass and arranged in twelve rows of twelve seats faced the throne from behind the supplication pedestals. On the aft side of the throne, balancing out the floor space occupied by the pedestals and witness seats, was a sparkling pool twelve feet deep inlaid with white onyx. The pool was ringed by exotic plants and graven images chiseled from black and white marble. The floor space beyond was occupied by concentric circles of similar graven images with six feet between each statue. The images depicted the history of the Egyptians, Assyrians, Babylonians, Persians, Greeks, and Romans; and were fashioned from brass, granite and marble. Shimmering crystal chandeliers provided brilliant interior lighting. The tiered chandeliers were suspended by polished brass chains, six rows across and six rows deep.

The temple grounds were planted with flowering trees among which were scattered life-sized marble figures of leopards, lions, bears, eagles, sphinxes, bulls and rams. Manicured shrubs of varying shapes and sizes were intermingled with the animal statues. Six granite walkways meandered through the grounds and circled back to the temple entrance. The structure and grounds occupied six hundred and sixty-six thousand square feet within the acreage where the papal palace had been located prior to the nuclear war. Romas marveled at the workmanship as he completed the tour and returned to his opulent private quarters on the east side of the temple grounds. Natas should be pleased, he thought happily. The temple was truly magnificent and a worthy habitation for the Prince of Darkness.

Romas' head swam in the midst of a drunken stupor as he reclined in his massive waterbed. The antique, hand-carved clock nestled in the north corner of the spacious bedroom registered 3:36 am. A raging expanse of flames appeared in Romas' subconscious, and reddish black smoke ascended from the midst of the fiery abyss. The flames sparkled with innumerable points of brilliant light as if billions of individual diamonds were reflecting the noonday sun. Cries of anguish and unspeakable agony mingled with screams of blasphemy and recrimination; a deafening din of human suffering that received no recognition as the tortured voices rent the outer darkness beyond the bottomless inferno.

Each point of light appeared to have its own voice and individual senses. Though no images appeared, each voice believed itself to be clothed with a human body that saw, heard, smelled, tasted, and broiled endlessly within the churning fire, searing every nerve and fiber as the smoke of individual torment drifted into the unfathomable blackness of unbounded space. Romas cringed with stark terror when he identified one of the voices begging for mercy. It was his own! He felt as if an invisible door had opened on a white-hot furnace and he had been cast headlong into the superheated interior. He was seized with indescribable pain throughout his entire being as he sank downward into the billowing fire. Yet, his body seemed weightless, rising and falling uncontrollably as the flames vomited him up and then received him again.

Then, the inky darkness above was pierced by a blinding light which gradually lessened until an image became discernible . . .a mighty angel held an open book in his left hand as he lifted his right hand toward heaven and cried out in a thunderous voice that transcended the wailing of billions of lost souls: "Give glory to him that created all things; for the mystery of God is now finished as he has declared to his servants, the prophets. . . and time shall be marked no longer. The kingdoms of this world have become the kingdoms of our Lord, and of his Christ and he shall reign forever."

Romas sat upright in the bed and rubbed his bleary eyes. His alcohol tortured stomach churned with fiery indigestion and his skull felt too small for his brain as he tried to focus his eyes on the clock. It was only a dream, he concluded with relief. . . just a stupid dream. He settled back into the mattress, closed his eyes again and thought about the resurrection of Natas. What a spectacle it was going to be when he personally answered the daily prayer of more than a billion loyal subjects.

The people were now completely united in their worship of Natas and all things contrary to that devotion had been purged from his kingdom. Every household outside of Israel worshiped before an image of Natas and people everywhere had psychologically prepared themselves for his return. They gave Natas credit for the disappearance of the mutant locusts, relief from the plague of noisome body sores, the reappearance of green grass and ground vegetation, and the absence of further natural disasters since the destruction of Wallace and his supporters. They also praised Natas for the return of normal weather patterns as the polluted oceans and seas gradually cleansed themselves. The loss of marine life had been compensated for by mass production of synthetic foods, and the desalinization plants had reduced the need for additional reductions in daily water rations.

A soothing feeling of power and well-being swept over Romas as he mentally rehashed the course of events since Wallace poisoned Natas. The people considered him to be Natas' true prophet, and it was of little consequence that his status would soon be reduced to that of the second most powerful man on Earth. He yawned contentedly and drifted off to sleep.

The midday sun blazed in the cloudless sky over downtown Rome as angry curses and threatening insults were directed at two men who stood in front of Natas' undedicated temple. Their sackcloth and sandals identified them as the two witnesses. They ignored the tumult raised by the onlookers as they turned about and raised their hands toward heaven. They stood with their backs toward each other; one facing east and the other looking west. The witness turned to the east entreated Almighty God in a powerful voice that echoed throughout the crowded streets:

"Behold the evidence of their blasphemy, Lord God Almighty! Look upon the children of Satan. Their fathers murdered the prophets and now they lust for the blood of your servants. Hearken unto the cries of those martyred in your holy name. How long, our Lord, holy and true, before you exercise judgment and avenge their blood upon them that dwell on the earth? In righteous judgment, stretch forth your hand upon the children of the enemy, and vex them in your sore displeasure."

Several dozen guards shoved a path through the crowd and approached the witnesses. The crowd cheered as the guards raised their weapons into firing position. Then, as if time suddenly stood still, the armed men froze in their tracks and there was dead silence among those gathered at the scene. The witness facing east turned about, faced his would-be executioners, sucked in his breath mightily, and exhaled a stream of fire that mushroomed into a whirlwind of destruction which scattered the onlookers and enveloped the stricken guards where they stood. As the roaring flames devoured the attackers, the witness looking westward addressed heaven in a resounding voice:

"Who is like unto God, and who is able to make war against heaven? Assemble yourselves and come. Draw near together, you that are escaped of the nations; you that have no knowledge, that set up the graven image, and pray to a god that cannot save. Look unto the Almighty, all the ends of the earth; for there is no other God unto whom every knee shall bow, and every tongue shall confess. He has sworn by himself. The word has gone forth out of his mouth in righteousness and shall not return unto him void. Who shall not fear you, Heavenly Father, and glorify your name? For you only are holy, and all nations shall come and worship before you.

Extend the arm of judgment and dip your finger of wrath into the rivers, lakes, and fountains of waters, and satisfy the thirst for blood among them that inhabit the earth; for they have shed the blood of saints and prophets and murdered the innocent. It is fitting therefore that they should have blood to drink; for truly they are worthy."

The crowd shrank back in terror as the two witnesses walked calmly through their midst and then vanished from sight.

Malinsky looked pale and worried as Romas welcomed him into his private study. Romas seated himself at his desk as Malinsky dropped into a cushioned armchair. "I understand that you lost forty or so men near the temple this afternoon," Romas remarked with a poker face. "And the two sorcerers eluded you again?" "The forty-eight men that got cremated are the least of our worries," Malinsky replied with a hangdog look. "Have you had a drink lately?"

"I had a little too much last night." Romas smiled pleasantly. "But I'll be happy to pour you one if that'll brighten your outlook. You appear less than confident in your abilities." "I was referring to our supplies of drinking water," Malinsky corrected him. "Everything is completely polluted. There's no fresh water anywhere. All the control centers are reporting the same mass corruption of rivers, lakes, wells, stored water, and streams. If we don't come up with a solution quickly, there's going to be public panic."

"We can begin by not thinking of blood in terms of pollution," Romas advised with a twisted grin. "If we don't think in those terms, then perhaps the public won't either." "You mean the waters really have turned into blood?" Romas looked blandly at Malinsky. "Do you have some lingering doubts about the chemistry?" "One of those loudmouths predicted that the waters would become blood! Do you think it's really true?" "There's no doubt about it," Romas conceded. "I ordered numerous samples tested and the results came back as pure human blood. Have you tried some? It really doesn't taste too bad, but I doubt that it mixes well with scotch or bourbon."

What an ignoramus! Malinsky concluded. He might take the matter a little more seriously if he drank less brandy. "How can all the fresh water on earth turn to human blood at the babbling of some idiots?" Malinsky asked with a scowl. "It simply isn't physically possible!" "Nothing is physically impossible once you raise your level of expectation above human limitations," Romas replied. "I'm not sure I'm on the same wavelength," Malinsky muttered. "What are our expectations?"

Romas adopted a thoughtful demeanor. "What is water composed of and from what source does its elements originate?" "Water is composed of two atoms of hydrogen gas and one atom of oxygen gas. When the hydrogen bond is formed between the two hydrogen atoms and the oxygen atom, a liquid molecule of water is created. Hydrogen and oxygen are plentiful elements that exist in our atmosphere and in other compounds."

Romas nodded agreement. At least he's studied high school chemistry, he mused. Maybe I can take him a step farther. "Where do the hydrogen and oxygen atoms come from? Where do the atoms of all the elements come from?" "I don't recall my chemistry and physics professors focusing on the origin of the atoms of any of the elements," Malinsky admitted. "What's your point?" "To understand my point, you must face up to the unanswered question . . . where do the atoms of the various elements come from?" "I have no idea as to the origin of the elements, but it has been amply demonstrated that all matter in our universe is composed of atoms that are listed on the periodic table of the elements. . . .including the nuclides."

Romas became slightly impatient. "Do you think the elements simply materialized out of nothing, or that they somehow created themselves? I think not. The very existence of the elements should prove to rational beings that some kind of creative force exists within our universe. The fault with evolutionary theories is the inescapable fact that such explanations do not even attempt to answer what is obviously a very elementary question: What is the source of matter? We all know that matter, which is composed of the various elements, cannot be destroyed but rather only transformed within time, distance and space by the application of kinetic energy which originates within the atomic structure of atoms. What is the source of that energy? We can describe the spinning electrons within the energy levels that surround the protons and neutrons. But, where did these atomic particles come from? And, how did the energy and motion within these particles of matter originate? To say that such energy comes from the sun is the height of baffle-gab; for we also know that the sun is a huge mass of hydrogen that is constantly being converted into helium by the heat of its own molecular weight within the vacuum of space. The loss of mass that occurs when hydrogen is converted to helium is given off as radioactive particles in precisely the same manner that a hydrogen bomb releases radiation in the form of subatomic particles of matter. Thus, the unanswered question remains. . . what is the source of atoms and the kinetic energy within those atoms?"

Malinsky pursed his lips and shook his head from side to side. "I don't have the foggiest idea, and I'm still missing your point. Why the physics lesson?" "I'm trying to help you understand that God is only a word that humans have coined to describe the essence of creative energy. . . the force that gave substance, form, motion and inherent energy to both organic and inorganic matter. . . matter that is no more than a selective combining of the atoms of the various elements fused together by the inherent energy therein. Wouldn't both blood and water fall within this scientific description?"

"Malinsky still looked confused. "Yes. I suppose so." "Do you then concede the quite obvious fact that some source of creative energy is responsible for the molecular structure of the universe. . . which certainly includes both blood and water?" "It would seem to be a rational conclusion." Finally! Romas thought. His head is a little thicker than I imagined. "Then, isn't it also within the realm of rational human thought to concede that this force, which we call God, is capable of altering molecular structure as well as creating it in the first place? And, if we must concede that such a force exists, why should we be surprised that water can be converted to the liquid which we know as human blood? Up to sixty-five percent of blood is plasma; and plasma is mostly water. Throw in a few elements that combine to form red and white blood cells, and various other elements that form the compounds which we know as blood nutrients, and the conversion is physically comprehensible to the most unwashed intellectual. Of course, we only need to turn on the faucet to see that water can indeed be turned into blood. Are you not astute enough to comprehend at this point that we are fighting against God, himself? That Natas is the incarnation of Satan? Or, perhaps you think that humans are the apex of the living beings into whom God breathed the breath of life? Do you not yet understand that we have become the servants of Satan; that we are forever branded with his mark, and that we shall share his eternal fate?"

Malinsky was stunned by Romas' outburst. "If we fight against God, as you say, how can we hope to prevail? Would it not be a futile effort?" "God has bound himself by his own creations. Satan's power is far beyond human understanding. . . just as we cannot comprehend the creative power of God which imparted to humans a free will which allows us to side with Satan against him. We have made our choice. We have chosen to reign in hell rather than to serve in heaven. But, from what I have seen of hell, we would be much wiser to enjoy the full measure of carnal lusts here on earth prior to our ultimate demise."

"You have seen hell?" Malinsky blurted out with a startled expression. "Yes." Romas answered quietly. "I saw it, or the lake of fire, in a dream this morning. I can assure you that reigning in hell doesn't count for much." "Who are these two so-called witnesses?"

Romas squeezed his chin with his right hand and gazed at Malinsky. "They are most likely Enoch and Elijah since neither of them experienced physical death. They have been sent back by heaven to worry us with plagues and to minister unto those who have refused to register at the control centers. Their mission must be to focus the attention of humanity on the struggle between God and Satan. The plagues are not meant to destroy mankind; only to capture the undivided attention of the world as the witnesses speak for God and we promote Satan."

Malinsky tried to hide the fear that clawed at his insides. He had never given much thought to spiritual concepts, but what Romas had said made a lot of sense. Both the witnesses and the plagues were real, and there had to be some rational explanation for their presence . . . just as the mere existence of the element's points to a creative force far beyond the intelligence of humans. Perhaps he had been premature in adjudging Romas to be an incompetent babbler. Still, it seemed a little asinine to wage war with God. To achieve what? The outcome surely was not in doubt. His sphincter muscles puckered as he studied Romas. "Assuming that you speak the truth, why are we engaged in a fight that we cannot possibly win? What purpose is served?"

Romas' eyes reflected resolute determination. "You say we cannot win, and I ask you: what is the measure of victory? Who won the nuclear war? Who won when the Jews committed suicide at Masada rather than surrender to the Romans. Who won in the Garden of Eden when mankind sided with Satan?. . .did Satan win when he brought about the physical death of humans. . . or did God win when he provided the means for spiritual redemption? Who will win the final battle for human souls? If the measure of victory is quantitative, then the outcome of the struggle is yet undecided. In any event, our fate is forever sealed. Nevertheless, if you are dissatisfied with your role during the remainder of your physical life, perhaps Natas can find a replacement."

The cold reality of Romas' logic calmed Malinsky's emotions. "No need to belabor your point. If the only possible strategy is to deceive as many people as possible, how do we proceed?" Romas settled back with a sneer. "Although the witnesses are probably Enoch and Elijah, they are subject to the physical limitations of human bodies. Consequently, your top priority should be to hunt down and kill those two thorns in our sides while

I convince the world that drinking blood for a few days has some positive benefits." Malinsky's face cracked into a devilish grin. "I suppose it'll help out with our food shortage. Some African tribes have survived prolonged drought and famine by drinking blood drawn in limited quantities from their cattle."

Romas beamed with self-importance. "I'll encourage everyone to pray to Natas for cleansing of the waters, for the death of the two witnesses, and for Natas' immediate return to earth. The networks will compete to broadcast my message. Then, when the plague has run its course, you kill the witnesses, and Natas is resurrected, the people will no doubt believe that their prayers have been answered."

Malinsky no longer doubted Romas' power to perform Satan's will. Watching the fiery death of Wallace and his men had left a lasting impression. He also began to visualize the power which the witnesses were capable of exercising. It would be prudent to remain in the background when those two were located again. He wasn't overly anxious to become a human torch. "When will Natas reappear?" "Very soon, I think," Romas replied. "Perhaps at the dedication of his temple."

The full moon illuminated the temple grounds as Romas strolled among the statues. An eerie foreboding haunted him, and he felt insecure although sentries were posted every thirty yards around the entire perimeter. He comforted himself by reflecting on his TV address three hours earlier. It had gone very well, and the media had been supportive of his explanation. The follow-up commentaries had praised him for his fearless leadership during difficult times and assured the public that it was safe to drink the blood for its water content.

Romas circled back to the temple entrance and admired the statue of Natas, fixated by the eyes that seemed to follow him regardless of the viewing angle. He shivered slightly as he entered the temple. Where was the frigid air coming from? It was eighty degrees outside and the air conditioning hadn't been turned on. He felt a strange presence and unseen eyes watching him. He ascended the steps to the throne and felt intense heat radiating from the golden seat. He felt compelled to withdraw as he backed down from the platform. The sight of the thick blood slopping against the sides of the pool behind the throne made him queasy.

He made his way back to the entrance and walked past the image of Natas without stopping. He was seized with an unknown dread and suddenly had the urge to flee. The sound of a resonant voice addressing him caused him to pause. “The time has come, Julius. I am ready to return." He turned and looked back at the statue of Natas. His heart jumped into his throat when he saw the lips of the image curl into a sinister smile. Goosebumps covered his skin as he turned away and hurried toward the comfort of his private quarters.

A gentle breeze bathed downtown Rome and a holiday spirit permeated the air. The streets teemed with thousands of spectators as media crews prepared to film the dedication of Natas' temple. Hundreds of security guards locked arms to hold back the crowd as Romas paraded in his full ceremonial costume through the temple grounds surrounded by media celebrities. The commencement of the dedication activities was still an hour away, but already there was standing room only and a hysteria of expectation.

Nancy Flack, the anchorperson from International Cable News, extended her portable microphone in front of Romas' chin. "Do you have any surprises in store for us today, Bishop?" Romas smiled politely for her camera operator. "Today belongs to the people. They have waited a long time for this dedication, and I think they will be quite pleased with the magnificent temple which they have helped to build through their personal sacrifices. They have much to be proud of, and I'm confident that Lord Natas will return unto us very soon. The people have been fervently praying for his return, and he surely will answer their prayers." Ms. Flack wiped away wisps of windblown hair from around her mouth with her left hand while her right hand steadied the microphone for Romas. "Do you think the witnesses might show up here and create a problem for you?"

Romas displayed his practiced nonchalant look for the camera. "It's hard to predict where those two fakers will pop up next. Should they attempt to intrude upon this joyous occasion, we have plenty of security people available to apprehend them." Ms. Flack wanted to hear something more controversial. "How long do you predict that the people will have to drink blood instead of water? Is there ever going to be an end to these plagues?" Romas changed his expression to that of the benevolent bishop. "I think the waters will be cleansed by Lord Natas in the very near future, and I also believe the plagues will end when those two sorcerers that you call witnesses are executed by our police force. It is just a matter of time before they show up at the wrong place."

Romas had retained the same production company that handled the trappings for the ceremony in front of Natas' tomb. Microphones, loudspeakers, and amplifiers had been set up, a colorful bandstand had been provided in front of the temple steps, and tens of thousands of brightly colored, helium-filled balloons were distributed to the crowd.

Behind the temple, more than a hundred crates of doves and white pigeons were being prepared for release at the right moment. Security guards escorted the musicians through the crowd to their seats on the bandstand. The excited chatter of the enormous gathering added to the atmosphere of celebration and merriment as men, women, and children packed themselves together shoulder to shoulder. During the long wait, mothers suckled their infants, and the toddlers were hoisted onto the shoulders of their fathers to enable the children to see over the heads of other adults.

Street vendors squeezed their way between the packed bodies to peddle ice cream, candy, popcorn, and soft drinks. The band began playing marching ballads, adding to the din of happy noise that was audible over a two-mile radius. The festive sounds drew more and more people into the streets as the final minutes ticked away. Media crews were allowed to set up inside the temple grounds to ensure the clarity of worldwide TV coverage. Outside of downtown Rome, people were glued to their television sets as the whole world watched the spectacle unfold.

The band music reached a crescendo and then began a drum roll as Romas mounted the speaker's podium which had been positioned some fifty feet forward of the midpoint between the temple arches. He looked masterful and in complete control bedecked in his impressive bishop's regalia as he lifted both arms skyward in recognition of the cheering crowd. The screams of excitement and praises shouted to Natas were deafening as Romas maintained his welcoming posture while the people vented their pent-up emotions.

Finally, the crowd settled down and people strained their necks to hear Romas' words: "In the name of our god, His Majesty, Oren Natas, I welcome you to this joyous event. We are gathered here today to dedicate the temple of our god and to entreat him to dwell among us again. Through the bountiful gifts given freely by faithful men and women around the world, we have erected a dwelling place befitting our divine king. It is fitting that our god should be surrounded by those things most precious to us, for thereby we demonstrate our loyalty and complete devotion. Throughout history, humans have worshiped false gods that are nothing more than graven images carved by those content to worship in ignorance and blind superstition. Prayers have long been offered up to gods with hearts of stone and ears that cannot hear. The world has already seen our god in the flesh and we have earnestly prayed for his return. His image has comforted you during his absence, and everyone knows that the image represents a living, breathing god whose ears are indeed open to our cries and our continuous prayers. We have prepared our hearts and our minds and labored diligently to become worthy of our god's physical presence."

Right on cue, thousands of white doves and white pigeons rose from behind the temple and flapped to freedom. Romas turned his back to the podium and faced the statue of Natas, lifted his arms skyward again and cried out mightily in an impassioned voice: "Lord God, Oren Natas, our benevolent ruler and divine king, behold the supplication of your faithful servants and come forth to minister unto us again!"

A breathless hush fell over all those assembled, and viewers throughout the earth gaped at their television screens as the image of Natas suddenly burst into flames. The only sound was the crackling of the fire as it completely engulfed the image, burned relentlessly for approximately three minutes and then died away as suddenly as it had appeared. Eyes blinked repeatedly, and mouths fell open at the sight of the incredible transfiguration that took place between the temple arches. Before the TV cameras and the eyes of the world, the undamaged statue was transformed into Oren Natas. . . in the flesh. He was dressed in the familiar white general's uniform that had adorned his corpse when he reposed in his casket at the Palace of Nations. Romas stepped aside with a pious expression as Natas stepped up to the podium and extended his arms toward the crowd, smiling a warm greeting from beneath his gold-braided military cap.

Worldwide pandemonium erupted as people everywhere screamed, cried and shouted hysterically. Romas stretched his arms toward the podium and began chanting loudly: "Natas! Natas! Natas!" As if directed by an invisible conductor, a resounding chorus of chants went up from the face of the earth: "Natas! Natas! Natas!"

David Solomon stared with disbelief at the television as Martha looked on wide-eyed and speechless. "God help us!" David exclaimed in a guttural voice. "He's back!" Martha found her voice and looked at David with fear in her eyes. "You were right!" David squeezed the remote-control button and the TV screen became dark and silent. "We don't have a prayer! Malinsky is a different breed from Wallace and will carry out Natas' orders without hesitation. We're trapped, with no one to help us." "You don't think there's any chance he'll honor the peace agreement?" Martha asked while looking down at her sewing. David's voice was quiet and resigned. "He didn't honor the compromise. Why should we believe that he'll be bound by the peace pact? All he wanted to accomplish was to disarm us . . . and Romas and Malinsky have done that for him. Before, the world considered him to be only a dictator. Now, they believe he is god. No one dared try to help us while he was considered mortal; and it's for sure that no one will back us now."

"Can't we make some more weapons?" David got up, stuck his hands in his pockets, and began pacing the living room floor. "It would require a major changeover in our manufacturing plants. With the inspection teams looking over our shoulder, there's no way we could secretly make the switch. The police are armed only with handguns and there are no munitions stores inside Israel. We can't go up against automatic rifles with nothing but short barreled pistols."

"There must be something that we can do," Martha responded, laying aside her needle and thread. She got up, walked over and embraced David. "There's always hope if we all stick together." David squeezed her tightly and kissed her cheek. "I need to talk to Hartstein and the other resistance leaders. Maybe, if we all put our heads together, we can come up with a strategy."

CHAPTER 10

Back From the Dead

Jack Roberts eased himself from under the cover, added some wood to the fire and walked to the spring. There was still nothing but crimson blood rushing by with a thick, sloshing sound. . . just like it had appeared in his dream. At first, he had discounted any meaning to the dream. . . until he remembered the prophecy in Revelation concerning the waters turning to blood.

After some raised eyebrows and strange looks, the others had humored him by filling every available container with water the evening before blood appeared in the spring. He stared at the sluggish stream and thought about their remaining supply of water. They had consumed the water out of the dishes, cups, and coffee pot first; and now three of Paul's four canteens were empty. None of them had been able to bathe or brush their teeth for five full days.

He heard the soft patter of bare feet coming up behind him. It was Paul. "Doesn't look very comforting does it?" he said as Paul stepped up alongside him and gazed at the spring with a disgusted frown. "You smell awful," Paul said, glancing sideways at Jack with a crooked grin. "You don't remind me of fresh flowers either. I've never wanted a bath so much in my entire life . . .but, I'm more concerned with our limited options when the last canteen's empty." Paul leaned his head backward and scratched an itch under his prickly beard. "I can't decide which I wanna do first ... bathe, shave, or brush my teeth. Think it might clear up today?"

"I sure hope so, but that's all it is. . . hope. The prophecy doesn't tell us how long the blood plague will last; only that its purpose is to force those who have shed so much blood to drink it as a symbol of their thirst for killing." Jack looked down at his watch. "It's coming up on 5:00 pm. One more hour will mark the end of the sixth full day." "Is there something significant about the seventh day?" Paul asked, raising his eyebrows with a hopeful expression.

Jack shrugged his shoulders and spread his hands. "Don't hold me to it, but there's always a certain predictability associated with specific numbers given in Biblical prophecy. Six is the number that pertains to mankind. Seven refers to a state of perfection or fulfillment of divine purpose. Forty generally indicates a period of testing or refinement. Seventy is used as a multiplier for the number seven whenever a series of events is involved and a repetitive cycle of years marks off the time intervening between each prophesied event. Twelve and twelve doubled or squared, relates to matters pertaining to faith and divine protection."

Paul stroked his chin with his right hand and nodded that he followed Jack's reasoning. "So, you think the blood might disappear today because the purpose of the plague is associated with the behavior of mankind?" Jack nodded and laid his left hand on Paul's right shoulder. "But, don't take it for granted. There's a big gap between predictability and certainty." Paul shook his head in agreement. "Sure hope the number association holds up. The women are getting more and more anxious. I doubt that any of them has gone this long without a bath since puberty. They smell as raunchy as we do."

The women awakened and busied themselves with breakfast preparations, wearing their robes and tennis shoes to help mask their body odor. Jackie and Marge broiled venison strips while Ruth and Mary poured a half cup of water for each person and arranged the place settings. Paul and Jack, decked out in their hunting attire, sat on flat rocks beyond the fire. Jack was sharpening his hunting knife and Paul was cleaning his pistol.

Paul looked toward the spring, whistled softly to get Jack's attention, turned toward the spring again, and cupped his right ear with his right thumb and forefinger. Jack stopped honing his knife and listened to the sound of the spring. It sounded different. . . . .lighter and swifter. As if on cue, both Paul and Jack jumped up and sprinted to the spring.

The women saw them running and ran behind them with frenzied excitement. When they caught up with Paul and Jack, they began squealing, crying, and hugging each other. "What a beautiful sight!" Paul shouted. "Praise God Almighty!" Sparkling clear water flowed by, and not a trace of blood was visible.

Oren Natas had an angry scowl on his face as he sat upon his throne thinking about the Children of Abraham. Wallace had failed him, and Romas had negotiated a peace pact that was more liberal than the original compromise. Everyone on earth now worshiped him except the defiant

Jews and the remaining Christians still in hiding. He gritted his teeth and cursed all Jews everywhere. Soon, he would go to Jerusalem, sit upon the Throne of David and force the seed of Abraham to worship him. Nothing that he had done impressed the Israelis, and the Jews that were deceived, both in Israel and around the world, despised him. The registered Israelis had taken his mark as part of the compromise provisions and for no other reason.

A foul taste fermented in his mouth and his head began to ache. One-third of the Israelis had not yet registered, much less rendered any homage to him. The rest of Jewry only paid him lip service while looking upon his mark as just a necessary evil to be endured in order to be able to buy and sell. Since the miracle of his resurrection had little impact upon those ignoring him, total extermination of all who refused to worship his image was the only way to establish an undivided kingdom.

His security forces had been inept in their attempts to capture and execute the two witnesses who mocked him and continued to plague his kingdom. That would have to change immediately or else his followers might begin to suspect his divinity. Even the angels in heaven did not ridicule the adversary of God, and he certainly wasn't going to allow humans to abase him.

The Captain of the temple guards approached and bowed down before him. "The reporters are all assembled, Divine Majesty. Do you wish to receive them?" "Have they been fully instructed concerning temple protocol?" "Yes, Divine Majesty." "Very well. You may allow them to enter."

The media correspondents entered the temple in single file with six feet separating each reporter. One by one, they bowed down in front of Natas and then took seats from left to right in the witness gallery. They had been instructed to maintain complete silence except for two questions per correspondent beginning in the order in which they were seated.

Natas sat motionless with his feet flat on the throne platform and his arms resting on the elevated sides of the throne seat. His fingers curled comfortably in front of the arm supports. He wore a jewel-studded royal robe woven from pure, white silk that fell around his kingly sandals made from pure gold and lined with diamonds and rubies. His head was adorned with a crown of gold encrusted with precious gems of all shapes and colors. He looked on passively while the assembly was properly accommodated. The only sounds that violated the complete silence were an occasional cough or sniffle. The first correspondent seated rose in front of her seat, bowed her head to Natas and began the round of questions:

"Divine Majesty, now that you have cleansed our fresh water supplies, can you tell us if we will have to endure more plagues?"

Natas gazed at her with a blank expression. "There are opposing forces within the spiritual realm which struggle for dominance. Humans are positioned only above the animals in the order of living beings and cannot comprehend the nature of the upper hierarchy of life. There will possibly be more plagues while I do battle with the opposing forces on behalf of mankind. Should more evil befall us, it must be endured until such time that I can overcome the enemy."

"Divine Majesty, would you tell us something about your origin and why you have chosen not to reveal yourself unto us until now?" The corners of Natas' mouth crinkled into a wry smile. "The eternal beings who look down upon humans are not concerned with the number of times Earth rotates on its axis or circles the nearest star. Such calculations have meaning only to mortal creatures whose lifespan is fleeting. For eons of time, I have defended my kingdom against those who would usurp my power. I neither hunger nor thirst nor desire the treasures which delight the eyes of humans. I sit at the top of the hierarchy of life and do battle where and when it pleases me. You see me now because this planet has become a divine battleground. Your mortal minds are not capable of grasping my origin, and so I will only speak of those things which are within your understanding."

The matronly anchorwoman bowed to Natas again and sat down. The distinguished gentleman to her right rose and bowed to the throne. "Divine Majesty, would you tell us by what physical process the waters became blood and how this pollution was so suddenly reversed?"

Natas' expression became icy and his eyes appeared to darken. "Humans are filled with unjustified vanity and consider that only those things which they have literally experienced are within the natural order of the universe. Suppose that from the beginning of measured time, great hailstones fell upon the earth, or the waters periodically took on the chemistry of blood, or swarms of mutant locusts emerged from the bowels of the planet. Would you be concerned with the question you have posed? Or, would you merely accept such phenomena as natural events governed by immutable laws of chemistry and physics? You ask me elementary questions that encompass what you perceive as a great mystery only because of your limited life experiences. The history of mankind upon the planet, Earth, is but one heartbeat within the past and future eons of existence. Thus, you have witnessed but a single scene in the unending drama of immortality which is played out beyond the scope of human reasoning. Both water and blood are composed of the elements which spring from eternal energy that behaves in accordance with divine will."

"Divine Majesty, will you tell us the source of the energy which forms itself into the atoms which make up our periodic table of the elements as we attempt to describe such energy?"

Natas looked upon him with condescending tolerance. "The hierarchy of eternal life emanated from the unison of divine wills so that such life preceded the formation of the energy that fills the space perceived by humans as well as regions unknown to mortal beings. Energy radiates from the upper hierarchy of life and forms what you call gases, liquids, and solids as a transitory phase within unmeasured eternity. The chemical composition and temporary appearance of gases, liquids, and solids as interpreted by the mortal senses of seeing, hearing, smelling, tasting and touching are changeable whenever divine will counteracts what you erroneously believe to be unalterable laws of physics, biology, and chemistry. Such laws have been postulated through your inability to recognize anything but your own life experiences and your lower position within the hierarchy of living beings. When divine tolerance allowed you to split the atom, you quickly acknowledged the destructive energy that constitutes what you call matter. Were you able to further divide particles of visible energy, you would find such particles continue to release inherent energy until the pure substance of motion, velocity and momentum are no longer discernible through your mortal senses. Since you cannot perceive the true nature of energy, it is your human vanity that causes you to ponder its origin."

The silver-haired gentleman bowed to Natas and sat down again. To his right, an attractive redhead who rose to celebrity status by using her brain rather than her sex appeal stood and bowed her flaming locks. "Divine Majesty, would you tell us whether human beings perish at death like the lower animals, or do we possess immortal souls?" Natas studied her and wondered if she really cared. "There is a spark of human immortality which survives the death of your physical bodies. You may use whatever word you believe best expresses that eternal state of which you are truly ignorant. You worship me now and you shall forever remain with me in my everlasting habitation. You may come to question the value of your immortality when physical death opens the eyes of your so-called soul. In the meanwhile, you would be well advised to satisfy your carnal desires within the permissiveness of our global law."

"Divine Majesty, are there such eternal habitations as heaven and hell? And if so, what are they like?" Natas' eyes twinkled with amusement. "You have coined the word heaven to describe different concepts such as the planet's atmosphere, the space beyond that atmosphere, the visible sky, the outer regions of space filled with galaxies, the dwelling place of divine beings, and a state of perpetual bliss. I assume that you are not requesting that I comment on all those diverse concepts, so I will answer by assuring you that all of those references to heaven are well founded. Living beings do indeed occupy habitations beyond Earth, and hell describes one of those dwelling places where the eternal state is rebellious rather than blissfully contented."

The next reporter stood and bowed to the throne. "Divine Majesty, is this place we describe as hell a habitation of endless and fiery torment?" Again, Natas indicated his indulgence of human limitations with a tantalizing smile.

"Your comprehension is diluted by the imperfection of your mortal senses. Torment for immortal beings is a state of discontent and separation from fellowship with those enjoying blissful servitude. The smoke and fire of such torment are indeed everlasting." "Divine Majesty, there are millions of people who are hiding out and refusing to join our new world society. They mock your authority and live as parasites off our natural resources. Do you plan to correct this problem?"

Natas' smile faded and his face turned to flint. "It is within the divine nature to be merciful and gracious. Hence, these dissenting vagabonds shall be given a final opportunity to come forth from hiding and voluntarily join my kingdom. Those who continue to rebel must be hunted down and executed. I have ordered Chief Malinsky to make this task his top priority and have further instructed him to assign sixty-six million of his men to a thorough and continuous search throughout zones one and two. I expect that the problem will soon be eliminated."

The next correspondent raised a similar question. "Divine Majesty, will you continue to allow the Jews inside Israel to worship another God? Will you honor the peace pact which Chief Malinsky and Bishop Romas were forced to negotiate because the Israelis refused to otherwise give up their military weapons?"

Natas masked his rage with an expression of benevolence. "Jerusalem must cease to be a burdensome stone and a yoke around the neck of law-abiding citizens. To that end, I will personally go to Israel and bring about global harmony."

"Divine Majesty, how is it that these self-proclaimed prophets, which some call witnesses, seem able to appear at any place of their choosing and yet elude the police?" Natas rose from his throne indicating that the audience was being terminated. "They are protected by the spirit world that opposes my kingdom but is not invincible. They are mere humans that will be sought out and executed. Anyone who harbors them or has knowledge of their location and fails to report that information will share their fate." Natas sat down again upon his throne while the correspondents stood, filed past the throne, bowed to him and headed toward the exit arch.

David Solomon traced the rim of his wine glass with his right index finger while listening with reservation to Aaron Hartstein. The old general was crafty, but sometimes overly cautious. David wanted to act more quickly before Natas launched an organized genocide campaign against the Jews. "If we wait too long, we will box ourselves in even more," he insisted. Hartstein placed his palms flat on his reading table and eased his weary body out of the cushioned leather chair. He circled his library and ended up at the liquor cabinet as David said nothing to permit Hartstein to ponder what had already been said. Such prolonged pauses were customary during their discussions, and David knew that his courtesy was deeply appreciated by his old friend.

Hartstein took another bottle of sherry from the cabinet, refilled their glasses, set the bottle on the table and sat down again while looking at David with squinted eyes and furrowed forehead. "We should do nothing that provides Natas with an excuse to attack us immediately. The world is aware of the peace agreement, and fear of adverse public reaction will hold Natas at bay for a while. Regardless of how the general population feels about the existence of the agreement, they would lose respect for Natas if he unilaterally breaches the peace. We need to formulate contingency strategy without doing anything that violates the provisions of the treaty."

Hartstein rubbed his tattoo again and thought about the fearless band of three hundred Spartans who defended a narrow mountain pass and held back the entire Persian army. "Chokepoints," Hartstein said with resolve. "We need to use natural terrain that limits access to our defensive positions. Since all military weapons have been destroyed, we don't need to fear artillery fire or aerial bombardment. Malinsky will have to move against us using ground forces armed with police rifles. If we hide within natural choke points, it won't matter how many men mill around below. We only have to be concerned with the number of men that have access to our positions at any given point in time. When the attack comes, we will have enough advance notice of troop movements to take up our defensive positions."

"But we still need something to fight with," David interjected. "Bare knuckles won't be much of a match for machine guns. We have to be able to kill each wave of attackers before we can pick up their weapons." "We can stockpile industrial explosives, acids, poison gases, and the like," Hartstein replied. "We still have our gas masks in storage and can make good use of them." "We can hurl dynamite and nitroglycerin down on them with homemade catapults," David suggested. "We can also use pressurized shoulder tanks to release poison gases and to spray acid. In addition, we have a wide variety of industrial chemicals that can be utilized to make crude bombs that can be thrown like grenades after being ignited."

Hartstein beamed with excitement. "When we consider all the industrial liquids, gases and powders that are routinely used by our industries, we can come up with a ready supply of items that are far deadlier than machine guns."

David was thrilled with the overall possibilities, but he knew that organization and discipline would be a major problem. "We need to use poison gas early on in order to get our hands on as many rifles as possible. Sniper fire from the heights is an excellent way to keep a large force pinned down while we hit them with everything else we can come up with. We need to lure a large number of their men into a trap where we can gas them and pick up their weapons. Matter of fact, we need to think about several such traps that could be sprung during the early phases of the attack before they catch on to our strategy. We need a simple, concise plan which every Israeli can follow without any hand-holding. When the alarm is sounded, everyone needs to know exactly where they should go and what they should bring along. We need to map out the details but keep it all under wraps until it becomes obvious to all of our people that Natas intends to murder us. We can use our former guerrilla organization to set the traps and to stockpile a supply of explosives, chemicals, and poison gases."

Hartstein's eyes glistened with resolute determination. "We'll also need a large inventory of canned foods, dried foods, drinking water, and canned formula for the infants plus baby food for the toddlers. We may all die in the end, but we can certainly exact a heavy price for our scalps. The guerillas can lay in the heavy supplies that I'll solicit from industrialists who are trustworthy. We'll all reduce our daily rations and start stockpiling food and water. We'll beef up our production of portable, pressurized containers and store the gases, acids and chemicals inside, and we can begin gathering up the explosives and then converting them into bombs and grenades. I'll also arrange for a supply of lumber, heavy coil springs, mechanical joints, and miscellaneous hardware for building the catapults. We can fabricate some heavy-duty slingshots for hurling sticks of dynamite, bottles of nitro, fist-sized bombs and other devices."

"We need to make up a list of items that are obtainable on short notice, and everyone except infants and toddlers needs a backpack," David added. "Each teenager and adult can shoulder at least fifty pounds and the children should be able to manage from five to thirty pounds depending upon their age. Homemade backpacks would be easy to come by. Clothing and blankets can be rolled into bundles, tied, and carried so that such necessary items don't take up space in the backpacks. Each family should carry as much food and water as possible, their gas masks, and at least five small bombs or grenades per adult. . . devices that can be made from household chemicals and consumer goods that are readily available. The supply list should include instructions on how to fabricate the explosives. That will provide us with several million small bombs and grenades in addition to the inventory stockpiled by the guerillas."

"We can put up one whale of a fight if we select the right places to hide," Hartstein predicted. "We need to study topographical maps and explore every conceivable option for laying the traps and establishing long-term defensive positions. We can certainly fortify Masada and use the ruins of Petra. Our main objective must be to control the heights and draw the enemy into the open terrain below. Since the rifle fire will be .30 caliber, it would help to round up all the bulletproof vests that we can locate, and outfit the men who will be on the forefront of the action. There won't be enough to go around, but every little bit helps."

"I wonder how the ten regional administrators, who have been ruling as kings, will react to Natas at this point," David remarked. "It's possible that they might rebel if Natas attempts to limit their power. Perhaps we could start some nasty rumors to the effect that Natas intends to strip them of the vast power they usurped during his absence. They're strong enough to divert some attention from us if we can somehow stir them up. We've finally deciphered the security code structure established for the control center computers. I'll have our inside contact transmit a series of false orders under Malinsky's code. That should create a little confusion and controversy."

"Excellent!" Hartstein agreed. "Let's get the rest of our key people together and lay out a definitive plan."

The electric powered motorcade left downtown Rome and headed for the airport. The morning sun was pleasant, and the air was refreshing. The atmosphere was virtually free of pollutants since nothing, but a limited number of aircraft could legally utilize conventional fuel. All other pollution was barred under global law, and the deadline for full compliance had expired.

The train of black limos sped along the uncluttered streets as cyclists and pedestrians looked on. A few other vehicles were visible, but rush hour traffic had become a thing of the past. Most people preferred not to make the large initial investment required to own a private, self-propelled vehicle but rather adopted walking, cycling or public transportation as their primary means of getting from one place to another. The majority lived within reasonable walking distance from their employers and were content with the anti-pollution law.

The population within each control center tended to concentrate close to manufacturing and service facilities, and government workers assigned to agricultural tasks lived in government housing provided on the farms where they worked. Electric buses provided shuttle service between all farm locations and urban centers. City neighborhoods were free of trash and slums following the elimination of unemployment, welfare, and the heavy tax burden formerly shouldered by factory and service employees. Once the penalty for tax evasion became immediate execution, the wide disparity between capitalists and their employees narrowed considerably.

The absence of any tax whatsoever at the minimum income level; the sixty-five percent tax on gross business profits; and the eighty percent tax on personal income above the minimum level had resulted in such a radical redistribution of wealth within global society that every citizen was able to enjoy a comfortable standard of living. Crime and all categories of street violence had disappeared completely, and people no longer bothered to lock their doors.

Although food and water were still rationed, everyone had an adequate share. A small percentage of capitalists managed to amass large fortunes even after paying all required taxes, but they maintained a low profile and did not flaunt their wealth. The super-rich deemed it more prudent to invest their assets in additional business ventures than call attention to themselves through a pompous or lavish lifestyle.

The limo carrying Natas was centered in a line of twenty-four security cars preceded by a truckload of men armed with automatic rifles. A similar truckload brought up the rear of the motorcade. Natas sat next to Malinsky behind bulletproof glass casually discussing issues involving Israel. Natas wore his temple attire plus a royal robe draped around his shoulders. Malinsky was dressed in one of his familiar business suits and gave off the fragrance of expensive cologne.

Malinsky was baffled by Natas' obsession concerning all Jews. He sensed that Natas would never be satisfied as long as any Jew was still breathing, but it simply didn't make sense. Why risk losing the respect of people who now worshiped him over a tiny nation that minded its own business and violated no laws?

All the Jews desired was to be left alone, and they had already shown their willingness to fight to the death when threatened. They were abiding by the peace agreement and were entitled to Natas' protection rather than his wrath. He felt a twinge of fear when Natas asked if he had developed a specific strategy for dealing with the Jews.

"My strategy will be shaped by what you wish to accomplish, Divine Majesty. Your ultimate objective is still unclear to me." Natas looked at Malinsky with obvious impatience "The seed of Abraham must be exterminated. None of them can be allowed to survive and propagate." "But why? Divine Majesty. Why is that so important?" "Didn't Bishop Romas answer your question?"

"He said that you're the incarnation of Lucifer, that you're Satan in the flesh; and that you are fighting against God Almighty." Mouthing the words brought a lump into Malinsky's throat. He swallowed hard and tried to remain poised. Something about Natas was terrifying, causing him to tremble on the inside.

The silence in the limo was uncomfortable as Natas' cold gray eyes studied him for what seemed like a lifetime. "Did he also tell you that your soul belongs to me. . . that I chose you because fleeting glory is more important to you than where you spend eternity?" Malinsky struggled to keep his voice from disclosing his fear. "If I possess such a thing as an immortal soul, then I concede the fact that I am more concerned with this present life."

Natas gazed at Malinsky with contempt. "Does it not trouble you that you place so little value on the very prize for which we labor?" "I labor to enforce your law, not to judge the value of what I cannot fathom."

Natas smiled with satisfaction. "That's why you are the right man for the job that must be done. You asked why it is so important to me that the Jews be eliminated. You desire to know not because you care about their fate, but only to satisfy your intellectual curiosity." "I confess that I have neither love nor hate for Jews, but if I understand the objective more clearly, then I can better serve you."

Malinsky's calculated responses pleased Natas and his demeanor became less threatening. "The battle for your soul has ended and you are forever joined to me. It is now worthwhile for you to perceive that the measure of my everlasting victory is human souls. Our mission is to ensure that more souls are joined to us than are redeemed by Christ. Divine battles are not waged for that which humans value, but for positions within the hierarchy of eternal life. I lost when I fought to become the master rather than remain a servant. Now, I battle to rob the victors of that for which God sacrificed even himself. . . the human souls upon which you place so little value."

Malinsky began to feel bolder and his tongue less timid. "Your words are too clever for me. Neither do I understand why killing Jews will accommodate your quest for souls. Isn't martyrdom the very essence of faithful servitude?" Natas cackled with devilish amusement as he considered the depth of Malinsky's ignorance. "Countless millions have willingly endured physical death for delusive principles or misguided faith in spiritual beliefs founded upon their own human vanity. To sacrifice one's mortal life in testimony to a false doctrine merits the reward for suicide rather than martyrdom."

Malinsky wrestled with the unanswered riddle posed by Natas. "But, Divine Majesty, don't the Jews refuse to worship any deity other than Jehovah. . . and if they willingly die rather than worship you, are they not true martyrs?"

A trace of mirth lingered on Natas' lips. "You put words into my mouth that I have not championed. When I sought to exalt my throne above God, I was brutally cast from the habitation of angels and Lucifer became Satan, the adversary of God. Nevertheless, I have become the god of this world, and all Jews will worship me or die. Their extermination will be mass suicide rather than collective martyrdom. Human souls are redeemed by acceptance of the sacrificial body and blood of Christ, not by recognition of Almighty God. A third of the angels never disputed his existence, yet they are imprisoned in the darkness of unmeasured space awaiting the outcome of the battle in which we are now engaged. The

Jews rejected Christ's words and besought the Romans to nail him to his cross. Yet, redemption for Jews through Christ can still be achieved by accepting his sacrifice prior to mortal death. Their stubborn rejection of their own Messiah is the lead goat that will march them to the slaughter."

The great mysteries of life, death and eternity began to unravel in Malinsky's mind. "You desire the death of all Jews in order to reign over their immortal souls?" Natas snarled his reply. "Death opens the eyes of the spiritually blind. The Jews shall inhabit my eternal kingdom along with those whose knowledge of Christ is subservient to enjoyment of their mortal life on Earth."

Malinsky mentally fitted another piece of the puzzle into place. He immediately saw why Natas was willing to be "merciful and gracious" to those refusing to worship him. Law enforcement had never been Natas' underlying motive. . . just a means to an end. He lusted for the souls of those who refused to register and accept his mark. If he executed them for exalting their faith in Christ above the value of their very lives, they would become true martyrs and be rewarded with redemption.

Natas intended to make it extremely difficult to profess Christ while he ruled over humanity. Understanding brought contentment. He was more than willing to serve Natas and to savor his own position of power and authority. A calmness swept over Malinsky and he no longer harbored any fear of Natas. He had already bartered away his soul, so there was nothing to lose. He might as well enjoy his fleeting glory.

The motorcade circled the Boeing 747 which had been isolated on the approach to the departure runway for security reasons. The guards emerged from the security cars, and twelve of them searched the aircraft while the others surrounded Natas' limo. The two truckloads of security troops fanned out and blocked all access routes to the departure apron.

One of the guards inside the plane appeared in the doorway and signaled to the men around Natas' limo. The sentries next to the limo doors formed a protective cluster around Natas and Malinsky as they climbed the passenger stairway and boarded the 747 followed by the rest of the escort assigned as bodyguards. The security troops remained in position on the ground while the mammoth plane taxied down the departure runway and headed for Tel Aviv-Yafo.

Samuel Goldstein shaded his eyes and watched the dot in the distant horizon take on the shape of an incoming jetliner. He turned and motioned to his security troops, and then watched the landing gear descend beneath the 747. He rehearsed his answers to the questions he expected from Lord Natas. The man responsible for all security forces inside Israel should know what was going on. The indigestion that had haunted him all morning backed up into his mouth as the aircraft settled onto the runway amid puffs of black smoke rising from the screeching tires.

His troops snapped to attention as the 747 slowly taxied from the landing runway onto the tarmac where a dozen limos and four trucks had been previously positioned. The front passenger door of the plane opened, and the ground crew locked the stairway into position. Thirty-six of Goldstein's men moved in and stood with rifles ready as the inside guards descended the steps and took up positions alongside the stairway. Then, Natas appeared in the doorway in his full splendor. The bright sunlight reflecting from the jewels embedded in his crown and golden sandals, and the royal purple robe that cascaded from his broad shoulders gave him the appearance of one worthy of worship.

Malinsky followed behind Natas as Goldstein waited next to a gleaming white limo surrounded by twelve guards. Four bodyguards manned the limo doors. "Welcome to Tel Aviv, Divine Majesty." Goldstein bowed humbly as Natas walked by and entered the limo.

Malinsky sat down next to Natas; and Goldstein, along with two bodyguards, climbed into the back seat facing them. Two more bodyguards positioned themselves next to the driver as the door attendants secured the limo.

The motorcade maneuvered into formation as Goldstein's troops mounted the waiting trucks. The passengers and crews inside the terminal buildings looked on in stony silence as the garish procession made its way through the airport grounds and headed for Jerusalem. Malinsky fixed his eyes upon Goldstein. "Has the Knesset building been thoroughly searched and secured?"

“Yes, Sir. Everything has been prepared and I personally screened the royal servants as well as all security personnel." “The spectators at the airport appeared a bit hostile,” Malinsky speculated. "I sensed that we're not overly welcome here. Are you expecting any sort of difficulty?"

Goldstein's palms felt clammy, but he refused to wither under Natas' gaze. "There won't be any uprising," Goldstein assured Malinsky. "The Jews will be less than hospitable, but that's as far as it goes. They'll do nothing to breach the terms of the peace agreement which would trigger an assault by my troops."

Natas voice dripped with contempt. "Your predecessor did not expect any reaction either. Yet, the Jewish rabble killed him and four hundred thousand armed troops in a single day. Are you prepared for such an attack?" The arrogant jackass! Goldstein resented the obvious sarcasm. What did he expect when he violated his written guarantees within a matter of days following Israeli disarmament? "We are mindful of the lessons to be gleaned from the Jewish reaction when negotiated treaties are unilaterally breached by signatories to the documents. They still do not trust us, but the situation is quite different now."

"In what regard?" Malinsky queried. "There are no rifles or munitions stored inside Israel. The police are armed with short barreled pistols and security measures do not permit any Jew to approach within thirty feet of a police officer. The automatic rifles carried by my troops today were brought in from Egypt and will be returned there upon His Divine Majesty's departure from Israel. The guerrilla organization has disbanded and those who masterminded the uprising are under continuous scrutiny. Israeli civilian leaders are managing internal affairs in strict accordance with the treaty which you and Bishop Romas negotiated with Hartstein and Solomon. The people are content with the status quo, so there is no reason for civil unrest unless you intend to breach the current treaty."

"Was there no adverse reaction when the Knesset building was converted into government property?" Malinsky asked with a note of skepticism. "The Knesset was symbolic of Israeli independence, and the people were outraged when the building was confiscated. It did not matter that their parliament no longer exists. It was a slap in the face that they have not forgotten, but most of them have become hardened to the indignity."

Natas became impatient with the dialogue between Malinsky and Goldstein. "Tell me about Solomon's Temple," he interrupted. "Has the restoration been completed?" "Yes, Divine Majesty. The priests are preparing for the re-dedication and to resume the daily oblation. Under the treaty provisions, the Israeli are permitted to worship as they please inside Israel."

"I am aware of those noxious details." Natas spat out the words. "Whom do you worship, Samuel?"

Goldstein was caught by surprise. Was his loyalty being questioned? He had faithfully served Natas, but he worshiped no one. He had been one of the first Jews in Israel to register and accept Natas' mark even though he suspected that Natas was just another gentile dictator, drunk with power and egomania. Since Natas stepped forth from his image after being dead and buried, he often pondered the origin of the creature now sitting across from him.

Did he have the ability to read a man's mind? What if he already knew the answer to the question? Goldstein took pride in his command of area security and dared not cross Natas. He decided that the best tact under the circumstances was complete honesty. "I am your faithful servant, Divine Majesty, and I most certainly do not worship another." The clever answer irritated Natas. "You speak the truth, Samuel, yet you evade the substance of my question. I want to know if you worship me."

"Perhaps I have never learned to worship, Divine Majesty. Wouldn't servitude and undivided loyalty be akin to worship?" "Do you believe that I am divine?" "I have no prior experience with divine beings, so I lack any basis for making a personal judgment. Your claim to divinity is not disputed by me." Natas cackled. "Suppose I told you that you must worship me as god or die. How would you react to that option?" "Compulsory worship would seem to have little value, but I would not trade my life for the dubious value of refusing such a command."

Natas felt compelled to elevate Goldstein to the proper perspective. "Since my mark is already in your forehead, it no longer matters whether you worship me. What matters is that you obey my orders when I put that same question to all Jews around the world. Can you handle that?"

Goldstein gazed at Natas without blinking. "Yes, Divine Majesty. I will obey your orders." "Do you think some Jews will fight to the death rather than worship me, Samuel?" "Yes, Divine Majesty. All of the unregistered Jews will resist to the death."

Malinsky chuckled with disdain. "What will they fight with?" His eyes raked Goldstein with ridicule. He wasn't the gladiator type. . . short, squat, partially bald, sagging chest with a pot belly, pale skin, blue eyes, a hooked nose and flat chin. He was in his mid-forties, married with four teenage children. "Perhaps they still have some hidden weapons?" "I think not," Goldstein replied flatly. "But they will fight anyway. . . with whatever they can find suitable for killing."

Natas glared at Malinsky and Goldstein. "You will tolerate no Jewish resistance whatsoever. Very soon, they will breach the peace, then you may legally exterminate them."

Natas sat in the private office formerly occupied by the Israeli Prime Minister. He looked over computer printouts supplied by Goldstein while four sentries posted outside the office door watched government personnel going about their daily routines. One of the sentries from the main entrance to the building approached and delivered a verbal message to the guards protecting the executive office, then returned to his post. The lead guard tapped on the door post. "Pardon me, Divine Majesty."

Natas stopped reading and looked up. "There's a small delegation of priests and rabbis at the main doors requesting an audience." "Perhaps they bring good tidings." Natas feigned a smile. "Make sure they are thoroughly searched and send them in." "Yes, Divine Majesty."

The guard returned along with two sentries from the main entrance escorting three priests and three rabbis dressed in their ceremonial garb. The delegation bowed silently before Natas and the sentries withdrew. "The audience is granted," Natas said curtly. "What is your purpose?"

The spokesman for the priests was a wizened old man with a gray beard and splotched skin. "Welcome to Jerusalem, Divine Majesty. I trust you have found the accommodations adequate."

"They will suffice for now . . . until something more suitable can be arranged," Natas replied smartly. "Why have you come?" "To make sure that there are no inadvertent misunderstandings concerning the intention of all Israelis to abide by your law, Divine Majesty . . . and to adhere to the terms of the peace treaty." The old man selected his words with care, speaking slowly and meticulously. Again, Natas forced a smile. "Why should I expect otherwise?"

"It is our desire to rededicate Solomon's temple tomorrow and to offer the daily oblation to Jehovah in accordance with our orthodox rituals. We wish to make it clear that such activity is not conducted with any disrespect to you, Divine Majesty, but rather as part of our ancient tradition and religious freedom which you have so graciously permitted."

"You speak about negotiations in which I was not involved," Natas replied tartly. "Your concerns would be more properly directed to Bishop Romas and Chief Malinsky." The eldest of the three rabbis spoke up. "But, Divine Majesty, surely your high priest and chief of security spoke with your authority during your absence. . . when you made your will known to Bishop Romas through divine revelation."

The smile disappeared from Natas' lips and his gaze became contemptuous. "The future is not forever bound by an agreement to resolve transient problems. The letter and spirit of such writings are subject to interpretation and renegotiation." "Surely divine will is not transient," the rabbi countered. "We find ourselves bound through a revelation of eternal purpose and not by human ambiguity."

Natas searched for a loophole in what he knew was a valid defense. "When divine will is disclosed by revelation, it is not uncommon for the recipient thereof to deliver an erroneous interpretation of the vision. Do not your own scholars debate the true meaning of your ancient law and prophetic writings? Do you take the position that gentiles are more perfect in their interpretations of such visions than Jews? How is it that you acknowledge error among yourselves, yet demand perfection of others? Is it not because you seek to gratify yourselves without regard to global peace and harmony?"

The rabbi was not cowed by Natas' icy response. "Do you wish to clear up possible misunderstandings drafted into the treaty, Divine Majesty?" Natas' tact became somewhat more subtle. "Tell me, Rabbi, is divinity a status enjoyed by any living being other than God?" "We do not believe so, Divine Majesty." "Is there more than one true God?" "We believe that there is but one God, Divine Majesty." "And such is the deity whom you call Jehovah?"

Too late, the rabbi saw the trap laid by Natas. "Yes, Divine Majesty." Natas grinned slyly. "Do you believe that I am Jehovah?" "We believe that Jehovah is Almighty God." "You come before me speaking from both sides of your mouths," Natas replied venomously. "You do not honor me as god, yet you refer to me as Divine Majesty. Then, you seek to bind me by the terms of a treaty which you claim to be immutable because it was inspired by divine revelation while claiming that only Jehovah is divine. By your own admissions, the treaty cannot be viewed by the parties thereto as divinely inspired because you do not believe that it issued from Jehovah. Therefore, it would seem that the agreement is subject to diverse interpretation by both sides and consequently open for renegotiation."

The old priest took up the cudgel. "We refer to your assumed title in order not to offend, Divine Majesty. You claim divinity and it is not our place to dispute that assumption. That matter rests between you and Jehovah. Your high priest has proclaimed that the treaty represents your will as revealed to him. Thus, you bind yourself by divine inspiration, and we have chosen not to dispute your high priest, but rather to accept his authority for the terms of the agreement. Thus, we speak not with a forked tongue, but with the voice of obedience to that which we have determined not to resist. We seek only to exercise those rights which the treaty confers upon us. If we have misconstrued the intent therein, then we stand ready to hear the true intent of the document."

Natas' expression changed to condescension. "I will make it known to you when such a clarification is appropriate. You may indulge yourselves in the meanwhile with the nonsense of your traditional ceremonies." "You are most gracious, Divine Majesty," the old priest replied with a subservient tone. The delegation bowed to Natas and filed out of the office.

"Chief Malinsky is waiting, Divine Majesty." "Send him in," Natas growled. Malinsky strode to the doorway and waited to be recognized. "Come in and have a seat," Natas commanded.

Malinsky sat down in a guest chair to the right of the well-worn executive desk, looking expectantly at Natas. "How many security troops can you move into Israel by tomorrow morning?" Natas inquired. "Half a million or so from Egypt, Syria, Lebanon, Jordan, and Saudi Arabia. That number would utilize all our transportation vehicles within a five-hundred-mile radius and allow twelve hours of travel time before dawn if the order was transmitted now." Natas gave him a deadpan look. "If you had three days, how many troops could you mass along Israel's borders?" Malinsky verbalized his mental calculations. "There are two hundred and ninety control centers in Africa, Iran, Iraq, Jordan, Saudi Arabia, Syria, and Lebanon within three days motorized travel time consistent with the transportation equipment available within the Middle East. We can pull four thousand troops from each center for a total of one million, one hundred and sixty thousand." "How many of them can be armed with machine guns?"

Malinsky raised his eyebrows and shrugged nonchalantly. "All of them can be equipped with .30 caliber automatic rifles." "I'll give you the three days," Natas snapped. "Give the necessary orders. I want your troops poised on the borders by nightfall three days from today. That will give you several extra hours to get organized. During the night hours after the borders are surrounded, move a forward force of three hundred thousand troops up and encircle Jerusalem." "It will be done, Divine Majesty."

The dawn air was wet from the misty October breeze that drifted over the eastern shore of the Mediterranean Sea. The air was cool in Jerusalem as the city began to stir. Bicycle traffic flowed casually along the streets as Jews and Arabs went about their normal Wednesday morning activities. A few electric powered automobiles mingled with the cyclists and small crowds waited at scheduled stops for the electric buses that provided public transportation.

The two witnesses walked leisurely along the pedestrian path leading to Solomon's Temple followed by curiosity seekers and a gathering of devout Jews who had risen early to attend to final details prior to the re-dedication ceremony. The witnesses were conspicuous by virtue of their sackcloth and sandals. The crowd burgeoned as word was passed along the streets that the witnesses were headed for Solomon's Temple.

The witnesses stopped twenty yards from the temple site and faced the crowd. The people milled around and waited to see what would happen. Angry shouts to the rear of the onlookers caused frantic jostling as a thirty-foot pathway was opened up for the thirty-six police officers who were rushing in to kill the witnesses.

None of the officers seemed able to raise a weapon as they pulled up and stumbled around a few yards from their intended victims. Another covey of police was approaching from the rear. The two witnesses calmly blew their breath toward the nearby officers and they burst into sizzling flames. A murmur of astonishment went up from the crowd as they watched the burning men stagger about helplessly and collapse, screaming in terror and agony. The police reinforcements turned tail and ran for their lives. The two witnesses turned away from the fiery corpses and looked toward the temple. They stretched their arms outward and the witness on the right cried out mightily:

"Violence is risen up into a rod of wickedness to destroy the impudent children of a hard-hearted people. None of them shall remain. Neither shall there be wailing for the slain. The sword is without and pestilence and famine within. They that escape shall be on the mountains mourning everyone for his iniquity. Horror shall be upon them and shame shall cover their faces. Wherefore, the Lord brings the worst of the heathen to cause the pomp of the strong to cease, and their holy places shall be defiled. Mischief shall come upon mischief, and rumor shall be upon rumor. Destruction is upon a rebellious people, and they seek peace, and there shall be none."

As the prophecy was spoken, a great wind scattered thick, dark clouds overhead, blotting out the sun. As the rumble of thunder sounded across the firmament, the witness on the left side spoke out:

"Come, my people, enter into your secret chambers and shut the doors. Hide yourselves as it were for a moment until the indignation be overpast. For behold, the Lord arises out of his place to punish the inhabitants of the earth for their iniquity. Even now, the hand of Almighty God is upon the sun, and the earth shall be scorched with a great heat. Look not upon the sun as it draws near unto the earth to execute the Lord's judgment." The media crews who had accompanied the crowd ran for cover as sheets of hail pounded the earth. Continuous flashes of lightning illuminated the spot where the witnesses had stood, but they were no longer there.

Chapter 11

Total Darkness and Blood to Drink

Oren Natas seethed with rage while Samuel Goldstein offered excuses for the failure of his men to eliminate the two witnesses. Perspiration dripped from Goldstein's armpits and his brow glistened with the moisture of his discomfort. "But we were not dilatory, Divine Majesty! My men closed in on them the moment they showed up. Three dozen troops surrounded them but were unable to fire their weapons. The witnesses cast some sort of spell on them and then burned them alive!" "Where did the fire come from?"

"No one could tell me, Divine Majesty. Some of the spectators said that the witnesses just blew their breath toward my men and they suddenly burst into flames." Natas grunted with disgust. "Do you believe that's what really happened? Did you conduct a subsequent investigation?"

"Yes, Divine Majesty. As soon as the hail ended, I personally went to the scene and saw the charred bodies of all thirty-six men. There is no doubt that they were burned alive, and I also spoke with a reporter who was there when it happened. He made a videotape of everything he saw, and the tape should be available within the next hour." Natas' gaze remained cold and penetrating. "Didn't anyone see where they came from . . . or try to follow them as they left the temple?"

"No one recalled seeing them before they were spotted near Solomon's Temple. Then, during the lightning and hail, they disappeared and haven't been seen since." “This fire trick of theirs must be some sort of sorcery or black magic,” Natas concluded. "Now that we have seen the extent of their defenses, we must devise an attack plan that can overcome their disappearing act and their ability to breathe out fire.”

"Can you give me some guidance, Divine Majesty?" "We know that they are mere men and can be killed,” Natas replied. "We also know that they will show up again somewhere. Once they appear, their babbling usually goes on for several minutes before they disappear again. We must be fully prepared regardless of where they pop up next. We could lay a trap by spotting men equipped with high-powered rifles and scopes throughout each control center. The snipers should be positioned at elevations overlooking city streets."

"We might get lucky," Goldstein agreed. "The odds are with us that they'll show up in the Middle East again since all the holy places recognized by both Jews and Christians are in and around Israel. I'll assign a thousand men from each of my control centers to the task." Natas' anger was somewhat soothed. "I'll brief Chief Malinsky and have him execute the same plan in all other control centers. We can't cover every street without robbing other projects of necessary manpower. But we can cover those locations where crowds are most likely to gather."

Aaron Hartstein sat across from David Solomon. "Are you sure this isn't just a ploy to trick us into breaching the peace?" David Solomon rubbed his chin thoughtfully with his right hand. "I don't think so. The orders were definitely transmitted to every control center under Malinsky's security code."

"It could still be a trick if they've discovered your inside contact." "I'll concede that remote possibility, but my man has never even been questioned. . . which leads me to believe that he's not under suspicion."

Hartstein stared at David and rubbed his hands together with resolve. "Natas doesn't miss a trick. Three days from the time the order was given means that the forward troops will advance toward Jerusalem Friday night, and the general slaughter will commence shortly after dawn on Saturday morning. He knows that the unregistered Jews will be occupied with observing the Sabbath from Friday evening until Saturday evening. The troop movements are less likely to be discovered after midnight on Friday and he figures his forces will catch us unprepared during solemn worship early Saturday morning."

"That's the way it looks," David agreed. "Eight hundred and sixty thousand troops armed with automatic rifles will encircle our borders by midnight on Friday, and Natas won't officially have breached the treaty until the three hundred thousand cross our borders and head for Jerusalem. Once the killing starts in Jerusalem, the troops massed along the borders will begin to move in, blocking all escape routes while machine-gunning our people as they're pushed into the center of a tight noose that keeps constantly shrinking."

"He makes Hitler look like a novice," Hartstein said. "Do you have a theory as to why he is sending an advance force into Jerusalem?" "He wants to cut off the head first," David surmised. "He knows that the brains behind our defense strategy is centered in Jerusalem." Hartstein gave David an affirmative nod. "Which way do you think the forward troops will be routed to Jerusalem?"

"They will most probably cross over from Jordan into the Rift Valley just south of the Dead Sea, then travel north along the Dead Sea to the northern end where they can approach Jerusalem from the east, north of Bethlehem and Judea through the Judean Hills. Of course, another possibility would be to ferry across the Jordan River from Amman and cut straight across the Judean Hills to Jerusalem. All other routes would significantly increase travel time and make it more difficult to avoid discovery."

"We'd better assume that both routes might be used," Hartstein cautioned. "Yes, I agree. We also need to pass a warning to Jews outside Israel. Malinsky has instructed control center supervisors to pull up a computer list of all Jews including addresses and places of employment. Within each center, the list will be broken down and individual Jews will be assigned to each member of the local security forces. When the slaughter begins inside Israel, the local troops within each center will begin executing the Jews outside Israel. Natas intends to kill every Jew."

"We don't have much time, Hartstein responded. "Have you come up with some strategy?" "Our first concern must be for the unregistered Israelis. We need to pass the word through our guerrilla network and flee to our defensive positions during the night hours on Thursday. Friday morning, we can leak Natas' genocide plans to the media. That should give all other Jews some advance warning. We can't trust the registered Jews with anything but a general warning until our guerrillas and their families have reached the mountains. I'll pack my cellular phone, so we can call the TV networks."

Hartstein got up and pulled a stack of maps from a library shelf. "By Friday morning, the troop movements will be well underway and the media can easily verify the information we phone in, so the story should break about mid-morning. By that time, we should be ready to fight." He opened the maps and spread them out before David.

"All of our people with motorized transportation will head for the Sinai Highlands by way of Elat. Everyone south of Beersheba will flee to the high ground overlooking the Ha-Arava Depression. Between

Beersheba and Ramla, the assembly areas will be in the highlands around Hebron and Bethlehem. "Between Ramla and Umm el Fahm, the defensive positions will be in the highlands overlooking the northern end of the Dead Sea and the Jordan River. North of Umm el Fahm, we will take up positions in the mountains around Galilee and on the Golan Heights. All the choke points are outlined in green and the areas where gas traps have been laid are marked in red. We have hidden hundreds of tons of poison gases, industrial explosives, deadly chemical powders, and homemade grenades throughout the highlands. The location of major inventories is penciled in orange. Our guerrilla command centers will be in the ruins of Petra and at Masada. We have over forty thousand guerrillas assigned to the routes leading to our strongholds from the Coastal Plains, the Judeo-Galilean areas, the Rift Valley, the Negev-Sinai Desert, and the Sinai Peninsula. These advance scouts know our general defensive strategies and where all supplies are stored. The greatest distance that anyone except our command group should have to travel is less than sixty miles. If we begin the evacuation at dusk on Thursday, everyone should reach the designated positions early Friday morning. We can justifiably proclaim that the ox is in the ditch, so everyone understands that traveling and fighting during the Sabbath hours are absolutely necessary. All of the food and water will be in place by Thursday evening."

"How many guerillas will be positioned along the anticipated invasion routes from Jordan to Jerusalem," David asked. "We had no shortage of volunteers," Hartstein answered. "We'll have over a hundred thousand men hidden in the highlands on the western side of the Dead Sea between the Ha-Arava Depression and the mountains east of Hebron. There will be another seventy thousand in the Judean Hills between the west bank of the Jordan River and Jerusalem. They'll have gas masks, bulletproof vests, grenades, heavy slings, catapults, and a goodly supply of poison gases in pressurized sprayers. They will also have dynamite, nitro, acids, and deadly chemicals. Every guerrilla will be committed to killing at least two of Malinsky's troops and salvaging their rifles and ammo."

"Every Israeli between the age of twelve and seventeen should be given a specific objective," David added. "Kill at least one of the invaders and then strip the body of arms and ammunition." "We'll pass that word along the escape routes," Hartstein promised. He looked at his watch. "Every minute is precious. Let's get organized."

The Thursday morning sun became visible in a cloudless sky. It appeared huge and unusually bright against the pale blue background of the firmament as Earth rotated eastward on its axis, turning darkness into light and light into darkness. The western hemisphere turned through the comfort of night as the eastern hemisphere caught the full brunt of the shift in the sun's position relative to the planet.

The enormous solar disk superheated the earth's surface, and noon temperatures exceeded one hundred- and forty-six-degrees Fahrenheit. The air itself became suffocating and skin exposed to direct sunlight burned within a matter of minutes. The massive output of radioactive solar energy triggered nausea, vomiting, fainting and heat strokes.

People fled indoors to escape the searing heat, but air conditioners labored futilely to cool their intake of blistering air. By mid-afternoon, a great panic seized the people within the eastern hemisphere; and the western hemisphere woke up to dire predictions being broadcast around the world by the TV networks. As the solar day wore on, anguished wails and angry cries echoed around the globe. Hospitals and morgues overflowed as the human race tried to hide from the relentless sun. . . screaming, crying, cursing and blaspheming.

Oren Natas sweltered as he sat in the confiscated office inside the Knesset building watching the TV coverage of the solar phenomenon. The newscaster's face streamed with perspiration and his clothes were wringing wet although an electric fan oscillated on each corner of his broadcasting desk.

The air conditioning system within the Knesset building hummed steadily at maximum speed, but several government workers inside the building had died from heat stroke and dozens more had fainted and were awaiting ambulance service. All emergency vehicles had been tied up since late morning transporting the sick and dying. Natas clicked the remote control to shut off the television as a door sentry rapped softly on the door post.

"There's some news correspondents requesting to see you, Divine Majesty." Natas looked at him blankly and shrugged his shoulders. "Frisk them and send them in." The sentry nodded and headed back toward the main entrance. Natas adjusted his crown and pulled the royal silk loose from his perspiring body, then wiped his face with a dry handkerchief.

The sentry returned with a woman and two men carrying notepads and wearing press badges. All three of them looked like they had just stepped out of a sauna as they bowed before Natas and the sentry returned to his post. "You may sit down," Natas said. "But, please be brief."

The two men sat down in guest chairs and the woman sank into the executive couch. Her hair was wet and stringy, and her cotton dress clung to her wet skin. The men's slacks and dress shirts looked like they had been sprayed with a water hose. The woman spoke up first. "I'm Nancy Flack, Divine Majesty, with International Cable News. Thank you for giving us an audience." Natas acknowledged her gratitude with a slight nod. Ms. Flack continued: "Can you tell us what's behind this terrible heat ... and how long it will last?"

Natas maintained his cordial expression. "As the astronomers correctly pointed out, a gravitational wave has created a disturbance within the solar system and temporarily pulled the sun closer to Earth. Such celestial events occur every two hundred million years or so. The culprit is most likely a large wandering planet with a heavy coating of interstellar ice so that its total diameter is much larger than the sun; and it is passing by close enough for the gravitational wave produced to affect the sun's motion, but perhaps a light year or so from Earth. Thus, the mass is not currently visible from this planet. As the invader moves on into outer space, the temporary gravitational bulge will be eliminated. How soon the bulge disappears depends upon the speed of the foreign mass. Therefore, the heat will last until the receding invader loses its gravitational influence."

Ms. Flack looked back at Natas through slitted eyes. "Then, you're saying that the two witnesses had nothing to do with this celestial event?" Natas grinned. "They apparently practice a little sorcery, but their magic falls a mite short of creating disturbances within the solar system."

"Isn't it true, Divine Majesty, that the witnesses accurately predicted that the sun would be drawn nearer to Earth?" "They do have some ESP capability," Natas answered. "But so do a lot of other human beings."

Ms. Flack wiped away the perspiration dripping from the end of her nose with her handkerchief. "But, Divine Majesty, it wasn't ESP that cremated the three dozen police officers. They also have the uncanny ability to disappear at their whim. Where does such power come from?"

Natas wiped his face again and forced a smile. "They are succored by the spiritual forces that war against me, but their power is limited. Apprehending them is a top police priority, so they will be caught and executed."

"Supervisor Goldstein says that a new strategy for dealing with them has been implemented. Can you tell us about that?" "Discussing such strategy with the media is not appropriate. We'd like those two to remain ignorant of our specific plans, which is not likely if you broadcast the details."

The two men appeared to be in their early forties; one was a Negro and the other of Oriental descent. They exchanged polite glances, and the Negro asked the next question: "I'm Nathan Washington, with the African Television Network. How long will you be staying in Jerusalem, Divine Majesty?" "Until the terms of the peace agreement have been clarified," Natas answered. "I discussed possible misunderstandings with priests and rabbis yesterday. We will continue our discussions and perhaps renegotiate certain provisions that are somewhat ambiguous. When such matters have been cleared up, my purpose in visiting Jerusalem will be accomplished."

"With respect to the provisions under scrutiny, Divine Majesty, does the controversy involve guarantees of religious freedom for the Israelis?" Natas wiped away beads of perspiration that had been dangling from his nose and chin. The reporters took the opportunity to wipe their faces and hands. Natas lowered his handkerchief and answered. "The issues under discussion affect world peace and spiritual unity which must be maintained in order for our global society to survive. Therefore, the manner in which the Israelis interact with the rest of the world is a proper subject for examination."

A puzzled look crossed the black man's face. "Isn't it a bit unusual, Divine Majesty, to reopen the terms of a treaty that disarmed a formerly independent nation during a time when that nation's military superiority was unchallenged?"

Natas attempted to sidestep the substance of the question. "Nothing is unusual in the interest of ensuring world peace." The answer had the ring of an overused platitude. "What can you offer the Israelis considering that they do not recognize your divinity, Divine Majesty? Obviously, they cannot rely upon guarantees that are so easily manipulated."

Natas fought off the urge to choke the insolent Negro. "It is not a matter that can be resolved by swapping concessions. The Israelis must not view the future as written in granite. New challenges are constantly evolving, and the problems associated therewith must be addressed at the appropriate time." Nathan Washington had made his point. The third reporter stopped scribbling on his pad and looked up at Natas.

"Chu Hsi Wong, with the Asian Syndicated Press, Divine Majesty. We hear complaints that the ten regional administrators have become virtual dictators within their respective territories. Now that you have returned, do you plan to limit their powers to necessary administrative functions?"

Natas hid his resentment toward such meddling with a courteous smile. "My appointees have all performed well under very difficult conditions. During my absence, it was necessary for them to assume those powers needed to maintain global law and order. I have not heard any complaints that they have abused that privilege. They will continue to report to me and coordinate regional matters with Chief Malinsky and Bishop Romas."

Natas' attempt to foreclose further questioning on that very delicate political issue fell upon deaf ears. Chu Hsi Wong happened to be the brother-in-law of Wang Souleng, one of the three regional administrators ruling in Asia.

"There are persistent rumors of a possible conspiracy among the regional administrators to retain their broad powers, and perhaps even usurp greater powers. In a showdown between you, Divine Majesty, and a coalition formed among your most powerful appointees, would Chief Malinsky be able to command the undivided loyalty of global security forces?"

The question further infuriated Natas. He had more important things on his mind. . . .killing the witnesses and exterminating the seed of Abraham. "Such rumors are fabricated by those who desire to sow discord within my kingdom. The security forces are dedicated to maintaining law and order, and they have never been disposed to participate in any activity that would produce a contrary result."

Chu Hsi Wong jotted down some notes and then raised another sticky subject. "You stated, Divine Majesty, that those still hiding out can voluntarily surrender and avoid execution. How long will you extend this stay of execution in exchange for willing servitude?" "Until such time that patience and mercy no longer serve any useful purpose. Now, if you'll excuse me, I have other matters to attend to."

The three reporters got up, bowed before Natas, and were escorted back to the main entrance. Natas motioned to the door sentry as he returned to his post. "Yes, Divine Majesty?" "Send someone to find Supervisor Goldstein and tell him to report to me immediately."

The Solomon family reached Hebron shortly before midnight. The temperature had fallen to one hundred and eight, Fahrenheit and all roads heading south were packed with fleeing Israelis. Most of them rode bicycles, but thousands traveled by foot, carrying backpacks and bedrolls. The electric automobiles passing by were jammed to capacity. The Solomons stopped along the roadside to rest for a few minutes.

Martha passed out fresh fruit while David gazed at the human tide flowing toward Ha-Arava and the Sinai Highlands. Mothers with infants either carried them in their arms, in chest slings or in small bassinets strapped to their bicycle handlebars.

Toddlers unable to keep up were carried by their fathers or other men traveling alongside the mothers. "Pray that your flight be not in winter, neither on the Sabbath day," David mumbled. "I'm sorry, I didn't understand you," Martha said. "I was remembering what Jesus said when he looked into the future and saw this day." Reuben stopped munching on his apple. "What did he say, Papa?"

David peeled an orange and looked sadly at his wife and sons. "When Jesus was teaching his disciples, he prophesied about our flight from Natas. He said we would only have time to run, and that it would be better for the mothers if their children had never been born. . . and that we should pray that we didn't have to flee in winter or on the Sabbath."

"How long will it take us to get to Petra?" Benjamin asked. "It's about ninety miles from here," David replied. "We should get there about this time tomorrow." "Why are we going to Petra, Papa?" Reuben inquired. "That's where General Hartstein will be," David said. "Petra is one of our guerrilla headquarters." He finished his orange and spat out the seeds. "We'd better keep moving. We've got a long way to go."

The small butane powered plane operated by International Cable News circled over the southern shores of the Dead Sea and headed northwest. The air temperature was a pleasant ninety-three degrees Fahrenheit on a bright Saturday morning as wispy white clouds drifted across the Rift Valley. The solar disk appeared friendly and normal for late October.

The pilot focused his high-powered binoculars on the terrain below and spoke into the microphone attached to the headset strapped over his gas mask. The slim steel shaft containing the microphone had been inserted through a special aperture in the side of his gas mask, and the surrounding space sealed with liquid plastic that hardened into an airtight patch.

"You were right, Nancy. All of the Israelis that I can see are wearing gas masks. The troop columns have been scattered by the poison gas, and it looks like tens of thousands have been killed. The guerillas are stripping the bodies of rifles and ammunition. Troops attempting to cross the Jordan are being bombarded with explosives launched from catapults. Throughout the highlands, I can see guerillas, including women and children, hurling what looks like some sort of grenades and dynamite at the troops below. They're also dumping some kind of chemicals into the lower elevations. Thousands of guerillas are spraying something into the air from metal tanks strapped onto their shoulders. It looks like the Israelis are massacring Malinsky's special forces."

"Good for them! Apparently, Thursday's sun screwed up the genocide time schedule. The forward troops were trying to reach Jerusalem before dawn. How many troops would you estimate are inside Israeli borders?" The pilot maneuvered his plane into a sweeping turn over the Judean Hills. "Hard to say, but my guess is around a quarter million." "How many do you estimate are massed along the borders?" "Between seven and eight hundred thousand." "How about the Israeli defenders. Can you estimate their present strength?" "It looks like at least a third of Israel's population is scattered over the highlands from the Sinai mountains to the Golan Heights. It's the craziest thing I've ever seen. Civilian men, women and children slaughtering professional troops armed with automatic rifles. Wonder where they got all that stuff they're using against the troops?"

"Probably from Israeli manufacturing plants. My heart goes out to them. I hope they kill all the invaders." "Well, it's for sure they're going to kill a bunch of 'em." "Keep up the good work, Mehier. I'm going back on the air and update the story." "Okay, Nancy. I'll get back to you in thirty minutes."

People around the world watching the International Cable News channel saw their TV screens blank out and then brighten again as a printed message ticked off from left to right: SPECIAL REPORT. . . SPECIAL REPORT. . . SPECIAL REPORT. . . JERUSALEM.

The printed announcement faded, and Nancy Flack appeared on the screen. The morning wind whipped her long black hair around her face and curled around the portable microphone she held to her mouth with her left hand as she pointed to Solomon's Temple with her right forefinger.

"Last Wednesday morning, the two witnesses appeared here outside the temple and predicted that the sun would scorch the earth and that the Israelis would be attacked. Well. . . Thursday's sun should still be fresh in our minds, and this morning the Israelis are under attack. This is now the second time that Lord Natas has unilaterally breached peace agreements with Israel while the Israeli people have been minding their own business and peacefully abiding by the spirit and letter of the peace pacts which twice disarmed the most powerful military force on Earth. Following the nuclear war, Israel possessed the world's largest and most destructive nuclear arsenal. They gave up that superiority in exchange for Lord Natas' guarantees of peaceful coexistence."

Nancy brushed hair away from her mouth and switched the microphone to her right hand. "Shortly thereafter, Lord Natas' appointees breached the peace agreement and the Israelis killed approximately four hundred thousand security troops inside their borders. They used kitchen knives, screwdrivers, ice picks and other tools to kill the enemy and salvage several hundred thousand automatic rifles. They also began manufacturing nuclear weapons and other arms. In a matter of weeks, once again the tiny nation became the world's most potent military force. Bishop Romas and Chief Malinsky negotiated another peace treaty with Israel wherein the Israelis were given similar guarantees which included freedom to conduct their own affairs within their borders and freedom of religion."

Nancy's camera operator panned around the temple site as she continued: "Early Friday morning, International Cable News received a telephone call from David Solomon, one of the guerrilla leaders who negotiated with Bishop Romas and Chief Malinsky. Mr. Solomon did not reveal his location but told us that Malinsky was massing troops along Israeli borders and had ordered three hundred thousand men armed with automatic rifles to move forward and surround Jerusalem by dawn today. We sent up our plane and our pilot reported a mass movement of troops toward Israel from Egypt, Syria, Iran, Iraq, Saudi Arabia, Jordan, Lebanon, and other Middle East population centers that surround Israel. As I speak, over a quarter million of Malinsky's troops are attempting to surround Jerusalem, and another seven to eight hundred thousand are massed along Israeli borders. The unbearable sun on Thursday apparently slowed down the surprise attack. After we verified the troop movements on Friday morning, we broadcast a warning at 10:38am that a genocide campaign was being launched against Jews and strongly advised all those listening to our broadcast to take heed."

The camera operator switched to a closeup of Nancy. "Well. . . it looks like the Jews inside Israel are not going to peacefully submit to mass murder. The Israeli guerillas and their families have fled to the rugged highlands and are attacking the invading troops using supplies obtained from Israeli manufacturing plants. They are killing the invading troops with poison gases, deadly chemicals, acids, industrial explosives, and homemade grenades. They're wearing gas masks and stripping automatic rifles and ammunition from the fallen troops. We cannot presently give you an accurate death toll on either side, but it appears that Malinsky's troops are being slaughtered. Jews outside Israel are not faring so well.

Local police are murdering our Jewish citizens around the globe. We have reports that local police have computer lists of all Jewish citizens within their control center and are methodically killing them on the streets, in their places of business and in their homes. The helpless victims are trying to defend themselves but very few have managed to escape. I'll have an update report for you within the hour. This is Nancy Flack, speaking for International Cable news . . . .on location in Jerusalem."

A gusty wind out of the northwest whipped across the southeastern Mediterranean Sea and carried the poison gases being released by the Israeli defenders across western Syria south of Damascus, throughout Jordan, and into north-central Saudi Arabia. The horizontal force of the wind kept the deadly gases from rising into the atmosphere over a distance of seventy miles east of the Jordan River and the Gulf of Aqaba. The Arab populations in Syria, Jordan, and Saudi Arabia had acquired gas masks when Saddam Hussein threatened to gas the Israelis. Consequently, the civilian death toll was less than one hundred thousand; and most of them were killed before the Arabs realized what was happening.

The invading troops were less fortunate. Since Malinsky's men assumed, they were being dispatched to a turkey shoot, gas masks weren't included in their standard equipment. The invaders ferrying across the Jordan and massed along Israel's northern and eastern borders were decimated by the gas attack. Israel's Coastal Plains between the Gaza Strip and the southern border of Lebanon, being bounded by the Mediterranean Sea, had not yet been invaded.

Malinsky had planned to send a hundred thousand troops from Egypt across the northern Negev-Sinai Desert, up the Gaza Strip, and into Israel's northwestern coastal plains. When the fighting began, those troops were concentrated along the Gaza Strip. Another two hundred and sixty thousand were distributed along Israel's southwestern border between the Gaza Strip and the northern end of the Gulf of Aqaba.

An additional seventy thousand formed a line across the Sinai Peninsula north of the mountains and south of Elat. The remainder of Malinsky's forces were strung out along Israel's eastern border from the Syrian side of the Golan Heights to the northeastern tip of the Gulf of Aqaba. The seven hundred and thirty thousand attempting to encircle Jerusalem and to seal off Israel's northern and eastern borders were massacred by the Israeli defenders.

The four hundred and thirty thousand troops poised on Israel's southwestern border crossed over and began moving north and east. The Israelis dug into the highlands hurled bottles of nitroglycerin, lighted sticks of dynamite, and an endless barrage of lighted grenades down on the troop columns stricken by the thick layer of poison gases.

The troops attempting to ascend the heights were doused from above with acids, deadly pesticides and a variety of other poisonous chemicals. Tons of explosives and homemade bombs came whizzing down from the heights, launched by catapults and heavy-duty slingshots.

By eleven o'clock in the morning, the battle for the highlands was over. The corpses of more than six hundred thousand troops were scattered below the guerrilla positions. The defenders had salvaged more than a half million automatic rifles and more than fifty million rounds of ammunition. . . an average of one hundred rounds per rifle captured. The surviving troops fled into Jordan, Syria, and Saudi Arabia.

Although the guerillas maintained control of the highlands, the four hundred and thirty thousand troops that crossed Israel's southwestern border continued to push north and east, methodically slaughtering every Israeli within rifle range. . . men, women and children. Over two million registered Jews with Natas' mark were scattered throughout Israel. They considered themselves to be Natas' subjects and entitled to his protection. Now, they ran for their lives with whatever food and water they could snatch up as the troops steadily moved forward.

Over sixty thousand Jews remained in Jerusalem although the continuous rattle of gunfire could be heard north, south, and west of the city. Those who refused to flee prayed for Messianic deliverance and stood their ground, believing that a last-minute miracle would save them. The temple priests carried out the temple re-dedication ceremony on schedule and were offering up the ritual sacrifices according to the law of Moses. Several hundred Jews were gathered before the temple engaging in solemn worship as the smoke from the sacrificial offerings ascended upward.

The sound of tramping boots interrupted the sacred event. Six hundred security troops marched on the temple led by Supervisor Goldstein and Oren Natas. His Divine Majesty wore his jeweled crown, royal garments, and diamond encrusted golden sandals. The front rank of troops was dragging six squealing pigs along with them. The swine averaged a hundred pounds each and were being pulled along with hemp ropes.

The troops suddenly broke ranks and surrounded the entire gathering. Goldstein, Natas and thirty-six men advanced toward the temple entrance.

The stunned Jews shrank back in horror as the encircling troops stood with rifles poised.

Several Jews tried to flee but they were immediately gunned down. The others made way for Natas' escort and milled around in fear and confusion. Twelve troopers followed behind, yanking the noisy swine forward. The temple priests locked arms and tried to block the temple entrance. The troops clubbed them to the ground with their rifle butts as the trapped Jews looked on helplessly.

The thirty-six men surrounded the temple porch and the twelve men with the six pigs clustered around the subdued priests. Natas stepped onto the temple porch between the pillars, turned and faced the Jews with his arms outstretched in a gesture of benevolence. Goldstein stood below the porch looking over the multitude. He raised his right hand straight up and shouted: "Behold your God, O Israel! Behold His Divine Majesty."

All the security troops began chanting in unison: "Natas! Natas! Natas!" As the chanting rose to a feverish pitch, a scattering of Jews tried to flee, and were shot dead. The troops encircling the Jews raised their rifles and took aim. The terrified Jews fell to their knees and joined the chanting: "Natas! Natas! Natas!"

The proclaimed god of the Jews savored the moment, then turned his back on the people, entered the temple, and made his way to the most holy place. The troopers with the pigs thrust the lead ropes into the hands of the battered priests and marched them into the temple as Goldstein proclaimed: "Behold the sacrifice to your God, O Israel!"

Natas positioned himself between the Cherubim and looked on while the priests slaughtered the six pigs and offered them up before Natas upon the altar by the holy oracle. As the stench of burning pork filled the temple, the multitude beyond sent up a continuous chant: "Natas! Natas! Natas!"

Roughly twenty miles from the Israeli border in the desert of southwestern Jordan overlooking the ancient overland trade route that once linked Arabia and the Mediterranean Sea, the ruins of the historic city of Petra buzzed with excitement. The rock cliffs appeared rose-red in the early afternoon sun that warmed the corpses of thousands of Malinsky's troops scattered in the small plain below the dwelling places carved into the colorful cliffs by the Nabataeans some five hundred years before Christ.

A large band of Israeli guerillas had fortified the red cliffs and taken up positions in the recesses hewn into the rocky heights above the plain. Before the invading troops gathered in the plain, the guerrillas had saturated the ground with a potent mixture of flammable liquids and combustible chemicals that combined to produce a blinding and deadly gas when ignited.

After the troops crowded into the plain, the guerillas hurled lighted dynamite and grenades from the heights, turning the lowlands into a death trap. The killing was over in less than an hour, and the guerillas, protected by their gas masks, scavenged rifles and ammunition from the corpses. Many of the rifle stocks were badly scorched, but the weapons were otherwise undamaged. Recovery of ammunition was somewhat tedious since some rounds had exploded from the searing heat. Nevertheless, the guerrillas salvaged over a million rifle cartridges.

At sunrise on Saturday, fourteen days after the swine were sacrificed in Solomon's Temple, the two witnesses casually walked along the way to the temple site. The people kept their distance as the witnesses stopped in front of the temple porch and conversed with each other. Natas was inside conducting an audience with Goldstein and the priests who now worshiped him. Goldstein's snipers assigned to the temple area were on duty with their high-powered rifles and scopes. The witnesses turned to face the temple, standing side by side with their arms uplifted. The one on the left called out in a strong, clear voice as if addressing those inside the temple:

"The day of the Lord shall be upon everyone that is proud and lofty, and upon every one that is lifted up; and they shall be brought low. They shall go into the holes in the rocks and into the caves of the earth for fear of the Lord and for the glory of his majesty when he arises to shake terribly the earth."

Natas and his bodyguards were transfixed, unable to speak or move as the witness continued to berate Natas: "You are forever fallen from heaven, O Lucifer, son of the morning! You are forever cut down to the ground. You shall be brought down to hell, to the sides of the pit. Those who see you shall narrowly look upon you and shall consider you saying: Is this he that made the earth to tremble. . . .that did shake kingdoms? Behold, the Lord prepares a great slaughter for your children of iniquity; that they do not rise, nor possess the land, nor fill the face of the world with cities. For the Lord of hosts shall rise up against them and cut them off and send horror upon the earth and sweep it with the broom of destruction."

The elevated snipers took aim at the witnesses and squeezed the triggers on their rifles, but nothing happened. The astonished assassins inserted new cartridges and peered through their scopes, but saw only darkness, and the weapons would not discharge. The frightened men ran for their lives as the second witness delivered his message to those cowering inside the temple and to all who had ears to hear:

"You have sealed up the sum, full of wisdom and perfect in beauty. You have been in Eden, the Garden of God. By the multitude of your transgressions you have filled the earth with violence and have done every abominable thing. Therefore, you are cast as profane out of the presence of God, and he shall humble you, O covering cherub; and will cast you into the midst of eternal torment. Your heart was lifted up because of your beauty. You have corrupted your wisdom by reason of your brightness, and you shall be forever cast down before the children of men that they may behold you. You shall not be a terror unto them, and never shall you rise anymore. The inhabitants of earth have made a covenant with death, and with hell, they have come to agreement. When the terrible scourge shall pass through, they think it will not come unto them; for they have made lies their refuge, and under falsehood have they hid themselves. Therefore, the hand of Almighty God is stretched out under the whole heaven and upon the face of the entire earth. There shall be darkness, even darkness that will be felt. The people shall not see one another, neither shall any arise from his place. They shall sit in thick darkness six days and gnaw their tongues in pain. The elements shall withhold their energy; neither shall there be light. The people shall endure the darkness and the cold, and they shall not die. Yet, in his tender mercy, the Lord shall make allowance for those who have rejected Natas. The elements shall warm them and give them light."

Having delivered their prophecy, the two witnesses casually strolled back in the direction from which they had appeared, and no one dared follow after them. Natas was both embarrassed and enraged by the audacity of the two witnesses and the inability of his forces to interfere with their testimony. He, himself, had also felt weak and powerless, and his fury escalated as he waited for Goldstein and the priests to orient themselves again. "Leave me!" Natas barked at them. "The audience is ended."

Goldstein and the priests bowed before Natas and withdrew from the temple. One of the snipers who had been assigned to watch the temple site met Goldstein just beyond the porch. "What happened?" Goldstein snapped.

The would-be assassin cradled his rifle across his chest and his hands were still trembling. "I don't know, Sir. Those two guys showed up, just like you figured, but we couldn't see through our scopes and our rifles wouldn't fire. Nobody could get off a shot at 'em."

"Did anyone try to follow them to see where they went?" "No, Sir. We were all too scared. None of us wants to get fried. Those two jokers are something else. Did you hear what they said?" "We heard," Goldstein snarled. "They sounded like they were standing in the temple door. They embarrassed all of us, including Lord Natas." "Why didn't His Divine Majesty do something? Is he afraid of them too?"

Goldstein spat on the ground to indicate his contempt. "They cast some sort of spell on us. We couldn't move or speak while they were squawking outside. We've got to figure out some method to get to those two troublemakers. There's gotta be a way."

Malinsky was sitting in Goldstein's private office looking over computer printouts. Goldstein stalked in, slammed the door behind him, and plopped down on his office couch. "Have a bad morning?" Malinsky chuckled. "If you're looking for something particular, maybe I can pull it up for you," Goldstein said with a scowl.

"Right now, I need a drink. Got any scotch?" "The booze is in the right-hand bottom drawer. Should be some Johnny Walker in there and some clean glasses."

Malinsky pulled out the drawer and found the scotch among an assortment of whiskey. He dug out two glasses and poured each one-half full. "I assume you're joining me," he said, passing one glass toward Goldstein. "Yeah. I can use it. Shall we drink to our divine leader?" "That's as good an excuse as any." Malinsky exhibited an ambiguous expression and tinkled his glass against Goldstein's. He swigged a mouthful and studied his subordinate. "How you getting along with the boss?" The large gulp of whiskey steadied Goldstein somewhat. "Okay, I guess, considering the way he feels about Jews."

Malinsky fished out a cigarette and lighter, fired up and inhaled deeply. "It's not you he's fuming about. It's your relatives up there in the rocks. They sure do make things interesting. Too bad they're not on our side." "They're a rowdy bunch," Goldstein snickered. . .and not real easy to kill. They're about as fond of Natas as he is of them." "They definitely know how to kill," Malinsky admitted, "and they'll be a lot meaner now with all those rifles. We'll eventually overwhelm them, but we're sure going to lose a lot of troops in the process." "Any possibility we can starve them out?"

Goldstein downed the rest of his scotch. "Pretty doubtful. They're strong enough now to raid food and water supplies anywhere in the Middle East, and our troops aren't too anxious to tangle with them after the mauling we've taken." Malinsky poured more scotch, then settled back with his feet on the desk. "What do you know about Solomon and Hartstein?"

"Hartstein is a concentration camp survivor who was regularly sodomized by a German officer. He's tough, fearless, and one of the best military minds around. He got his military training in the United States and in the school of hard knocks. He's highly respected by all those who've served under him. He generally knows the answers to the questions he asks but has a way of making subordinates feel like the ideas are all theirs. The best thing we can hope for when it comes to Hartstein is that he'll die soon. His health has been going downhill for the past several years. Solomon is Hartstein's right-hand man, and he gets his kicks by personally killing the enemy in hand-to-hand combat. He's also a brilliant and creative intelligence officer who always manages to come up with whatever information Hartstein wants. You certainly don't want to meet up with him on his turf. The combination of Hartstein and Solomon is about as bad as they come. That little trick they pulled off to get the first half million rifles is a good example of their capability."

"You got any suggestions as to what our strategy should be?" "The best strategy would have been to honor the peace treaty. Now that peace is a moot issue since Natas' demand that they worship him, we probably should bring in enough troops to lay siege to their positions thereby keeping them from replenishing their food and water supplies. It'd take a lot of troops, but we've got plenty if we draw from all fourteen thousand control centers. The logistics would be a little hairy and require a lot of tedious planning."

"It would also take time, and Natas wants immediate results. On the other hand, it's better than any other option I can think of. How many men do you think we would need?" Goldstein rubbed his mouth and chin with his right hand and thought about the area that would have to be covered. "We'd have to throw a pretty big circle considering that they're dug into the highlands along the entire eastern border from the Golan Heights to the Sinai Mountains. My guess is that we'd need five million troops." Malinsky swigged his drink. "We can get the men with no problem. Transporting them to Israel and then keeping them supplied for two or three months will be the stumbling block." Suddenly, it became totally dark and the sound level changed. All power sources became silent and unresponsive, and there was not a trace of light. "What happened?"

Malinsky gasped. He felt for his lighter, pulled it out, and thumbed the wheel, but not a single spark was visible. "What's going on?" he repeated himself. He got up and felt his way to the office door, opened it and heard nothing but the sound of confused human voices. He could see absolutely nothing. He felt his way back to the desk and sat down. "Are you there, Goldstein?"

"Yes. I'm here." The voice was timid and unsteady. "What happened?" "I don't know. There's no sun, no lights, no power. . . nothing." "How can that be? I don't understand?" "There's a flashlight in the center drawer. Can you feel it?" Malinsky found the flashlight, pushed the switch forward, and shook the casing when nothing happened. "It doesn't work!" "Try the matches." Malinsky found the matches and tried to fire one up. Nothing happened. He tried striking several more but got no result. "They won't strike!"

"We're in big trouble!" Goldstein exclaimed. "It's really happening!" "What? What's really happening?" "The two witnesses said this morning that the elements would withhold their energy; that there would be no heat, no light, just total darkness." "You gotta be kidding me!" "I wish I were. That's what they said. . . that the darkness will last for six days, and that people will gnaw their tongues because of pain and the cold."

Malinsky's voice sounded like a scared child. "Pain. What Pain? What do you mean?" "They didn't say. . . just indicated there would be a lot of pain, and that people would have to endure it because they won't die. Maybe they were talking about pain from lack of heat. It's going to get mighty cold with no sunlight or any source of energy of any kind." "How can that be? It's not physically possible!" "I wouldn't bet on it! Everything else those two predicted has happened, exactly like they said it would. You don't see any light, do you? Or maybe you think you just went blind. When the temperature starts dropping, I think you'll discover that the problem isn't blindness."

"What are we gonna do?" "Beats me! I'm just gonna sit here a while and see what happens." "Shouldn't we be doing something? Six days! We need food, water, blankets, and so forth. We can't just sit here for six days! We need supplies!" "From where? And how you gonna get there? You'd be lucky to find your way out of this building . . . and if you did, you'd have absolutely no sense of direction. You'd be totally lost. We're better off to stay put and simply wait it out."

Malinsky fumbled for the whiskey, found it, and gulped from the bottle. The liquor didn't quench the terror that crept throughout his being.

His mind raced over all the events that had occurred since he became Chief of Police. Everything seemed so unreal. He felt very small and insignificant.

Goosebumps covered his skin as his arrogance and pride vanished. He trembled uncontrollably in the stifling darkness and wondered what hell would be like. He felt a warm liquid along his left thigh and realized that he had just urinated on himself. He fought against the compelling urge to vomit. His head began to pound, and his bowels wrenched with stabbing cramps. He tried to focus his eyes on his hands as he spread them in front of his nose. Nothing! The pain in his head and bowels became more intense as he felt himself falling headlong into a bottomless hole. His stomach rushed up into his mouth and his face contorted into a scream, but he had no voice.

He kept falling faster. . . down, down, down into the terrifying blackness of nothingness. His brain seemed to explode as his silent screaming took away his breath. Then, as if some unknown hand pulled his entrails out through his mouth, he heard the sound of his voice. . . a pitiful childish wail that escaped from his inner being and disappeared into the all-consuming darkness.

"What is it, Malinsky? What's the matter?" Goldstein croaked hoarsely. He heard no response, only an anguished groan that made his toes curl inward. He tried to get up and feel his way to Malinsky, but his legs felt like dead weights. His skin began to tingle as if his body had become covered with living creatures. He stared wide-eyed into the impenetrable darkness and slapped at his stomach and sides with his palms. His heart fluttered as he felt something curl around his ankles and a slithering movement across his shins.

He felt something crawling around on his scalp and inside his ears. He swiped at his hair and beat his hands frantically about his face and neck as he felt tiny legs up and down from the top of his head to his armpits. He held his breath when he felt something crawling on his upper lip below his nostrils. As he tried to rake his lip with his right forefinger, he felt tiny teeth ripping at his flesh, eating him alive. His masculinity no longer mattered, and his self-control crumbled. He defecated in his clothes and gnawed at his tongue in the prolonged grip of his hallucination, each passing second a lifetime of horror and excruciating pain.

Paul Roberts uncovered a peephole at the cave entrance, but he couldn't see a thing. He rubbed his eyes and tried again. Still nothing. He opened up a crawl space and stuck his head outside. It was pitch black without a trace of light. He turned his face toward the sky. No moon, no stars, nothing! He could feel the crusty covering on the ground, but he couldn't even see the snow!

He spread his fingers in front of his eyes and couldn't see them. Even with the heaviest overcast, he knew he should be able to see the snow. . . and his fingers! He pulled the radio from his pocket, turned it on and held it toward the sky. It was totally dead. He covered up the hole, picked up the radio and headed back through the dark tunnel toward the inner room.

Jack had gotten the fire going and the women were preparing dinner. Jack saw Paul returning and assumed that he had spotted some danger outside. "See something out there?" he called to Paul. The women stopped to listen with concern on their faces. Paul looked at his watch. "What time have you got." Jack checked his watch. "Quarter past five." "That's what I thought. It should still be twilight outside!" "You mean it isn't?" "It's pitch black, not a speck of light! I couldn't even see the snow or my fingers in front of my nose. It's really weird, I've never seen it so dark! Wonder what's going on."

"Must be the darkness plague," Jack surmised as Paul sat down by the fire. "Did you try the radio?" "Yep. Couldn't get a thing, not even static." "What's happening?" Marge asked, walking over to Jack and Paul. The other women gathered around to listen. "The earth's totally dark," Paul answered. "There's no light of any kind. . . no twilight, no moonlight, no starlight, nothing."

"How come?" Jackie queried. "How can that be?" "Jack thinks it's the plague of darkness prophesied in the book of Revelation," Paul responded. "I don't understand," Mary complained. "What are you talking about? What darkness plague?"

Ruth stepped over to the fire to continue broiling the meat, and the other women sat down with Jack and Paul. "It's like the other plagues we've seen," Jack said. "God is vexing Natas and his followers with total darkness to demonstrate that Natas is not what he claims to be, and to encourage those who have refused to take Natas' mark or to worship him. It's more or less like the plagues that fell upon Egypt when Pharaoh refused to free the Hebrew slaves. The plagues humbled Pharaoh and encouraged Moses and the slaves."

"How long will the darkness last?" Jackie asked. "Probably several days, maybe six." "That means no more news for a while," Paul added. "The radio doesn't pick up anything."

"How long will these plagues continue?" Marge inquired. "Right up to the great battle between Christ and Satan just prior to the millennium reign of Christ," Paul answered. "And they get progressively worse." "I'm sure glad I'm in here," Marge said. "The best day of my life was when Jack found me and brought me in. It's bad enough to be tricked into taking Natas' mark. I can certainly do without anything else because of him." "The meat's done," Ruth called out. "Let's eat."

At 8:48 am Jerusalem time, exactly one hundred and forty-four hours after the blackout of the planet, Earth, a joyous shout went up from the human race. As if a giant curtain had suddenly been pulled aside, the celestial lights once again scattered the thick darkness within the vacuum of space surrounding Earth. The full lunar orb in a star-speckled sky lit up the mountains around Boise, Idaho and the morning sun lighted the Middle East with glorious rays of solar energy. Around the globe, the inhabitants of the earth bearing Natas' mark began stirring from their places where they had endured continuous torment for six days. They had urinated and defecated upon themselves and were weak from dehydration, gnawing hunger and exposure to frigid temperatures. Although many had the look of complete insanity, no one had died from causes related to the darkness plague. They ate and drank and cleaned themselves while cursing the two witnesses for tormenting them.

CHAPTER 12

Genocide by Divine Proclamation

Oren Natas sat upon the throne inside the temple in Jerusalem awaiting the arrival of Chief Malinsky. His thoughts were preoccupied with the demise of the Israeli defenders dug into the highlands along the northern and eastern borders of Israel. The unregistered Jews and the Christians in hiding were his only real concerns.

Some of those bearing his mark might turn against him, but such rebellion was of no consequence if he could root out the remaining Christians and exterminate the Jewish resistance. Everyone with his mark was doomed anyway, and he could care less how they felt about his persecution of the Jews. The battle was for human souls, not for human praise, and his subjects had shown themselves to be fickle and unpredictable when bartering away their souls.

He tapped his fingertips together impatiently as the captain of the temple guards approached, drew near to the throne, bowed low and then stood tall and attentive. "Chief Malinsky is waiting, Divine Majesty." "I thought perhaps he had found something more pressing to attend to. Send him in and send a messenger to fetch Supervisor Goldstein." "Yes, Divine Majesty."

Natas' disposition worsened as he watched Malinsky moving toward him. Since the six days of darkness, the man seemed withdrawn and insecure, and the coming conflict called for a leader possessed with neither fear nor indecision. Malinsky bowed humbly and then stood with stooped shoulders. "Your obedient servant, Divine Majesty." Natas frowned at Malinsky. "Are the rebellious Jews prepared to surrender?" Malinsky fixed his eyes on Natas' jewel-encrusted sandals and pondered the amount of gold squandered to fashion the royal footwear. "I don't believe they're thinking in those terms at the moment, Divine Majesty." "Have you devised a plan to alter their confidence level?" "Yes, Divine Majesty. We are in the process of bringing the matter to an end."

"May I assume the engagement will be concluded before you die of old age?" "Yes, Divine Majesty. We are laying siege to the Israeli positions with five million troops and will deplete their food and water reserves. That seemed more prudent than sacrificing a million or so troops during a frontal assault. We should be able to both dehydrate and starve them within sixty to ninety days. None of them will escape."

Natas considered the full range of Malinsky's options under the circumstances which had evolved since his surprise attack had fizzled. "I'll leave the matter in your hands for ninety days." "Ninety days will be adequate, Divine Majesty." "How many among the criminals in hiding have surrendered?"

Malinsky stood taller and returned Natas' gaze. "One million, four hundred and twelve thousand, three hundred and twenty-nine have surrendered and have been resettled within the appropriate control centers, Divine Majesty. We have captured and executed three million, two hundred and eleven thousand, nine hundred and seventeen."

"And how many continue to defy you?" "We are unsure at the present time, Divine Majesty. Based on information obtained from those flushed out, it appears that a significant number went into hiding before and during the nuclear war. Therefore, the statistics necessary to estimate their numbers were never entered into our computers."

Natas' jaws clenched, and his eyes narrowed. "Those souls are more precious to us than the Jews. We must become more efficient by concentrating our efforts." "Do you have something specific in mind, Divine Majesty?" Natas' voice took on a friendlier tone. "The load has become too heavy for you alone to bear. Supervisor Goldstein will report to me and be responsible for executing the witnesses and pursuing those still in hiding. You will continue to report to me and direct your undivided attention to the siege of Israeli strongholds. Other security matters can be attended to by area supervisors until your victory over the Jews is achieved. I will coordinate matters between the regional administrators and Bishop Romas. We need to conclude the projects at hand and prepare for the coming conflict which will require the concentration of all our resources."

"Yes, Divine Majesty. I will brief Supervisor Goldstein on the status of our search activities."

Bishop Romas took a quick shower, put on his official attire, and had just picked up the paper when Henri Werner showed up. Romas opened the door and greeted him: "Hello Henri, your timing is perfect. Come on in." Werner shook Romas' extended hand with a polite smile. "I appreciate your hospitality." "May I take your coat and offer you some brandy?" "Oh, thank you. I'd love a little brandy."

Romas hung Werner's coat in the foyer closet and guided him to the living room. "Make yourself at home, Henri, while I fetch the brandy." Werner sat down on Romas' plush couch while Romas poured the brandy and placed the snifters on coasters atop the convenience table in front of Werner. "I trust everything is going well for you, Henri." Romas smiled graciously and sat down across from him in an overstuffed chair within easy reach of the snifters.

"Things only run smoothly in the absence of stupidity," Werner replied with a hint of frustration. Romas picked up his snifter and extended it toward Werner with an accommodating expression. "Then, let us drink to the speedy resolution of mutual problems." "And to more sensitive leadership," Werner added. "Do you think that's possible at this point?" "I'm beginning to wonder, Bishop. What on earth is our divine leader trying to prove. . . that he can murder at his whim? Has he gone completely mad?"

"The media seems to think so, Henri. People like Nancy Flack are really stirring up a nasty public mood. The first time that an opportunity arises, there's going to be a mass revolt against the government unless the press can be reigned in." "Are you suggesting censorship?" "No. People today are too sophisticated to stand for that. The velvet hammer approach might ease the situation somewhat."

"I believe things have gone too far, Bishop. The people in my region no longer trust the government to protect them. Moreover, they see the security forces as inept. Malinsky marched over a million men into Israel and lost two-thirds of them while the unregistered Israelis barely got scratched. Then, when the police started indiscriminately murdering law-abiding Jews, both in and outside of Israel, all remaining respect for the government vanished. Even if the press never said another derogatory word about either Natas or Malinsky, the mistrust and insecurity among the people will not go away."

Romas sipped his brandy and considered Werner's remarks. How many other regional administrators has reached the same conclusion as Werner? The ten regional strongmen were already immensely powerful and extremely wealthy. Corruption had become rampant after the death of Wallace, Walker, and Wirtman; and neither he nor Malinsky had been in a position to control the regional kingpins during Natas' absence. Now, they were fearful that a rebellion against the government might oust them also. Werner was as dangerous as any of them which made his appearance deceitful.

His bald head, rubbery nose, beer belly, squat frame, and pale blue eyes seemed more compatible with a carnival hawker than the most influential man in Europe. At sixty-three, he had suffered a mild stroke that left a permanent droop in the right corner of his mouth making it necessary to frequently wipe away the accumulated spittle with his handkerchief. “Do you sense a division of loyalty among the security forces, Henri?”

Werner swallowed some brandy and took time to wipe his mouth, letting Romas know that he had carefully considered whether he dared confide in Natas’ henchman. “It is risky at best to assume where one’s loyalty lies when disputes are resolved by force rather than adjudication. The war horse under bridle and saddle still yearns to run free, and the most trusted mount may dump its master when pricked by the sword. Malinsky’s humbling by the Israelis doesn’t exactly inspire awe and blind obedience.”

Romas decided to probe the waters a bit deeper. “For the purpose of evaluating potential confusion of loyalties, Henri, let’s assume that five of the ten regional administrators unite in an effort to overthrow Natas. What sort of alignment would you predict among the security forces?”

“That would be a risky bet to place and the outcome would be greatly influenced by the solidarity within the chain of command. The rank and file tend to always follow immediate supervisors in whom they place their trust and confidence. I am persuaded that the majority of supervisors will cast their lot with regional command and that the majority will sway the minority through the reality of one-sided firepower. Our divine leader’s recent behavior and his rout by Israeli guerillas lead many to question his authenticity.”

The deeper the probe, the hotter the water, Romas surmised. He decided to go a step farther. “If such a division did arise, Henri, would your regional troops remain loyal to you?” The immediate response indicated that Werner knew the question would be raised.

“My subordinates were carefully chosen to ensure their complete support. Their commands will remain intact.” "And if Lord Natas continues his present behavior, would you join in an effort to oust him?" Werner wasn't quite ready to expose his cards. "You pose a choice upon which one gambles his life. How would you choose, Bishop? Would you side with a majority of the regional powers against Natas and Malinsky?"

Romas felt confident that Werner knew the precise bounds of the growing conspiracy to unseat Natas. "The present course of events will lead to utter chaos, and I much prefer the peaceful enjoyment of life's pleasures. I see no value in an untimely death while pursuing that which has already been determined."

Werner picked up the brandy bottle and refilled both snifters. He held his drink in his left hand and passed the other to Romas. "Then, let us drink to the return of law and order." He extended his snifter as Romas returned the gesture. The tinkling of delicate crystal belied the suspicion that lingered in the minds of both men.

The two witnesses made their way along the ancient cobblestone streets winding through the section of Eastern Jerusalem known as the Old City. Massive stone walls forty feet high and two and a half miles long dating back nearly five centuries enclosed four ethnic neighborhoods: Armenian, Christian, Jewish and Muslim.

The pattern of life along the narrow cobblestone lanes continued much as it had since the days of the Byzantine Empire. Camels and donkeys labored under their burdens of merchandise along streets too narrow for motor vehicles. Shopkeepers debated current events with friends and opponents as they lounged on stools and benches in front of their places of business.

Under the huge stone arches connecting buildings on opposites sides of the crowded passageways, pedestrians strolled by, enjoying the sights and sounds of the city that served as the seat of Jewish government a thousand years before Christ.

The witnesses seemed to be sightseeing as they casually ambled westward, taking in all the activity and aroma around them. All those present in the vicinity of the witnesses gawked in amazement as they continued on in the general direction of the hill in eastern Jerusalem where Solomon's Temple was situated. The more stouthearted fell in behind the witnesses, albeit at a distance, to see what would happen.

The haphazard formation of spectators caught the attention of reporters and, within a matter of minutes, camera crews could be discerned among the jostling crowd that trailed behind as the witnesses unhurriedly approached the temple. Police officers mingled with the onlookers, but none of them seemed willing to overtake the dangerous characters.

Snipers overlooking the temple vicinity waited for the right moment to sight in on their victims. The two men arrayed in sackcloth displayed neither fear nor a sense of urgency as they turned about facing their audience and lifted their hands toward the firmament above. Media cameras and sound equipment were quickly focused on the pair as one of them called out in a voice that was audible to all those assembled:

"The day is upon man that shall burn as an oven, and the people shall be as stubble cast into the fire of the Lord's anger. He that stretched forth the heavens and laid the foundation of the earth shall make Jerusalem a cup of trembling unto all the people round about in the time of siege. Jerusalem shall be a flaming sword and all that burden themselves with it shall be cut in pieces. . . though all the people of the earth be gathered together against it. The Lord shall smite the armies with astonishment and the rulers with madness and all of Natas' host with terror. He shall deliver them as wood to the furnace and Jerusalem shall be inhabited again, and Christ shall sit upon the Throne of David. The day of the redeemed draws nigh and the Lord's word has been proclaimed through the mouth of his anointed servants." A defiant murmur rippled through the crowd and the police cautiously inched forward. The snipers chambered their rifles and began adjusting the fuzziness out of their scopes as the second witness continued the prophetic utterance:

"Rome, the city of whoredom, is fallen and is become the habitation of demons, and the hold of every foul spirit. Come out of her, all that are unmarked, that you be not partakers of her sins and that you receive not of her plagues; for her sins have reached unto heaven and God has remembered her iniquities. He shall reward her double according to her works. She has glorified herself and lived deliciously, proclaiming herself a queen that knows no sorrow. Therefore, shall her plagues come in one day. . . death, mourning and famine; and she shall be utterly consumed with fire. Thus, with violence shall that great city be thrown down and shall be seen no more; for in her was found the blood of the prophets, and of the saints, and of the righteous that were slain upon the earth."

A volley of shots rang out from the sniper positions causing the crowd to scatter at the sound of the high-powered rifles. The two witnesses crumpled under the withering barrage of bullets, their blood gushing from fatal wounds inflicted in their heads, faces, necks, chests and stomachs. A victorious shout echoed from the sniper positions as the police among the spectators ran forward and riddled the bodies of the fallen witnesses with their rifles, shotguns and handguns. A hysteria of delight enveloped the crowd when they realized that the witnesses who had repeatedly plagued the earth had just been shot dead.

The TV cameras zoomed in on the two corpses as the vehement multitude surged forward to desecrate the bodies. They circled the mutilated victims, dancing with glee, stomping and kicking the corpses in a frenzy of excitement. Many bowed low to spit upon them, and others dipped their fingers in the witnesses' blood, then smeared their crimson trophies upon their own foreheads and cheeks.

Goldstein drew near to the throne with elation and a newly found confidence, feeling secure in the wake of his victory over the two witnesses. He bowed before Natas, then stood erect with a sheen of pride in his eyes. "You sent for me, Divine Majesty?" Natas gave him a look of appreciation. "You have performed well, and your status must be elevated."

"I'm more than content to serve you in my present capacity, Divine Majesty." "Nevertheless, you shall be richly rewarded. You have made my subjects most happy and it is my desire that their rejoicing remains unrestrained. Proclaim an extended holiday that one and all may indulge themselves with feasting and merriment and view their corpses on television." "Yes, Divine Majesty. It will be a most joyous occasion."

Around the world, the global television audience cheered and offered up praises to Natas in thanksgiving that the source of their misery had finally been vanquished. Everywhere, people poured into the streets, singing and dancing with exultation. Within each control center, trucks laden with assorted foods and alcoholic beverages circulated throughout the noisy streets distributing their cargo as government gifts to enrich the convivial occasion. Fires were kindled, and the people roasted sides of beef, choice cuts of pork, and assorted fowls. They shouted and danced; ate and drank; slept in drunken stupor; then arose to continue making merry. For three days, the partying continued without interruption; government workers joining in as soon as their trucks were emptied.

Throughout Israel, the registered Jews, who now worshiped Natas, pressed into Jerusalem to view and desecrate the corpses of the two witnesses. The bodies were horribly mutilated and dripping with spittle as captured by the electronic eyes of media cameras.

The merrymakers were staggering drunk and slovenly. Some of them openly urinated upon the remains of the witnesses. Natas had retired to his private chamber within the temple to view the television coverage. He cackled with laughter as he watched the abominations unfold.

Eighty-four hours had ticked by since the witnesses had been shot down less than sixty yards from Solomon's Temple. During that three and a half days, unmanned electronic equipment focused on the site while media crews joined the partying, only returning to the equipment to monitor audio and video discs and to make sure the cameras and recording devices were operating properly. It was 4:06 am Jerusalem time, and the clear sky overhead sparkled with stars beyond the lighted quarter of the lunar orb.

The extended holiday was winding down, and people were expected to report to their jobs within a matter of hours. The camera and sound crews were now manning their equipment, taking close-up shots of the mangled corpses along with the background noise as the partying petered out. The wind was calm, and the predawn air was seasonably comfortable. Suddenly, a rumbling voice that sounded like thunder echoed across the firmament: "Come up hither!"

The media crews cried out in terror as the remains of the witnesses began to stir. The people looking on were transfixed with stark fear and astonishment as all signs of mutilation and desecration disappeared from the bodies of the two witnesses. They shook themselves mightily and rose upon their feet with their arms stretched toward the starry sky. Continuous claps of thunder sounded overhead, and dazzling bolts of lightning illuminated the entire city of Jerusalem.

Before the terrified eyes of all those assembled and the cluster of whirring TV cameras, the two witnesses began to ascend upward. As they rose above the city, an expanse of white appeared beneath their feet, seeming to speed their ascent into the firmament where they disappeared from earthly view.

David Solomon felt like shouting as he listened over his cellular telephone to his control center contact calling from west Jerusalem. David decoded the information as fast as it was relayed to him. Natas' kingdom had just been ripped asunder. Five of the regional administrators had declared their territories to be totally independent and self-governing. They also had recalled all their security troops that had been ordered to participate in the siege of Israeli positions in the highlands.

The five rebels no longer recognized any authority other than their own within their respective regions. Malinsky had temporarily halted his advance and had left for Jerusalem to confer with Natas.

David listened with joy to Hartstein: "We know that the regional rulers now aligned against Natas and Malinsky are the most powerful among the ten regions: Mahatma Ghane in India; Chou Huang in China; Wang Souleng in Indonesia; Henri Werner in Europe; and Sumo Komoto in the Far East. Furthermore, it is now rumored that Malcom Allie in Africa might declare his region to be independent; and, if so, that Jahamal Sadatie in Africa might follow suit. There is no indication thus far as to how Bishop Romas might align himself. In any event, the siege will be delayed and severely hampered by such a major split which will give our guerillas additional time to raid government food and water inventories. If we set up a defensive line stretching from the Sea of Galilee due west to the Bay of Haifa, we can choke off any troop movements from the south. Our line would be protected on the west side by the Mediterranean Sea and on the east side by the Sea of Galilee. We're already in control of the Golan Heights and we can secure all remaining highlands along our border with Lebanon. If we mass additional firepower along our border west to the sea, we can create defensive positions completely surrounded by natural choke points. We'll also have control of our northern coastal plain above the Bay of Haifa as well as the fertile valleys around the mountains of Galilee thereby eliminating our concerns over adequate food and water."

David immediately saw the workability of Hartstein's proposal. They could take over the existing crops and force the local population to fight alongside them. The women and children could perform the necessary agricultural activities while the men held the defensive lines.

"That's absolutely brilliant, General! But we'll have to move fast before Malinsky gets himself reorganized. All of our people south of the Dead Sea will have a long way to travel. However, the troops currently available in Israel, Jordan and Saudi Arabia won't attack us if we travel in large numbers."

Goldstein looked up from his computer printouts as Malinsky entered, perched on the arm of the office couch, and fumbled for a cigarette. "Hi, Goldie. Tell me what's happening here so Natas doesn't catch me totally cold." Goldstein gazed at him sympathetically. "I just heard some bad news you should be aware of before you talk to him. The Israeli guerillas have pulled out of their positions south of the Dead Sea and are moving north." "What are they up to now?" Malinsky asked with an irritated look.

"Probably a repositioning designed to make your siege strategy ineffective," Goldstein replied. "They're apparently going to consolidate their forces around Galilee and the Golan Heights." "How's that going to help? It'll just reduce my perimeters and require fewer troops."

"That was also my first reaction until I realized what they're intending to do. They're going to seal off the northern tip of Israel, so they have a captive supply of food and water. You'll be blocked off by water on the east and west sides of their new position; and by the Golan Heights to the northeast. They'll concentrate their forces along the narrow northern border with Lebanon and throw up a heavy defensive line from the Sea of Galilee to the Bay of Haifa which will cut you off from the south. That will create an easily defended perimeter enclosing the coastal plain north of the bay and the valleys between their defensive line to the south and the northern border with Lebanon. They'll have enough food and water to make a siege futile."

"Can we attack them before they get repositioned." "They're moving in a disciplined defensive line armed with over a half million automatic rifles, more than fifty million rounds of ammo; poison gas, explosives, and other goodies. You don't have enough troops in the right places to attack them before they reach their goal. . . and, if you attack with what's presently available, you'll be massacred."

"I'm in trouble," Malinsky sputtered. "I get the picture. Natas is going to blow a fuse." Goldstein shrugged and bit at his lower lip. "You'd be much better off to forget about them for now and prepare for an attack from Europe and Asia. . . and pray that Africa doesn't join the rebellion." Malinsky looked stunned. "You think that's a serious possibility?" "Yes ... they probably think blacks come right behind Jews in Natas' genocide plans. It's a predictable suspicion considering what they've seen him do to other law-abiding citizens."

Malinsky mentally calculated his remaining troops if Africa joined the independence movement. The rebels would control twelve thousand, two hundred and thirty-four control centers with roughly one hundred and seven million, three hundred and sixteen thousand armed men. On the other hand, his command would shrink to one thousand, seven hundred and sixty-six control centers with approximately fifteen million, four hundred and ninety-two thousand security troops. He would be outnumbered nearly seven to one. Worse yet, eleven hundred and fifty of his control centers were in Australia, North American and South America, creating a logistical nightmare with respect to a major conflict centered in the Middle East.

Over sixty-five percent of his total forces would have to be shuttled by air or sea using commercial ships and planes; which were in short supply. He felt cold and clammy as he sought additional advice from Goldstein. "Is there anything we can do at this point to convince the Africans that they're better off with us than against us?"

Goldstein snorted with disdain. "I suspect they wouldn't be impressed with any sort of guarantees. They've already seen precisely what Natas' guarantees are worth. . . less than nothing! His solemn pledges serve only to disarm prior to attack without warning and without justification."

"There must be something we can do. . . " Malinsky wheedled. Goldstein looked resigned. "Back off from this unreasonable and inexcusable persecution of the Jews that survived his initial murderous attack while they were relying on his guarantees of complete protection. Let the regions that have declared their independence know that they can do their own thing without any interference from Natas. In time, most of the people will disregard what Natas has done. Just as the world soon forgot what Hitler and Stalin did, the people will put the matter out of their minds and convince themselves that it really never happened. At least we'd be able to hold on to what's left of the kingdom."

Malinsky knew he was getting sound advice, but he also knew what was driving Natas. "He'll never go for it. We'll just have to make the best of a bad situation, and hope that things will work themselves out without a full-blown war."

"You're dreaming," Goldstein replied with a negative wag of his head. "But I'd be interested in hearing what our divine leader has in mind." Malinsky stubbed out his cigarette, stood up, and flashed a friendly grin. "Thanks for filling me in on the maneuvering by Hartstein and Solomon, and for sharing your honest opinion. I won't forget it, and I'll let you know what the boss plans to do next. I'd better move along before he sends someone after me. Our god doesn't like to be kept waiting."

Natas appeared relaxed and poised as Malinsky bowed before the throne and the temple guard retreated. "You appear not as one who comes victorious," Natas said with a hint of sarcasm in his voice. "I come with unwelcome news, Divine Majesty, and to ask for a portion of your wisdom to help me carry out your divine will." "The division within my kingdom will not deter us from our unchanging purpose, and the rebellious Jews have not devised an impregnable position."

Malinsky was surprised by Natas' opening remark. He already knew everything that had transpired and was foreclosing any suggestion that a retreat from his objectives was acceptable. "The weak link in the new Israeli position is their southern defensive line stretching from the Sea of Galilee westward to the Mediterranean Sea. They're protected by the seas from attack from the east and from the west, and the Golan Heights block an attack from the northeast. Their defensive line along the northern border with Lebanon would be as difficult to overrun as the Golan Heights. It seems more desirable to break through their southern defensive line using a superior concentration of troops." "So be it," Natas answered. "How much time do you need?" Time? Malinsky wondered how Natas had risen to the rank of general. Time would take care of itself. He was more worried about troop movements and how the Africans would react when he ordered them to send three million security troops to help kill men, women and children who were merely trying to defend themselves against cold-blooded genocide. Even if the Africans didn't rebel, Jahamal Sadatie and Malcom Allie might refuse to send troops into Israel.

Blacks were favorably inclined to honor peace treaties and to cheer for the underdog. Hanni Solanni in Pakistan would probably think twice before bucking Mahatma Ghane, Wang Souleng, Chou Huang and Henri Werner. Ramos Warez could be counted on to play along, but he was halfway around the world from where the clash would occur.

That left only Mohammad Mousani to save his bacon, and Arabs generally didn't fare too well against the Israelis. The odds were also pretty good that the Eurasian rebels would attack while he was preoccupied with killing Jews. Time was not his enemy. Natas' passion for conquering those without his mark was going to get Boris Malinsky killed.

"If the Africans remain loyal, Divine Majesty, I will need fifteen days to gather the necessary troops and begin the assault upon the Israeli position. Otherwise, I will need ninety days to shuttle our forces from the western hemisphere using commercial ships and all available aircraft."

A mystic smile played at the corners of Natas' mouth. "You concern yourself with that which is untimely. The rebellious spirits have truly gone forth to gather all flesh to the final conflict, but the hour of reckoning is yet within the womb of time. Our victory does not turn upon the shifting of human loyalties but rather is measured by the sum of those who accept my mark or worship my image. The struggle that must be won rages beyond the realm of mortal contests, and the appointed time for ending the conflict within the hierarchy of eternal life will be neither hastened nor stayed. The remnant of Abraham's seed must die while their hope is yet in vain, and the remaining Christians must be persuaded to accept my mark or worship me. Therein lies the everlasting treasure for which we will sacrifice all that is precious to humanity, and it matters not how many fights against us once their souls have been claimed. Nevertheless, the passing of time does not favor us. Redemption through Christ is being preached to those who are counted as Abraham's seed by men of great stature among the remnant who must perish. Though your days are numbered, the full measure of your glory is undecided. Draw near to the throne that your fear may be vanquished."

Natas' words were like sharp spikes driven through Malinsky's skull and into the depths of his brain. He felt the urge to flee from Natas' presence and to cast himself headlong from the nearest precipice, but a force beyond his control moved his legs forward and compelled him to kneel before Natas. Something dark and evil slithered from within his inner being and formed words in his mouth. "Your will be done, Divine Majesty."

The touch of Natas' right hand upon the top of his head seemed to melt his brain and turn his heart to flint. His entire body threatened to burst into flames as he heard the voice of Lucifer speaking through the mouth of Natas. "Go forth and hide the light of salvation in the darkness of vanity and drown the voice of reason in its own blood."

David Solomon and Aaron Hartstein concluded their morning prayers and focused their attention on the topographical maps where David had marked out the positions taken up by Malinsky's troops. The latest reports from the lookouts indicated no change in strategy.

"He's got us boxed in pretty good," David conceded. "We're outnumbered six to one including our women and children. His men along the border with Syria and Lebanon are staying out of rifle range which also makes our slings and catapults useless. Although they're not wearing them yet, it's a safe bet that all of his troops are equipped with gas masks."

Hartstein looked a little glum. "We're kinda between a rock and a hard place again . . . and our southern line will eventually be breached. Looks like he's willing to sacrifice a sizable portion of his troops in order to break inside our defensive perimeter. If we try to stand toe to toe with him, we're going to be massacred. Our best bet is to try and pull off something unexpected."

"Like breaching his lines before he breaches ours?" David suggested by way of a question. Hartstein smiled with appreciation. "Something like that. The seas have now become our enemy. We're not equipped to attempt an escape by water where he has the weakest concentration of forces. We'd need an armada of ships which we don't have. . . and we certainly can't swim that far. His strongest position, like ours, is to the south where we're outgunned at least three to one. Our most viable option would be around the northern shore of the Sea of Galilee. That would put some distance between us and his troops positioned north and south. He's pretty well strung out on the eastern border along the Golan Heights which provides an opportunity to punch through between the sea and the heights. We'd only be facing about twenty percent of his troops scattered along the eastern border blocking the sea. We could no doubt overcome his forces between the sea and Nawa."

David's mind was racing ahead. What does a capable general do when fighting a far superior force? Run and fight . . . run and fight! To stay ahead of Malinsky's troops once they breached his line between the Sea of Galilee and the Golan Heights, they'd have to make a dash due east before turning northeast to cross the Euphrates bridge at Al Hadithah. "A running battle all the way to Russia?" David asked with arched eyebrows.

"Yes. Malinsky has drained the control centers of troops in Syria, Iraq and Iran to man his present attack force. As long as we can stay ahead of his pursuing army, we'll have little resistance in front of us. . . and he won't dare follow us into Russia for fear of an attack by Chou Huang and Henri Werner. Huang and Werner will protect us once we cross the border from Iran into Russia, and they won't care how much killing and scavenging we do along the way."

David flipped the maps open and began tracing an escape route due east from the northern tip of the Sea of Galilee. "We'll have to provide a rear-guard delaying action while we strip Nawa to resupply ourselves. That would be roughly thirty miles inside the Syrian border. Then, we continue due east about thirty-five miles to Shahba and confiscate additional supplies to make it across the Syrian Desert. We maintain the rear-guard action and continue eastward across the Iraqi border to Ar Rutbah, picking up supplies there. Then, we head northeast and cross the Euphrates at Al Hadithah, and the Tigris at Baiji. We call in our rear guard when we cross the rivers and blow up the bridges behind us. From the Tigris, we continue northeast to Kirkuk and take on more supplies. Then, we proceed on northward across the Iranian border and along the western side of Lake Urmia to Khvoy, Iran. We take on more supplies at Khvoy and head northeast the remaining sixty-five miles or so to the Russian border."

"Judging by the maps, it appears to be eight hundred and seventy miles or so from our breakout point to the Russian border along that route," Hartstein observed. "But we don't have a closer path where we can hope to stay ahead of his pursuing troops. All we have to do is travel faster than they do. We'll assign our strongest, fastest sharpshooters to the rear-guard action and load them down with nitro, dynamite, and grenades so they can set a few traps along the way. We'll keep enough nitro and dynamite in reserve to blow up the bridges and for miscellaneous demolition. We'll also scavenge every camel, donkey and horse from the local populations to provide mounts for the women, children and older adults who'll have trouble keeping up with our young men. Wherever the terrain is suitable, we'll provide our rear guard with whatever motor vehicles we come across. By stripping the local populations and burning everything else behind us, Malinsky's men will have to make periodic detours to find enough food to maintain their pursuit, and they'll have a tough time crossing the rivers. While they're delayed rounding up supplies, we'll be moving full speed ahead."

"With a scorched earth strategy, there's no reason we can't stay well ahead of them," David said with a look of great confidence. "We have to eat, drink, rest and sleep, but so do they. . . and our rear guard will make sure they don't sleep too soundly."

"We need to break out about two o'clock in the morning," Hartstein advised. "Malinsky is poised to attack at dawn. We'll send out an advance force under cover of darkness to attack his sleeping troops three miles on either side of our exit point. Our best trained guerillas will dispatch his sentries and then, after the advance force opens fire on his groggy troops, the guerillas can dynamite any supply vehicles we can't take along. Our main body can then move out and cut down the troops close enough to commence an immediate pursuit." Hartstein checked his watch. "It's ten after nine. We've got nearly seventeen hours to get organized. Let's get our division commanders briefed and begin preparations to move out."

A heavy web of security had been spun around the administrative offices of Wang Souleng in downtown Hong Kong. Inside the executive conference room on the top floor of the twelve story building, five men were gathered to make decisions affecting the human race. Henri Werner chaired the meeting, and around the table sat Wang Souleng, Mahatma Ghane, Chou Huang, and Sumo Komoto.

The center of the round table was laden with delicate china platters filled with fresh fruits, pastries and miscellaneous delicacies to please the palate. A white-coated waiter moved silently around the table serving gourmet tea and coffee from gleaming silver pots. The men chatted casually, waiting for the waiter to withdraw and for Werner to begin the conference. Chou Huang's jeweled fingers sparkled as he sipped his tea and fastened his slanted eyes upon Werner.

"Did the good bishop offer to share his future plans with you, Henri?" Werner looked back with a straight face. "No. He seems to be sifting priorities." Huang's chuckle shook his rotund belly as he rubbed his bald head with his right palm. "He's a most interesting man with many vices and seems to have plenty of time to enjoy them." "He's fallen from grace with Natas and would like to align himself with us," Werner replied.

"What does he have to contribute to our alliance?" "He knows how Natas thinks and what drives him, and perhaps what his weaknesses are. That could prove to be useful information in unforeseen situations." "Can we trust a man whose loyalties shift so quickly?"

Werner smiled wryly. "He's guilty of no more disloyalty than the rest of us. We also turned on Natas rather suddenly. I think Romas is more concerned with protection from Natas' propensity for homicide than with shifting loyalties."

Huang's expression became more serious. "Then, it might benefit our cause to offer him protection in exchange for reliable information. He's not in a position to drive a hard bargain."

Mahatma Ghane had been listening to the banter between Werner and Huang. He sat tall and straight with his hands folded on the table, ignoring the culinary delights. He was dressed in a black business suit with white silk shirt and pale blue tie. A man of simple taste, he disdained jewelry and displayed only a wristwatch and tie clasp. At sixty years of age, his frame was still thin with narrow, rounded shoulders. He spoke softly with measured politeness. "Would not Bishop Romas' allegiance to us sway the common people even farther from Natas. Many of them still look to him for spiritual guidance."

Because Ghane seldom voiced trivia, everyone listened when he spoke up. Wang Souleng studied him thoughtfully. Unlike Huang, Souleng was a petite Oriental with shiny black hair, manicured mustache, small bone structure, wizened face, and serious, dark eyes. He was sixty-two years old, and an astute politician.

"That is an excellent point, Mr. Ghane. Like our Indian brothers, my people do not change their spiritual leaders like dirty underwear. Romas' personal lifestyle is not common knowledge in my region."

Sumo Komoto nodded agreement with a gracious smile. Like most Japanese, he exhibited meticulous manners and never interrupted another's comments. He resembled Hirohito, the former emperor of Japan: small frame, wiry build, square jawed, broad forehead, wrinkled skin with sunken, watery eyes, and black hair flecked with gray. He was sixty-three years old and had spent thirty-two years climbing up the political ladder. "It is so among my people. If Bishop Romas wishes protection, then let us provide it for him. His defection from Natas will be welcome in the Far East since we do not look with favor upon blatant genocide."

Werner and Huang nodded their heads up and down when Komoto concluded his remark. Everyone at the table knew the issue was now settled. Bishop Romas would be given protection in exchange for his unwavering support of the alliance.

Henri Werner cleared his throat and called the meeting to order: "Shall we begin, Gentlemen?" He glanced around the table to ensure that everyone was prepared to commence. "The first item on the agenda is our planned response to a possible attack by the combined security forces from those regions which have not declared their independence. I propose that an attack upon any one of us be considered an act of war against all five of our regions and that we respond accordingly. I further propose that the five of us form a war council with one vote each; that the will of the majority forms the battle plan that each of us passes down in his respective region; and that each of us command his own forces to achieve the objectives set by our war council."

For thirty of his fifty-nine years, Chou Huang had wanted to be a general. He had served ten years in the Chinese military beginning at age nineteen and had risen to the rank of Lieutenant Colonel before deciding to enter politics. "You're proposing that the council function as a general over our combined forces, and that the regional commanders carry out the council's orders?" "Yes." Werner agreed. "You have expressed the intent most clearly."

"That is an excellent proposal," Souleng chimed in. "We each retain complete control of our regional forces but can count on the combined strength of all five regions if any of us are attacked. The majority votes on the council will determine the overall strategy for any situation where our combined forces are committed."

"How many men could Malinsky put in the field against us?" Komoto inquired. "As long as the other five regions remain loyal to Natas, Malinsky has approximately forty-eight million security troops at his disposal," Werner answered. "That's out of a total population numbering approximately five hundred million, and eighty-eight million of them are between the ages of eighteen and thirty-five."

"No single region could risk facing that potential," Komoto reasoned. "But, standing together, we can maintain our complete independence." "We have a younger population throughout Asia," Souleng pointed out. "Approximately thirty percent of our people are draft age. Including our existing security forces, we could muster a combined army of more than two hundred million men. That gives us an advantage of sixty-four million troops . . . nothing to sneeze at when it comes to all-out war."

"Are we then prepared to vote?" Werner prodded. He looked slowly around the table to see if anyone wanted to comment further. "Okay, then. All in favor of the proposal as submitted signify by raising your right hand."

Five hands went up in unison. "We all bear witness to each other that the proposal has been adopted," Werner said solemnly. "Before moving to the economic portion of our agenda, there is a related and pressing issue that we should discuss. The Israelis have broken through Malinsky's blockade and are fighting a running battle across Syria toward the Iraqi border. The Israelis are greatly outnumbered but are staying ahead of the pursuing troops by stripping the countryside as they pass through to resupply themselves and burning what's left behind them. They are apparently trying to seek refuge in an independent region, and judging by their present course, they'll cross the Euphrates and head north through Iran to the Russian border. I'd like to see them make it and propose that we provide them refuge once they cross into Russia. To discourage Malinsky from pursuing them, I further propose that we mass sufficient troops along the Russian border with Iran to beat back his forces if he attempts to cross the border."

Chou Huang was the first to respond. "Now is as good a time as any to clearly demonstrate that we intend to maintain the integrity of our regional borders. I'd love to have Hartstein and Solomon join my security forces along with their men." "Are we willing to risk war in order to help the Israelis?" Souleng asked. "That's not the critical issue," Werner replied. "The question is really whether we're going to allow Malinsky to violate our borders regardless of the circumstances." "But we can refuse to allow the Israelis to cross," Souleng countered.

"That's true," Werner agreed. "However, are you prepared to do battle with the Israelis so Natas can practice genocide?" "Absolutely not!" Souleng replied. "I'm just making sure that we all consider the possibility of war if we provide them refuge. Personally, I'd rather fight Malinsky than Hartstein and Solomon." "Let's give them protection," Komoto ventured. "They are not our enemy," Ghane said softly. "Let them in." "Let's have a formal vote," Werner admonished.

Again, all five hands went up in unanimity. "So be it," Werner said with a ring of finality. "I am prepared to order all my security forces in Baku, Sumgait, Yerevan, Leninakan, Kirovabad, Batumi, Tbilisi, and Astrakhan to take up immediate positions along the Iranian border; and begin shuttling additional troops by air to Baku and Yerevan from eastern Europe, central and south Russia. Based on the distance covered thus far, it will take the Israelis another two weeks to reach the Russian border. That gives us enough time to ship backup troops across the Black Sea and the Caspian Sea. If we make use of all our commercial planes and ships capable of transporting troops, and are currently within the logistical parameters, we should be able to place enough of our forces in position to keep Malinsky from entering Russia. If this strategy is acceptable to everyone, I suggest we take a break at this time and transmit the necessary orders to our regions. Does anyone wish to propose an alternative strategy?" Werner looked at each man and waited patiently.

"We will incur some significant commercial losses," Souleng pointed out. "Shall we agree to equally share those losses?" "That is acceptable to me," Huang committed. Ghane and Komoto indicated agreement with an affirmative nod.

"Very well," Werner responded. "Let us confirm our mutual understanding with a formal vote concerning the adoption of the military strategy proposed and the equal sharing among our regions of all commercial losses incurred as a direct result of implementing that strategy. All those in favor of the proposal as stated, please raise your right hand."

As he spoke, Werner raised his right hand. The other four men followed suit. Werner displayed a pleased expression. "Okay, then. Let's take a short break and confer with our control centers before moving on to the economic agenda."

The Iraqi population fled before the oncoming human tide as the Israelis swept into Ar Rutbah and began sacking the city's food and water supplies. The sound of continuous gunfire echoed through the Syrian Desert where the rear guard ambushed the pursuing troops. The proximity of the rifle fire worried David Solomon. Malinsky's men had been steadily gaining ground since they hadn't yet slowed down to forage for supplies.

"There's got to be some way to slow them down." David voiced his thought as he pulled out the route maps. His right index finger traced their route northeast from Ar Rutbah to Al Hadithah. The pipeline! They had crossed a major oil pipeline which the map showed they would parallel as they traveled between the two cities. They could rupture the pipeline and create a burning lake of oil behind them. That should encourage the pursuing army to consider a suitable detour!

No matter whether they turned aside to the northwest or the southeast, they should be delayed long enough for us to reach the Euphrates at Al Hadithah ahead of them and blow the bridges, including the bridges at Anah and Hit. When the others moved on from Ar Rutbah, he would lag behind and wait for the rear guard. While he waited, he'd rupture the line and start flooding the terrain.

The troops doggedly pursuing the fleeing Israelis covered an area twenty miles wide and five miles deep. They moved like an army of scurrying ants across the Syrian Desert fifty-three miles due west of Ar Rutbah. Most of the men traveled on foot, followed by a caravan of track driven vehicles hauling food and water. Thousands of desert vehicles packed with troops raced over fifty miles ahead of the main body and were periodically attacked by the Israeli rear guard waiting in ambush.

The guerillas salvaged all vehicles that remained operational and moved on to the next defensive position. For more than sixty miles along the Israeli escape route to the west and to the east of Iraq's border with Jordan, the desert was littered with human corpses. The bodies of several thousand Israeli guerrillas were scattered among nearly a quarter million of Malinsky's fallen troops. By the time the weary Israelis gathered enough food and water to pull out of Ar Rutbah, the rear guard was battling motorized troops in the outskirts of the city.

The main body of Israelis followed the pipeline northeast toward Al Hadithah while the rear guard took up a position along the pipeline northeast of Ar Rutbah and continued beating off the motorized pursuers. Meanwhile, the ruptured pipeline behind them poured millions of gallons of crude oil into the path of the army advancing on foot. The growing oil slick oozing westward and toward the southwest flowed beneath burning vehicles into which the Israelis had thrown small bottles of nitroglycerin or lighted sticks of dynamite.

Mangled bodies were strewn about the wrecked carriers and more than forty thousand Israeli rifles fired a withering hail of bullets into the oncoming transports. Exploding vehicles and ruptured fuel tanks spewed billowing fireballs of burning fuel across the gigantic oil slick as the ruptured pipeline continued to vomit out a huge torrent of oil. As the subsequent waves of motorized troops piled up west and south of the wall of flames, David Solomon and the Israeli rear guard moved on northeast along the pipeline.

Boris Malinsky traveled with his main force and he rode comfortably aboard the lead supply transport. He felt nauseated as the string of bad news was relayed from Ar Rutbah. How could the Israelis travel so fast burdened down with women, children and old people?

Somehow, they continued to stay nearly fifty miles ahead of his main force and were slaughtering his motorized troops. The carnage he saw strewn in the desert behind the Israelis was appalling. How could they consistently maul his forces like that? The scenes had destroyed the morale of his infantry and he knew they weren't anxious to close the distance with Solomon and Hartstein. Still, they maintained the pace he demanded of them even though it was clearly apparent they would never catch up to the Israelis before they crossed the Euphrates and blew up the bridges.

Neither would his motorized troops be able to stop them. Less than fifty thousand guerillas had lagged behind to ambush and decimate those forces. What would happen to those same troops if they did run up on the rest of the guerillas. . . and faced a half million rifles rather than a mere fifty thousand?

He was beginning to understand how a couple million Jews established the nation of Israel while completely surrounded by Arab nations totally committed to exterminating them. Israel's military had not been defeated since the nation was reestablished in 1948, and it didn't seem to matter how badly they were outnumbered.

Mowing down unarmed women and children peaceably going about their business on the streets was one thing; chasing after a half million fearless guerillas escorting armed women, children and elderly folks was quite a different story. The twelve-year olds and the seventy-year olds would blow your brains out just as efficiently as the fierce young men.

How was he going to explain his humiliating failure to Lord Natas? He had the entire guerrilla force bottled up in a trap and surrounded by six million men. If he couldn't take them then, how would he ever manage to get the job done?

Now, he was out in the middle of nowhere, running out of supplies, being outdistanced by his quarry, suffering heavy losses, being ridiculed by his own men; and the outcome of the battle had already been determined. The unmarked Jews were going to make it to the Russian border well ahead of him. He'd have to travel twice as fast as Hartstein and Solomon in order to overtake them before they reached Al Hadithah, and that was highly unlikely. Once the rear guard blew the bridges over the Euphrates and the Tigris, he was stalled. He'd have to either detour thirty miles to other bridges or hang around with his thumb up his nose while his troops repaired the bridges sufficiently to allow passage.

Either way, he'd lose a full day. A thirty-mile detour would put him an additional sixty miles behind, and the Jews would no doubt travel that far if he stopped to repair the bridges. He'd lose at least ten hours at the Euphrates, and another eight hours at the Tigris. Moreover, since Hartstein and Solomon had adopted a scorched earth strategy, he'd have to make several detours for supplies between his present position and the Zagros Mountains.

There was no doubt about it. The guerillas were going to cross over into Russia, and there wasn't a thing he could do about it. Up ahead, he saw his general communications contact waving his arms to flag him down. He motioned to his driver to pull over. The heavy rig turned aside and stopped as the communications officer climbed onto the track below Malinsky's window. "Yes ... what is it?" Malinsky inquired.

"I'm sorry, Sir. The men up ahead are requesting permission to turn back. Less than three hundred vehicles are still operational, and the men feel it's suicidal to clash with the guerillas again with our main force so far behind. We've sustained better than fifty percent casualties, and many of the survivors are now on foot. In addition, a large number have suffered severe burns and need emergency medical attention. Our medics can't possibly handle all the gunshot and burn victims. We're losing too many men for lack of medical care." "Shall we simply retreat like whipped dogs with our tails between our legs?" Malinsky barked. "Maybe you'd like to explain such a defeat to Lord Natas."

The officer hung his head for a moment and then stared back at Malinsky. "It's no use, Sir. They've beaten us. We don't have enough troops in the control centers ahead of them to even slow them down. . . and we can't follow them into Russia."

"Why not?" "Our man in Goris reports that Henri Werner and Chou Huang are rushing troops to the border to keep us from entering Russia. We'd be facing a superior force in addition to the Israelis." Malinsky silently cursed Werner and Huang. "You think the rebels would actually attack us?" "Yes, Sir. I don't think there's any question about that. They'll have enough men in those mountains to pin us down until reinforcements arrive. . . then we'll be looking up at more rifles than we'd care to count."

The stark reality of his dilemma smothered Malinsky's ego. He had driven the Jews to heroic efforts that captured the admiration of Huang and Werner. Hartstein and Solomon had whipped him again, and if he tried to run them down inside Russia, Huang and Werner would give him a royal thumping. . . which wouldn't be any easier to explain to Natas than letting the Jews get away. He wasn't prepared for war with the independent regions.

"What shall I tell them, Sir?" Malinsky leaned his head forward and massaged his forehead with the fingertips of both hands as he faced the inevitable. "Tell them to turn back," he said in a resigned tone. "This mission is terminated. Let's get these clowns turned around and back to their control centers."

CHAPTER 13

Torture and Decapitate All Christians

"What's going on between you and Natas? Have you heard from him recently?" Werner asked Romas. He sipped at his third brandy since arriving at Romas' home forty minutes earlier. "Not a thing since your last visit. He's still preoccupied with killing Jews and torturing Christians. He doesn't have much need these days for my services."

Werner grinned widely. "The Israelis that defied him are certainly a stouthearted bunch. They've kicked Malinsky all over the Middle East. They'll soon be safe from Natas. I'm offering them sanctuary in my region." "I was sure you would, Henri. How long before they reach the Russian border?" "They slowed down a bit when Malinsky turned back, so they're still south of Lake Urmia. The pace they had maintained since fleeing northern Israel was killing off some of the elderly. None of Malinsky's control center forces in Iran or Turkey will dare try to stop them. If Malinsky couldn't subdue them with six million men while he had them completely surrounded, it would be nothing short of gross stupidity for a few hundred thousand troops to pursue them in open country."

Romas laughed softly. "I pity the poor idiots dumb enough to try. That same bunch of guerillas has already killed well over a million of Malinsky's men, and the arms they're carrying now make them a lot deadlier." "It beats anything I've seen in my lifetime," Werner replied. "It boggles my mind what they've accomplished considering they were totally disarmed when Natas first tried to pounce on them." "I wonder if they could have pulled it off without Hartstein and Solomon," Romas remarked. "Those two are worth an entire division."

Werner grinned from ear to ear. "I guess we'll never know the answer to that, but Hartstein and Solomon can dine at my table any time. . . and I hope they never become my enemies." "Are you still massing troops on the border, Henri?"

"I'm not shuttling any troops by air or sea, but I'm leaving the ones in place that were pulled from nearby control centers. I want to be sure Malinsky and Natas get the message, and the men already in place would like to welcome the Israelis into the region. They're as proud of them as I am."

"Do you think the Israeli guerillas will want to join your security forces, Henri ?" "That's hard to say right now. I think they really want to just live in peace and provide for their families. But, they're welcome to join if they wish." Werner looked thoughtfully at Romas. "Tell me, Julius, how do you truly feel about Natas? Are you prepared to completely abandon him?"

Romas took his time in answering. He knew why Werner was asking and he didn't want to appear overly anxious. "He has gone too far to ever regain the trust and loyalty of the masses. They now see him as a fraud and look to the regional administrators for leadership." "But, how do you see him, Julius?" "I see him as a complete egomaniac that threw away his kingdom for the opportunity to persecute the Jews. In doing so, he proved himself to be a liar and cold-blooded killer. I neither respect him nor wish to maintain any sort of relationship with him."

"How do you think the masses see you at this point?" Romas drank more brandy. Would his alignment with the independent regions depend upon his ability to sway the masses from a spiritual perspective? Would the people reject him because he had proclaimed Natas to be divine? If so, would the alliance have any use for him? Would anybody? He decided to be noncommittal. "I truly don't know how the people feel about me, Henri. I've intentionally maintained a low profile since Natas began his rampage. . . hoping that it wouldn't rub off on me. We both know that the people want a living, breathing spiritual leader, even if they don't believe in any life hereafter. Whether I can continue to fill that need remains to be seen. I have done nothing to suggest that I approve of what Natas has done since he breached the peace with Israel."

Werner carefully studied Romas' eyes and believed that he answered honestly. "Wang Souleng, Mahatma Ghane and Sumo Komoto seem to believe that their populations have not turned on you. Chou Wang and I have heard nothing overly derogatory from any sizable percentage of our people. I think perhaps there's a lot of confusion that needs to be cleared up. All five of us feel that you could play an important role should war break out between the alliance and Natas. It is imperative that our populations maintain some common faith. No one can remain in power once the masses rally against them. That fact has been amply demonstrated from the French Revolution to the dissolution of the Soviet Union."

Romas nodded his head up and down slowly to indicate agreement with what Werner was saying. "I'm willing to give it my best effort, and quite frankly, Natas scares me. Who knows what he'll do next." "If you don't know, Julius, who would? You've been closer to him than anyone."

"I'll share my insights into his basic nature with you, but I don't know how helpful that will be since he is quite hard to understand and very unpredictable." "That's all we ask, Julius. We're not looking for any miracles from you. . . just honesty and loyalty." “You can count on that, Henri.”

Romas was bubbling inside although his face didn't show it. "Do you think that war is probable in the near future, Henri?" Werner sipped his brandy and scratched his right cheek. "The five of us have no interest in trying to overthrow Natas for the benefit of the other regions. If they want to continue worshiping him, that's their business and their choice. However, if he attacks us, we're prepared to wage war. . .which brings up an issue concerning which I'd like to hear your opinion. Do you think Natas will resort to manufacturing military weapons?"

Romas shook his head. "He's much too clever to attempt that. On the other hand, he understands that people are quite willing to kill each other with clubs, knives, rifles, and handguns over such things as political boundaries, natural resources, personal wealth; and to obtain relief from oppressive government. They will also rally behind their government for what they consider just causes and follow their favored political leaders to war. The nuclear war did not change basic human nature but rather instilled within the masses the unshakable resolve to forever ban all categories of military weapons. It's okay to wage war when necessary, and to kill each other. . . but not too many at once, and never civilians."

Werner nodded agreement. "I'm glad to hear you reinforce my own conclusion. I also am convinced that the quickest way to be ousted from power is to even suggest the production of military weapons." Werner drained his snifter and filled it half full again. "I have one more question, Julius, before we return to more pleasant things. "Do you think the Africans will stick with Natas?"

Romas had already reached a conclusion on that question, but he gave the impression that he pondered it before answering. "The blacks are a loyal race by nature and seldom revolt against a government that rules them fairly. Therefore, I believe they'll remain loyal to Natas until he does something they perceive as threatening to them. As long as they don't rebel, they'll also follow him to war to keep him in power."

Werner reflected on Romas' opinion. Africa represented the core of Natas' remaining power since the continent contained thirty-four percent of all control centers outside the alliance. If the Africans could be coaxed into declaring their independence, the balance of power would be tipped heavily in favor of the alliance, even if Africa chose to remain an independent population with no political entanglements outside the continent.

The alliance already controlled more than half of the world's total population and nearly seventy percent of the earth's resources. Oil was no longer a key factor within the global economy. Since petroleum-based fuels had been banned under global law, except for tightly rationed aviation and marine fuels, the oil market had been reduced to non-energy consumer products, leaving Europe and the Asian regions controlled by Huang, Souleng and Ghane the major players in the world market.

Werner scratched his bald head and decided to run up a trial balloon. "There must be some way to prod Jahamal Sadatie and Malcom Allie into declaring African independence. You said the blacks won't rebel unless they feel threatened, Julius. Do you have any thoughts on how we might disturb their comfort level?"

Romas poured himself a fresh drink and adjusted the level in Werner's snifter. He knew precisely what Werner was suggesting. The crafty old goat was dangling a tempting bait under his nose. He'd swallow it, but first the pot needed to be sweetened up a bit. He flashed Werner his most accommodating smile. "When is a nasty rumor most likely to be believed, Henri?" Werner grinned with the look of a fox in the hen house. "When the source is perceived as unbiased and honest." "Then, if you want an entire race to accept the rumor as fact, what else becomes necessary?"

"Generally speaking, I would think the rumor must be connected with something that the targeted population is prone to believe anyway, and something that stirs their emotions more than it stretches their common sense." "Like unreasonable and unjustified persecution?" "That would certainly be fertile ground." Now is the time to raise the ante, Romas gambled. He arched his eyebrows and gazed intently at Werner. "Does it matter to the alliance who controls Africa as long as the continent declares its independence?"

Werner considered Romas' motivation and conceded the point. "No. What matters is whether Africa turns against Natas." "That could be decided by stirring up the population to the point where Sadatie and Allie are forced to declare Africa independent or be ousted from power." "I agree," Werner replied. "How do you propose that we jointly accomplish that objective, Julius?"

Romas savored his brandy and pretended meditation, then finally showed his cards. "I can make a public statement on television that Natas has turned aside from his divine mandate to maintain world peace because of his innate hatred for Jews and blacks; that he has already demonstrated his intent to kill the Jews; and that he is planning to move against the entire Negro race. I can publicly denounce him for his madness, unfitting even a divine being, and make a plea for blacks to unite against him before it's too late. Should Natas vehemently deny my statements, who will believe him? His murderous campaign against the Jews will speak louder than his denial."

Werner became visibly excited. "After your public statements, each of the alliance members will echo your concerns. That should turn up the heat on Sadatie and Allie. The African people will clamor for independence from Natas. Then, if they're slow to respond to the public outrage, a power vacuum will be created which I assume you would like to fill." "I believe the Africans would follow someone they respect and trust," Romas speculated, "especially if that person is trying very hard to protect them from genocide. I can fit nicely into that role."

"The timing of your TV statements and our corroborating speeches must be carefully coordinated," Werner cautioned. "We need to ensure the continuity of fear and outrage to keep the people in a perpetual uproar until the desired result is achieved. I'll relay our strategy to the rest of the alliance. I think they'll all support it one hundred percent." Romas extended his snifter toward Werner. "Shall we drink to our mutual ambitions?" Werner lifted his snifter and clinked the rim against Romas' drink. "To a long and loyal relationship."

Boris Malinsky waited in Goldstein's office, chain-smoking cigarettes and drinking straight scotch from an eight-ounce glass. Goldstein was in the temple updating Natas on his progress in rooting out the Christians hiding from the security forces. Malinsky hoped the scotch would help calm him while he explained to His Divine Majesty how the unmarked Jews managed to escape into friendly territory. He looked at his watch. If Goldstein didn't get back soon, he'd have to head for the temple without any warning as to Natas' mood. He drank the glass dry, poured it full again, stubbed out his cigarette and lit another. He wondered how

Goldstein was making out with the stubborn Christians. He laughed to himself. What Goldstein called "rooting out" was a nice term for unmitigated torture. Natas didn't want the Christians to martyr themselves. He wanted them to worship him and renounce Christ in exchange for amnesty. He had heard how Goldstein's troops encouraged Christians to accept amnesty. They began by ripping out fingernails and toenails one at a time. Next, they chopped off fingers and toes. If the victim didn't give in by that time, they carved up the genitals, hacked off arms and legs, and punched out the eyes. Even then, most of the fanatics refused to exchange their hope in Christ for Natas' stay of execution. What would it take to make Goldstein give in if the roles were reversed . . . the first glimpse of the pliers?

He snickered to himself, gulped more scotch and cursed the Jews. Too bad Goldstein didn't have to deal with the Israeli guerillas instead of fanatical Christians hiding out in small groups all over the world! The Israelis would teach Goldie a few lessons in humbleness. He still found it hard to believe they killed so many of his men while running like scalded turkeys. Well, at least a few of them died in the process.

Goldstein walked briskly into his office, pulled out his chair and plopped down behind his desk. "Hi, Boris. What's going on?" "Is your hide smoking, Goldie?" Malinsky asked with a chuckle. "Not really," Goldstein replied with a scowl. "He just thinks I should be getting more results. He believes that anybody will do anything to avoid extended physical torture." "Have you found that to be the case?" Malinsky asked without any mirth.

Goldstein shook his head, sighed and stared up at the ceiling. "I've seen parents close their eyes while their children were mutilated beyond recognition; women raped to death while they prayed, and their husbands were forced to watch before being hacked into pieces; people burned alive; and any other atrocity you can imagine. In spite of everything we do to break their wills, only a fraction of the Christians give in. I've had about all I can stomach. How about you?"

Malinsky lit another cigarette and finished off his scotch. "I helped myself to a couple of glasses. . . hope you don't mind." "You're welcome to it. Want another?" "I'd better not. My tongue's thick as it is." Malinsky got up from the guest chair, handed Goldstein the glass, and sat down on the corner of the desk. "I guess you heard how the Israelis outran me?"

Goldstein dug out the scotch and poured himself a stiff drink. "I heard they're headed into Russia and left a lot of dead men behind them. It's hard to believe. You had them trapped and outgunned better than six to one." "That's what Natas will want to know and I don't have an intelligent answer. They simply outfoxed me." Malinsky checked his watch again. "I'd better head that way. What kinda mood's he in?"

"Hard to tell about him," Goldstein replied. "When I left, he seemed fairly relaxed. I wouldn't worry about it too much. Just go in and tell him the truth. The Israelis pulled a surprise maneuver that you didn't anticipate, and they got away. He'll understand, and if he doesn't. . . he'll eventually get over it." Malinsky got up and headed for the door. "Thanks for the pep talk, Goldie. I'll let you know how it goes."

The sixteen ounces of scotch deadened Malinsky's senses as he bowed before Natas. "Your obedient servant, Divine Majesty." Natas smiled pleasantly from his golden seat between the outstretched wings of the Cherubim. "I presume that, as you promised, none of the Israelis escaped?"

Malinsky's tongue felt like a wad of fat meat. "I regret to inform you, Divine Majesty, that I promised more than I delivered. The guerrillas broke through my lines and have escaped to Russia with their families. We managed to kill a few thousand, but the rest have been given refuge by Henri Werner."

Natas boiled inwardly but maintained a friendly face. "The race is not always to the swift, neither the battle to the strong; but time and chance happens to us all. Those are the words of King Solomon, whose blood runs in David Solomon's veins. Do not pound your breast over what is past or carry past failures into the future. There is yet time to catch the fox, but weary hounds delay the hunter. It is time for you to refresh yourself and resume your full command."

Malinsky was uplifted by Natas' attitude toward his error in judgment. "I would rather pursue the fox, Divine Majesty." Natas forced himself once more to exhibit patience and utter words of consolation. "Let us not hasten to the battle before the appointed time, nor let the enemy choose the terrain. The fox will become fat and lazy and perceive not that the hounds are upon him. Let the matter rest until time lulls the quarry to untroubled sleep. In the meanwhile, the dogs of war howl beyond the northern horizon. Trouble not yourself with their ceaseless yapping. The armies of the rebels will come to us in due season. Go forth and lay your hands upon the Christians and offer them the gift of amnesty according to our unchanging purpose."

A mighty shout went up from more than a million Israeli throats as David Solomon and Aaron Hartstein passed the word that the Russian border was less than two miles away. The joyous sound echoed across the mountains and stirred the emotions of the troops waiting to welcome the heroic guerillas and their families. The massed troops sent back thunderous shouts and cheers that reverberated from the mountains and valleys along the Russian border, continuing without ceasing as the Israelis drew nearer. They stretched out as far as the eye could see; appearing as a monstrous snake advancing across the rugged terrain.

Henri Werner and Chou Huang had arranged for resettlement camps in the nearby valleys where ample supplies of food and water, bedding and extra clothing were waiting under billowing tents. Government workers had been assigned to the camps to help register the Israelis and to provide medical attention. The registration number was unique to the refugees and bore no meaning nor relationship to Natas' mark nor his number. After rest, medical examinations, food, water and sleep, the happy Israelis were provided transportation to nearby cities where they were assigned government housing and government employment.

Aaron Hartstein took an adjoining apartment in Baku next to David and Martha Solomon. It was the end of an uncertain and miraculous flight from death. Aaron ate with them and visited frequently, praying with them and awaiting the end of Natas' reign. David worked for the government in the computer center at Baku, and Aaron, being of retirement age, was given a full government subsidy. Their days were filled with comfort and quiet fellowship while the wrath of Natas was directed toward the Christians.

Throughout the continent of Africa, angry blacks gathered around their televisions, watching and listening as Nancy Flack hosted a special broadcast by International Cable News Network. For the previous six days, the network had encouraged all Africans to mark the time and date at which Bishop Julius Romas would personally appear at the network studio in Africa to broadcast a message of vital importance to every African.

There had been broad hints that the bishop had separated himself from Lord Natas and that he was deeply concerned about the safety of every Negro. From all the fragments of information being doled out by Romas to International Cable News, a dark rumor had emerged that Lord Natas, lacking the nerve to pursue the Israelis into the independent regions controlled by Chou Huang and Henri Werner, now planned to persecute the Negro race which he deemed inferior to whites. Of course, it was just a rumor and Bishop Romas was expected to clear the air.

Ms. Flack reviewed the events leading up to the flight of the Israeli guerillas and the massive casualties they had inflicted upon Malinsky's security forces. She ran film clips of armed police murdering Jews and the desecration of Solomon's Temple. Then, she rehashed the numerous battles between the security troops and the unmarked Israelis from the second breach of the peace agreements with Israel to the final exodus into Russia. She speculated about Natas' true nature and then introduced Bishop Romas.

Romas wore his black bishop's robe that fastened around his throat but displayed no other religious garb. He conjured up a sad countenance leavened with a sprinkling of spiritual benevolence as he looked into the main TV camera and spoke slowly to add a measure of conviction to his words:

"Good evening to all our citizens around the world and may your homes be filled with love, peace, and unity of spirit. I feel a personal obligation to come before you and to confess a heavy burden which truly breaks my heart. I have been continuously concerned about Lord Natas' unjustified persecution of the Jewish people and his apparent willingness to commit cold-blooded murder at the hands of Malinsky's security forces. I have only limited insight into the forces of good and evil that wrestle within the person of Lord Natas, but genocide is not to be tolerated . . . even from one clothed with the vesture of divinity. I have been stricken with astonishment as we have seen the evil within his divine nature evolve into an all-consuming paranoia that has driven him beyond the realm of human compassion to the point where his wisdom and ability to govern have been subjugated to whatever power now darkens his original vision of world peace and security." Romas looked into the cameras with self-willed watery eyes.

"I have completely set myself apart from him and feel compelled to resist his further oppression of law-abiding citizens. I am especially concerned about our black citizens in Africa and around the world. There is now little remaining doubt that Lord Natas intends to exterminate all blacks as well as Jews. I cannot give any rational explanation for his intended genocide. I can only warn all black citizens that the persecution is sure to come. Thus, it is with great sadness and a contrite spirit that I implore black citizens around the world to rise up with one voice against this madness and to stand together in mind and body to resist Natas' forces. We have already seen that he is not invincible when his intended victims close ranks against him. The Israelis now enjoying their complete freedom within the independent regions have demonstrated to us that fearless men and women joined together in a common defense can withstand awesome forces. The African continent contains more than enough black citizens to overpower any force that Malinsky can muster, and the time to prepare is now. I will do everything within my power to help black people everywhere resist the evil that has somehow turned Lord Natas into a hideous demon that I know not. We must not let this unexplained transformation of Lord Natas sway us from our devotion to each other and our desire to live together as one global family within a world society where every person is equal and entitled to mutual respect. Now, more than ever, we must maintain our unity of spirit to repel any threat to our future peace and security. It is my sincere hope that you will allow me to lead you into this future. Thank you for this opportunity to come into your homes this evening and to unburden my heart."

Jack Roberts awoke at 5:12 pm and pushed back the covers. His eyes slowly focused in the cool darkness illuminated only by the small flame dancing on the end of a single torch hanging at the north side of the spring. He and the others had been asleep since around ten in the morning, and it was time to roust up to get ready for dinner and another long night of foraging for edible plants and roots. His back still ached from hauling five frame loads of wood the previous night. The fresh tracks he and Paul had seen in the rain-soaked woods indicated that the searchers had been back for the tenth day in a row, and Jack knew that the chances of remaining undiscovered were getting slimmer with each passing day.

From all the signs they'd examined during the past week, two to three dozen troops had passed within a hundred yards of the entrance three times. Sooner or later, they would find the cave if they kept coming back. Why were they continuing to search the same terrain? The Sawtooth Wilderness area covered a lot of territory.

What had they seen that encouraged them to keep looking? He and Paul had seen absolutely nothing to indicate that anyone else was hiding out within a five-mile radius of the cave. . . so what had attracted attention to this particular neck of the woods? Had someone spotted Paul and him out hunting without them being aware of it? Not likely. . . unless a camouflaged individual had been posted close enough to spy through high-powered binoculars on the areas, they hunted and foraged in. If so, and he or Paul had been spotted, it would most likely have been several weeks ago when they were still going out during daylight hours.

Then, another possibility crossed Jack's mind. It was necessary to use the ax and saw when cutting wood since all the loose wood had already been scavenged, and the sound of either the ax or saw would carry a long way during the stillness of night hours. Suppose some of the troops had been camped close enough to hear the noise? What if they were equipped with an infrared spotting device and had seen them heading back toward the cave? It would be convenient for some members of a search party to camp out during warm weather if they were campers at heart. It's for sure something piqued their interest, or they would move on somewhere else, Jack reasoned. Well, there was nothing much he and Paul could do about it except be extremely careful and hope for the best. He got up, stirred up the few live coals remaining from the morning fire, then added just enough dry wood to broil some meat.

Paul sat up, scratched his chest and squinted at Jack. "Guess it's about that time. . . unless you want me to stay behind and stoke the fire." "Time's wasting," Jack countered. "Hustle on outta there, and let's get at it."

The women awakened, got up and went to the spring. Paul joined Jack by the fire. "Think those human hounds were sniffing around again today?" "I've been giving that matter some thought," Jack answered. "I think we've been spotted from a distance. . .either hunting or cutting wood. They know we're here somewhere and are gonna keep looking until they find us."

Paul didn't seem surprised. "I came to that conclusion some time ago but didn't want to say anything for fear I might be voicing undue alarm." "I think we might as well face up to it, Paul. That's the only plausible explanation I can think of that would explain why they're not moving on." "Yeah. . .I know. I tried to envision myself in the shoes of whoever is the brains behind the searching and asked myself what strategy I would employ."

Jack nodded up and down, pursed his lips and frowned. "Let's see if I can guess what you came up with." He positioned the grill over the fire and stoked the wood. "You figured it'd make more sense to post observers with high-powered binoculars along the elevations providing the best view of suspicious areas rather than just tromp around on a random search. You also allowed for the possibility that anyone familiar with the wilderness might forage mainly at night to minimize the chances of being spotted. . .so you figured it'd be worthwhile to keep some men posted during the night hours and furnish them with infrared spotting scopes."

The worried look that deepened in Paul's eyes indicated that Jack had read his mind. "You're scaring me more than I care to admit. That's exactly what I would do, and there's no reason to think that the guy responsible for running us down isn't smart enough to think along the same lines."

"Think it would make any difference if we pull outta here at night, stay close to the ground in the tree cover and find another hideout?" "I doubt it, Jack. That really wouldn't solve the problem as long as they're searching this entire wilderness area using the same strategy. We'd still have to have food and firewood, and they'd spot us wherever we relocate as easily as they can here. Unless we move to a different mountain range, we're probably just as well off to stay right here." "I guess you're right," Jack conceded. "Every control center has troops searching out wilderness terrain. The risk of being spotted while trying to relocate is extremely high, and I doubt very much if we could come up with a place harder to find than this cave. The fact that they haven't found us yet, even though we assume they know we're here someplace, is a pretty good indication that we outta stay put." "I agree. Let's not say anything right now to worry the women."

The evening twilight had given way to darkness when Jack uncovered a peephole at the cave entrance and listened to the night sounds in the nearby woods while Paul waited behind him. Patches of dark gray clouds drifted past the quarter moon making it difficult to see very far. Jack watched and listened for roughly ten minutes. "Let's give it a whirl. I think it's okay."

They uncovered the entrance, laid aside their deerskin bags, and replaced the rocks and brush. A soft breeze rustled through the shadowy evergreens causing them to sway like giant sentries in the miserly moonlight. Paul and Jack scanned the woods in all directions looking for any sign of searchlights or campfires. The only sounds they heard were the mating calls of insects and the hopeful howl of a coyote several hundred yards to the northwest. The darkness blanketing the distant horizons was unbroken by manmade light. They shouldered their bags and headed for the hollow southeast of the cave where the ground was soft enough to gather roots, and the sunlit spaces continuously sprouted large, edible mushrooms during the spring and summer.

Inside the hollow, Paul and Jack searched only the open spaces where the moonlight filtered through, knowing that those same areas were sunlit during the day. They had gathered their first bag full and were just heading back toward the northwest when they heard the sound of a motor vehicle beyond the south rim of the hollow. Moments later, they saw the beam of headlights approaching from the southwest. Coming from behind the headlights was the unmistakable sound of cooped up bloodhounds.

"Whoa!" Jack exclaimed. "They're starting to wise up. We're gonna have to kill some dogs. If we head back, those stinking hounds will be digging at the entrance in a half hour." Paul nodded. "We're gonna have to leave them a hot trail to the northwest and then ambush the dogs along with whoever is with them." "Let's watch them get out and see how many we're up against. They can't drive across the hollow the way they're coming in."

The full-sized pickup lumbered into view along the southwest rim and began its descent into the hollow. Paul and Jack checked their handguns as the pickup angled toward the northeast until it reached the impassible gully between the north and south slopes approximately two hundred yards below Paul and Jack. The driver killed the engine and six men exited the back of the pickup with four bloodhounds on leashes. Two more men climbed out of the cab carrying hand lights. All eight men were armed with rifles fitted with banana clips.

"I think that's all there is," Jack whispered. "I don't hear any more vehicles. Hold on to your sack, and let's hustle about three hundred yards northwest to that rocky depression where we can see them coming. You kill everything on the right, and I'll take the left side. Kill the men first, then we'll take care of the dogs. Taking them by surprise, we should be able to kill four men each before they know what's happening."

Paul nodded and began sprinting alongside Jack toward the ambush point. Behind them, they heard the baying of all four hounds as the dogs immediately picked up their scent. Paul and Jack reached the rocky depression, pulled out their pistols and knives, and then laid flat on their stomachs. They clasped the knives in their left hands and the pistols in their right hands. "Let's wait till they get within twenty-five yards, so we can be sure of our targets," Paul whispered. "Those rifles are strapped, so they'll probably be carrying them on their shoulders. I only saw two lights, so they'll be pretty close together." "Okay," Jack whispered. "Let's send them back to Satan."

Jack and Paul laid motionless, peeking over the tops of the limestone rocks as the hounds approached, straining at their leashes. The men were four abreast and the four men holding onto the bloodhounds had their rifles slung over their shoulders. The four men trailing behind were right next to the men with the dogs. The two center men in the rear carried the lights. Paul and Jack were invisible in the dim moonlight, but the swinging hand lights gave them a clear view of all eight silhouettes.

As the men and hounds came closer, Jack and Paul cocked their hammers back and took deliberate aim. "Now!" Jack whispered. The .45 and .357 rounds exploded simultaneously in two successive bursts, downing the four men in front in less than two seconds. The men behind clawed at their rifles, but they never had time to recover from their initial confusion within the fleeting seconds between life and death. Four more shots rang out from the heavy caliber pistols. In four seconds, all eight men had been fatally wounded, and the hounds milled around the fallen men with mournful howls.

Paul shot two dogs and quickly reloaded his .357, but it wasn't necessary. Jack's .45 boomed out twice more and the other two hounds caught slugs in the back of their heads. Paul and Jack ran up and checked the bodies to make sure that each man was dead, then checked the hounds. One of the dogs shot by Paul was still alive and bleeding from its mouth. Paul bent down and slit the dog's throat with his hunting knife. "I'll gather up the rifles and all their ammo and see if they're carrying any other supplies we can salvage." "Okay," Jack answered. "I'll bring the truck around and we'll load up. Check the pockets first for the keys."

Paul searched for the keys while Jack reloaded his .45. "Here they are," Paul said as he fished the keys from the driver's pocket. He tossed the keys to Jack. "I'll strap the rifles together with their belts, so we can carry 'em easier." "Hang loose. I'll be right back," Jack said. He trotted toward the hollow as Paul continued searching the bodies.

Approximately twenty minutes later, Jack arrived with the pickup. It was a government vehicle with two cases of ammunition in the rear, extra batteries in the glove box, and another rifle hanging behind the truck seat. Jack and Paul heaved all the bodies along with the dogs into the rear bed and fastened the tailgate.

Paul had bundled up everything he had salvaged from the bodies inside one of the men's shirts. "I'll drive you within a quarter mile of the entrance, so you can haul this stuff in while I ditch the truck and these bodies over the cliff," Jack suggested. "That's far enough from here that nobody should come looking around this area after they find the truck and cargo. I'll be able to dump these guys and walk back in less than two hours."

The women were chattering around the fire when Paul came out of the tunnel carrying both deerskin sacks stuffed with roots and mushrooms. The sight of Paul alone and carrying both sacks frightened them. "Where's Jack!" Ruth cried out in a fit of panic. "He's okay! He's okay!" Paul assured them. "We ran into a little trouble and Jack's dumping some stuff over the cliff. We'll tell you about it when Jack gets back. In the meantime, I've got to go out again with my frame." He dropped the sacks by the fire. "I'll be back by the time you sort these goodies."

The women washed the roots and mushrooms in the spring while Paul hauled in the rifles, ammunition, and other items. He set the heavy load down in the tunnel about ten feet from the inner room so that the women wouldn't see the rifles before Jack returned. The glow from the fire was sufficient to keep Jack from stumbling over the frame

Paul sat down on a rock to the right of the fire and watched the women finish up at the spring. He thought about how different things might have been if the men and dogs had showed up at another time. . . like after he and Jack had recently been out and returned to the cave.

If the searchers continued to use dogs, it would just be a matter of time until the animals sniffed them out. They couldn't forage outside the cave without leaving a scent the dogs could pick up, and they had to replenish their supplies. They had enough wood for another month or so and enough meat for maybe three months. Then what? Besides, if they let those supplies dwindle too low, they would give up a margin of safety that had kept them from starving several times.

The women stashed the food and then gathered around Paul. "Are you guys going back out when Jack comes in?" Ruth asked. "Probably not," Paul answered. "We ran into a search party, and there's a possibility that more may show up before morning. We'll discuss it some when Jack comes in." "There he is now," Jackie announced. Paul looked toward the tunnel and saw Jack coming in with the frame on his back. He got up and helped Jack set the frame down by the fire. The women gasped when they saw the nine rifles. "Hey Hey!" Marge exclaimed. "What happened out there?"

"The searchers are using bloodhounds," Jack explained. "They came up through the hollow where Paul and I were foraging. If they had shown up an hour later, the dogs would have tracked us straight to the entrance." "Wonderful!" Jackie responded. "Dogs! What next?" "We'll just have to be a lot more careful," Jack replied. "Where are the searchers and dogs now?" Mary asked anxiously. "We killed them," Paul answered. "We had no choice."

Ruth stared at the nine rifles in wonderment. "Nine men! Nine men with automatic rifles?" "There were only eight men and four bloodhounds," Jack explained. "They had an extra rifle in the pickup. We left a hot trail to the northwest, so the dogs wouldn't backtrack us to the entrance. The hounds led the men after us, and we ambushed them at close range. Paul got four and I got the other four. Then, we shot the dogs. We loaded all the dead bodies and the dogs into their pickup and then I rolled the truck over a cliff a couple of miles away while Paul hauled in everything we could salvage."

"That's incredible!" Mary exclaimed. "You guys took on eight men with those rifles with nothing but your pistols?" "We got lucky," Paul said modestly. "We were well hidden in the dark, and they were all lit up by their hand lights. We let them get right on top of us, then blasted all eight. Four shots each by Jack and me, and they were all down. The four with the dogs never had a chance. The four in back of them were startled and had trouble getting a bead on us. We cut them down while they were fumbling with their rifles." The women were flabbergasted, but both thankful and delighted. "Wow!" Marge squealed. "You guys are something else!"

Paul blinked his eyes repeatedly and grinned. "Before you girls get too worked up, let's go through this stuff and see what we've got." He pulled out the shirt bundle first, laid it on the ground, began untying the ends, and glanced up at Jack. "Got a little surprise for you in here I think you might like." He spread the shirt out and fished two packets of pipe tobacco from among the watches, batteries, folding money, coins, cigarette packs, lighters, pocket knives, loose .30 caliber cartridges, and two pocket-size radios. One tobacco pouch was unopened, and the other was nearly full.

Paul looked happily at Jack. "The driver was a pipe smoker. I found these on the same body as the truck keys. I brought along all the cigarette packs to convert the tobacco." "Oh, man!" Jack responded. "I can sure use that!" He picked up the opened pouch, unrolled the top, spread the flaps apart, and inhaled the tobacco aroma. "Pardon me while I find my pipe." Ruth's eyes glistened as she watched Paul unbuckle the belts around the rifles. "Take a look at these beauties," Paul invited. "They'll fire sixty rounds faster than you can count to six."

He handed each woman a rifle, and then laid the other five on the rocks. While the women admired the rifles, Paul lifted out the two metal cases of ammunition, opened one and took inventory. He whistled softly as he counted the layers of cartridges. The heavy case contained ten layers with one hundred rounds in each layer. "Not bad! Two thousand rounds plus five hundred and forty in the rifles and another couple hundred loose cartridges. We've got enough ammo to eliminate a lot of intruders."

Jack puffed on his pipe while examining one of the rifles. It was a .30 caliber with two thirty-round clips fitted together with a soldering iron. Paul finished emptying out the frame while the women watched, chatting among themselves after leaning the four rifles against the rocks. Paul dug out two battery operated hand lights, a carton containing twelve flashlight batteries and four six-volt batteries. "Anybody ready to eat?" Ruth inquired. "I'm sure ready. Why don't you guys find a place to store this stuff and wash up? Mary and I will cook up some meat and boil some mushrooms."

After the meal, Paul talked with Jack while the women played a word game around the fire. Jack fired up his pipe again and honed his knife as he considered the problems posed by the searchers. "I think we should each carry one of those rifles when we go out in addition to our pistols. They're far superior to hunting rifles and shotguns. With a hundred and twenty rounds between us without reloading, we could maul a pretty large search party from ambush."

"I agree," Paul replied. "And another thought occurred to me. All of us need to take turns watching and listening while we're sacked out. If the dogs do sniff us out, the searchers will have to come through the tunnel, and it's long and narrow enough to limit the amount of men that can crowd in at one time. It doesn't matter how many are outside. We've now got enough firepower to keep the tunnel clear as long as we have a little advance warning that they are coming in."

"Matter of fact, as long as we have enough ammo, they never would be able to take us," Jack concluded. "We need to teach the women how to operate the rifles without wasting rounds." "About the only thing they could do would be to blow up the tunnel and try to seal us in," Paul reasoned. "In any event, with those rifles we can keep them from coming in. It'd be a worse massacre than Wounded Knee."

Jack put down his honing rock and checked the edge on his knife. "We need to start teaching the women how to handle the automatics immediately. There's a good possibility that somebody knows exactly where those eight we killed were planning to search. If so, there'll be another search of this vicinity soon as those corpses are found.... which'll probably be within twenty-four hours. A few hours after they fail to return to their base, you know good and well there will be search parties combing this entire wilderness."

"No doubt," Paul agreed. "We'd best stay inside a week or so until things cool off some." "Yeah," Jack replied. "We've made it this far. Let's not get careless." "I'll second that!" Paul said. He glanced at Marge.

"Wonder if Marge is marking off the months and knows how close Natas is to the end of his reign?" "She knows," Jack replied. "She tries not to think about it to avoid depression. She's really a sweet woman. It's too bad she got deceived into taking Natas' mark, but there's nothing she can do about it now ...... just try to enjoy the time she has left."

The discontent in Africa boiled over into widespread violence. Throughout the continent, angry, protesting mobs attacked government facilities, tearing down and burning anything displaying homage to Natas. Across the Mediterranean, less than four hundred miles from northern Tunisia, Rome basked in unprecedented splendor. The city had been the capital of the world before five of the ten regions comprising the world's surviving population declared total independence.

Rome was still the trading center of global society and remained a stronghold of support for Natas. The population density was higher than any other area on earth, and Natas' Temple was regularly visited by a large percentage of the local population.

Henri Werner paid handsome sums to African agents to encourage the rioting natives to sack and burn Rome. The sacrifice of the extravagant mercantile hub was deemed a modest price to pay for the destruction of Natas' Temple and the alienation of all Africa. Werner gradually drained Rome of security forces as the agitated natives formed a disorganized army of more than twelve million rioters determined to cross the Mediterranean Sea to Rome.

The seething mobs gathered along the coast of northern Africa from the Strait of Gibraltar to Tripoli. Rumors abounded that the riches of Rome were up for grabs, including the several tons of gold, silver and precious stones adorning Natas' Temple. Mercenaries, desiring to share the spoils, chartered ships and planes to transport the rampaging Africans on a coordinated swoop into Rome.

The vast armada of ships set out for the west-central Italian coast, followed by a swarm of chartered planes. The ships and planes made continuous round trips and the mercenaries scheduled and grouped the invading Africans into a deadly weapon aimed at the city. Less than two hours after the last plane landed, the lawless rioters were loosed upon the defenseless metropolis. Roughly half of the city's population had fled to northern and southern Italy, but the rest stayed with confident expectation that neither Natas nor Werner would allow Rome to be destroyed.

The undermanned security forces deserted Rome as the screaming, bloodthirsty invaders poured into the city streets, indiscriminately robbing, raping, torturing and killing. In less than one day, the entire city was looted and set ablaze. Everything of value was traded to the mercenaries for a fraction of its real value in hard cash, then quickly loaded aboard the ships and planes. The smoke of Rome's burning blackened the evening sky, and the flames was visible over a fifty-mile radius from downtown streets.

Natas' Temple was systematically stripped to its marble foundation, then defecated and urinated upon by the pillagers. Stores of food and alcoholic beverages throughout Rome were piled into the streets to fuel the drunken orgies played out by the light of burning structures as Rome was reduced to a smoldering heap of unwanted rubble. The evening horror continued all through the terrifying night until only black faces greeted the smoke-filled morning twilight. Rome had indeed fallen to rise no more. The city had become a sprawling, charred skeleton embracing the mutilated corpses of its once affluent citizens.

When their fury was totally spent, and the killing frenzy satisfied for the time being, the Africans gorged themselves with the remaining food and drink; slept, and arose to more feasting. The mercenaries returned to transport them back to Africa in exchange for a goodly portion of the hard cash which had been previously doled out for Rome's treasures.

The back of Boris Malinsky's knees itched as if tiny spiders were circling his joints as he bowed before Natas. "You sent for me, Divine Majesty?" Natas looked down at him with amused contempt. "The shadows lengthen, and our task remains unfinished. Nevertheless, it is time to prepare for the gathering of all flesh, and to answer the ancient question. The fires have long been kindled and await our coming. Our final battle will determine the tally of those who shall dwell among the flames in mockery of the everlasting covenant. Do you hear the sound of tramping feet, Boris?"

"Rome has been destroyed, Divine Majesty, and the Africans have joined the rebels. A mighty army advances from beyond the Euphrates. The Asian regions have assembled a force of two hundred million soldiers." "And how many do you have to fortify the Middle East?" "Approximately thirty-six million, five hundred and ninety-nine thousand, Divine Majesty. We appear to be hopelessly outnumbered. Werner, Sadatie, and Allie will send forty million or so against us, and there's still the Far East region to consider. Komoto will certainly send his forces to appease his alliance partners. I'm afraid that our cause is lost."

Natas' face cracked into an evil smile that chilled the marrow in Malinsky's bones. "All that draw near to the final battle will fight against him whom they know not and swords that cannot be turned aside. The essence of our striving is to lay the trap with care. The rebels have garnered all their young warriors to push against the sword, and we shall do likewise. Conscript the loyal regions to swell our forces for that is truly the final jest. The entire Middle East will encompass the battle for the throne in Jerusalem, and the beckoning graves in Armageddon will be inundated with a river of blood offered in hope of that which is already lost. They come because it is time to come, and they fight for that which has no value. The dominion of Earth by humans is forever ended, and we shall hasten their immortality to the eternal furnace."

"I have prepared for the battle, Divine Majesty. We will force the rebels to come to us over a battlefield bounded by eighty miles on one side and thirty miles on the adjoining side. Twenty-four hundred square miles will host four hundred million troops. After the initial volleys, the ranks will close into hand-to-hand combat. There will be no time for reloading once the killing margin shrinks to a few square feet."

"Where will you concentrate your strength?" "The seat of our government is Jerusalem, and we will protect the throne. We will draw the enemy into the Plain of Esdraelon in the north; into the Jordan Valley to the east; along the Coastal Plains to the west; and into the Negev Desert southward from the Ha-Arava Depression to Al Qusaymah."

"And where will your riflemen be concentrated?" "They will be the inner protection, Divine Majesty. We will saturate the Judeo-Galilean Highlands, and entrench in Jericho, Bethlehem, Bet Shemesh, Ram Allah, and along the northwest side of the Dead Sea. This will forge a protective ring around Jerusalem." Malinsky looked expectantly up at Natas. "We can alter that strategy, Divine Majesty, as you deem wise."

Natas laughed within his being but gazed at Malinsky with steadfast eyes. "Your net has been laid with care and will entice the prey onward. It is around Jerusalem that death will feast. All who fall under her shadow shall fight against him who died that they might live. Do you not find that a challenging thought, Boris; to perish at the hand of him who first suffered your fatal wounds? Who purchased with his own blood the redemption that you perceived as lacking in value?"

"Your riddle is too wonderful for me to perceive, Divine Majesty. I'm just an obedient servant." "You have spoken truly, Boris. In the passing of eons, your perception will improve. The struggle that is upon us will not alter the visage of eternity, but we shall steal a measure of its sweetness.

Go now, and stand your ground, for the fox has returned and the dogs are salivating for blood."

"Shall I discontinue the search for Christians, Divine Majesty, and gather those forces to battle?" Natas blinked with wonderment at the thickness of Malinsky's ignorance. "No, Boris. One of those unmarked is more precious than the whole of all who will fall in battle. All who are running to this slaughter have been tallied and claimed. Their death will have no significance other than to flout their numbers. One Christian who can be encouraged to accept our amnesty is worth all their blood mingled together." "Yes, Divine Majesty. We will continue the search."

Mahatma Ghane said nothing as he listened to the other members of the alliance war committee voice their opinions and predictions concerning the imminent war against Oren Natas. They were cocky and confident that the outcome was not in doubt. The alliance forces outnumbered Malinsky's troops approximately three to one. The battle would be bloody and the casualties high, but now was the time to strike. The Africans would no doubt join in the struggle on the side of the alliance if war was declared now.

If they waited, Sadatie and Allie might be able to calm the natives and remain loyal to Natas. The Arabs governed by Mohammad Mousani were still reeling from their humiliating defeat by the Israeli guerrillas and had little heart for confronting the vastly superior alliance army. Ramos Warez's troops were green and totally unfamiliar with Middle East terrain. If they pushed the issue now, only Haini Solanni's troops would be ready for immediate action.

On the other hand, if they waited and clung to the shaky hope that war could be averted by extended negotiations, Natas would only grow stronger; Warez's army could be better trained and equipped; the Arabs would become bolder, and the Africans might settle down. Gambling on maintaining peace through negotiation would permit time to change the odds and make the outcome of a future war somewhat uncertain. War was sure to come anyway, so why not get it over with now while they had the upper hand? They could divide up the rest of the world among the alliance partners, and Romas would be their puppet.

Komoto had not offered any opposing opinion and Ghane wasn't sure just where Komoto stood, but it didn't matter. Huang, Souleng, and Werner could carry the necessary majority votes. He listened with reserved skepticism as Werner traced the positioning of Malinsky's army on the wall maps. Werner's red-tipped pointer drew a line from north to south, west of the Jordan River. "From this line westward, Malinsky will concentrate

Warez's green troops to bear the brunt of our frontal assault. Along this eighty-mile front, he hopes to absorb our rifle fire and then slow our advance by hand-to-hand combat."

The pointer drew a line westward thirty miles into the Negev Desert, then northward from Mount Ramon to the port city of Haifa. "Inside this wedge, he will scatter his more experienced troops throughout the high ground, allocating to them the bulk of his rifles and ammunition. As our forces break through their eastern front, they will face continuous rifle fire from the highlands. His crack troops will form a tight ring around Jerusalem here."

The pointer drew an oblong loop passing through Bethlehem, Bet Shemesh, Ram Allah, and Jericho. "The Judean Hills will be crawling with riflemen, and the high ground between Ram Allah and Janin will be heavily fortified. Between Janin and Mount Meron, he will draw into the Plain of Esdraelon all our troops that breach the eastern front between Bet Shean and Qiryat-Shemona. The deciding battle will thus be waged on the battlefield of Armageddon and within a thirty-mile circle of Jerusalem. He has chosen the terrain and will not yield those positions to carry the fight to us. Although he will put up a desperate defense and bloody our noses, he cannot possibly prevail against our overwhelming forces. We shall simply storm those positions and put an end to Natas' reign."

Ghane now felt compelled to speak. "By the time our men break through Malinsky's eastern defensive line, they will be well scattered, fatigued, and depleted of ammunition; and they will be looking up at millions of rifles. It is worth remembering that Malinsky's forces outnumbered the Israeli guerrillas by six to one. Yet, the guerrillas suffered only minor losses while dealing Malinsky a heavy blow. A sizable numerical advantage does not necessarily assure victory."

Sumo Komoto was nodding his head up and down politely as Ghane voiced his concerns. Now, he too spoke up. "I suggest that we pool all our ships to transport our European forces across the Mediterranean Sea to attack the Coastal Plains from A Naqurah to Ashqelon, with the heaviest concentration between Pardes Hanna and Haifa. We can pool all our aircraft to fly my Far East forces to Damascus and other Syrian airports north and east of Malinsky's eastern line. The Africans can be ferried across the Suez Canal, then march along the northern edge of the Sinai Peninsula and up the Gaza Strip to attack Jerusalem from the southwest. Our troops from western Asia can march through Turkey and Syria and attack from the northeast. The bulk of our forces drawn from the rest of Asia can march through Pakistan, Afghanistan, Iran, Iraq, and Jordan to overwhelm Malinsky's eastern defensive line. Then, we quickly tighten the noose to end the conflict. We now have two hundred million troops massed along the borders with Iran, Afghanistan, and Pakistan. They can reach and bridge the Tigris and Euphrates while our forces are being shuttled across the Mediterranean and from the Far East to Syria."

Werner was impressed with the input from Ghane and Komoto. "That makes good sense. We can stall the movement of troops in the sea, up the Gaza Strip and southwestward from Syria until our main force crosses the Tigris and Euphrates rivers, and has moved into southwestern Syria and western Jordan. Then, we launch a coordinated attack forcing Malinsky to fight on four fronts simultaneously. We will also be strongest where he has spent his strength. . . . at Armageddon and at Jerusalem."

Huang and Souleng looked pleased with the overall strategy. Huang rubbed his rubbery, bald head with his right palm and gazed at the maps. "We should also allow time for our advancing troops to subdue the populations in Natas territory that we march through, so they don't rise up against us later. We can also strip them to supply our troops. Since Malinsky won't budge from his chosen positions, we can take our time in arraying our forces against him while we confiscate the wealth of regions opposing us. If we loot them completely, they will be unable to launch a campaign to reclaim the territory."

"I agree," Souleng added. "If we allow our troops to rape and pillage along the way, they will be even more bloodthirsty when they close with Malinsky's forces. That should give us a bigger edge in the hand-to-hand fighting." Werner laid aside his pointer, returned to his seat and looked around the table. "Do we have any dissenting opinions concerning Mr. Ghane's, Mr. Komoto's, Mr. Huang's, Mr. Souleng's, and my collective recommendations; or the input from Mr. Huang and Mr. Souleng concerning the subjugation of hostile populations?" The silence of acquiescence followed Werner's question. "Then, let us seal our agreement with a formal showing of hands." The alliance war committee had reached a unanimous decision affecting the human race.

The sky cleared, and the full moon illuminated the woodland by the time Jack and Paul hauled the fifth load of wood inside the tunnel and set the loaded frames down. They went back to the cutting site and used pine branches to smooth away their tracks in the wet ground vegetation from the pine stumps to the cave entrance. They sealed up the entrance and then carried the loaded frames through the tunnel and into the inner room. The women reacted with joy and relief when they saw Paul and Jack.

"Thank God!" Ruth cried out. "What took so long? We were scared out of our wits!"

Jack and Paul lowered the frames alongside the fire, and Jack tossed a log atop the coals. "We worked up two whole trees and dumped them inside the tunnel. Why don't you ladies unload the frames while we dry off?" "Yeah," Paul agreed. "I think my skin is wrinkled all the way to my bones."

The men shucked their wet gear and rubbed themselves down with dry towels at the fire while the women unloaded the frames. "You guys must be starved," Jackie said. "How about some broiled moose?" "Broiled anything sounds good to me right now," Paul answered. "I'm definitely in need of some chow."

Following a healthy portion of meat and casual conversation around the fire, Jack and Paul put on their tennis shoes to haul the wood in from the tunnel. Jack hung a torch along the tunnel where the wood was strewn about to facilitate loading the carrying frames. The men hauled four frame loads to the fire and rested after each trip while the women unloaded and stacked the wood. While Jack and Paul were gathering up the last load a few feet inside the entrance, Jack abruptly stopped working and motioned to Paul for silence. Paul heard the faint noise that sounded like trailing hounds.

Jack hurriedly uncovered a hole at the entrance and listened intently. "Bloodhounds! And coming this way!" "They're sure to find us!" Paul responded. "That wet ground will hold our scent for hours." "Bring our clothes and guns while I try to get a better fix on them," Jack urged. "There's still time to lead the dogs off if we hurry!"

Paul sprinted to the inner room, grabbed up dry clothes, socks and boots, slung the gun belts and two rifles around his shoulders, then ran back toward the tunnel. The women called to him frantically, asking what was happening. "Bloodhounds! Searchers and bloodhounds! Keep those rifles handy! We're gonna try to lead them off!" Paul ran back through the tunnel to the entrance, laid the gun belts and rifles aside, handed Jack his gear, stripped off his robe and tennis shoes, and began yanking on his hunting clothes. "How far away are they now?"

"Can't tell for sure," Jack answered. He tossed aside his robe and tennis shoes, then quickly dressed. "It sounds like they're circling to the northwest from the hollow where they jumped us the other day. I'll head them off above those fresh stumps if I can. You cover the entrance and head north a quarter mile, then cut due east. I'll lead them farther north, then turn back southeast. Kill the dogs. We can lose the men in the dark."

"Okay," Paul agreed. "We'll meet up by the lake after shooting the dogs, then lead the men toward Galena Summit until we lose them, then cut back to the cave." "Be careful," Jack said softly. "And don't worry about me." He buckled on his gun belt, grabbed one of the automatic rifles, then disappeared into the night. Paul carefully recovered the entrance, checked his .357, shouldered the other rifle, and began running due north. He raced ahead a quarter mile before turning east. As he changed directions, he heard the hounds northwest of the fresh stumps. Then, he heard something else that caused him to pause. Beyond the lake, to the southeast, another bunch of hounds were audible.

Wow! Paul thought. That complicates things. He decided to double back, circle the lake, then lead the incoming dogs northwest toward Jack. If he didn't kill them all, maybe Jack would get in on the action.

North of the fresh stumps, he heard the continuous chorus of four to six bloodhounds. Jack had coaxed the first bunch of dogs to follow him due north.

A short burst of rifle fire rang out from Jack's direction, followed by four single shots in rapid succession, then three more single shots. Those shots were mingled with a volley of return fire from eight to ten automatic rifles. The only dogs Paul heard after the gunshots were behind him. He trotted onward to a small clearing lighted by the full moon, moved to the dark side, and took up an ambush position by lying flat on the ground beneath a drooping hemlock. He pulled out his .357, laid it to his right, then sighted his rifle into the center of the clearing, and waited for the hounds to appear.

CHAPTER 14

Battle of Armageddon

Here I am," Paul muttered to himself. "Come and sniff me out." A couple of minutes later, three hounds burst into the clearing from the south side. When the dogs bounded toward him, Paul shot them at point-blank range with a volley of twelve rounds. Two more dogs appeared, stopped at the dead hounds and began sniffing them. Paul shot each dog in the head, then rolled over several feet to his left and sighted in on the far side of the clearing. Might as well discourage them a little more, Paul reasoned. A few dead men might spoil their sporting night out. He waited patiently until six men appeared in the tree line beyond the dogs.

They stopped and stood motionless, afraid to enter the moonlit space. Paul could make out their silhouettes enough to mark the distance from left to right. He positioned his sights at chest level and squeezed the trigger while swinging the rifle barrel through the marked distance. The chatter of his rifle was followed by agonized groans and the sound of running feet. He rolled farther into the darkness to his left and watched the clearing. The sound of the fleeing men faded away and he heard nothing more. He rolled back to his right, picked up his .357 and jammed it back into its holster.

Paul waited another ten minutes before getting up and circling around in the dark to the far side of the clearing. He found five dead men along with their rifles. While he was removing the clips from their rifles and loose rounds from their pockets, he heard a slight rustle off to his right. Paul froze and then relaxed at the sound of Jack's voice. "It's okay, Paul. It's just me. Hang loose." Jack stepped out from behind a white pine and quickly moved up to Paul. "Did you get all their dogs?" "I think so," Paul replied. "Five was all I saw."

"I got all six of the ones after me," Jack said quietly. "I never saw any of the men, but they fired in my direction. Guess they hightailed it when I plugged their hounds." He cradled the rifle under his right arm and patted the barrel with his left fingers. "These are right handy little peashooters.

Think those clowns got the idea that we don't like being chased with dogs?" Paul chuckled. "Thirteen dead men and fifteen butchered hounds ought to be an adequate hint. . .unless they're slow learners. Think we ought to salvage their rifles?"

"Might as well," Jack said. "We may burn up some barrels if they try to storm the tunnel." He bent down and began removing the belt off one of the dead men. "Let's strap the rifles together and get back to the cave."

Paul and Jack hiked back to the entrance, uncovered it, set the rifles inside, then swept out their tracks. They recovered the hole, finished loading the frames, draped their robes and tennis shoes on top; shouldered the frames, picked up the torch and rifles, then walked on toward the inner room.

As they rounded the last bend, Jack called out: "Don't shoot, Ladies! It's Jack and Paul." The women laid their rifles aside and ran to meet Paul and Jack, clustering around them with excited chatter as the men made their way to the fire and set down their loads. "Tell us what happened," Marge implored. "Are the dogs still around?"

Paul unstrapped the rifles and laid them on the floor. "No. We shot all the dogs and there are five men who don't need those rifles anymore. The rest of the men took off after we killed their hounds." "Think they'll be back before morning?" Mary asked.

"I doubt that they'll try again tonight," Jack answered. "But you can rest assured they'll be back at first light. We'll rest up a few hours, then leave false trails all around and continue shooting their dogs. Maybe they will decide we're not worth all the grief." "Right now, we need a bath and some shuteye," Paul added. "We need to be up and at it two hours before daylight."

Paul and Jack left the cave at 3:45am and walked toward the southeast. "Let's get three-quarters of a mile away, then completely circle the cave," Jack suggested. "That'll leave a hot trail any hound worth his chow can stumble onto. Then, we'll do a figure eight to the north, south, east and west to muddle things up a bit. After that, we can crisscross between the trails to slow the dogs, even more, so we can count them and get a look at the men behind them. After we see what we're up against, we'll set up an ambush from the thicket in the hollow to the northeast."

"That should work out," Paul replied. "Let's each walk half the main circle and meet each other. That should make the hounds paw and scratch some. I'll do the figure eights north and west while you work south and east. After that, we can meander around awhile and then pick a spot to watch from." He fingered the five extra clips stuck under his gun belt. “I feel like a Mexican bandit with all this ammo."

"You may need it all before the day is over,” Jack said with a chuckle. "They should be really mean by now. No telling how many will be after us today." "There will be fewer by noon," Paul replied. "See you in the hollow.” “I’ll be along,” Jack promised. "Take care of yourself. Things wouldn't be nearly as exciting without you.”

The songbirds were beginning to twitter as Paul and Jack rested at lookout points and waited to see what the morning would bring. Each of them had selected clubs to eliminate any hounds that came upon them prematurely. They deemed it better to kill advance dogs silently rather than alert the searchers by gunfire. They could easily stun the dogs with the four-foot clubs, then slit their throats. During daylight hours, it was far wiser to kill the men first, then worry about wasting the hounds.

The sun had risen when Jack and Paul heard dogs sniffing out the three-quarter mile circle around the cave. They listened carefully to count the dogs and determine how fast they were traveling. The chorus of canine voices indicated a dozen or so hounds on leashes. Their progress was too slow for dogs running free. Both men moved around to glimpse the dogs and spot the search party. There were twelve hounds on leashes and thirty searchers trailing after them. Six of the dogs appeared to be bloodhounds, and all of the men with them carried automatic rifles with extended clips.

Paul and Jack met as planned in the thicket of evergreens with a clear view of the deepest section of the hollow lying northeast of the cave. Jack looked a little worried. "How many did you spot?" "A dozen dogs on leashes and thirty or so men,” Paul answered. "They're all carrying automatic rifles."

"We've got to wait until they're all in the hollow," Jack reasoned. "The dogs will follow our tracks right down to the bottom. The men are staying close behind the hounds and will all be below the west rim before the dogs start up the slope toward us. We'll be completely hidden with a clear shot at everything below us. We know these rifles will fire sixty rounds in roughly six seconds. None of the men can get out of this hollow that fast and they’ll be busy scrambling to get a fix on us when they catch a bullet. You take the left and I'll take the right. With a total of a hundred and twenty rounds each, we should be able to put all thirty men down. Then, we switch clips and I'll make sure every man is dead while you start blasting the hounds. Don’t worry about the dogs that run off. They are leash hounds, so they'll come back to the hollow.”

"It's only sixty yards to the west slope and thirty to the bottom," Paul said. "At that range, we should be deadly." Jack and Paul laid on their stomachs in the thicket and positioned their rifles, waiting quietly for the bloodhounds to sort out the maze of trails. The yelping grew steadily louder, and less than seven minutes later the dogs came boiling over the west rim of the hollow. The sturdy hounds yanked their handlers forward as they lunged to the bottom and started up the east slope. The rest of the searchers were caught between the midpoint of the west slope and the bottom when Jack and Paul opened fire.

Within the span of six seconds, the entire search party was down and scattered along the bottom and sides of the hollow. Jack and Paul jerked out their spent clips and inserted full clips. Jack riddled the fallen men with additional rounds while Paul mowed down the hounds that stayed near their handlers. Four of the dogs fled during the first volley of rifle fire but returned to the hollow while Paul and Jack were salvaging the ammunition from the dead men. Paul killed the returning hounds and then resumed the salvage activity.

Jack stripped the shirts off four of the dead men and began dumping loose rounds from their pockets onto one of the shirts. Paul stripped all thirty rifles of their full clips and piled ten clips on each of the other three shirts. While Paul tied up the shirt bundles, Jack searched the bodies for tobacco and came up with two pouches of pipe tobacco and nine packs of cigarettes. He untied one of the bundles and dropped the tobacco inside, then retied the shirt and walked over to where Paul was examining the dead hounds.

"Sure is a shame to waste such fine animals," Paul commented. "Yeah," Jack agreed. "I also hate to leave all those rifles behind, but we've got all we really need. Let's get on back with this load of ammo." Paul and Jack hung a bundle on each end of their rifles, balanced the load over their shoulders and headed back to the cave with over two thousand .30 caliber cartridges.

Maggots were feasting within the eyes, mouths and noses of the dead men slain by Paul and Jack Roberts. Huge green flies buzzed about the corpses, drawn by the aroma of rotting flesh. The search party that discovered the massacre picked their way among the slaughtered men and dogs, picking up the rifles and gathering identification from the bodies.

The blue-coated supervisor stood back from the carnage with a look of bewilderment. A member of the party approached him and pulled down his face mask. "We have identified all of them, Sir. The only thing apparently taken from the bodies was loose ammo. All of the rifles have been recovered, but the clips are missing. We also found the ambush site. Looks like just two men laid up in that thicket with the same type rifles we're carrying. Man! I'd hate to meet up with those two dudes. It makes me nervous just being in the same county with 'em. That makes forty-three men they've killed . . .that we know about, plus twenty-seven of our best dogs."

"They've got fourteen of our rifles and at least four thousand rounds of ammunition," the supervisor replied. "From the looks of things here, they also know how to use the equipment. We're coming back with five hundred men and do the job right."

A heavy mist blanketed the surface of the sea, shrouding the thousands of ships ferrying alliance troops toward the Middle East battlefield. Six cargo planes per minute arrived at airports in western Syria, discharged an average of two hundred and forty troops per plane, then headed back to the Far East for another load as part of a circular shuttle that would continue for several days. Ten rectangles of alliance troops marched toward Malinsky's eastern defensive line. Each rectangle measured six miles across and twelve miles deep.

Three rectangles crossed the Russian border and marched through southern Turkey and northern Iran toward the Tigris and Euphrates rivers. Six rectangles marched through Pakistan and Afghanistan, then across central Iran toward the Tigris and Euphrates. Another rectangle crossed the Iranian border near Meshed and headed due west toward the Tigris. The marching troops broke ranks periodically to cross rugged terrain and to squeeze through narrow mountain roadways. They also took detours to rob, rape and slaughter the local populations, leaving a desolate wilderness behind them. The troops shuttled by air into Syria from the Far East massed along the southwestern Syrian border.

An endless wave of African troops ferried across the Suez Canal and marched across the northern Negev-Sinai Desert toward southwestern Israel. Millions of Africans crowded into the Gaza Strip; looting, raping and killing as they swept the local population across the Israeli border. Gradually, like a poisonous tide, the Alliance forces aligned themselves along a gigantic battlefield measuring roughly eighty miles from north to south and thirty miles from east to west encompassing most of the northern half of Israel.

The alliance troops shuttled across the Mediterranean poured into the Plain of Esdraelon and the Plain of Sharon. As both Malinsky and Werner had predicted, the strength of the opposing armies centered in Armageddon and around Jerusalem. It was shaping up to be the greatest slaughter of humans by humans since the nuclear war. This time, however, the killing would not be done at a distance by planes, tanks, missiles or other mechanical wonders. The fighting would be at close quarters using small arms, knives, clubs and other primitive weapons.

Jack and Paul Roberts returned to the cave a half hour before dawn laden with nuts, berries, and edible plants. For weeks, they had foraged only at night to elude the five hundred searchers that continued to canvass the entire Sawtooth Wilderness area during daylight hours. The women were preparing breakfast as Jack and Paul emptied their sacks by the south end of the spring and undressed for their morning bath. Jack laid aside his hunting gear, stepped into the spring, and glanced back at Paul as he approached with soap and towels.

"Those tracks past the entrance were made less than four hours before we went out," Jack surmised. "Looks like forty or so passed within twenty feet of the camouflage." "You know they're eventually going to stumble upon the entrance if they keep passing by," Paul replied, stepping into the spring. "Our luck can't continue to hold with hundreds of men searching these mountains every day."

“I know,” Jack acknowledged. "But we won't have to hide much longer. The armies are on the move in the Middle East, and the great tribulation period is coming to its end. Soon, it will be behind us and Christ will mount the throne in Jerusalem."

"That suits me just fine," Paul replied, "I'm anxious to see him and hear his words." Both men exited the spring, dried off, slipped on their robes and tennis shoes, then joined the women at the fire. "Hear any news?" Ruth asked, handing full plates to Jack and Paul. Mary filled their cups with cold spring water and then sat down with her portion. Jackie and Marge filled their plates and sat down next to Mary.

"The war is about to begin in the Middle East," Jack answered. “The armies are poised to pounce on each other, and millions of refugees have been raped and murdered by the gathering troops. It appears that Natas' reign is about over."

Ruth sat down next to Marge and slipped her right arm around Marge's waist. "I don't regret a moment that we've shared here together. I never dreamed that I could love anyone as much as I've come to love everyone here." The others nodded, indicating that Ruth's words expressed their sentiments. The tender moment was interrupted by the howl of a bloodhound coming from inside the tunnel. Jack and Paul sprang to their feet and grabbed their rifles. "Whoa!" Jack exclaimed. "They tracked us with one lousy hound! Lay out the rifles and ammo! Let's go get 'em, Paul!"

Jack shouldered his rifle, strapped on his gun belt, and stuck five full clips under the belt. Paul did likewise, and the women scrambled for their rifles as Paul and Jack ran toward the tunnel. Three dozen searchers carrying torches pressed into the tunnel behind the man holding on to the leash of an excited bloodhound. As Paul and Jack rounded the second bend from the inner room, they could see the glow from the torches, causing them to retreat back into the darkness. "Wait till the hound gets almost to the turn," Jack whispered, "then we'll stick the rifles around the corner and blast 'em!"

“Okay,” Paul whispered back. "You hold neck high, and I'll hold chest high. I'll get the dog!" The yelping bloodhound lunged toward the bend, followed by his handler and thirty-six men. Jack and Paul poked their rifles around the turn and held the triggers back. The automatic rifles spat out sixty rounds each. Shouts of surprise and death screams were heard above the chilling rattle of gunfire. Paul and Jack jerked out their empty clips, jammed in full ones and raked the tunnel with another hail of bullets.

The searchers had come in two abreast and eighteen deep. The survivors in the rear hugged the tunnel floor and fired wildly into the darkness ahead. Paul and Jack loaded a third clip and peppered the tunnel floor. The return fire died away, and the wounded hound thrashed about on the floor. Paul moved up, whipped out his .357 and shot the dog between the eyes, then backed up to Jack. "Gimme your full clips and bring us some more. I'll watch here till you get back."

Jack handed Paul two full clips, then raced back to the inner room, calling out: "It's Jack! Don't shoot!" The women lowered their rifles as Jack ran up, grabbed six clips, jammed them under his gun belt, then cradled six more clips in both hands. "Follow me!" Jack advised. "We're holding them off at the second bend! Bring as many clips as you can carry!"

The women slung their rifles over their shoulders, snatched up two full clips in each hand, and ran behind Jack into the tunnel, stopping in the darkness behind Paul. "Hear any more?" Jack whispered, handing Paul six full clips. "Some crawled in behind the dead bodies, then backed out again. I'm not sure what they're up to," Paul whispered back. "Let's position the women and get ready. . .just in case."

"Okay." Jack responded, turning to the women. "Paul and I are taller, so we'll stand. Ruth and Mary can lie on the floor, and Jackie and Marge can squat in the middle. Point your barrels about four feet above the tunnel floor and move them from left to right the full width of the tunnel. Don't fire until I give the word. No need to waste any ammo."

The six of them waited silently as nine long minutes ticked away. Suddenly, the darkness in the tunnel ahead exploded with a volley of rifle fire amidst dozens of individual muzzle flashes. Jack, Paul and the women simply shielded their bodies around the bend as hundreds of bullets pelted the tunnel walls and floor ahead of them. "They're crawling along the floor!" Jack cautioned. "Sounds like three or four dozen moving up two abreast. When I give the word, spray the floor from left to right while raising your barrels one inch every sweep. Don't fire more than two clips. That should be enough for this bunch." Jack silently counted to ten. "Now!" he whispered.

Jack, Paul and the four women crisscrossed the tunnel floor with seven hundred and twenty bullets in less than eight terrifying seconds. Bloodcurdling cries and curses indicated that the rounds were not wasted. There was a sputtering of return fire, then the sound of running feet followed by loud, angry voices coming from the cave entrance, then silence.

"Stay here with the women, Jack. I'll load up our ammo in my carrying frame, so we have plenty," Paul whispered. He leaned his rifle against the tunnel wall. "I'll also bring six more rifles in case our barrels get too hot."

Nothing happened during Paul's round trip to the inner room. He returned with all eight remaining rifles and the balance of their ammunition. "Thought I'd better bring the other two in case of jam-ups," Paul said quietly. He removed the rifles and cartridges from his carrying frame, positioned them alongside Jack and the women, then set the frame out of the way and returned to his firing position.

"Think they're taking a nap?" Paul joked to ease the tension. "Maybe they don't want in as badly as they thought. We musta killed fifty already."

"We got enough to make them think twice," Jack replied. "They're probably trying to figure out how much ammo we've got left. While we're waiting, we'd better stuff our empty clips."

"You in the cave!" a raspy voice bellowed through a bullhorn. "We're authorized in the name of Lord Natas to offer you amnesty. If you come out voluntarily and register at the nearest control center, we'll guarantee you safe passage and full citizenship. You've got fifteen minutes to decide

. . .then we're going to fill your cave with poison gas. It's up to you. I'm not wasting any more men. Come out or we'll gas you."

"Well, now we know why they stopped coming in," Jack said. "Anybody want to bow down to the Antichrist?" During the silence that followed Jack's question, Marge eased backward in the darkness, raised her rifle and sprayed the positions occupied by the others with a full clip of bullets. Knowing precisely where each person was, and at point blank range, Marge's treachery was effective. Amid surprised cries and groans, the riddled bodies of her companions collapsed onto the tunnel floor. Marge loaded another full clip and sprayed the bodies again, guiding her rifle by its muzzle flashes.

She dropped the rifle and began feeling her way toward the entrance. "Hey, out there!" Marge called out. "I'm coming out. My name is Marge Rosen. I'm both registered and marked. Don't shoot! I've been a prisoner! I'm coming out! Don't shoot!"

Marge repeated her lines as she worked her way forward over the bodies littering the tunnel floor. She reached the entrance and stepped out with her hands lifted. Four men grabbed her while the blue-coated supervisor looked her over. "Bring up the portable scanner," he commanded. "Let's see if she's telling the truth."

Two of the searchers walked to a nearby jeep, lifted out the portable scanner, then approached Marge. "It's on the back of my right hand," Marge advised.

"She's telling the truth, Boss," the man holding the scanner said. "She's marked all right." "How did you wind up with this bunch?" the boss queried.

Marge frowned at him. "I was just picnicking on my day off and ran into Dr. Roberts. He knew I'd turn him in, so he kidnapped me and made me live in that stupid cave with his family and a friend. I managed to steal one of their rifles in the dark and shoot them while they were distracted by your threat to gas them."

"You didn't do us any favor, Lady. The whole idea was to get them to accept amnesty. . .not kill them." "I've been with them long enough to know that they'd never take the mark or worship Natas. Why should I let you gas me along with them? I saw my chance. . .and I took it."

"Well, I guess I can't blame you. You say that's Dr. Roberts in there . . .Dr. Jack Roberts, the orthopedic doctor from Boise?" "Yes," Marge answered, "with his wife, his brother and his wife, and a friend named Jackie Mason."

"Well, how about that!" the boss said. "Dr. Roberts set my boy's leg once after a bicycle accident. His brother, Paul, was a fighter pilot. I saw his picture in the doc's office."

"They were a couple of real stallions," Marge volunteered. "Too bad they were also religious fanatics." "You got any idea how many of my men they killed?" the boss asked with a hang dog expression. "Forty-three as of last night," Marge answered. "How many did they kill today?"

"More than I want to think about. You're a gutsy lady to do what you did. You probably saved a bunch of my men since I don't have any poison gas, and I wasn't leaving without bringing them out." He squeezed Marge against his side with his right arm and looked over his shoulder. "Bring up some fresh torches, and let's drag the bodies out."

www.ingramcontent.com/pod-product-compliance
Lightning Source LLC
Chambersburg PA
CBHW070749280626
47162CB00018B/2792